Carpe Demon

"Smart, fast-paced, unique—a blend of sophistication and wit that has you laughing out loud!"

—Christine Feehan, *New York Times*
bestselling author of *Dark Demon*

"This book, as crammed with events as any suburban mom's calendar, shows you what would happen if Buffy got married and kept her past a secret. It's a hoot."

—Charlaine Harris, *USA Today*
bestselling author of *Dead as a Doornail*

"Sprightly, fast-paced . . . readers will find spunky Kate hard not to root for in spheres both domestic and demonic."
—*Publishers Weekly*

"Kenner scores a direct hit with this offbeat, humorous adventure."
—*Romantic Times*

"This book was so much fun to read. I highly recommend this exceedingly entertaining read!" —*Midwest Book Review*

"A fun netherworld thriller that readers will treasure."
—*The Best Reviews*

"A+ . . . I am very ready for the next installment in Kate Connor's life." —*The Romance Reader's Connection*

"You're gonna love this book! . . . Terrific . . . lots of humor and crazy situations and action." —freshfiction.com

"Fast pacing and in-your-face action. It's a good read. Give it a try. Kate's a fun character, and keeps you on the edge of your seat." —SFReader.com

Carpe Demon

Adventures of a Demon-Hunting Soccer Mom

Julie Kenner

JOVE BOOKS, NEW YORK

THE BERKLEY PUBLISHING GROUP
Published by the Penguin Group
Penguin Group (USA) Inc.
375 Hudson Street, New York, New York 10014, USA
Penguin Group (Canada), 90 Eglinton Avenue East, Suite 700, Toronto, Ontario M4P 2Y3, Canada
(a division of Pearson Penguin Canada Inc.)
Penguin Books Ltd., 80 Strand, London WC2R 0RL, England
Penguin Group Ireland, 25 St. Stephen's Green, Dublin 2, Ireland (a division of Penguin Books Ltd.)
Penguin Group (Australia), 250 Camberwell Road, Camberwell, Victoria 3124, Australia
(a division of Pearson Australia Group Pty. Ltd.)
Penguin Books India Pvt. Ltd., 11 Community Centre, Panchsheel Park, New Delhi—110 017, India
Penguin Group (NZ), Cnr. Airborne and Rosedale Roads, Albany, Auckland 1310, New Zealand
(a division of Pearson New Zealand Ltd.)
Penguin Books (South Africa) (Pty.) Ltd., 24 Sturdee Avenue, Rosebank, Johannesburg 2196,
South Africa

Penguin Books Ltd., Registered Offices: 80 Strand, London WC2R 0RL, England

This is a work of fiction. Names, characters, places, and incidents either are the product of the author's imagination or are used fictitiously, and any resemblance to actual persons, living or dead, business establishments, events, or locales is entirely coincidental. The publisher does not have any control over and does not assume any responsibility for author or third-party websites or their content.

CARPE DEMON

A Jove Book / published by arrangement with the author

PRINTING HISTORY
Berkley trade paperback edition / July 2005
Jove mass-market edition / November 2006

Copyright © 2005 by Julie Kenner.
Cover design by Annette Fiore.
Text design by Stacy Irwin.

All rights reserved.
No part of this book may be reproduced, scanned, or distributed in any printed or electronic form without permission. Please do not participate in or encourage piracy of copyrighted materials in violation of the author's rights. Purchase only authorized editions.
For information, address: The Berkley Publishing Group,
a division of Penguin Group (USA) Inc.,
375 Hudson Street, New York, New York 10014.

ISBN: 0-515-14221-2

JOVE®
Jove Books are published by The Berkley Publishing Group,
a division of Penguin Group (USA) Inc.,
375 Hudson Street, New York, New York 10014.
JOVE is a registered trademark of Penguin Group (USA) Inc.
The "J" design is a trademark belonging to Penguin Group (USA) Inc.

PRINTED IN THE UNITED STATES OF AMERICA

10   9   8   7   6   5   4   3   2   1

If you purchased this book without a cover, you should be aware that this book is stolen property. It was reported as "unsold and destroyed" to the publisher, and neither the author nor the publisher has received any payment for this "stripped book."

For Allison and Kim.
Thanks for letting me take Kate and run with her!

Acknowledgments

That I do not speak Italian became painfully apparent when I e-mailed my pieced-together-from-Internet-research dialogue to the fabulous Eloisa James with SOS in the subject line, and she very politely told me that I had it all wrong. Even better, she fixed it for me! So a special thanks to Eloisa for saving my linguistically challenged rump. (But if there are mistakes, blame me and not her!)

That I do not know Latin became painfully apparent way back in high school. I didn't even try the Internet route in that regard, just sent out an SOS to the Novelists, Inc. e-mail loop (a *wonderful* list!) and heard back almost immediately from Eve Gaddy (who couldn't answer my question but who put me in touch with a man who could). Thanks to John Harris, Ph.D., who pulled it together for me. I don't think I've ever taken quite so much pleasure in watching someone analyze the linguistic nuances of telling the dead to rise!

That I know little about fencing became painfully apparent when the fencing scene was filled with more XXs than text, indicating all those places where I needed terminology. Thanks to Stefan Leponis for helping me fill in the blanks and giving me wonderful insight into the world of fencing. And thanks to Helen for noticing my "I need fencing terminology" whine in my blog and sending her husband, Stefan, to my rescue!

That I know little about karate . . . well, you get the drift. Special thanks to the wonderful and talented Lexie for helping me out with uniforms and other details (and, if memory serves, getting to stay up a bit past bedtime to filter answers back to me through her mom), and to Nancy Northcott for outlining some of the moves she learned in class.

Also thanks to Deacon Ron Walker, St. Mary's Parish, Austin, Texas, who helped with the Cathedral layout and other Catholic-related stuff that I really should have known. . . .

Again with the caveat: All mistakes are my own. And they were on purpose. Really. Call it literary license. *Really . . .*

And, finally, a special thanks to Don, Kim, Kassie, Allison, Dee, and Kathleen, who all loved Kate from the moment they met her. And that means the world to me!

One

My name is Kate Connor and I used to be a Demon Hunter.

I've often thought that would be a great pickup line at parties, but with a teenager, a toddler, and a husband, I'm hardly burning up the party circuit. And, of course, the whole demon-hunting thing is one great big gargantuan secret. No one knows. Not my kids, not my husband, and certainly not folks at these imaginary parties where I'm regaling sumptuous hunks with tales from my demon-slaying, vampire-hunting, zombie-killing days.

Back in the day, I was pretty cool. Now I'm a glorified chauffeur for drill-team practice and Gymboree playdates. Less sex appeal, maybe, but I gotta admit I love it. I wouldn't trade my family for anything. And after fourteen years of doing the mommy thing, my demon-hunting skills aren't exactly sharp.

All of which explains why I didn't immediately locate and terminate the demon wandering the pet-food aisle of the San Diablo Wal-Mart. Instead, when I caught a whiff of that telltale stench, I naturally assumed it emanated exclusively from the bottom of a particularly cranky two-year-old. My two-year-old, to be exact.

"Mom! He did it again. What are you feeding him?" That from Alison, my particularly cranky fourteen-year-old. She, at least, didn't stink.

"Entrails and goat turds," I said absently. I sniffed the air again. Surely that was only Timmy I was smelling. . . .

"Mo-om." She managed to make the word two syllables. "You don't have to be gross."

"Sorry." I concentrated on my kids, pushing my suspicions firmly out of my mind. I was being silly. San Diablo had been demon-free for years. That's why I lived here, after all.

Besides, the comings and goings of demons weren't my problem anymore. Nowadays my problems leaned more toward the domestic rather than the demonic. Grocery shopping, budgeting, carpooling, mending, cleaning, cooking, parenting, and a thousand other "-ings." All the basic stuff that completely holds a family together and is taken entirely for granted by every person on the planet who doesn't happen to be a wife and stay-at-home mom. (And two points to you if you caught that little bit of vitriol. I'll admit to having a few issues about the whole topic, but, dammit, I work hard. And believe me, I'm no stranger to hard work. It was never easy, say, cleaning out an entire nest of evil, bloodthirsty preternatural creatures with only a few wooden stakes, some holy water, and a can of Diet Coke. But I always managed. And it was a hell of a lot easier than getting a teenager, a husband, and a toddler up and moving in the morning. Now, *that's* a challenge.)

While Timmy fussed and whined, I swung the shopping cart around, aiming for the back of the store and a diaper-changing station. It would have been a refined, fluid motion if Timmy hadn't taken the opportunity to reach out with those chubby little hands. His fingers collided with a stack of Fancy Feast cans and everything started wobbling.

I let out one of those startled little "oh!" sounds, totally pointless and entirely ineffectual. There was a time when my reflexes were so sharp, so perfectly attuned, that I probably could have caught every one of those cans before they hit the ground. But that Katie wasn't with me in Wal-Mart, and I watched, helpless, as the cans clattered to the ground.

Another fine mess . . .

Alison had jumped back as the cans fell, and she looked with dismay at the pile. As for the culprit, he was suddenly in a fabulous mood, clapping wildly and screaming "Big noise! Big noise!" while eyeing the remaining stacks greedily. I inched the cart farther away from the shelves.

"Allie, do you mind? I need to go change him."

She gave me one of those put-upon looks that are genetically coded to appear as soon as a girl hits her teens.

"Take your pick," I said, using my most reasonable mother voice. "Clean up the cat food, or clean up your brother."

"I'll pick up the cans," she said, in a tone that perfectly matched her expression.

I took a deep breath and reminded myself that she was fourteen. Raging hormones. Those difficult adolescent years. More difficult, I imagined, for me than for her. "Why don't I meet you in the music aisle. Pick out a new CD and we'll add it to the pile."

Her face lit up. "Really?"

"Sure. Why not?" Yes, yes, don't even say it. I know "why not." Setting a bad precedent, not defining limits, blah, blah, blah. Throw all that psycho mumbo jumbo at me when *you're* wandering Wal-Mart with two kids and a list of errands as long as your arm. If I can buy a day's worth of cooperation for $14.99, then that's a deal I'm jumping all over. I'll worry about the consequences in therapy, thank you very much.

I caught another whiff of nastiness right before we hit the restrooms. Out of habit, I looked around. A feeble old man squinted at me from over the Wal-Mart Sunday insert, but other than him, there was nobody around but me and Timmy.

"P.U.," Timmy said, then flashed a toothy grin.

I smiled as I parked the shopping cart outside of the ladies' room. "P.U." was his newest favorite word, followed in close second by "Oh, *man!*" The "Oh, *man!*" I can blame on Nickelodeon and *Dora the Explorer.* For the other, I lay exclusive blame on my husband, who has never been keen on changing dirty diapers and has managed, I'm convinced, over the short term of Timmy's life, to give the kid a complete and utter complex about bowel movements.

"You're P.U.," I said, hoisting him onto the little drop-down changing table. "But not for long. We'll clean you up, powder that bottom, and slap on a new diaper. You're gonna come out smelling like a rose, kid."

"Like a rose!" he mimicked, reaching for my earrings while I held him down and stripped him.

After a million wipes and one fresh diaper, Timmy was back in the shopping cart. We fetched Allie away from a display of newly released CDs, and she came more or less willingly, a Natalie Imbruglia CD clutched in her hand.

Ten minutes and eighty-seven dollars later I was strapping Timmy into his car seat while Allie loaded our bags into the minivan. As I was maneuvering through the parking lot, I caught one more glimpse of the old man I'd seen earlier. He was standing at the front of the store, between the Coke machines and the plastic kiddie pools, just staring out toward me. I pulled over. My plan was to pop out, say a word or two to him, take a good long whiff of his breath, and then be on my way.

I had my door half open when music started blasting from all six of the Odyssey's speakers at something close to one hundred decibels. I jumped, whipping around to face Allie, who was already fumbling for the volume control and muttering, "Sorry, sorry."

I pushed the power button, which ended the Natalie Imbruglia surround-sound serenade, but did nothing about Timmy, who was now bawling his eyes out, probably from the pain associated with burst eardrums. I shot Allie a stern look, unfastened my seat belt, and climbed into the backseat, all the while trying to make happy sounds that would calm my kid.

"I'm sorry, Mom," Allie said. To her credit she sounded sincere. "I didn't know the volume was up that high." She maneuvered into the backseat on the other side of Timmy and started playing peekaboo with Boo Bear, a bedraggled blue bear that's been Timmy's constant companion since he was five months old. At first Timmy ignored her, but after a while he joined in, and I felt a little surge of pride for my daughter.

"Good for you," I said.

She shrugged and kissed her brother's forehead.

I remembered the old man and reached for the door, but as I looked out at the sidewalk, I saw that he was gone.

"What's wrong?" Allie asked.

I hadn't realized I was frowning, so I forced a smile and concentrated on erasing the worry lines from my forehead. "Nothing," I said. And then, since that was the truth, I repeated myself, "Nothing at all."

For the next three hours we bounced from store to store as I went down my list for the day: bulk goods at Wal-Mart—*check*; shoes for Timmy at Payless—*check*; Happy Meal for Timmy to ward off crankiness—*check*; new shoes for Allie from DSW—*check*; new ties for Stuart from T.J. Maxx—*check*. By the time we hit the grocery store, the Happy Meal had worn off, both Timmy and Allie were cranky, and I wasn't far behind. Mostly, though, I was distracted.

That old man was still on my mind, and I was irritated

with myself for not letting the whole thing drop. But something about him bugged me. As I pushed the shopping cart down the dairy aisle, I told myself I was being paranoid. For one thing, demons tend not to infect the old or feeble. (Makes sense when you think about it; if you're going to suddenly become corporeal, you might as well shoot for young, strong, and virile.) For another, I'm pretty sure there'd been no demon stench, just a particularly pungent toddler diaper. Of course, that didn't necessarily rule out demon proximity. All the demons I'd ever run across tended to pop breath mints like candy, and one even owned the majority share of stock in a mouthwash manufacturer. Even so, common sense told me there was no demon.

Mostly, though, I needed to drop the subject simply because it wasn't my problem anymore. I may have been a Level Four Demon Hunter once upon a time, but that time was fifteen years ago. I was retired now. Out of the loop. Even more, I was out of practice.

I turned down the cookie-and-chips aisle, careful not to let Timmy see as I tossed two boxes of Teddy Grahams into the cart. In the next aisle, Allie lingered in front of the breakfast cereal, and I could practically see her mind debating between the überhealthy Kashi and her favorite Lucky Charms. I tried to focus on my grocery list (were we really out of All-Bran?), but my brain kept coming back to the old man.

Surely I was just being paranoid. I mean, why would a demon willingly come to San Diablo, anyway? The California coastal town was built on a hillside, its crisscross of streets leading up to St. Mary's, the cathedral that perched at the top of the cliffs, a focal point for the entire town. In addition to being stunningly beautiful, the cathedral was famous for its holy relics, and it drew both tourists and pilgrims. The devout came to San Diablo for the same reason the demons stayed away—the cathedral was holy ground. Evil simply wasn't welcome there.

That was also the primary reason Eric and I had retired in San Diablo. Ocean views, the fabulous California weather, and absolutely no demons or other nasties to ruin our good time. San Diablo was a great place to have kids, friends, and the normal life he and I had both craved. Even now, I thank God that we had ten good years together.

"Mom?" Allie squeezed my free hand, and I realized I'd wandered to the next aisle, and was now holding a freezer door open, staring blankly at a collection of frozen pizzas. "You okay?" From the way her nose crinkled, I knew she suspected I was thinking about her dad.

"Fine," I lied, blinking furiously. "I was trying to decide between pepperoni or sausage for dinner tonight, and then I got sidetracked thinking about making my own pizza dough."

"The last time you tried that, you got dough stuck on the light fixture and Stuart had to climb up and dig it out."

"Thanks for reminding me." But it had worked; we'd both moved past our melancholy. Eric had died just after Allie's ninth birthday, and although she and Stuart got along famously, I knew she missed her dad as much as I did. We talked about it on occasion, sometimes remembering the funny times, and sometimes, like when we visited the cemetery, the memories were filled with tears. But now wasn't the time for either, and we both knew it.

I squeezed her hand back. My girl was growing up. Already she was looking out for me, and it was sweet and heartbreaking all at the same time. "What do you think?" I asked. "Pepperoni?"

"Stuart likes sausage better," she said.

"We'll get both," I said, knowing Allie's distaste for sausage pizza. "Want to rent a movie on the way home? We'll have to look fast so the food doesn't spoil, but surely there's something we've been wanting to see."

Her eyes lit up. "We could do a Harry Potter marathon."

I stifled a grimace. "Why not? It's been at least a month since our last HP marathon."

She rolled her eyes, then retrieved Timmy's sippy cup and adjusted Boo Bear. I knew I was stuck.

My cell phone rang. I checked the caller ID, then leaned against the grocery cart as I answered. "Hey, hon."

"I'm having the day from hell," Stuart said, which was a poor choice of words considering that got me thinking about demons all over again. "And I'm afraid I'm going to ruin your day, too."

"I can hardly wait."

"Any chance you were planning something fabulous for dinner? Enough to serve eight, with cocktails before and some fancy dessert after?"

"Frozen pizza and Harry Potter," I said, certain I knew where this was going to end up.

"Ah," Stuart said. In the background I could hear the eraser end of his pencil tapping against his desktop. Beside me, Allie pretended to bang her head against the glass freezer door. "Well, that would serve eight," he said. "But it may not have quite the cachet I was hoping for."

"It's important?"

"Clark thinks it is." Clark Curtis was San Diablo's lame duck county attorney, and he favored my husband to step into his shoes. Right now, Stuart had a low political profile, working for peanuts as an assistant county attorney in the real estate division. Stuart was months away from formally announcing, but if he wanted to have any hope of winning the election, he needed to start playing the political game, shaking hands, currying favors, and begging campaign contributions. Although a little nervous, he was excited about the campaign, and flattered by Clark's support. As for me, the thought of being a politician's wife was more than a little unnerving.

"A house full of attorneys," I said, trying to think what

the heck I could feed them. Or, better yet, if there was any way to get out of this.

Allie sank down to the floor, her back against the freezer, her forehead on her knees.

"And judges."

"Oh, great." This was the part about domesticity that I didn't enjoy. Entertaining just isn't my thing. I hated it, actually. Always had, always would. But my husband, the aspiring politician, loved me anyway. Imagine that.

"I tell you what. I'll have Joan call some caterers. You don't have to do anything except be home by six to meet them. Folks are coming at seven, and I'll be sure to be there by six-thirty to give you a hand."

Now, see? That's why I love him. But I couldn't accept. Guilt welled in my stomach just from the mere suggestion. This was the man I loved, after all. And I couldn't be bothered to pull together a small dinner party? What kind of a heartless wench was I?

"How about rigatoni?" I asked, wondering which was worse, heartless wench or guilty sucker. "And a spinach salad? And I can pick up some appetizers and the stuff for my apple tart." That pretty much exhausted my guest-worthy repertoire, and Stuart knew it.

"Sounds perfect," he said. "But are you sure? It's already four."

"I'm sure," I said, not sure at all, but it was his career, not mine, that was riding on my culinary talents.

"You're the best," he said. "Let me talk to Allie."

I passed the phone to my daughter, who was doing a good impression of someone so chronically depressed she was in need of hospitalization. She lifted a weary hand, took the phone, and pressed it to her ear. "Yeah?"

While they talked, I focused my attention on Timmy, who was being remarkably good. "Nose!" he said when I pointed to my nose. "Ear!" I pointed to my other ear.

"More ear!" The kid was literal, that was for sure. I leaned in close and gave him big wet sloppy kisses on his neck while he giggled and kicked.

With my head cocked to the side like that, I caught a glimpse of Allie, who no longer looked morose. If anything, she looked supremely pleased with herself. I wondered what she and Stuart were scheming, and suspected it was going to involve me carpooling a load of teenage girls to the mall.

"What?" I asked as Allie hung up.

"Stuart said it was okay with him if I spent the night at Mindy's. Can I? Please?"

I ran my fingers through my hair and tried not to fantasize about killing my husband. The reasonable side of me screamed that he was only trying to help. The annoyed side of me retorted that he'd just sent my help packing, and I now had to clean the house, cook dinner, and keep Timmy entertained all on my own.

"Pleeeeeeze?"

"Fine. Sure. Great idea." I started pushing the cart toward the dairy aisle while Timmy babbled something entirely unintelligible. "You can get your stuff and head to Mindy's as soon as we get home."

She did a little hop-skip number, then threw her arms around my neck. "Thanks, Mom! You're the best."

"Mmmm. Remember this the next time you're grounded."

She pointed at her chest, her face ultra-innocent. "Me? In trouble? I think you have me confused with some other daughter."

I tried to scowl, but didn't quite manage it, and she knew she'd won me over. Well, what the heck. I was a woman of the new millennium. I'd staked vampires, defeated demons, and incapacitated incubi. How hard could a last-minute dinner party be?

•   •   •

Mindy Dupont lives at our exact address, only one street over. Once the girls became inseparable, Laura Dupont and I followed suit, and now she's more like a sister than a neighbor. I knew she wouldn't care if Allie stayed over, so I didn't bother calling ahead. I just bought a chocolate cake for bribery/thank-you purposes, then added it to Allie's pile as she set off across our connecting backyards to Laura's patio. (They're not technically connected. A paved city easement runs between us, and it's fenced off on both sides. Last year Stuart convinced the city that they should install gates on either side, so as to facilitate any city workers who might need to get back there. I've never once seen a utility man wandering behind my house, but those gates have sure made life easier for me, Laura, and the girls. Have I mentioned I adore my husband?)

A little less than ten minutes later I had Timmy settled in front of a *Wiggles* video, and I was pushing a dust mop over our hardwood floors, trying to get all the nooks and crannies a judge might notice, and ignoring all the other spots. I was pretty certain there was a dust bunny convention under the sofa, but until the conventioneers started wandering out into the rest of the house, I wasn't going to worry about it.

The phone rang, and I lunged for it.

"Allie says you're doing the dinner party thing. Need help?"

As much as I loved her, Laura was an even more harried hostess than I was. "I've got it all under control. My clothes are laid out, the sauce is simmering, the appetizers are on cookie sheets ready to go in the oven, and I even managed to find eight wineglasses." I took a deep breath. "And they match."

"Well, aren't you just a little Martha Stewart? In the pre-scandal, domestic-goddess days, of course. And the munchkin?"

"In his jammies in front of the television."

"All finished with bathtime?"

"No bath. Extra videos."

She released a long-suffering sigh. "Finally, a flaw. Now I don't have to hate you after all."

I laughed. "Hate me all you want for managing to pull this together. It's a feat worthy of your hatred." I didn't point out that I hadn't actually pulled it off yet. I wasn't counting this evening as a success until the guests went home happy, patting their tummies and promising Stuart all sorts of political favors. "Just don't hate me for dumping Allie on you. You sure it's okay?"

"Oh, yeah. They're locked in Mindy's room trying out all my Clinique samples. If they get bored, we'll go get ice cream. But I don't see boredom in their future. I've got two years' worth of samples in that box. I figure that works out to at least four hours of free time. I'm going to make some popcorn, pop in one of my old Cary Grant videos, and wait up for Paul."

"Oh, sure, rub it in," I said.

She laughed. "You've got your own Cary Grant."

"And he'll be home soon. I'd better run."

She clicked off after making me promise to call if I needed anything. But for once, I actually had it under control. Amazing. I tucked the dust mop in the utility closet, then headed back to take a final look at the living room. Comfortable and presentable. Some might even say it had a casual elegance. The dancing dinosaur on the television screen really didn't add to the ambience, but I'd close up the entertainment center as soon as Timmy went to bed.

In the meantime, I needed to go finish the food. I gave Timmy a kiss on the cheek, got no reaction, and realized he'd been completely mesmerized by four gyrating Australian men. If he were fifteen, I'd worry. At twenty-five months, I figured we were okay.

I was running through my mental checklist as I headed back into the kitchen. A flash of movement outside the kitchen window caught my attention, and I realized I'd forgotten to feed Kabit, our cat.

I considered waiting until after the party, decided that wasn't fair, then crossed to the breakfast area where we keep the cat food bowl on a little mat next to the table. I'd just bent to pick up the water dish when the sound of shattering glass filled the room.

I was upright almost instantly, but that wasn't good enough. The old man from Wal-Mart bounded through the wrecked window, surprisingly agile for an octogenarian, and launched himself at me. We tumbled to the ground, rolling across the floor and into the actual kitchen, until we finally came to a stop by the stove. He was on top of me, his bony hands pinning down my wrists, and his face over mine. His breath reeked of rancid meat and cooked cauliflower, and I made a vow to never, *ever* ignore my instincts again.

"Time to die, Hunter," he said, his voice low and breathy and not the least bit old-sounding.

A little riffle of panic shot through my chest. He shouldn't know I used to be a Hunter. I was retired. New last name. New hometown. This was bad. And his words concerned me a heck of a lot more than the kill-fever I saw in his eyes.

I didn't have time to worry about it, though, because the guy was shifting his hands from my wrists to my neck, and I had absolutely no intention of getting caught in a death grip.

As he shifted his weight, I pulled to the side, managing to free up my leg. I brought it up, catching his groin with my knee. He howled, but didn't let go. That's the trouble with demons; kneeing them in the balls just doesn't have the effect it should. Which meant I was still under him, smelling his foul breath, and frustrated as hell because I didn't need this shit. I had a dinner to fix.

From the living room, I heard Timmy yelling, "Momma!

Momma! Big noise! Big noise!" and I knew he was abandoning the video to come find out where the big noise came from.

I couldn't remember if I'd closed the baby gate, and there was no way my two-year-old was going to see his mom fighting a demon. I might be out of practice, but right then, I was motivated. "I'll be right there!" I yelled, then pulled on every resource in my body and flipped over, managing to hop on Pops. I scraped at his face, aiming for his eyes, but only scratched his skin.

He let out a wail that sounded as if it came straight from the depths of hell, and lurched toward me. I sprang back and up, surprised and at the same time thrilled that I was in better shape than I realized. I made a mental note to go to the gym more often even as I kicked out and caught him in the chin. My thigh screamed in pain, and I knew I'd pay for this in the morning.

Another screech from the demon, this time harmonized by Timmy's cries and the rattle of the baby gate that was, thank God, locked. Pops rushed me, and I howled as he slammed me back against the granite countertops. One hand was tight around my throat, and I struggled to breathe, lashing out to absolutely no effect.

The demon laughed, his eyes filled with so much pleasure that it pissed me off even more. "Useless bitch," he said, his foul breath on my face. "You may as well die, Hunter. You surely will when my master's army rises to claim victory in his name."

That didn't sound good, but I couldn't think about it right then. The lack of oxygen was getting to me. I was confused, my head swimming, everything starting to fade to a blackish purple. But then Timmy's howls dissolved into whimpers. A renewed burst of anger and fear gave me strength. My hand groped along the counter until I found a wineglass. My fingers closed around it, and I slammed it down, managing to break off the base.

The room was starting to swim, and I needed to breathe desperately. I had one chance, and one chance only. With all the strength I could muster I slammed the stem of the wineglass toward his face, then sagged in relief when I felt it hit home, slipping through the soft tissue of his eyeball with very little resistance.

I heard a *whoosh* and saw the familiar shimmer as the demon was sucked out of the old man, and then the body collapsed to my floor. I sagged against my counter, drawing gallons of air into my lungs. As soon as I felt steady again, I focused on the corpse on my newly cleaned floor and sighed. Unlike in the movies, demons don't dissolve in a puff of smoke or ash, and right as I was staring down at the body, wondering how the heck I was going to get rid of it before the party, I heard the familiar squeak of the patio door, and then Allie's frantic voice in the living room. "Mom! Mom!"

Timmy's yelps joined my daughter's, and I closed my eyes and prayed for strength.

"Don't come in here, sweetie. I broke some glass and it's all over the floor." As I talked, I hoisted my dead foe by the underarms and dragged him to the pantry. I slid him inside and slammed the door.

"What?" Allie said, appearing around the corner with Timmy in her arms.

I counted to five and decided this wasn't the time to lecture my daughter about listening or following directions. "I said don't come in here." I moved quickly toward her, blocking her path. "There's glass all over the place."

"Jeez, Mom." Her eyes were wide as she took in the mess that was now my kitchen. "Guess you can't give me any more grief about my room, huh?"

I rolled my eyes.

She glanced at the big picture window behind our breakfast table. The one that no longer had glass. "What happened?"

"Softball," I said. "Just crashed right through."

"Wow. I guess Brian finally hit a homer, huh?"

"Looks that way." Nine-year-old Brian lived next door and played softball in his backyard constantly. I felt a little guilty blaming the mess on him, but I'd deal with that later.

"I'll get the broom."

She plunked Timmy onto his booster seat, then headed for the pantry. I caught her arm. "I'll take care of it, sweetie."

"But you've got the party!"

"Exactly. And that's why I need to be able to focus." That really made no sense, but she didn't seem to notice. "Listen, just put Timmy to bed for me, then head on back to Mindy's. Really. I'll be fine."

She looked unsure. "You're sure?"

"Absolutely. It's all under control. Why'd you come back, anyway?"

"I forgot my new CD."

I should have guessed. I picked Timmy back up (who, thankfully, was quiet now and watching the whole scene with interest). "Put the munchkin down and you'll be doing me a huge favor."

She frowned, but didn't argue as she took Timmy from me.

"Night, sweetie," I said, then gave both her and Timmy a kiss.

She still looked dubious, but she readjusted her grip on Timmy and headed toward the stairs. I let out a little sigh of relief and glanced at the clock. I had exactly forty-three minutes to clean up the mess in my kitchen, dispose of a dead demon, and pull together a dinner party. After that, I could turn my attention to figuring out what a demon was doing in San Diablo. And, more important, why he had attacked *me*.

But first, the rigatoni.

Did I have my priorities straight, or what?

Two

The appetizers were in the oven, the table was set, the wine was breathing, and I was dragging a demon carcass across the kitchen floor when I heard the automatic garage door start its slow, painful grinding to the top. *Shit.*

I stopped dead, my gaze darting to the clock on the oven. Six twenty-five. He was *early*. The man who'd been ten minutes late to our wedding (and this after I told him it started thirty minutes earlier than it did) had actually managed to make it home on time.

I scowled at the corpse in my arms. "This really is a day of wonders, isn't it?"

He didn't answer, which I considered a good thing—you can never be too careful with demons—and I shifted my stance, grunting as I maneuvered him back toward the pantry. Knowing our garage door, I figured I had at least two minutes before Stuart stepped into the kitchen. Stuart keeps meaning to fix the thing, and I keep pestering him to hurry up and do it, but right then I was supremely grateful that my husband could procrastinate with the best of them.

My original plan had been to get the body out the back door and into the storage shed where I knew neither Stuart nor Allie would dream of wandering. I'd already left a message for Father Corletti telling him about the demon and the cryptic Satanic army message, and as soon as he called me back, I'd insist he send a collection team *stat*.

In the meantime, I resigned myself to throwing a dinner party with a demon in my pantry. I heard the familiar *clunk* of the garage door coming to a stop, then the purr of the Infiniti's engine as Stuart pulled in. I listened, frantically shoving cat-food bins aside to make room for the body.

The engine died, and then a car door slammed.

I shoved the demon where the cat food belonged, then slid the bins back in front of him. No good. I could still see the demon's white shirt and blue pants peeking up behind the bins.

The doorknob rattled, followed by the squeak of the door leading from the kitchen to the garage. I grabbed the first thing that looked remotely useful—a box of Hefty trash bags—and ripped it open. I pulled out bag after bag, whipping them open and tossing them over the body and the bins. Not perfect, but it would have to do.

"Katie?"

My heart beat somewhere in my throat, and I leaped across the pantry in a move that might have been graceful had it not been so desperate. I stuck my head around the open door, smiled at my husband, and hoped to hell I looked happy to see him.

"I'm right here, sweetie," I said. "You're home early."

He aimed a trademark Stuart Connor grin my way. "You mean I'm home on time."

I stepped out of the pantry, then shut the door firmly behind me. "With you, that is early." I planted a loving, wifely kiss on his cheek. Then I took his briefcase, pressed a firm hand against his back, and aimed him out of the kitchen. "You must have had a hard day," I said. "How about a glass of wine?"

He stopped moving, turning to look at me as if *I* might have been possessed by demons. "Kate, the guests will be here in half an hour."

"I know. And this is an important night for you. You should be relaxed." I urged him forward. "Red or white?"

He didn't move. "*Katie.*"

"What?"

"*Half an hour,*" he repeated. "And you're not dressed, and—" His eyes widened, his mouth shut, and I knew exactly what he was looking at.

"Brian got a homer," I said, then shrugged. Mentally I cursed myself. I'd cleaned up the glass, then drawn our sheer curtains for camouflage, but there was nothing I could do about the breeze blowing in, kicking the flimsy material up like so many dancing ghosts.

He looked at me. "Have you called a glass shop?"

Okay, *now* I was annoyed. I cocked an eyebrow, planted a hand on my hip, and glared at him. "No, Stuart, I haven't. I've been a little busy throwing together a last-minute dinner party."

He looked from the window to me, and then back to the window. "The kids okay?"

"No one was nearby when it shattered," I lied.

"Where's Tim?"

"Already asleep," I said. "He's *fine*. We're all fine."

He studied me for a minute, then pushed a stray curl behind my ear. He stroked my temple, and I winced.

"You call this fine?"

I exhaled. I didn't know if I'd been cut by the glass or scratched by the demon. "It's just a nick," I said. "No biggie."

"It could have got you in the eye."

I shrugged. It could have done a hell of a lot worse than that.

He squeezed my hand. "I'm sorry about tonight. I didn't realize you'd be cleaning up a disaster area in addition to cooking a meal. Do you need any help?"

Okay, I'd been mildly irritated with him, but that faded right then. "I've got it under control," I said. "Go do whatever you need to do. You're the one on the hot seat tonight."

He pulled me into his arms. "I really appreciate this. I know it's last-minute, but I think it'll pay off big-time."

"Campaign contributions?"

"Possibly. But I'm hoping for endorsements. Two federal and two state judges. That's a lot of clout."

"How can they not be impressed with you?" I asked, tilting my head back to look at him. "You're amazing."

"*You're* amazing," he whispered in that soft voice that he really shouldn't use unless he was planning to take me to bed. His lips closed over mine, and for a few sweet seconds I forgot about demons and dinner parties and rigatoni and—

The appetizers!

I broke the kiss. "The oven!" I said. "I need to take the appetizers out." I couldn't serve a federal judge burnt mini-quiches. I'm pretty sure that would be social and political suicide.

"I'll do it. And I'd better cover that window. It's supposed to rain." He looked me up and down. "I'm already dressed, but you need to change. They'll be here soon, you know."

As if I could forget.

I peeled off my PTA T-shirt on the stairs and slid out of my bra as I jogged down the hall to the double doors leading to our bedroom. Inside, I dropped the clothes on the floor, then shimmied out of my ratty sweatpants. I kicked the bundle out of my way, then grabbed the outfit I'd laid across the unmade bed. I'd picked up a cute little flower-print sundress during a T.J. Maxx shopping spree at the beginning of the summer (swimsuits and shorts for Allie, yet another growth spurt for Timmy). With its fitted bodice, tight waist, and flared skirt, it was both festive and flattering. Considering I mostly lived my life in T-shirts, jeans, or sweatpants, this was the first chance I'd had to wear it.

With one eye trained on the digital clock next to the bed, I shoved my feet into some light blue mules, ran a brush through my hair, and stroked some mascara onto my eyelashes.

I never got ready this quickly, but today I had incentive, and the whole process took less than three minutes. Didn't matter. I could tell the second I raced into the kitchen that I'd taken too long. Way too long.

"What the hell is this?" Stuart said. He was standing just inside the pantry, so I couldn't see his face, just part of his arm and the back of his head.

His voice didn't help me, either. He sounded vaguely mystified, but that could as easily be a reaction to a new brand of cereal as it was to a dead body behind the cat food. If he was questioning my switch from Cheerios to Special K, then *That's an incapacitated demon, dear. I'll get rid of him by morning* would be an entirely inappropriate response.

I'd sprinted across the room, and now I put a hand (wifely, supportive) on his shoulder and peered around him into the pantry. As far as I could tell, there was no visible demon. Just dozens of trash bags blanketing the small room.

Big relief.

"Um, what's the trouble?"

"This mess," he said.

"Yes, right. Mess." I was babbling, and I stood up straighter as if good posture would force more oxygen to my brain. "Allie," I said, jumping on my first coherent thought. First Brian, now Allie. Had I no shame? "I'll talk to her about this tomorrow."

I could tell he wanted to belabor the point—my husband is a total neat freak—so I urged him out of the pantry and shut the door. "I thought you were fixing the window."

"That's why I went looking for the trash bags," he said with a scowl. "Rain."

"Right. Of course. I'll bring you some." I pointed to the clock. "Thirty minutes, remember? Less now."

That got him moving, and in a whirlwind of male efficiency, he had the broken window covered in under fifteen minutes. "It's not a very attractive job," he admitted, finding me in the living room where I was arranging the tiny quiches on our tangerine-colored Fiestaware platters. "But it'll keep the weather out."

But not the demons. I fought a little shiver and glanced in that direction, but all I could see was thick black plastic. I made a face and tried not to imagine a horde of demons crouched below the windowsill, just waiting to avenge their compatriot.

Enough of that. I forced the thought away, then stood up and surveyed the rest of the room. Not bad. "Okay," I said. "I think we're ready for battle. If we can keep everyone corralled in the living room, the den, and the dining room, I think we'll be okay."

"Oh," Stuart said. "Well, sure. We can do that."

Warning bells went off in my head, and I thought of the piles of sorted laundry in the upstairs hallway, the disaster area Allie called a room, and the wide assortment of plush animals and Happy Meal toys that littered the playroom floor. Also, I was pretty sure the CDC wanted to quarantine the kids' bathroom, hoping to find a cure for cancer in the new and exotic species of mildew growing around the tub.

"You want to show someone the house?" I asked, in the same tone I might use if he'd suggested I perform brain surgery after dessert.

"Just Judge Larson," Stuart said, his voice losing a bit of steam as he watched my face. "He's looking to buy a place, and I think he'd like the neighborhood." He licked his lips, still watching me. "I'm, uh, sure he won't mind if the place is in some disarray."

I raised an eyebrow and stayed silent.

"Or we can do it some other time."

"Yes," I said with a winning smile. "Some other time sounds fine."

"Great. No problem."

That's another thing I love about Stuart. He's trainable. "So who's Judge Larson?" I asked. "Do I know him?"

"Newly appointed," Stuart said. "Federal district court. He just moved up from Los Angeles."

"Oh." Keeping track of all the judges and attorneys that cross Stuart's path is next to impossible. "You can show him the kitchen and the study if it's important to you. But don't take him upstairs." I bent down and moved the fruit plate slightly to the left, so it lined up nicely with the row of forks I'd set out.

We didn't decide whether a downstairs tour was on the agenda or not, because that's when the doorbell rang. "Go," I ordered. "I still need to put out the wineglasses." I started running down a list in my head. Appetizers—*check*; wine—*check*; napkins—

Oh, shit. *Napkins.*

I knew I had cocktail napkins somewhere in this house, but I had absolutely no idea *where*. And what about tiny plates for the appetizers? How could I have forgotten the tiny plates?

My pulse increased, gearing up to a rhythm that more or less mimicked my earlier heart rate when I'd fought the demon. This was why I hated entertaining. I always forgot something. Nothing ever went smoothly. Stuart was going to lose the election, and his entire political demise could be traced to right here. *This* moment. The night his wife completely screwed up a dinner party.

And forget using demons as an excuse. No, I would

have forgotten the napkins and plates even without Pops. That's just the way I—

"Hey." Stuart was suddenly beside me, his lips brushing my hair, his soft voice pulling me out of my funk. "Have I told you yet how amazing you are, pulling all this together on such short notice?"

I looked up at him, warmed by the love I saw in his face. "Yeah," I said. "You already told me."

"Well, I meant it."

I blinked furiously. My husband might be the sweetest man on the planet, but I was *not* going to run my mascara. "I don't know where the cocktail napkins are," I admitted, sounding a little sniffly.

"I think we'll survive the tragedy," he said. The doorbell rang again. "Pull yourself together, then meet me at the door."

I nodded, calmed somewhat by the knowledge that my husband loved me even though I was a total domestic failure.

"And, Kate," he called as he moved toward the foyer, "check the buffet, second drawer from the left, behind the silver salad tongs."

Clark arrived first, of course. And while he and Stuart did the political he-man thing—dishing about the upcoming campaign, bitching about various idiocies being implemented by the newly installed city council—I took the opportunity to round out my role as a domestic goddess.

I hauled out the cocktail napkins (right where Stuart said they'd be), brought in seven wineglasses (I'd used the eighth to kill the demon), and checked on the dessert.

Throughout all of this, I kept looking toward the flimsily repaired window, half-expecting to see a demon army come crashing through. But all seemed quiet. Too quiet, maybe?

I frowned. On a normal day I'd say I was being melodramatic. But I no longer knew what normal was. For fourteen years, normal had been diapers and bake sales and Bactine and PTA meetings. Demons—especially the kind that are ballsy enough to just out-and-out *attack*—were not normal. Not by a long shot.

And yet years ago, that had been my life.

It wasn't a life I wanted back. Wasn't a life I had any intention of letting my husband or kids see.

But here that life was. Or, rather, *there* it was—in my pantry, dead behind the cat food.

It wasn't the dead demon that bothered me so much (okay, that's not entirely true), but it was its words that had really thrown me—*You may as well die, Hunter. You surely will when my master's army rises to claim victory in his name.*

I rubbed my bare arms, fighting goose bumps. Something was happening here, something I didn't want to be a part of. But want to or not, I had a feeling I was already in it up to my eyeballs.

"Katie?" Stuart's voice drifted in from the living room. "Do you need help, sweetheart?" Elizabeth Needham, another assistant county attorney in Stuart's division, had arrived a few minutes ago, and now she and Clark and Stuart were doing the war-stories thing. Stuart's offer was genuine, I'm sure. But I could tell from his tone that he was also voicing a request that I get my butt in there and join them.

"I've got it, hon," I said. "I'll be right there. I just want to call Allie and say good night."

Stuart didn't answer, so I couldn't tell if he thought that was odd or not. It was. Allie stayed with Mindy and Mindy stayed with us on such a regular basis that Laura and I were basically surrogate parents for the other's kid. I knew Laura would call if anything was out of the ordinary.

Reason, however, was not part of the equation. I wanted to talk to my daughter, and I wanted to do it right then.

I dialed and waited. One ring. Two rings. Three, and then the familiar click of Laura's answering machine. I waited through the message, tapping my fingers on the counter as Laura spelled out her family's vital statistics—name, phone number, can't get to the phone right now, yada yada—and then finally I heard the high-pitched little beep. "Laura? You there? Give Cary Grant a rest and pick up. I want to tell Allie something."

I waited, still tapping on the countertop. "Laura?" I stopped tapping, noticing that I'd now chipped the manicure that had managed to survive a demon attack.

Still no answer, and I could feel that cold rush of panic growing in my chest. Surely demons hadn't gone after my daughter. . . .

"Come on, girl," I said to the machine, fighting to keep the panic out of my voice. "I need—"

I shut my mouth and my eyes, exhaling deeply as I realized what a fool I was being. Not demons. *Ice cream.* Makeup might keep Mindy occupied for hours, but my daughter was a different breed. Forty-five minutes, tops.

"Never mind," I told the still-open line. "Just have Allie call me when you guys get back."

I checked the clock. Seven-ten. If they went to the mall, they wouldn't be back until at least eight. I could keep my paranoia in check for fifty minutes.

Stuart stepped into the kitchen just as I was hanging up the phone. "Anything wrong?"

He said it in a tone that suggested he almost hoped there'd been some horrific tragedy—because that would explain why his hostess wife was camped out in the kitchen ignoring her guests.

"I'm sorry." I slammed the phone down. "Just mommy paranoia."

"But everything's all right?"

"Fine," I said brightly. He was angling for an explanation and I didn't have one to give. The oven timer dinged and I lunged for a hot pad. Saved by baked Brie.

I'd just slid the Brie onto a plate and passed it off to Stuart when the doorbell rang again.

"Well," I said. "We'd better go see to our guests."

I led the way out of the kitchen, my baffled husband following. In the living room, Stuart slid the plate onto the coffee table next to the fruit as I breezed past on my way to the front door, an efficient hostess smile plastered to my face.

I opened the door to reveal one of the most distinguished men I'd ever seen. Despite his years—I guessed he was at least sixty—he had the bearing of a self-confident forty-year-old. His salt-and-pepper hair gave him an air of distinction, and I was absolutely certain that this was a man who never second-guessed his decisions.

"Judge Larson," Stuart said from behind me. "So glad you could come."

I held the door open wider and ushered him in. "Welcome to our home. I'm Kate, Stuart's wife."

"It's a pleasure to meet you, my dear," he said. His voice had a gravelly Sean Connery–esque tone. I may be only thirty-eight, but I'll confess to a tiny bit of debonair-lust. I could only hope that Stuart would be that sexy and sophisticated when he hit sixty.

"You have a beautiful home," he added. We were still in the entrance hall, and as he spoke, he was passing me, close enough that I could smell the cologne he'd apparently bathed in. I wrinkled my nose. Sexy, maybe. But I think age must have degenerated his olfactory nerves.

And that's when I caught it—a foul, garlicky stench hidden under wave after wave of Old Spice. *Holy shit.*

Forget attraction. Forget sophistication. Forget the fact that I had a party to host.

The judge in my foyer was a demon—and there was no way he was getting out of my house alive.

Three

Instinct and long-ignored training took hold, my muscles springing into action. I twisted at the waist, planning to kick back and ram my heel into the demon's gut.

I didn't make it.

At the same moment that my foot left the floor, common sense flooded my brain, and I jerked to a stop. *Too late*. My sudden shift in direction threw off my equilibrium, and I landed with a *plunk* on my rump, the ceramic tile cool through the thin material of my dress.

Stuart cried out my name, but it was Judge Larson who bent down and extended a hand. I stared at him, blinking, mentally reminding myself that I had demons on the brain and not everyone who desperately needed a Certs was Satan's henchman.

"Mrs. Connor? Are you okay?"

"Fine. I'm fine." Wary, I took his hand, encouraged when he didn't immediately yank me to my feet and try to rip off my head. That had to be a good sign, right?

With Judge Larson holding my hand and Stuart gripping my elbow, the men helped me to my feet. "I'm so sorry," I mumbled, my cheeks on fire. "I must have slipped on something. I'm terribly embarrassed."

"Please," the judge said. "Don't be."

By this time, Clark and Elizabeth had come in from the living room to see what all the commotion was about, and two more guests were coming up the walkway. How lovely. The entire gang was there to witness my mortification.

I tugged my hand free from Larson and focused on my husband. "I'm okay. Really."

The worry I saw on Stuart's face appeased my fear that my acrobatics had made a farce of the evening. "You're sure? Is your ankle sprained?"

"It's *fine*," I said again.

It wasn't fine, of course. It wasn't fine at all. For all I knew, I was about to serve my famous rigatoni (famous because it's the only dish I do well) to a demon. And right at the moment, I had no way to confirm Larson's humanity.

I cast a sidelong glance Larson's way as Stuart led us all toward the living room. I'd figure it out, though. He couldn't keep his identity from me forever.

And if Larson turned out to be a demon, then there really would be hell to pay.

"More Brie?" I held the tray in front of Larson, leaning forward like some little flirt showing off cleavage. If he wasn't a demon, he probably thought I was hitting on him. Stuart, bless his heart, probably assumed I was having a psychotic episode.

But I was determined to get another whiff of the man's breath. At the moment it was all I had to go on.

"No, thank you," he said as I inhaled through my nose. No use. He'd already helped himself to quite a bit of the Brie, and now the pungent cheese odor masked whatever other stench might linger on his breath.

Frustrated, I slid the Brie back onto the table and took my seat next to Stuart. He and Judge Robertson, one of the late arrivals, were deep in a scintillating discussion of California's three-strikes law.

"So, what do you think of three strikes?" I asked Judge Larson. "I'm all for it," I went on, "except for those truly evil creatures that just deserve to be taken out, no matter what the cost." I could see that I'd caught Stuart's attention, and he was looking at me with some surprise. His platform was tough on crime, but not *that* tough.

"Vigilante justice?" Larson asked.

"In certain circumstances, yes."

"Katie . . ." Stuart's voice held a *What are you doing?* tone.

I smiled at him, but directed my words at Larson. "Just playing Devil's advocate, honey."

"Kate can debate with the best of them," he said to the group. "And she's got very firm views on crime."

"Good and evil," I said. "Black and white."

"No shades of gray?" Elizabeth asked.

"Some things are uncertain, sure," I admitted with a glance toward Larson. "I just find those things supremely frustrating."

They all laughed. "Maybe your wife's the politician, Stuart," Judge Westin, a newly elected state court judge, said. "Be careful or *she'll* be the new county attorney."

Stuart rubbed my shoulder, then leaned over and planted a light kiss on my cheek. "She'd keep a tight rein on crime, that's for sure." He smiled broadly at the group, and I knew the politician had returned. "Of course, so will I."

"All I intend to keep a tight rein on is some pasta." I stood up, gesturing for the guests to stay seated. "I need to go finish dinner. If you'll excuse me . . ."

In the kitchen I sagged against the counter, my heart beating wildly. I never used to be such a ditz about demon-hunting. Of course, I'd never entertained demons in my house before, either. In the past I'd been given an assignment and I'd carried it out. Simple. I never had to actually locate the demons; my *alimentatore* handled that part. I just did the dirty work.

And as dangerous and as messy as my old job had been, I think I preferred it to my current situation.

I pulled a wooden spoon from the drawer by the stove and stirred the sauce, feeling a little guilty that I wasn't playing the perfect wife role to a T. At least the sauce had turned out great. Maybe a really kick-ass meal would make up for the fact that Stuart's wife was a nutcase. (Just how important *was* a sane wife to a politician, anyway?)

I ran the evening's events back through my mind and decided that Stuart's career was still on track. Our guests probably just thought I had a little color and was tough on crime. I could live with that. More important, *Stuart* could live with that. Keep acting like a space case, though, and I'd blow his shot before he'd even announced his candidacy.

Think, Katie, think. There had to be a way to figure out for sure if Larson was a demon without ruining my marriage, Stuart's political aspirations, or the dinner party.

I turned the heat down under the sauce, then dumped the pasta into the boiling water, all the while considering my options. Unfortunately, there are very few foolproof litmus tests for identifying demons. If a demon has *possessed* a human while the human is still alive, it's easy. Then you have a Linda Blair situation and there's this whole raging battle inside the person. Very messy. Very easy to spot. And very *not* my job (former job, that is).

If you're possessed, don't call a Hunter. For that, you need a priest. It's a painful, ugly, scary proposition involving lots of nasty invectives by the possessing demon, a multitude of body fluids, and utter and complete exhaustion. I know. I watched two as part of my training. (There's nothing like a possession to get a Hunter in tune with *exactly* why we want to eradicate the nasty little demon bugs from the face of the earth.) It's not something I want to see again.

But there wasn't any battle raging inside Judge Larson. No, if I'd guessed right, Larson wasn't possessed. Instead, he actually *was* a demon. Or, rather, a demon had moved in and the real Larson's soul, like Elvis, had left the building.

It's a sad fact that there are lots of demons inhabiting our world. Thankfully, most of them can't do much in the way of annoying or harming humans. They're just out there, floating around in a disembodied state, spending eternity looking for a human body to fill. A lot of them want to be human so badly that they go the possession route.

But it's the ones with more patience that I worry about. These demons inhabit a body at the moment of death. As the person's soul leaves, the demon slips in, just like Pops in my pantry. You've heard the stories of folks who couldn't possibly survive a car wreck . . . but did? Or the person on the operating table who against all odds managed to pull through? Or the heart attack victim who collapsed . . . and then got right back up again with no apparent damage whatsoever?

Well, now you know.

Of course, it's not as easy as all that. The timing has to be *just right*. Once the soul is gone, the entry point closes and, poof, no more opportunity. (That's not *entirely* accurate. There's a later point where the body is once again ripe for takeover. I think the decay opens a portal or something. I'm not a theologian. All I know is by that time, there are issues of rigor and worms and all sorts of gross stuff. Demons do resort to that on occasion, and I've fought a few zombies in my time. But since Larson clearly wasn't a zombie, that really wasn't my concern.)

The other thing about using a human body is that demons can't inhabit the faithful. Those souls *fight*. So it's not like a demon can just hang around a hospital waiting for folks to head out to the Great Beyond. It's a lot harder than that. Which, when you think about it, is good news for all of us.

So, while there aren't that many demons walking around in human shells, the ones that *are* out there are hard to spot. They blend in perfectly. (Well, there is the bad-breath thing, but how many non-Hunters clue in to that?) And disposing of them is a real pain in the butt.

But those demons *do* have certain idiosyncrasies that are useful to Hunters for identification purposes. I'd already tried the breath test on Larson. And while I thought he'd failed, I couldn't get a good enough second whiff to confirm. And, frankly, even if his breath was so bad it knocked me over, that really wasn't reason enough to stab him in the eye. It's difficult enough covering up a demon killing. The accidental death of a nondemon judge was not something I wanted to explain.

Which meant I needed to find another test.

The best test was holy ground. Your run-of-the-mill demons can't bear to enter a church. They can physically make it through the doors, but it just about kills them to do it. Major pain and suffering, and it only gets worse the closer they get to the altar. And if the altar happens to have incorporated the bones of a saint (which is pretty common), then we're talking extreme depths-of-hell-quality torture. Not a pretty picture. But since there was no way I could convince Stuart, Larson, and the gang to take a little field trip to the cathedral, that test was pretty much useless.

Frowning, I turned on the tap. I needed to wash my hands and get dinner on the table. Demon detection could wait until after dessert.

And that's when it hit me. *Holy water*. The answer was so obvious, I felt like an idiot for not thinking of it earlier. Just like in *The Exorcist*, holy water burns the shit out of demons. (And I've got to say that there's very little in this world more satisfying than seeing those welts appear on a demon you've been stalking. Vengeful? Absolutely. But so very true.)

The timer dinged, which meant the pasta was ready. I

dumped the pot into the colander, mixed the rigatoni with my secret sauce in one of the fancy serving bowls we'd received as a wedding present, then carried the dish to the table. I hesitated there, glancing toward the stairs, shifting my weight from foot to foot. My hunting gear was locked up in a trunk in the attic, but every good Hunter keeps a few essentials nearby, even after fifteen years. And I was pretty sure that if I looked in the bottom drawer of my jewelry chest, I'd find an oversized crucifix and at least one small bottle of holy water.

At least, I hoped I would.

I gnawed on my lower lip. Would they notice if I disappeared upstairs? Surely not. After all, I'd only be gone a second.

I was just about to risk it when Elizabeth stepped into the dining room, looking fabulous in something that I'm sure cost at least a month's salary. (Her husband is a partner at McKay & Case, a personal injury firm. Let's just say they don't need to pinch pennies.)

"Can I help?"

I considered letting her finish putting the food on the table while I ran upstairs, but a burst of sanity vetoed that plan. I didn't need the holy water this very instant. If Larson was a demon, I'd know soon enough. And in the meantime, he wasn't going anywhere. (And what would I do if he *was* a demon, anyway? Killing him during dinner would be a social *faux pas* from which I'd never recover.)

As I finished preparing the table, Elizabeth called in the men. They came, and I seated myself next to Larson, pretending not to notice the chair Stuart held out for me.

We had the salad first, and I actually managed to participate in the conversation. ("Why, yes, I heard some developer wants to put in a mall on Third Street. I hope it falls through. That's *so* near the beach." "Actually, Allie grew the basil, Elizabeth. I'll tell her how much you enjoyed it."

"Thank you. We certainly love our neighborhood." Mundane. Boring. You get the drift.)

People tend to get more involved in eating once they get to the main course, abandoning polite small talk in favor of their stomachs. And that's when I made my move. I cocked my head to the side and made a show of furrowing my brow. Then I leaned forward, meaningfully meeting Stuart's eyes. "Did you hear that?"

"What?" Confusion and a hint of concern splashed across his face.

I pushed my chair back, dropping the napkin in my seat. "I'm sure it's nothing," I said. I was up and around the table, heading for the doorway. "I thought I heard Timmy." I smiled at our guests. "Excuse me. I'll be right back."

Stuart was halfway out of his chair. "Should I—"

"Don't be silly. He probably had a bad dream. I just want to check."

That appeased him, and I headed off. As soon as I rounded the corner and was out of sight of the dining room, I took off at a run, bounding up the stairs two at a time.

I didn't breathe until I hit the bedroom, and once I did, I took the most direct route to my jewelry box, bouncing across the bed in a way that would have earned Timmy a scolding. I yanked the bottom drawer out and dumped it, scattering odd bits of jewelry and memorabilia over the rumpled bed linens.

A charm bracelet, a broken pocket watch, a silver crucifix in a velvet case, a box of Allie's baby teeth, and—tucked in the back—a single bottle of holy water, the metal cap still screwed on tight.

Dear Lord, thank you.

I didn't even hear Stuart come up behind me. "Kate?"

I yelped, then shoved the bottle down the bodice of my dress, where I could feel my heart pounding against it.

"Shit, Stuart, you scared me to death." I slid off the bed and turned around to face him, not quite meeting his eyes.

"I thought you were checking on Tim."

"I was. I did. He's asleep."

Stuart lifted his brows and looked pointedly at the mess on the bed.

"I, um, realized I wasn't wearing any earrings."

Nothing.

The silence grew so thick that I was afraid he wasn't going to answer. Then he moved toward me and stroked my cheek, finally cupping my chin in his hand. With the utmost tenderness, he tilted my head back. "Sweetheart, do you feel okay?"

"I'm fine," I said. As fine as anyone could be who had to deal with demons and a dinner party and keeping secrets from her husband. "I'm sorry. I'm just distracted."

It hit me then that we were both upstairs, and the kitchen was unguarded. What if someone spilled something? What if they went looking for paper towels? *What if they looked behind the cat food?*

I grabbed his hand. "I guess I felt a little overwhelmed," I said as I tugged him down the hall. "I'm not much of a Jackie O."

"I don't want Jackie O.," he said. "You've done a fabulous job. Just be yourself and everyone will love you. I know I do."

I forced a smile, but I couldn't force any words. Because for the first time, the honest to God's truth hit me: My husband, the man who'd fathered my youngest child and who shared my bed every night, didn't really know squat about my life.

And if I had my way, he wasn't ever going to.

My opportunity presented itself during dessert. "Would anyone else like some water?" I asked, rising. No one did, so I headed into the kitchen, pulled down our smallest glass (one of Timmy's with faded purple dinosaurs) and poured in the holy water. Not even half an inch.

I eyed the tap, wondering if it was sacrilegious to mix holy water with the water provided by the City of San Diablo. Even more important, I wondered if it would render the water ineffective.

Since it wasn't worth the risk to either my soul or my plan, I returned with my tiny bit of water in my tiny little glass. Stuart looked at me, and I shrugged. "We never seem to have enough clean glasses," I said.

Judge Larson looked amused. "You're not very thirsty," he said. "Or are you sneaking a shot of liqueur while the rest of us gorge ourselves on your delicious apple tart?"

I laughed. "Exceptionally thirsty," I lied. "I polished off most of the glass just walking back." As I spoke, I headed for my seat, planning to trip over my own feet and dump the water on Larson as soon as I was in range.

The phone rang, and Stuart pushed his chair back, blocking my path and spoiling my plan. "That might be Judge Serfass," he said, referring to the one no-show who'd called to say her plane was late. He answered, but his expression quickly turned to confusion. "I can't hear you," he said, in that overly loud voice people use on bad connections. "I can't understand a word you're saying."

Another few seconds passed as he shook his head, looking confused and frustrated. Then he shrugged and hung up the phone.

"Who was it?"

"No idea. Sounded foreign. Italian, maybe. The connection was terrible, but it had to be a wrong number."

Father Corletti.

Out of instinct, I turned to look at Larson, *and found him looking right back at me.*

Oh, hell, it was now or never. I pushed past Stuart's chair toward my own. As I did, Larson stood. He reached down as if to pull my chair out for me, but before I realized what was happening, he bumped my arm and the glass went flying.

Water splashed harmlessly on the tile. But not a single drop touched the man.

"Oh, look at that. I'm so sorry," he said. "How incredibly clumsy of me."

"You did that on purpose," I hissed as I bent to pick up the glass.

"*What?*" That from Stuart. *Oops.* The comment I'd meant only for Larson had apparently been louder than I'd thought.

"I said he really knows how to startle a person." I stood up and met Larson's eyes, my smile cold. "No harm, no foul. Water's certainly replaceable. Tap water, mineral water, bottled water. All kinds of water."

He didn't answer me. He didn't have to. We both knew the score for that round. Demons—one. Me—*nada*.

Another hour of chitchat and political hocus-pocus and then the guests were finally ready to hit the road. Parties often come to an end in a bustle of bodies gathering purses and car keys, and this one was no exception. We all migrated to the foyer, then stepped out onto the front porch where hands started shaking and good-byes started flying.

In the flurry, Larson took my hand, his skin rough against my own. "It's been a lovely, enlightening evening, Mrs. Connor. I'm sure we'll see each other again soon."

His eyes reflected a deep intensity. Not necessarily evil . . . but the man definitely looked as if he knew my secrets.

I shivered, fighting revulsion and a hint of fear. "Yes," I managed. "I'm sure we'll cross paths again soon."

"And I'm so sorry I didn't have the chance to meet your daughter. I imagine she's just like her mother."

My chest constricted and I realized I couldn't breathe. It

was almost eleven o'clock. The mall had been closed for an hour. And I hadn't heard a word from Laura or Allie.

Oh, shit, oh, shit, oh, shit.

"I hear Timmy crying," I muttered, ostensibly to Stuart, but I didn't bother to see if he heard me. I raced back into the house, tossing "thank you all for coming" over my shoulder as I disappeared inside.

"Pick up, pick up, pick up." I had the phone in my hand and was pacing the kitchen. Laura's voice, that damn message, the beep, and then, "Allie? Laura? Where are you guys? Hello?"

No one was answering, and I was on the verge of slamming down the receiver and racing to Laura's back door when the machine beeped and I heard Mindy's voice, laced with giggles. "Mrs. Connor?"

"Mindy." I exhaled, and my legs gave out. I sank to the ground and hugged my knees to my chest, my back pressed against the dishwasher. "Where's Allie?"

"She's on the treadmill. We both had double scoops, so that means we have to burn like three hundred calories or something to make up for it."

I closed my eyes and decided I'd save the eating-disorder lecture for another time. "Can you put her on?"

Mindy didn't bother to answer, but I heard the clatter of the cordless phone changing hands. "Mom! Mrs. Dupont took us to an Adam Sandler movie! Isn't that cool? He is *soooo* funny."

"I didn't realize you guys were going to be gone that long," I said. "I thought you were just getting ice cream."

I could practically hear her shrug. "We kinda begged. But, Mom, it was such a slammin' movie."

I assumed that meant she liked it. "Any reason why you didn't call to let me know where you'd be?"

"Huh? I was with Mrs. Dupont, remember?"

Okay, I wasn't being fair. "Sorry. I just got a little worried when I couldn't find you."

"Then let me have a cell phone."

My daughter, the pragmatist.

"So," I said brightly, "why don't you and Mindy come over here tonight. I'm wired from coffee. If you're still up for that Harry Potter marathon, I'm game."

"Um . . ."

Not the enthusiastic response I'd wanted. "Come on, Al. It'll be fun. You two can stay up as late as you want."

"Yeah?" A pause. "Why?" Suspicion laced her voice. Smart kid.

"Because you're my kid and I love you and I want to spend time with you." *And protect you.*

"Oh." I held my breath while she thought it over. "We don't have the movies."

"I'll send Stuart out to get them."

"And we can really stay up for all of them?"

"Absolutely." I could be magnanimous in victory.

"Cool." A pause, then. "And, Mom?"

"Hmmm?" I was distracted by the realization that I now had to convince Stuart to schlep to Blockbuster.

"I think the guy at the concession stand likes me."

No more distraction. "Which one? That blond guy who looks like he plays college football?" I'd wring his neck if even looked at my baby girl that way.

"*Nooo.*" I got the verbal eye roll. "He's probably about sixteen and he's got glasses and curly dark hair. He's cute."

"You don't need a boyfriend, Allie," I said. "Believe me. There's time enough for that later."

"Oh, *Mo-om.* Anyway, I wouldn't want *him* as a boyfriend." Which begged the question of whether there was a particular boy she *did* want. "I said he liked *me.* He's cute and all, but he's a little bit of a dweeb. And he's got really gross breath."

My blood turned to ice. "Allie," I said, my voice as sharp as a knife. "I'm going to drive over and get you both right now." I drew a breath, then tried to cover. "Otherwise," I added, "we'll be watching movies until dawn."

Despite their enthusiasm for our impromptu marathon, Allie and Mindy only lasted through the first half of *Chamber of Secrets*. I left them camped out on the floor of the den, then circled the house, checking all the doors and windows, and making sure all the alarms were activated, including the motion sensor on the first floor. We rarely use that feature (inevitably the cat trips the alarm), but tonight I considered it essential. If anyone (or anything) came through the window, I wanted to know about it.

I considered moving the body, but feared I'd wake someone up. Better to send husband and kids out tomorrow with a list of Saturday morning errands, and leave me alone to do the dirty work. If I gave them the option of shopping or cleaning the bathrooms, I could pretty much guarantee they'd depart the house willingly.

I planned to go back to sleep on the couch beside the girls, but Stuart woke up while I was checking Timmy's room, and he tugged me back into bed with him. We spooned together, the same way we had for years, but I couldn't sleep. Instead I lay there, my mind in a muddle. I tried to reach out, to grasp some coherent thought and make some sense of the day's events, but I was too exhausted.

And, really, there was no sense to be had. I simply didn't have enough information.

I glanced at the clock, the digits swimming through my bleary-eyed vision. Just after four. I eased away from Stuart and sat up, swinging my bare feet to the floor. Then I padded into the guest room and shut the door.

Time to make a phone call.

Even after fifteen years I could still dial the number from memory, and I punched it in, then waited through the funky beep-ring that always made me think that European phones were more of a toy than a telecommunications device. After four rings the Vatican operator picked up.

"Sono Kate Andrews. Posso parlare con Padre Corletti, per favore?" I said, giving my maiden name. Of course, Father also knew me by my first married name—Crowe—but Father had been like a parent to me. I'd always be Katherine Andrews around him.

The operator put me through, and after a few seconds, Father Corletti picked up. *"Katherine?"* His voice, once so firm and commanding, seemed weak and feeble. *"Katherine? Sei tu?"*

"Si." I closed my eyes, suddenly fearful that Father would be no help to me at all. But he had to be. If I couldn't turn to the *Forza Scura*, then there was nowhere else to go.

"I am so pleased," he said, his accent thick. "When I could not reach you earlier, I feared the worst had come."

I licked my lips. "Tell me what's happening."

"It is you who are there, in San Diablo. Perhaps you should tell me."

I did. I started from the beginning, going into more detail than I'd left in my earlier message, and ending with Larson's parting comment and Allie's revelation about the stinky concessionaire. "They can't be after my little girl," I whispered. "Please, Father, that isn't happening, is it?"

"They seek something," Father said. "Something in San Diablo."

"You didn't answer my question," I accused.

"I have no answer, my child."

I closed my eyes and fought tears. I was *not* going to lose Allie. Not now. Not ever. "What? What do they want?"

"That, we do not know."

"Then find out," I said. "Or better yet, just eradicate the problem. Surely you have Hunters in place here already."

"There are no Hunters there."

"Then send some," I hissed. I fought to keep control, to

keep from yelling at him. My nerves were on edge, my emotions raw, and I had to remind myself that my family was sleeping, and I didn't want to wake them.

"Ah, Katherine," he said. "I have, perhaps, been unclear. No? But I think that you do not understand. There is no one we can send to you." He drew in a breath. "This battle, you must fight on your own."

Four

"*Excuse me?*" I held the phone out as I spoke, glaring at it as if the handset had just personally delivered the bad news. "I can't handle this. I have kids. I have a car pool. I have *responsibilities.*"

"You have always had responsibilities," Father said.

"Oh, no, no, no." I kept my voice low—a concession to my sleeping family—so I wasn't sure that I was adequately displaying the depths of my displeasure. Ranting and screaming would have been so much more effective. "I'm *retired*, remember? The *Forza* isn't my life anymore. I'm demon-free, and I like it."

"Apparently, child, you are not."

I thought of the demon in my pantry and had to admit Father had a point. I kept quiet, though, waiting for him to say something else. When he didn't, I kept quiet some more, in the foolish hope that I could outwait him.

Nothing.

"Dammit," I said, when I couldn't take it anymore. "Why is this *my* problem?"

"The demon came to you. That makes it your problem, no?"

"No," I said, but without conviction. I was caving. I knew it, and he knew it.

He said nothing.

I sighed, anger finally succumbing to a much stronger surge of exhaustion. It had been a hell of a day. And from the sound of things, it was shaping up to be one hell of a weekend, too.

"Okay, fine." I finally spoke, in part to quiet the overloaded silence emanating from Rome. "But at least tell me why I'm on the hot seat." I asked the question even though I didn't really need an answer. Whatever the reason, I already knew the only part that mattered—no one was coming to help me, and I had been, quite without fanfare, *un*retired. The why of it was completely academic.

Still, I was curious, and I listened with a perverse fascination as he explained in depressing detail the recent dwindling of *Forza Scura*'s resources and the unsettling implications that followed.

"Young people today," he said. "They are more interested in television and—what do you call it?—Nintendo. The life of a Hunter has no appeal, and the *Forza*'s numbers are dwindling."

"You've got to be kidding me," I said. "Have you *watched* television? Played those games?"

From what I could tell, it was a rare kid that wasn't willing to plunk his or herself down in front of the television and do the dirty work.

"Many young people have the desire," Father admitted after I spewed out my theory. "It is the rare student, however, that has the stamina."

That made a little more sense. My own daughter's attention span tended to increase or diminish in direct proportion to the number of boys in the vicinity. "All right," I said, conceding the point. "I'll buy that recruiting has fallen off. But I can't believe there aren't *any* Hunters. I mean, there's still a need, right?"

That was my not-too-artful way of asking if demon activity had fallen off in the last few years. I couldn't imagine that it had, though. I might be retired, but I still watch the evening news. And believe me, there are demons among us.

"*Numquam opus maius*," Father said. My Latin sucks, but I got the gist. The need was greater than ever. "And, yes, there are other Hunters, though not many. As you are aware, the mortality rate is high. We have fewer Hunters now than we did when you were active."

"Oh." Although the information was hardly news, it was still sobering. "And the Hunters you do have," I pressed, "I suppose they're otherwise occupied?"

"*Sì.*"

"Shit." And then, "Sorry, Father."

His low chuckle seemed to wash over me, and I wrapped myself in a sudden, unexpected memory. Me, laid up with the flu, propped up in my dorm-room bed with a box of tissue and a jar of Vicks VapoRub. And Father Corletti, sitting beside me, the flimsy cot buckling even under his negligible weight, as he told story after story of life within the *Forza Scura*. Serious business, he'd said. God's work. But still, he was able to find a bit of humor. And by the time my cold had disappeared, I was more eager than ever to get back to my training.

Father Corletti had been the closest thing I'd had to a parent, and until Eric, the *Forza* was the only family I'd known. So if Father needed me to drop everything and go kill demons, I would. I might not like it, but I'd do it.

"You will not be completely alone," Father said, and I fought a smile. He'd always had an uncanny ability to read my mind.

"Okay," I said. "Who?"

"An *alimentatore*," he said.

"You've got a spare *alimentatore*, but not a Hunter? Sounds like the Vatican human resources department isn't exactly doing a stellar job of keeping the proper balance among employees."

"Katherine . . ."

"Sorry."

"He will meet you at the cathedral tomorrow at noon."

"Fine," I said, knowing not to push. "Fine." Then I thought about it a bit more. "Tomorrow? It's the middle of the night here. You mean later today?" I knew he did. "How are you getting him here so fast?"

"He is already there."

"Already—"

"You will learn what we know tomorrow. In the meantime, rest . . . and conserve your resources. I fear that you shall need them."

Once again I held the handset out and stared at it, only this time I wasn't glaring. This time I was completely befuddled. "You *knew* about this? You already know what's going on here? Dammit, Father. Don't you dare make me wait until tomorrow!"

"Child, now is not the time." He paused, and I held my breath, thinking foolishly that he might change his mind. "You have of course kept up with your training?"

He'd turned the statement into a question. And though his tone was casual, I could tell the query was completely serious.

"Sure," I lied. "Of course I have." Like hell, I have. The only physical training I got these days was chasing a two-year-old, and my most recent mental exercise consisted of debating Allie about just how slutty the gotta-have-it outfit of the moment really was.

Not exactly at the top of my game, I had to say.

"Good."

That one word scared me more than anything else he could have said. "Father, I know you won't tell me everything, so I'm not even going to try. But—"

"Goramesh," he said, the demon's name turning my blood to ice. "We believe he may have come to San Diablo."

I stared at the phone once again, and this time realized my hand was shaking. *Goramesh*. The Decimator. One of the High Demons.

The old-man-demon's voice echoed in my head—*when my master's army rises up . . .*

Forget scared; now I was terrified.

I crossed myself in the dark, then said good-bye to Father Corletti. I didn't go back to Stuart, though. Instead I sat there on the guest bed, my knees under my chin and my arms wrapped around my legs. And then, as the first hint of sunlight fired the sky outside the window, I closed my eyes, bared my soul, and prayed.

"*There* you are. Jeez, Mom, Mindy just left, and Stuart and I've been looking *everywhere* for you."

Allie's voice pulled me from a not-too-sound sleep that had been filled with dreams of demons, death, and Eric. He'd been my partner, my strength. But he couldn't help me with this newest battle, and so I woke with tears in my eyes and the bitter fear that came with being completely alone.

"Mom?"

Worry filled her voice, and my emotions shifted, guilt now taking the strongest foothold. I held out a hand, and she came to me, her expression wary as she eased onto the bed. I pulled her to me and closed my eyes, breathing in the scent of Ivory soap and Aveda shampoo. I *wasn't* alone, and damn me for wallowing in self-pity. I had Allie and Timmy and Stuart, and I loved them each desperately.

"Were you thinking about Daddy?"

Her words cut through me like a knife, and I heard myself gasp.

"It's okay," she said. "It's okay to miss him."

She was repeating my own words back to me. My baby girl. *Eric's* baby girl. She'd grown so much since he'd died. He'd missed so much. I reached and stroked her cheek, determined not to cry.

"You okay?" she asked, tiny lines of worry creasing her forehead.

I took her hand and squeezed. "I'm fine," I said. "But when exactly did you grow up?"

The worry lines faded, replaced with a smile that was almost shy.

"Does that mean we can add an extra hour to my curfew?"

She spoke lightly, with a little impish grin I recognized as my own. I reflected it right back at her, my mood already remarkably lighter. "I'll take it under advisement," I said.

"In mom-speak, that means no."

"Not only did you grow up, you grew wise."

"If I'm so smart, how come my curfew's so early?"

I swung my feet over the side of the bed. "That's one of the great mysteries of the universe," I said. "I could tell you, but then I'd have to kill you."

"Mo-om." She rolled her eyes, and just like that, life went back to normal. Or at least as normal as possible under the circumstances. After all, I had a demon to hunt and a body to dispose of. I'd already accidentally overslept. Now I really had to get with the program.

The scene that greeted me in the kitchen was almost as scary as my encounter last night with Larson—Stuart standing in front of a griddle, spatula in hand, French toast sizzling in front of him. And the pantry door behind him standing wide open. *Yikes!*

I leaped across the room, managing to avoid a plastic

Tonka truck and half a dozen LEGOs. My hand closed around the knob to the pantry, and I slammed the door shut, then leaned against it, breathing hard.

"Wait!" Stuart called, leading with the spatula as he took a step toward me.

My heart stopped beating.

"I need another loaf of bread from in there."

Thump-thump, thump-thump. Okay. I was going to survive after all. "There's a loaf in the bread box," I said.

"Not anymore."

I grimaced. How could he go through an entire loaf of bread and still not have enough French toast to feed two adults, a teenager, and a toddler? Even I could manage that.

"I'll grab it for you," I said brightly. "After all, I'm right here."

He raised his eyebrows. "So I see. That's why I asked you."

"Right." I smiled, hoping to forestall any chance of my husband thinking I was nuts.

"Momma Momma Momma." Timmy's little voice managed to fill the entire downstairs. "Where you at, Momma?" The patter of footie-pajama feet, and then my little man appeared in the kitchen, a sippy cup in one hand and Boo Bear in the other. "Go potty, Momma. Go potty."

Shit. Not the most apropos of curses, I supposed, because Timmy had no interest in the whole potty-training experience. He just liked to sit on his little-bitty toilet fully clothed while he tossed things into the tub. Unfortunately, this activity required the presence of a mommy for full enjoyment potential.

"Go ahead," Stuart said. "I'll get the bread."

"Allie, can you take him to the bathroom?"

"Oh, Mom, do I have to?" Allie had plunked herself down at the kitchen table and was now engrossed in the pages of some magazine.

"Yes," I said, even as Timmy started up again, belting out a rousing chorus of "Mommamommamomma" without any musical accompaniment whatsoever.

"Timmy, honey, go with Allie."

"No."

"Allie . . ."

"He doesn't want to go with me."

"Kate, just take the boy. I can handle getting a loaf of bread."

Not in this lifetime. I pointed a "don't move" finger at Stuart, shot a "forget that extra hour at curfew" glance toward Allie, then slipped inside the pantry. I grabbed a loaf of bread and reemerged. I was in there just long enough to see that my demon was still covered and, thankfully, still dead. Always a plus.

I shoved the bread at Stuart, who looked a little bewildered. "Here. Cook." Then I grabbed Timmy's hand. "Come on, kiddo. Where are we going?"

"Bafroom! Potty!"

"Lead the way," I said, letting him tug me along, clearly delighted to have Mommy's undivided attention.

As soon as we reached the bathroom he shared with Allie, I collapsed onto the closed toilet seat while Timmy proceeded to position Boo Bear strategically on the little plastic potty we'd bought optimistically on his eighteen-month birthday. Now, seven months later, the kid had yet to christen the thing.

In the kitchen I could hear the sizzle of battered bread in my electric griddle then the scrape of a spatula against the Teflon surface. I exhaled, congratulating myself on keeping my husband in the dark.

At the same time, though, I wondered if it would really be that terrible if Stuart knew my secret. I intended to tell Allie the truth eventually, just not soon. After all, she had a right to know about her father, and she couldn't really understand her dad without knowing about *Forza Scura*. Stuart, though . . .

He was my husband. I loved him. And I didn't want to have secrets from him. But at the same time, I didn't want him to know *this*. I eased my conscience by falling back on the rules—my identity as a Hunter was secret, the oath of silence absolute. But that was only a crutch. I didn't *want* Stuart to see me as a Demon Hunter. As soon as he learned the truth, he would never see just Kate anymore. And I didn't think I could stand that. I had a sneaking suspicion a marriage counselor would find a huge red flag in my logic, but that was a risk I'd have to take.

As Timmy gleefully tossed every clean washcloth we own into the still shower-damp tub, I rested my elbows on my thighs and put my head in my hands.

Father Corletti was right. I should have kept up my physical training. I was pooped. Physically and mentally. Not a good sign. Especially since I still had to find the energy—not to mention the time—to dispose of one dead demon and stop an evil demon from taking over San Diablo, not to mention the world.

I checked my wristwatch—just past nine. I had a feeling it was going to be a *very* long day.

To Stuart's credit, he managed to pull off some pretty amazing French toast. Just enough cinnamon in the batter, a light dusting of powdered sugar (a culinary accoutrement I'm frankly amazed we had in the house, much less that he found it without discovering Mr. Demon). We four sat at the Fifties-style Formica table and wolfed down mass quantities of the breakfast confection, washing it down with tall glasses of ice-cold apple juice, a constant staple in our house due to its toddler-taming propensities.

Allie checked her watch. "If we leave right after breakfast, we'll get there when the mall opens."

I gaped as she flipped open the spiral notebook that had

been sitting closed and innocent by her plate all through breakfast. I'd completely forgotten that she'd been planning a school wardrobe shopping extravaganza for today.

"I made a list," she explained, tapping her pen against the page. "We can hit the Gap first, just to check any sales. Then the Limited and Banana Republic. I'll snag whatever deals I can, then fill in the gaps with stuff from Old Navy. Then we can move on to the department stores to check for any awesome markdowns. I figure we'll start with Nordstrom and work our way down to Robinsons-May."

"Don't forget about the carousel," I added, thinking quickly. "Timmy loves it."

Allie was looking at me as if I'd grown two heads. "We're *taking* him? I thought he was staying home with Stuart?"

"Kate," Stuart said, "you know I've got things to do around the house." He'd been hidden behind the metro section of the San Diablo *Herald*, but now he snapped the paper down, his frown almost as deep as Allie's. "That window, for instance. I won't get any of it done with Timmy underfoot."

Timmy perked up, apparently realizing he'd actually let most of a conversation pass without a significant contribution. Deciding to remedy that, he began to sing "If You're Happy and You Know It, Clap Your Hands" at the top of his lungs.

"I'll handle the window," I said to Stuart, dutifully clapping my hands on cue. We did need to get it fixed, of course, but I have to confess that after passing the night without incident, my paranoia quotient had dropped dramatically. "I was thinking that *you* could take Allie and Timmy to the mall."

He stared at me as if I'd gone mad, and Allie's expression mirrored his. For two people without a single genetic bond between them, at the moment they were doing a good impression of twins.

Allie spoke up first. "Mom, no way. Shopping with Stuart? He's a *guy*."

"Yes, he is," I said. "And he has wonderful taste, don't you, darling?"

"No," he said. "I mean, yes. My taste is fine." His eyes narrowed to tiny slits. "Are you mad at me? Did I do something to tick you off?"

I stifled the urge to bang my head against something hard and instead pushed back from the table.

"Momma Momma Momma. Where you going, Momma?"

"Just right over there, sweetie," I said, pointing to the wall that separates our breakfast area from the living room. "Finish your toast."

I tugged Stuart with me into the living room. I won't say he came willingly, but he did come, and the second we were out of sight from the kids, he let me have it. "Are you insane?" he stage-whispered. "The *mall*? You want me to go to the *mall*? What did I do? Seriously, I'll make it up to you. A trip to Paris. A day at the spa. You name it. Just not the mall."

I confess to being somewhat moved by his plea. If Stuart didn't make it in politics, I saw a bright future for him in acting. The man had melodrama down to a science. "Be serious," I said. "I thought about this a lot, and I think it's a wonderful idea." All of which was true, just not for reasons that I could share. I grasped for a Stuart-worthy reason. "You and the kids need some bonding time. Especially Allie."

"What's wrong with Allie? We get along great." His brow wrinkled. "Don't we?"

"Sure," I said. "*Now* you do. But she's fourteen. Do you remember fourteen?"

"Not very well."

"Well, I'm a girl, and I do. Fourteen's a hard age." Not that my fourteen had been anything like Allie's. I'd impaled my first demon at fourteen. That isn't something a girl is likely to forget. "She needs father-daughter time."

"But shopping?" He looked vaguely terrified by the prospect. "I couldn't just take her out to dinner?"

I gave him a sideways glance. "Stuart . . ."

"Fine. Fine. The mall it is. But you can't expect me to take Timmy, too."

Timmy was trickier, I have to admit. While I'd managed to concoct a psychologically sound argument for Stuart accompanying Allie to the mall, there really was no reason for a two-year-old to tag along for the ride.

I resorted to righteous indignation, the ultimate fallback for every stay-at-home mom. "Stuart Connor," I said, propping one fist on my hip and fixing my very best glare on him. "Are you telling me that you're incapable of spending time with the same two children I spend every single day with? That you can't find the time or energy to take your own son out for the morning? That you—"

"Okay, okay. I get the drift. I guess it's Daddy's day out."

My stern face dissolved, and suddenly I was all smiles. I raised up on my tiptoes and kissed him. "You're the best."

Stuart did not look ecstatic, but he wasn't apoplectic. Score one for Kate. We wandered back into the kitchen to find that Allie had already put all the dishes in the dishwasher and was now going over Timmy's face (and hair and hands and clothes) with a washcloth, trying to eradicate all signs of powdered sugar and syrup. Even on a bad day, Allie's pretty good about helping with Timmy. Add in the promise of a new wardrobe, and the kid becomes positively saintlike.

Another ten minutes and they were settled in the van, Stuart armed with credit cards, Allie with her list, and Timmy with Boo Bear. As they pulled out onto the street, I headed back to the front porch. I leaned against one of the wooden posts and waved, hoping they couldn't see the way my body sagged with relief. I love my family, really I do. But as I watched the van pull out of the driveway, I had to admit that a little alone time was awfully nice.

Even if I was alone with a dead demon.

Five

Fifteen minutes later a fresh pot of coffee was brewing on the kitchen counter, the pungent aroma of Starbucks Sumatra reminding me of the caffeinated reward that awaited me once my task was complete. At the moment I was hunched over, my fingers tight around the old man's arms as I dragged him from the kitchen toward the French doors at the back of the house.

My meeting with my *alimentatore* was at noon, and I couldn't wait. Ever since Stuart and the kids had left, I'd been fighting the creepy sensation that I was being watched. I'd checked the window first and found no demons (or mortal-variety Peeping Toms) lurking about. The plastic had come loose in a couple of places, but I attributed that more to the cheap off-brand duct tape I'd bought than to the forces of evil.

I'd shoved my uneasiness aside and got on with the job at hand. The truth is, I would have preferred to simply keep the demon in the pantry, then bring my mentor back with me to provide sound and useful advice about how to get rid of the remains. But since I couldn't be certain that Timmy's good mood or Stuart's shopping stamina would last that long, I had to get the demon out of the house and tucked away in our storage shed. In my old life, once I'd done away with a demon, one simple phone call to *Forza* would dispatch a collection team to take care of the demon carcass, leaving me blissfully unaware of that portion of the job. How lucky I was to now get this peek at demon-disposal methods. (That, in case you missed it, is called sarcasm.)

Though small and wizened, the old man still managed to be quite a burden. He was, after all, dead weight, and I was huffing by the time I reached the French doors. The curtains were drawn, and I pushed one panel aside, peering out into our backyard as if I were a fugitive. I'm not sure what I expected to see. An army of demons? The cops? My husband pointing a finger and accusing me of keeping secrets?

I saw none of the above and breathed a sigh of relief. My paranoia quotient had increased, however, to the point that the sound of the dishwasher changing cycles made me jump.

I left the body in front of the doors, then trotted up the stairs, taking them two at a time as I mentally sorted through the contents of my linen closet. I needed something big enough to wrap the man in, but it also had to be something I didn't mind tossing out. I didn't care how good the local dry cleaner was; there was no way I'd ever sleep on a demon shroud, freshly pressed or not.

I grabbed a fitted sheet (100 thread count, so no great loss) and raced back downstairs. Perfect. The elasticized corners even helped keep the floral print shroud attached to the body as I rolled it over and over until it was well co-cooned. I doubted my efforts would fool anyone who might be peering over my fence (a body wrapped in a sheet pretty much resembles only a body wrapped in a sheet), but the process made me feel better. And despite my rampant paranoia, I didn't *really* believe anyone would peek into my backyard in the time it would take me to get the body stowed in the shed.

As it turned out, it took longer than I'd expected.

Getting the body from the house *to* the shed was remarkably easy (I remembered Timmy's Radio Flyer wagon and put it to good use), but getting it *into* the shed was not. The little building was literally crammed to the gills, and I couldn't have stuffed a toaster in there, much less a body.

It was still early, so I wasn't in full-tilt panic mode. Yet.

I had a hefty adrenaline buzz going as I pulled out boxes and furniture and assorted bits of life junk, then stacked it all outside the shed for the single purpose of reorganizing it in a manner more conducive to the hiding of corpses. As soon as I'd made a big enough dent, I climbed inside, then bent down and grabbed the mummy. I slid him inside, discovering that he fit nicely under Allie's old twin bed. Then I hopped down and started to replace everything I'd just removed. Nietzsche would have made some pithy comment about exercises in futility, but not me. I just wanted the job done. And it was precisely because I was so in the zone that I didn't hear anyone coming up from behind me until it was too late.

A hand closed over my shoulder, and I yelled. Without thinking, I fell into a crouch and pivoted, ignoring my aching muscles as I whipped my leg straight out to catch my assailant just below the knee before pulling myself back up to attack position. It was a beautiful, brilliant move, and one that I managed without even pulling my hamstring. (Who knew I still had it in me?) The move would, in fact, have been perfect . . . had I managed to fell a demon. Instead, I found myself looming over Laura, hands fisted at my sides, blood pounding through my veins, and my chest about to explode with the suppressed urge to hit someone.

Fortunately, I *did* manage to suppress the urge. Pummeling my best friend would require a lie far beyond my powers of fabrication, particularly in my current state of mind. I bent over and drew in deep breaths, my hands propped just above my knees. Laura was on the ground in front of me, the heels of her hands pressed into the pea gravel that makes up the western half of our yard, surrounding the shed and Timmy's playscape. From the diameter of her eyes, I could tell I'd surprised her as much as she'd surprised me. For a moment, neither of us could speak. I recovered first.

"*Jesus*, Laura. Don't sneak up on me like that."

She blinked, winced. "I'll remember," she said, then reached down to rub her calf. "Where'd you learn to do that?"

"Neighborhood watch," I said. "The cop showed us all some techniques last month." A ridiculous answer, but she didn't seem to notice; she was too intent on flexing her leg and wiggling her ankle.

"So what were you doing, anyway? Hiding the family gold?"

I ignored the question, instead leaning over to put my hand on her calf. "How bad is it?"

She grimaced. "I'll live," she said. I helped her up and she gingerly put her weight on the leg. "But what *were* you doing? I don't think I've ever seen you so intense."

"Oh. Right." I scrambled for a reply, finally settling on the only thing I could think of that would keep her from asking too many follow-up questions. "I had another dream about Eric last night. And since Stuart and the kids are at the mall . . ." I trailed off, assuming (rightly) that she'd pick up the thread.

"Going through old things?"

I shrugged. "Sometimes I just miss him."

Her forehead creased, and I saw real concern in her eyes. The truth was I did dream of Eric, more frequently than I liked to admit. And Laura had been my confidante on more than one occasion. Today, though, I couldn't share my real burden, as much as I might like to. "Want to talk about it?"

"No." I looked at the ground, afraid of what she might see in my eyes. "I'll be okay. I need to pull myself together anyway. I have an appointment at noon."

She glanced at her watch, then at the boxes that still littered my yard, then at me, still in sweats and a T-shirt with no makeup and unwashed hair. "I'll help you put the shed back together."

I wanted to turn down the offer, but it was already getting late. Besides, I knew it was Laura's way of helping me out about Eric even though I didn't want to talk. And since the odds of her thinking that the bundle under the old twin bed was anything other than a rolled-up rug (or, for that matter, thinking about it at all) were slim, I graciously accepted.

"What have you got going on at noon?" she asked as she passed me a box.

"Nothing important," I said, trying for casual and pretty sure I came off like a bank robber swearing he had no idea where the money was hidden. "An old friend's in town. I'm going to meet him. Catch up. Trade family pictures. That kind of thing."

"Oh, that sounds like fun. How do you know the guy?"

"Eric and I knew him," I said, jumping on the first answer that popped into my head.

She sighed. "Oh, sweetie. You're getting inundated on all fronts, aren't you?"

"Pretty much." I couldn't quite meet her eyes as I took another box from her.

"Can I help?"

"Wish you could," I said. "It's just my past. Sometimes your old life sneaks up on you, and even though you weren't expecting it, you still have to deal with it."

She nodded and we finished the job in silence. I shut and locked the shed doors, then dusted myself off before looking pointedly at my watch. "Thanks for helping," I said. "But I should probably hop in the shower."

"Sure. I ought to get going, anyway. I promised Mindy I'd take her to the mall for new clothes today. I've spent the summer avoiding the thought."

I laughed. "I enlisted Stuart."

"You married a keeper," she said with a small frown. She patted her pockets and pulled out her key ring. She fidgeted, twirling the keys on her finger. "You know, I'm going to be a wreck after an entire day at the mall. Want to have a glass of wine later and wind down?"

I recognized the proposal for what it was—an offer to be an ear after my emotionally charged afternoon with my dear old friend.

She might be wrong about the cause, but she wasn't wrong about the end result—by the time today was over, I was certain I'd be in desperate need of a drink. Or two.

"Sounds like a plan. Besides, I'm sure the girls will want to compare wardrobes and coordinate for the first day of school."

"True enough. We'll need a bit of a buzz to survive the teenage walk of fashion." Her gaze drifted to the right, and I could picture her mentally inventorying her wine cabinet. "I've got a nice Moscato. I'll chill it and bring it over, along with my daughter and half of Nordstrom." (As the CEO of a very successful chain of fast-food restaurants, Paul makes significantly more money than Stuart. His daughter would not be shopping the sales.)

Her gaze drifted toward my back door. "Do you have time for me to snag a cup of coffee? I'm out of everything except decaf, and I've been dragging all morning."

"You came to the right place." Remembering the freshly brewed coffee perked me up.

We went inside and I grabbed one of Stuart's commuter mugs for Laura. She took it, then headed to my refrigerator for cream. As soon as she opened the door, I heard it—a light scratching at the plastic that was covering the broken window. My heart started beating double-time as adrenaline surged through me, readying my body for action. What was it? A demon intending to complete the job Pops left unfinished? Or maybe a hellhound, sniffing around outside before it lunged and ripped my throat out?

"Mind if I use your Hazelnut Coffeemate?" Laura asked, her head in the fridge.

I didn't answer. I was too busy watching the plastic. *Not now . . . not yet.* I didn't want Laura around when the thing attacked. I didn't want her involved. I didn't want—

YEEER-OOOO!

"Oh, shit!" Laura screamed.

Something small and lithe leaped through the window, half-sheathed in a loose section of plastic garbage bag, screeching in an unearthly way that made the hairs on my arms stand on end. I lunged forward to catch the beast and my fingers grabbed something soft, and—

"Yer-owwwwwl."

I stopped short, my mind finally catching up with what my hands already knew. No demon. No hellhound. Nothing bad at all—just Kabit, our overweight, overly grumpy, supremely opinionated tomcat.

Kabit glared at me for a long moment, his fur sticking straight up, his tail three times its normal size. Then he marched to his food bowl and started eating, the picture of quiet dignity. I wanted to laugh, but couldn't quite manage.

"Sorry," Laura said, bending down to pick up the Coffeemate container she'd dropped. "He scared me to death."

I looked down at the mess, and suddenly the laughter bubbled up. "Yeah," I said, breathing through my chuckles, "I guess so."

Laura's sheepish expression faded as she joined in my laughter. Together, we sank down to the floor, our backs against the cabinets as we shook with mirth. The situation wasn't really funny, though, and I knew that my laughter stemmed more from raw nerves than from humor. Today, Laura had only been startled by my cat. Considering the turn my life had suddenly taken, I couldn't help but wonder if, before this whole mess was over, Laura would see something truly scary.

If she did, would I be there to protect her?

St. Mary's Cathedral was built centuries ago as part of the California mission trail. The original cathedral building still stands, though Mass is only held there on High Holy Days, a concession to the ongoing renovations to the beautiful building. In the meantime, the Bishop's Hall serves as a temporary place of worship.

From a purely personal perspective, I'll be happy when the renovations are complete. The inside of the cathedral is awe-inspiring, whereas the inside of the newer Bishop's Hall lacks some of that holy *oomph*. And, yes, I go to Mass regularly (well, more or less). I've witnessed exorcisms, staked vampires, and put down demons with nothing more than a plastic swizzle stick from Trader Vic's—so, yeah, I'm a believer. I even got roped into doing some committee work a few months ago. Of course, the project—which was supposed to have been finished during the summer—is still dragging on. What's that saying about no good deed going unpunished?

The cathedral is perched on San Diablo's highest point, the church grounds looking out over the Pacific and the Channel Islands. Like any church, the worship hall is holy ground. But St. Mary's Cathedral has an added little *zing*. Everything beyond the communion rail—the sanctuary, the altar, even the basement below and the ceiling above—was built with a mortar that was heavily infused with the bones of saints. It's pretty common to work a saint's bone into an altar (well, it's not as common now as it used to be), but that much saintliness was unique even centuries ago.

Eric and I had believed that such a powerful sanctuary explained San Diablo's low demon quotient. Sure, demons could still wander free in the town—or on the nonconsecrated church grounds, for that matter—but we'd opined that the cathedral gave off a strong antidemon vibe. Apparently that bit of conjecture was hogwash.

Anyway, I had no idea of the identity of my new *alimentatore*; according to tradition, a Hunter knows nothing about his or her mentor until the two actually meet. I find that particular tradition to be not only archaic, but also downright idiotic. Unfortunately, I'm not on the Rules Committee for *Forza Scura*, and no one asked my opinion.

Even though I couldn't know whom I was supposed to meet, I dearly wished that I had asked Father Corletti for more details on the exact location. For all I knew, my mentor might be sitting in Father Ben's rectory office twiddling his thumbs and wondering where I was.

The thought sparked another—my mentor might actually *be* Father Ben.

I rather liked that idea. Although Father Ben is only a few years out of seminary, he seems on the ball and his homilies are never yawners. Still, the likelihood that I was intended to meet up with Father Ben was slim. Father Corletti might have been vague, but he'd definitely said that *Forza* had "sent" an *alimentatore*. Since Father Ben had taken the position of rector years ago, unless *Forza* had been aware of Goramesh's interest in the cathedral far longer than Father Corletti let on, Ben wasn't my man.

I decided that the actual cathedral building was my best bet, and maneuvered the Infiniti into one of the nearby parking spaces. I confess to taking a devious pleasure in saddling Stuart with the more kid-friendly van, and part of me wanted to just sit in the lot, engine running, as I basked in that clean car smell that involved no hint of sour milk or spilled grape juice. Unfortunately, I didn't have time to wallow. I shifted into park, killed the engine, and abandoned the air-conditioned comfort for the equally agreeable Southern California weather.

I followed the stone path to the cathedral, letting my hand reach out to graze the birds-of-paradise that lined the walkway like sentries. The double doors—heavy wood with tarnished brass hardware—were closed but unlocked, and I tugged the door open and plowed on in, crossing first through the small foyer, then slowing as I moved over the threshold into the worship area. The stone receptacles that usually held the holy water at the entrance had been packed away as part of the renovation, replaced with simple wooden stands topped with gold-plated bowls. The floor was still damp, probably from the earlier rain, and I walked carefully so I wouldn't slip. I dabbed my finger in the basin of holy water, made the sign of the cross, then genuflected toward the tabernacle.

The pews were empty, and I considered heading over to the hall to see if my rendezvous was there. But I'd actually arrived a few minutes early, so it seemed silly not to wait.

I'd brought an empty glass vial, and I filled it with holy water, replenishing my stock. That errand completed, I just stood there, idly flipping through a missal, and checking my watch about every twenty-four seconds. At eleven-fifty-seven I heard the creak of a door, followed by footsteps. Because the room's acoustics were designed more for singing hymns than pinpointing sound, I had no idea which direction to look. I turned a full circle and was walking toward the communion rail when the mystery was solved—Father Ben passed through a velvet curtain to appear on the sanctuary in front of me.

He carried a clipboard and a pen and didn't seem to realize I was there.

I cleared my throat, and he looked up, startled. His face

cleared almost immediately, though, and he smiled broadly. "Kate Connor. What brings you here today?"

Okay. So he definitely wasn't my *alimentatore*. I let loose my preplanned excuse. "I'm picking up some more inventories to type. But the message on my cell phone was garbled, so I'm not sure who called."

Since our project involved reviewing and indexing the extensive donations received by the cathedral's sizable archives, I assumed there was a list somewhere waiting to be typed. Thus, I was not actually lying to a priest.

Father Ben rubbed his chin. "Well, I'm afraid I can't help you. Delores would know, but she's not here today," he added, referring to the committee chair.

"Oh. That's too bad." I frowned and tried to look suitably flummoxed. "I was hoping to get started on the pages tonight." I turned a bit, looking around as if I expected someone to materialize in a pew. "You haven't seen anyone else around, have you?"

"Sorry."

"I'll go check the Bishop's Hall. If someone is looking for me, would you let them know I'm there?"

"Of course."

I made polite good-bye noises and headed out the door. I popped into the Bishop's Hall, looked around, and found no one except the janitor, who was mopping the floor. I backed out quickly, careful not to muck up his work.

The adrenaline rush that had accompanied the thought of meeting my new mentor was being fast replaced by annoyance. I had at least three loads of laundry piled up at home. Not to mention a body that was going to get pretty ripe if it stayed in my shed much longer. I decided to head back to the cathedral in case we'd been passing each other in a not-so-funny comedy-of-errors kind of way. I'd just stepped onto the walkway when I heard footsteps behind me. I turned, but didn't see anyone. I called out, but no one answered.

I reached the church doors at the same time Father Ben did. His face lit up instantly, and this time I could tell that I was exactly who he wanted to see.

"Oh, Kate, I was just going to look for you. I bumped into a gentleman looking for you in the parking lot."

"You did?" My gaze automatically shifted toward the lot. I saw five cars, but no people. "Who?"

"I'm afraid I don't know his name," Father said. "He said he'd just looked for you in the hall, but that the floors were wet."

"They are. I was just there."

"He asked me to direct you to the courtyard if I saw you."

"Great. Thanks."

We parted ways, him entering the church, and me heading around the building toward the courtyard, a small sitting area bordered by the cathedral, the rectory offices, and the Bishop's Hall. Primarily used by church staff as a place to sit and eat lunch, the courtyard boasts nothing much more than a few concrete benches and some potted plants. A decorative iron fence marks the entrance. The gate was open, and I walked through. I saw no one. The concrete benches had been bleached to near white from day after day of California sunlight, and I thought absurdly of bones in a field picked clean by vultures and left to bake. I shivered, as if someone had walked over my grave, and I turned my gaze to the statue of the Virgin Mary, looking for comfort. "Give me strength," I whispered, closing my eyes only briefly as I crossed myself.

This cloak-and-dagger routine was irritating. I had a cell phone, a fax, a Palm Pilot, and high-speed Internet access. Was it really necessary to skulk around the cathedral grounds when one simple e-mail message could have set out an exact time and meeting place? Another glance at my watch revealed that it was now ten past noon. Father Ben had just seen the man, so where the Devil was he?

"Hello?" I called, feeling stupid since there was obviously no one there. Then I muttered the kind of curse you really shouldn't say in a churchyard, and headed back in the direction I'd come. My blood was boiling as I turned, my entire body tight with pent-up frustration. I wanted to hit something, to lash out and let my frustration find some tangible release. The reaction surprised me. For a decade and a half, I'd worked so hard to stifle those urges, and to live by a different set of rules. I'd succeeded, too; suburban life making it easy to bury my past. I repeatedly tell Timmy not to hit, bite, kick, or scream; hitting isn't nice, hitting doesn't solve anything.

Except sometimes hitting *does* solve things.

Sometimes, hitting saves your life.

I may have buried my years of training, but I never truly lost them. And now I felt my old instincts clamoring to the surface, my blood burning and my strength returning. And, even more, I felt the desire. To fight. To win. To live.

A twig snapped behind me, the sharp crack reverberating through the courtyard. I spun around, fists raised, muscles tight. I truly expected nothing more than my tardy *alimentatore*, but I'd crossed some line; I couldn't simply turn and say "Hi, there."

And thank God for that.

He was right there. Larson. Looming not two feet behind me.

"Son of a bitch," I howled as I launched myself at him. I wasn't consciously thinking, but satisfaction still tickled in my head. I'd been right all along! He was a demon, he'd found out about this meeting, and somehow he'd delayed (or killed) my *alimentatore*.

On top of all that, I simply didn't like the man. His comments about Allie had pissed me off, and it was with an absurd breed of joy that I tackled him.

His eyes went wide as he saw me coming, and he held out his hands at the last minute as if to stave off my assault, but the reaction came too late. I hit him with the full force of my body, and down we went. Not the most artful of moves, I'll admit, but my primary concern had been to get him before he got me.

He recovered quickly from his initial surprise and twisted violently to the left, managing to toss me off in the process. He was much stronger than I'd expect for a sixty-something man of the judiciary, and that only confirmed my belief that he wasn't a man at all.

His parry had sent me crashing to the cold stone ground, the motion sending my purse flying. My stuff spewed out like the payload from a suburban bomb. I clambered to my knees, clawing at the debris, my hand closing around the first solid thing I found—a Happy Meal action figure, complete with a molded plastic sword. Not great, I admit, but I could make do.

I climbed to my feet, and saw that Larson was doing the same, pushing himself up to a standing position. He wasn't there yet, though, and I took advantage, landing a solid kick somewhere in the general vicinity of his kidneys.

The bastard didn't stand a chance. He went down, and I lunged, landing on top of him and wrestling him into a chokehold. I'd won, and we both knew it. There was fear and defeat in his eyes, and the thrill of victory pounded in my ears. I moved in for the kill, bringing the Happy Meal action figure closer to his left eye.

"For the love of God, Kate, stop! I'm your *alimentatore*!"

Six

"Like hell you are," I said, keeping the plastic sword just millimeters from his eyeball. We were on the ground, my other arm tight around his neck, his head pressed near my chest. If he moved, my makeshift weapon would penetrate the sclera to sink deep into the vitreous fluid like a hot knife through butter. If he were a demon, he'd be dead. Human, he'd be blind.

At the moment, that was a risk I was willing to take.

"Kate, think about what you're doing. *Forza* sent me to assist you." He pulled back away from the sword, his head pressing against my breasts. He was cold with fear, practically trembling.

I tightened my grip around his neck. "Explain yourself," I said. "Explain the dinner party."

Nothing. Just silence. I gave him a little shake, meant to jostle his enthusiasm for spilling his story.

"Test," he finally sputtered, the word so low and raw I could barely understand.

I released my hold on his neck just a little, but my fingers tightened around the Happy Meal toy. "Bullshit."

He coughed, started to speak, then coughed again. I steeled myself to remain unmoved by his apparent discomfort.

"Talk," I said.

"You've been out of touch for a while. I needed to know what we were dealing with. How much training you needed. What your skill level was."

"So you came to my house and impersonated a demon? I could have killed you."

"But you didn't." He cleared his throat and sucked in a breath. I realized I'd loosened my hold even more. "You passed that test, at least." He started to get up, but I jerked him back. He winced. "Although I may still modify that grade."

"You deliberately baited me. The breath. The comments."

"The breath I'll concede," he said. "A week of eating garlic and not brushing my teeth. The comments, though . . ."

He trailed off.

"What?"

"I never said a single thing that was damning. You assumed I was a demon and heard what you wanted to hear."

I tried to think back over the evening, to see if what he said was true. But it was too much of a blur. All I could remember was what he'd said about Allie—that he'd been sorry he hadn't met her. That she was probably a lot like me.

Shit.

He was right. Unless he was one of Satan's minions, that was pretty damn innocuous.

Without letting go, I leaned over and took a good long sniff. He opened his mouth helpfully. Minty fresh.

I released the hold from around his neck, and he sat up, rubbing his shoulders and doing head rolls.

"Apology accepted," he said.

"I haven't apologized." I kept the toy poised near his face. I was pretty sure he was okay, but I wasn't positive.

He groaned, either in frustration or pain, I couldn't tell, and shifted slightly to the left. "Refilled your supply?"

I had no idea what he was talking about, then I turned in the direction he was looking. My checkbook was lying open near the base of a bench, a vial of holy water half-buried beneath it. I couldn't reach it without letting him go, and I did a quick run-through of my options. It might be a trick. He might be planning on attacking me (or running like hell) the moment I let go. But since I couldn't sit there forever, that was a risk I was going to have to take.

"Don't move," I said, as if I could keep him there by force of will alone.

"Wouldn't dream of it."

I scooted backward, retrieved the vial, and moved back to crouch over him again. I still held the toy, but a bit less enthusiastically. He hadn't moved a muscle during my scramble for the water, and now he watched me, his face impassive, as I unscrewed the metal cap. "Truth time," I said, tossing the water at him without preamble.

He didn't even flinch, and I knew right then what the result would be. Nothing. No ripped and burning flesh. No screams emanating from the depths of Hell. Not even a little pop and fizzle. I felt my body relax.

No demon could tolerate a direct dousing of holy water in the face.

Larson wasn't a demon. He was just a man, bemused and dripping.

I sighed and passed him a crumpled tissue from the back pocket of my jeans. He started to dab water off his face. "Okay, then," I said. "I believe you."

"I would hope so." He started to stand. I took the opportunity to crawl around, looking for my various personal belongings.

"So you were testing me," I said, now stating the obvious. "At the party, I mean."

"I was."

I shoved my checkbook in my purse, then started collecting loose coins. "Did I pass?"

He peered at me. "Let's just say there's work to be done."

"Right. Of course." *Damn.*

I don't like being wrong, and, frankly, I've gotten used to being right pretty much all of the time. I'm the mom, and Mom is always right. So it would not be an exaggeration to say that I was taking my error about Judge Larson's identity a bit less than gracefully.

Fortunately, he seemed to understand, and while I sulked, he drove to the county dump, the demon carcass in his trunk and me in the passenger seat brooding quietly. Not that I'd been sulking the whole time. After a few vigorous *mea culpa*'s on my part (I can't believe I drenched my *alimentatore* with holy water!), we'd headed to my house. I'd parked the Infiniti out front, while Larson pulled his Lexus into the garage. We tugged the body from the storage shed, schlepped him back though the kitchen, and filled Larson's oh-so-pristine trunk with one geriatric dead demon.

I learned it costs twenty-five dollars to enter the dump, and no one writes down your name, license plate number, or anything. One grizzled old man was guarding the entrance, but he was more interested in *The Price Is Right* playing in grainy black-and-white than he was in us. Considering the ease with which we entered—dead body in tow—I had to imagine that a whole plethora of murderous fiends had come this way before us. Not a pretty picture.

Larson parked behind a pile of debris, shielding us from the view of anyone who might wander down the road. The place wasn't exactly hopping, though, so I wasn't that worried about onlookers. Together, we hauled Pops out of the trunk, then stuffed him into a space we'd carved among the debris. The stink factor was significant, but with two kids (one still in diapers) my gag reflex is well under control.

We rearranged the trash to cover the body, dusted ourselves off, then headed back out the way we came. With any luck, no one would ever find the body. Or, if they did, they'd never figure out who left it there.

"Are you still annoyed with me?" Larson asked after we'd been driving for a while.

"Yes," I said. "But I'll get over it."

"It was necessary," he said.

"I understand," I said, and I *did* understand. "It just irks me that you felt compelled to test skills I haven't used in years. I mean, how would you like it if your Property professor dropped by unannounced and quizzed you on the Rule Against Perpetuities?" For the record, I have no idea what that is, but whenever Stuart invites his lawyer friends over for drinks, they inevitably bring it up, and complain about what a bitch it was to understand, and then say how glad they are they don't write wills for a living. Larson's eyes crinkled in a very Paul Newman–esque sort of way. "Point taken," he said. "I wouldn't like it at all." He stopped at a traffic light, then held his hand out to me. "Truce?"

I took it. "Truce." The light changed and we were under way again. A few minutes later, he turned onto Rialto Boulevard, the cypress-lined street that leads into my subdivision. I twisted in my seat to face him. "So how pathetic was I?"

"Actually, under the circumstances you were surprisingly resourceful. Not that I'd expected any less. I've read your file and I know Wilson would not have been lax in his training."

If he was trying to snare my attention, he'd succeeded. "You knew Wilson?"

Wilson Endicott had been my first and only *alimentatore* until the day I'd retired. The eldest son of some British bigwig, he'd forfeited his inheritance when he left home to join *Forza*. Where Father Corletti had been like a father to me, Wilson had been like an older brother. I'd trusted him, looked up to him, and I missed him terribly.

A shadow crossed Larson's face. "He was as good an *alimentatore* as he was a friend. His passing is a great loss."

"He'd probably have been mortified to see the way I reacted to you."

Larson shook his head ever so slightly, then reached out to gently touch my hand. "On the contrary. I think he'd have been very proud."

I focused on my fingernails. "Thanks."

"I'll be sending a positive report back to *Forza*, Kate. You did well. Truly."

"Oh." I sat up a little straighter, trying to pull myself together. "Well, that's great. How come you didn't say so earlier?"

He glanced quickly in my direction and I saw a grin sparkle in his eyes. "If memory serves, you had a miniature swordsman aimed at my eye."

"Right. Sorry about that."

"No offense taken," he said. He flipped down his visor to reveal a pack of Nicorette gum. He unwrapped a piece and popped it in his mouth, then aimed a frown in my direction. "Harder to quit than I thought," he said.

"So how are you going to find Goramesh?" I asked, getting down to business. "That's the plan, right? You find him, I exterminate him, and life goes back to normal." I squinted at him then, my comment spurring another thought. "Are you really a judge? Stuart's going to have a fit if it turns out you can't really endorse him."

He laughed. "I assure you, my place among the judiciary is quite secure."

"So, what? You moonlight for the Vatican?"

I was being sarcastic, but he nodded. "Something like that."

"No kidding?" Back in my day, Hunters and *alimentatores* were full-time, full-fledged *Forza* employees. Outside employment wasn't even an option.

"I was twelve years out of law school when I contacted Father Corletti about training as an *alimentatore*," Larson told me.

"Really?" I couldn't help the incredulous tone in my voice. *Forza* is supersecret. I'd never heard of anyone contacting the organization out of the blue.

"Father thought it was unusual, too," he said. "But I'd been doing some reading on my own about demons and the infiltration of the Black Arts into mainstream society, and I ran across a vague reference to the group in an ancient text. I was intrigued, and the more I poked around, the more determined I was to find out if the organization was real or a product of someone's imagination."

"I'm impressed."

"It took five years, but I managed." His mouth turned up into a wry grin. "Interesting years, those. Amazing the characters you run across if you're searching for an elite group of Demon Hunters."

"So Father brought you on board and the rest is history?"

"Something like that. I worked out of Rome until the new policy went into effect about ten years ago. Once we were permitted to hold a second job in addition to our *Forza* duties, I returned to Los Angeles and took up my law practice."

Eric and I had made the same transition, retiring first to Los Angeles after our wedding, then moving up the coast to San Diablo when we found out I was pregnant. "And then you became a judge?"

"Exactly. Three years later I was appointed to a superior court seat." We were on my street now, and he pulled into my driveway, put the car in park, then turned to me. "As you can imagine, my new position was quite useful to *Forza*. The criminal justice system provides a fascinating snapshot of demon activity."

"I'll bet," I said. His tone had been matter-of-fact—like a meteorologist discussing the weather, or a doctor relaying lab results. Just the general trappings of his workaday world, but I felt a knot in my stomach. It wasn't workaday to me. It hadn't been for a long, long time.

And yet here I was. The man next to me was in the business of tracking demon activity and studying methods of defeating them. I was *back* in the business of killing them.

I felt suddenly cold and overcome with the urge to hear my kids' voices. Goose bumps rose on my arms as I rummaged in my purse for my phone. As Larson watched, I punched in Stuart's cell number. One ring, two, and then his voice: "Please tell me you're coming to rescue me."

I was instantly on alert. "Why? What's wrong?"

Larson turned to me, alarm coloring his features as well, and my hand closed around the door handle, releasing the latch.

Stuart laughed. "Nothing's wrong. Sorry to scare you. Were you afraid I'd lost the kids somewhere between the parking lot and the food court?"

"Something like that," I said. "Can I talk to them?"

"Sure, if you want to get Tim all worked up. He's on the carousel right now with Allie. He's doing great, but if he hears Mommy's voice . . ."

"Right. Never mind." I hardly needed for Timmy to throw a fit and for Stuart to schlep everybody home. "So what's your ETA back home?"

"Not sure. Right now Timmy's happy, so I'm willing to stick it out for as long as Allie wants."

I felt my brow lift in surprise. "You are?"

"Sure. Why not? I already told Allie we'd do a late lunch at Bennigan's."

"Really?" Stuart's not a chain-restaurant kind of guy, but Allie loves the place, and it's easy to find food for Tim there. "You're going to score some major points."

"I know," he said, and I could practically hear him grinning. "And it's better than dealing with that damn window. How's that going, by the way?"

"Fine," I lied. I'd completely forgotten about the window.

We wrapped up the conversation, and then I tucked the phone back in my purse, oddly unsatisfied.

"Everything okay?" Larson asked.

"Sure," I said. But it wasn't. I don't know what I'd expected—Stuart to have somehow magically discerned my distress and assured me that all would be well? A promise from my kids to never talk to strangers or demons? Whatever I'd needed, I hadn't gotten it. I got out of the car and headed for the house, Larson following in my wake. "You never answered my question about how you're going to find Goramesh," I said as we went inside.

"You never gave me the chance," he said.

He had a point. "I want him dead. I want this over with. I want my kids safe."

"It will be over soon," he said. "That's why I'm here. To assist you and bring this situation to a speedy conclusion."

"Good." I thought about what he said. *Situation* wasn't the word I would have chosen, but I couldn't quibble with *speedy conclusion.* The quicker life got back to normal, the better. "Yeah, that's great," I added.

We were in the kitchen now, and the digital clock on the stove flashed the time—just past two. I'd forgotten to ask if Tim had napped in the stroller, but I had to assume the answer was no. Timmy's not at his most charming on anything less than a two-hour nap, and at the first sign of serious toddler crankiness, I knew Stuart would drag the whole crew home. "We'd better get on with it," I said. "If you're here when Stuart gets back, I don't know what we'll say."

I opened the refrigerator, grabbed two bottles of water,

handed him one, then headed toward the living room. I was just opening the door to the back porch when I realized Larson wasn't following. "You coming?"

"Coming where?"

"Aren't we training?" I made a swishing motion, like Bruce Lee. "Hand-to-hand? Weapons training? Maybe throw in a little sword practice?" I unsheathed an imaginary sword, only to realize he wasn't amused by my pantomimes. I sighed. "I'm almost fifteen years out of practice, Larson. I need to train. Either I practice, or I'm dead."

"You were quite adequate in the churchyard," he said.

"Adequate isn't going to cut it."

He cleared his throat, but didn't say anything.

I leaned against the doorjamb. "What aren't you telling me?"

"*Forza* is concerned less about Goramesh and more about finding what he seeks."

"Stop Goramesh, and it won't really matter what he's looking for, will it?"

"And how do you propose to do that?"

"Fighting, remember?" I waved impatiently in the general direction of the backyard. "The kind of maneuvers *Forza* spent years teaching me to do—that's what Father expects, right? For me to take care of this problem? To stop Goramesh?" I wasn't angry so much as scared. Scared that this life I'd built and loved would come crashing down around my ears, and I'd be thrust back into a world of dark and shadows. "I just want to *nail* him, Larson. I want it *over*."

"And, again, I have to ask. *How*?"

"Apparently not with your help." My temper flared. "Why are you here if you're not going to help me? I need to train. I'm in lousy shape, and I—"

Oh. I closed my mouth.

Something clicked in my head, and suddenly I understood. "Goramesh isn't corporeal, is he?"

"Not to *Forza*'s knowledge, no."

"That puts a little kink into my plan, then," I admitted. If the demon hadn't taken a human body, I could hardly kill him.

Larson made a little *hmmm* noise, and I grimaced.

"So what do *you* suggest?" I demanded, sounding churlish.

"In this endeavor, we will prevail through brains, not brawn. We need to determine what Goramesh seeks, and get to it first."

"Great. As soon as you figure out what and where it is, I'll be more than happy to snatch it." As I thought about it, the fact that Goramesh was floating around as an unembodied demon was actually *good* news for me. Without a body, there wasn't anything for me to hunt. And research was an *alimentatore*'s job. "Point me toward a demon, and I'll kill it," I said. "But except for the one we just buried, I haven't seen any around." I grinned, suddenly happier than I'd been all day. "As they say, my work here is done."

Larson didn't appear to share my joy. "And Goramesh?" he asked. "We need to ascertain what he wants."

A finger of guilt poked at me, but I held firm. "No, *you* need to figure that out."

"Kate—"

"What?" I crossed my arms over my chest. "Come on, Larson. *Every* demon wants something. But unless he's got someone in San Diablo doing his dirty work—mortal or demon—then I'd have to say that we're not exactly at Code Red, you know?"

"That's hardly responsible."

"Responsible?" It had been a hellacious twenty-four hours, and the last thing I needed was a lecture on responsibility. "I'm drowning in *responsible*." I started ticking off on my fingers. "Car pool, playdates, PTA. Not to mention making sure my family has food to eat and clothes to wear and—if they're lucky—no science experiments breeding in the bathtub. *Those*," I said, "are my responsibilities."

He opened his mouth, but I wasn't finished.

"And *your* responsibility is to handle the research side of the relationship," I said. "Or did *Forza* change that policy, too?"

"All right." He nodded slowly. "You make a good point. But my ability to work will be hampered by my job. The records I'd like to review are in the cathedral archives, and I'll be in court most days working."

That finger of guilt poked harder. I sighed, on the verge of caving. "Research isn't exactly my thing. I didn't even finish high school." More accurately, I didn't even *go* to high school. The Church provided tutors, of course, but it was a nomadic, hit-or-miss kind of education. I spent my youth never expecting to make it to the next sunrise. "This is a little out of my league."

"I'm hardly asking you to translate ancient texts, Kate. You will only have to review what's already in the archives. And I've already done some of the legwork. I have a few leads. With your help, I can track them down."

That should be easy enough. I could tell Delores that I'd like to add another layer of responsibility to my volunteer work. So long as I didn't cut back on the secretarial duties, she'd probably welcome my additional help. The Church had hired actual archivists to work on the rare and valuable stuff. But there were tons of donations still to sort through. From there, I figured I could wrangle a peek at whatever records Larson might be interested in. "All right," I finally said.

"Excellent."

I held up a finger, wanting to hold him off until I was sure we were on the same page. "I'll help with the research, but until we see some *solid evidence* that Goramesh has demons on the case, I'm not rearranging my whole life. For all we know, we just buried his only corporeal minion. Fair enough?"

His brow furrowed, but he nodded. "Of course. You

make an excellent point. Until circumstances indicate that alacrity is called for, there's no need to rush through the research."

I gave him credit for being perfectly agreeable. I, however, felt like a prickly bitch. "Good. Great."

Except it wasn't good or great. I couldn't be absolutely certain that I'd killed San Diablo's only walking, talking demon. And no stinky-breathed fiend was going to put my kids in danger. Not if I had any say in the matter. "Wait here," I said. I trotted to my pantry, grabbed a Swiffer dust mop and a Swiffer wet mop, and brought them back to the living room with me. I handed the wet mop to Larson.

From his expression, I could tell he thought I was in the throes of some sort of mental breakdown.

"I've got two kids and a husband who have no clue what's going on. If there are any more demons in San Diablo, I intend to be ready for them."

I'd never fenced with Swiffer handles before, and I'm certain that Larson hadn't, either. But he didn't protest (well, not too much) as I led him to the backyard. For the record, I actually do own real equipment. Unfortunately, I'd buried it all years ago in the very back of the storage shed, and I had no intention of tackling *that* project again. The Swiffer handles would work well enough, at least for the quickie session I had in mind.

I marched into the graveled area of the yard, came *en garde*, and waited for Larson to catch up. "Don't hold back," I said as he took his own position. "And while we spar, you can fill me in on everything you already know about Goramesh."

As it turned out, he was pretty damn good, giving me quite a run for my money, and working me hard enough that neither one of us was doing much talking. We'd been at it for about ten minutes—my footwork cutting geometric paths in the gravel and the Swiffer handles doggedly hanging in there during our lunges and ripostes—when I heard the van pull up, followed by the telltale churning of the garage door opening.

I looked at my watch, quite unable to comprehend that they were home already. I caught Larson's eye, unreasonably peeved to see that he didn't look the least bit flustered.

"What should we tell them?" I asked.

"Not the truth," he said.

"Gee, you think?"

"There's no need for sarcasm, Kate."

"On the contrary, I think the situation practically demands it."

"We'll simply say I came over looking for Stuart. To discuss his campaign. Don't worry. It won't be as bad as you think."

Seven

To his credit (and to my relief), it turned out that Judge Larson could bullshit with the best of them. We were back in the house and he was seated at the kitchen table when Allie barreled through the door, almost plowing me over in the process.

"Mom! Mom! Check it out!" She waved a shopping bag at me as I dumped out the old morning coffee and started a new pot, hoping I looked like I'd been doing nothing more than puttering around the house all day. "I got *five* Tommy Hilfiger shirts at Nordstrom. They had a whole table marked seventy-five percent off and Stuart said I could have one of each, and I got a couple for Mindy, too, and—" She clamped her mouth shut, finally noticing the man sitting at the table. "Oh. Hi."

I could tell she was trying hard to be polite by not demanding to know who he was. I stepped in to fill the gap, but Larson got there first.

"You must be Allie," he said, standing. "I've heard so much about you. I'm Mark Larson."

"Oh." Allie looked at me, and I smiled in an encouraging mom manner. She hesitated, then held out her hand. "Nice to meet you."

"Katie?" Stuart's voice drifted in from the garage as I heard the van door slide shut. "Whose car is that? Have you got compan—*Judge*." Stuart stood in the doorway, Timmy clinging to him like a baby monkey. Stuart recovered quickly enough, then stepped all the way into the room. "Judge Larson. Sorry. I wasn't expecting to see you." He kissed me, but the gesture seemed distracted. I couldn't blame him. As for me, I was holding my breath. How did spouses who cheat handle it? One tiny little indiscretion and I was already sweating bullets. (Okay, maybe the indiscretion wasn't so tiny, but still . . .)

I held my arms out for Timmy, and Stuart passed the munchkin to me, then went over to shake hands with the judge. "When did you get here? Have you been waiting long? I'm sorry I wasn't here. I didn't realize you'd be coming over." His sentences crashed over one another, and under other circumstances I might be amused. Today, I wasn't.

Before Larson could answer, Stuart frowned, then looked toward me. I busied myself with kissing Tim (who was quietly begging for Teddy Grahams, but any minute would surely erupt into full-fledged howls). "Actually," Stuart said, turning back to the judge, "I suppose I should ask *why* you're here."

Larson laughed, the sound hearty and cordial. "I apologize for barging in like this. I was in the neighborhood looking at a few houses, and I noticed your car in the driveway." He gestured at me. "Kate explained that you'd switched cars, but she was nice enough to offer me a cup of coffee while I waited for you."

Stuart-my-husband may have been surprised to find Larson in the kitchen, but Stuart-the-politician stepped seamlessly into the fray. "This is good karma on a number of levels," Stuart-the-politician said, pulling out the chair across from Larson and sitting down. "I didn't think we had nearly enough time to chat last night, and I'd been planning on giving you a call Monday morning. I was thinking we might talk more over lunch or drinks."

"I'd like that," Larson said. "Clark speaks so highly of you."

They segued into a political banter that I was beginning to find familiar, and I put Timmy down, grateful to relieve myself of his thirty-two pounds of girth. He immediately started tugging on the kitchen cabinets, testing the child-proof latches in a familiar daily ritual. When he came to the one cabinet I keep unsecured, he pulled out two saucepans and a wooden spoon and gleefully settled in for the afternoon concert.

"Hon?" Stuart's voice rose over the din.

"Sorry." I leaned over Tim. "Come on, buddy. Let's get you out of here."

"No. Mine. *Mine*." He grabbed hold of the pots and didn't let go. The amount of strength contained in the hand of a two-year-old never ceases to amaze me. I aimed a *he's-your-son-too* look at Stuart as I resorted to that age-old mothering trick—bribery. "We can watch Elmo."

That got him. The little bugger abandoned his makeshift studio and trotted happily toward the living room.

I looked around for Allie, hoping to enlist her as a babysitter, but she'd managed to slip away. Probably already on the phone to Mindy. No problem. Elmo could handle babysitting duty.

I shoved Tim's favorite tape into the VCR and waited until he was entranced. As soon as he'd calmed down enough, I'd take him upstairs and try to urge him into a late-afternoon nap. Until then I left Elmo in charge and headed back to the kitchen and the men. Not the most conscientious parenting option, I know, but I was desperate. And if I'm being honest, I park the kid in front of the television for lesser reasons all the time. As far as I can tell, he isn't warped yet.

Actually, I couldn't get back to the kitchen fast enough. I'd left Larson and Stuart alone, and that didn't sit well. Stupid, I know. It's not like Larson was going to accidentally mention there were demons in town any more than he was going to casually announce that back in my prime I could easily kill a dozen of them before breakfast.

No, there wasn't anything tangible fueling my discomfort. But I was determined to be present nonetheless. (This was my crisis, after all. And if I wanted to sit in on the deathly dull political chitchat and convince myself I was preventing some catastrophe, then by God, that's what I was going to do.)

Five minutes later I was regretting my decision. They were talking about Gallup polls and voting districts and a bunch of other political mumbo jumbo. I tuned out. I'm not even sure what I was thinking about—though I'm pretty sure demons were involved—when Stuart tapped the table in front of me.

"Honey?"

I jumped, my hand flying to my throat. "Timmy?" I could tell immediately he was fine. I could see him standing on the couch facing the backyard as he jumped up and down, singing "C is for Cookie" in time (more or less) with Cookie Monster.

"No, sorry. It's just the back door. It's probably Mindy."

"Oh. Right. Sure."

From the breakfast table you can see most of the living room, but not the back door. (Thus my odd perspective of the jumping child who was obviously, now that I had all the information, greeting Mindy in his own exuberant little way.) The layout's the major downside of this house, actually. I have to move to the living room if Timmy is playing on the back porch—otherwise I can't see him. Which means using the backyard as a distraction while I put away dishes doesn't work. Not unless I want my kid wandering free in the wild like Tarzan.

As it turns out, Stuart was right, and I opened the door to Mindy and Laura. "Hey," I said. "Come join the party." I noticed that Mindy was schlepping not only three paper shopping bags (Nordstrom, Saks, and The Gap), but she also had her familiar canvas duffel slung over one arm. Apparently the kid was here for the long haul.

"You don't mind, do you?" Laura said, catching the direction of my gaze.

I waved a hand. "Of course not," I lied. I usually didn't mind having Mindy sleep over. Tonight, though, I was craving peace and quiet. I had a feeling it might be a long time before I had another shot at that again. "Allie's upstairs," I added to Mindy. "In fact, I'd assumed she was talking to you on the phone."

"She was," Mindy said. "But we figured I might as well come over. Can we really watch a movie and have pizza after we show off our clothes?"

"Absolutely," I said, hoping no one else could tell that I'd completely forgotten my earlier plans with Laura for a pizza and fashion extravaganza.

Oh, well. Quiet is highly overrated anyway.

As Mindy bounded toward the staircase with an energy I envied, Laura eyed me with curiosity. Like a reflex, I rubbed my upper lip, as if I might have an errant smear of chocolate there. "What?"

She shook her head, looking slightly discombobulated, and I felt myself begin to worry. About what, I wasn't sure. But of late, I was trusting my instincts. And something was going on with my friend. Something that I desperately hoped was of the nondemonic variety. "Come on, Laura," I said. "Spill it."

We were still by the back door, and now I reached down to lock it, the familiar ritual all the more important lately.

"It's nothing. Really. Or at least it's none of my business."

"What's not?" Her comment was cryptic, but it made me feel better. Nosiness I could handle. She leaned against the wall facing me, her back toward the kitchen. Beyond her, I could hear the scrape of chairs against the tile as Larson and Stuart continued their conversation. "I feel like an idiot even saying something."

I held on to the doorknob like a crutch. Now that my fear had dissolved, I was both curious and amused. "Come on," I said. "Give."

"It's silly." She made a fluttery motion with her hands, and her cheeks actually flushed. I felt my brow furrow. This was weird. Then she took a step forward, her cheeks flaming. "Is everything okay with you and Stuart? I mean, you aren't, um, having an . . ." She trailed off, her head bobbing back and forth in a fill-in-the-blank kind of way.

My mind riffled through the possibilities, my own face flushing when I realized what she had to be thinking. "Of course not!" I said. "Everything's fine with me and Stuart. Everything's great!" I sounded overly enthusiastic even to my ears. Everything *was* okay. But I still had guilt. Because even though everything was just fine in the way Laura was thinking (an *affair*?!), I *was* keeping secrets from my husband. Secrets of the big, juicy variety. "Why on earth would you ask that?"

Relief flooded her features. "Thank God. I knew it was an idiotic question. I just . . ." She shrugged, then shook her head, then tossed up her hands. She looked a little bit like a puppet controlled by a spastic master.

"Laura . . ."

"Well, I didn't know what to think. I saw you in the yard sparring with that older man, and you guys looked so familiar, and I just thought that *something* must be going on."

Something was, but not that. "If you'd found me crawling around under the house, would you have assumed I had a thing for the plumber?"

"Hardly. But your fencing partner didn't seem like the butt-crack type."

"Don't dis plumbers," I said. "You'll find yourself with a backed-up sink on Christmas Day, and then where will you be?"

"I take it back," she said, holding up three fingers in typical Boy Scout fashion. "But what were you *doing*? I mean, fencing in the backyard with that man? I didn't know you fenced. And you weren't even using swords."

"Fencing?" *Stuart's voice.* Followed quickly by the man himself as he stepped into the living room from the kitchen, Judge Larson at his side.

I stifled the urge to curse, and pasted on a happy-homemaker smile as I considered all the possible lies I could tell. None sounded very convincing.

Laura was still facing me, and she mouthed *I'm sorry*, before turning around to face Stuart. I could tell by the way her shoulders stiffened a half second later that she hadn't expected to see Larson there, too. And I couldn't really blame her when the words "Oh, *you*" flew from her lips.

I cleared my throat. "Laura Dupont, meet Judge Mark Larson."

Because Laura is well trained, she moved toward him, her hand held out in greeting. If I'd hoped that such pleasantries would distract Stuart, though, I was sadly disappointed.

"This may sound naïve," he said. "But why on earth were you two fencing? *Were* you fencing?"

"Ah," I said, and then closed my mouth, realizing I had nothing to say. I twisted slightly, looking to Laura for help, but she'd already dropped Larson's hand and was now backing toward the stairs. "I'm going to go check on the girls," she said. *Yeah, Laura. Thanks a bunch.*

I returned my focus to the problem at hand, a rather lame "um" the only response I could come up with. Not exactly at my bullshitting best. Larson laid his hand on

Stuart's shoulder, giving it a gentle squeeze. He was pulling out all the grandfatherly stops, and I figured I owed him one for that.

"Self-defense," Larson said, and I decided we were now even. *That* response I could have come up with.

"Self-defense," Stuart repeated.

"Right," I said, because now that he'd put it out there, I was stuck. "And, um, exercise."

Stuart continued to stare at me, his expression perplexed but interested. Fortunately, I saw no signs that he was contemplating having me committed or, worse, that he thought I was having an affair with Larson (where the *heck* did she get that idea?).

The silence hung there, and I kept waiting for Larson to fill it. When he didn't, I jumped into the breach. "It's a crazy world out there. And, um, I should know how to take care of myself." Since Stuart was still silent, I rushed on, warming to my theme. "You're working longer hours, staying late to confer with Clark, and I'm home alone with the kids." I started ticking points off on my fingers. "Allie will have tons of after-school activities this year. I'll be picking her up late—with Tim in the car. It just seemed reasonable that I be prepared."

"And so you were fencing with Judge Larson?" He wasn't being sarcastic, just confused. I couldn't really blame him for that.

"Ah, no. Self-defense classes. I'm going to sign Allie and me up."

"Oh, awesome!" Allie's voice echoed from the stairwell, and a moment later my own little Britney Spears appeared, decked out in a too-tight T-shirt that plunged so low I could see the lace of her bra and stopped so high I could see her belly button, form-fitting black Lycra pants that clung to her hips (and the rest of her), and white Keds with lace-topped socks. Fortunately, I didn't see any evidence of tattoos or body piercing.

I scowled at Stuart as she made her way over, Mindy and Laura bringing up the rear. "This is your idea of a school wardrobe?"

He held up his hands and took a step backward away from me. Smart man. "I just drove and paid."

"We're really gonna take a self-defense class?" Allie asked, clamoring to a stop beside me. "No kidding?"

"No kidding," I said, already wondering when I'd find time to sit Allie down for the *this-is-not-appropriate-attire* conversation.

"I'm so psyched," she said. "And you're really going to do self-defense stuff, too, Mom? Like kicks and everything?"

I tackled the righteous indignation part of the equation first. "Yes, I'm really going to do it. What, you don't think I have it in me?"

"Well, you know. You and Stuart are old." She shrugged. "No offense and all."

"None taken." I glanced at Stuart, pleased to see that the perplexed expression had now been replaced by amusement.

"Apparently your mother isn't completely crippled by the ravages of age yet," Stuart said. "She and Judge Larson put on a little fencing exhibition earlier for Mrs. Dupont."

"Very funny," I said, even as Allie said, "No shit?" then clapped her hand over her mouth. "Oops. Sorry!"

"Allie!" I said, more happy for the diversion than I was upset about her language.

"You were really fencing?" All remorse about her language had died, drowned by waves of curiosity.

"Yes." I could hardly deny it, much as I might want to.

"That's so cool."

I beamed. My fourteen-year-old thought I was cool. Old and creaky, but cool.

"Why?" she asked.

The glow from offspring adoration faded, replaced by the frustration of being interrogated. I sighed. "I already explained to Stuart. Woman. Alone with children. It just seemed—"

"No, no. I heard all that. I mean, why *fencing*. And why with *him*?" She avoided looking at him, and from her tone, you'd think it was Larson who was the spawn of Satan.

"Allie." There it was again—my Shocked Mother Voice. The second time in so many minutes. I turned toward Larson. "She's fourteen," I said, by way of explanation, even as I wondered if she'd overheard Laura's suggestion of an affair.

"Mo-*ther*."

"Alison Elizabeth Crowe," I said. "Did you lose your manners at the mall?"

"I'm sorry," she said.

"Don't tell me."

She drew in a long, labored breath, then tilted her head up to Larson. "I'm sorry. I didn't mean anything personal, really. I just . . . I mean . . . well, why's my mom fencing with *anybody*?"

"A very good question," Stuart said, and Allie moved two paces closer to him, apparently sensing an ally. Laura and Mindy, I noticed, had faded backward into the living room and were now staring at the television, as if they were as enraptured by Elmo and the gang as my son. Cowards.

"I really don't understand why everyone's so worked up about a little fencing," I said.

"Kate simply mentioned her plan to take a self-defense class," Larson said, his voice coming off smooth and reasonable compared to my high-pitched protestations. "I told her I used to fence, she asked if a fencing class would be worthwhile for her purposes, we started chatting, and before we knew it, we were sparring with the cleaning products."

Stuart frowned. "Cleaning products?"

"Swiffer handles." Laura volunteered the info from

across the room. Apparently she wasn't as absorbed in *Sesame Street* as I'd thought.

"Why—"

I held up a hand, cutting Allie off. "It doesn't matter. The point is, Judge Larson was kind enough to show me a few fencing moves. It seems like a fun sport, but not nearly practical enough." That was true, actually. While this conversation had started as a giant bullshit session, it also underscored one undeniable truth—this world is filled with dangerous people, of both the human and demonic variety. My little girl was growing up (too fast, if that outfit was any indication) and if she was going to be out there in the world, I wanted her as safe as possible. Why not teach her to kick a little butt? I figured that was the least a concerned mother could do.

I aimed a measured look at Stuart and Allie. "We'll start classes next week," I said. "Kickboxing or aikido or something. I'll look into what's available." What I really wanted was a sensei who could teach her all the basics—and who could work with me on an advanced level when Allie was in school. Not likely, but I could hope.

"You really mean it?" Allie asked. "I'm gonna go out for cheerleader, so we have to make sure the class times are okay, but oh, wow, this is so cool!"

"Glad you think so." Who knew the promise of working up a sweat would be so appealing?

"That's a lot of activities," Stuart said, looking not at Allie but at me. I tempered the urge to tell him that I was a hell of a lot more concerned about my daughter staying alive than I was about her grades. He had a point, though, and part of my pissy knee-jerk reaction was that I hated when I made a Responsible Parent misstep. (And, yes, I know that's one of the reasons that having two parents is a good thing. But—dirty little secret time—no matter how much I love Stuart, Allie belongs to Eric and me. She just does. So I always get a little tense when Stuart picks up the parental slack where Allie is concerned. Stupid and unfair, I know, but there you have it. And if Allie ends up revealing all on *Jerry Springer* some day, I'll have no one to blame but myself.)

"Mom?" I was getting the puppy-dog look now.

"Stuart's right," I said. "If your grades fall, something will have to give, and since I think this is important, that something will be cheerleading or drill team or drama or whatever activity you're fascinated with that week. Understood?"

Her head bobbed. "Oh, yeah, sure."

I tried to look stern. "So long as we're clear, we can start the classes. But this is high school, kiddo. It's a whole new ball game."

"I know." She crossed her heart. "Really. I'll totally be Study Girl. You'll see." She cocked her head toward the living room. "Can Mindy take classes with us?"

Mindy had been tickling Tim, but now she leaned forward, my apparently boneless child limp across her lap as he squealed for "More tickle! More tickle!"

"Can I, Mom?" she asked, turning her own set of puppy-dog eyes on Laura. *"Pleeeeze."*

"You could come along, too," I said to Laura, already into the idea of Laura and Mindy joining the party. So long as I'd decided to get my daughter into fighting shape, I might as well help our friends gain that competitive edge, too.

"Not bloody likely," Laura said. "But if you're willing to schlep two kids, I'm willing to fork over her tuition."

"Whoo-hoo!" Mindy gave Tim another big tickle, then escaped out from under him to half-run, half-bounce toward Allie.

"You sure?" I said to Laura.

"I can barely get through the basic twenty-minute Pilates workout. I think kickboxing is a little beyond me."

I'd encountered Laura's philosophy of exercise before—basically, Laura considered pushing the grocery cart from the checkout stand to the car to be a killer aerobic workout—so I knew better than to press. "Okay, girls," I said. "Looks like you're going to be mixing it up pretty soon."

As Allie and Mindy leaped around the room, kicking and chopping at each other like rejects from the next *Charlie's Angels* movie, I shot a quick frown at Larson. A tiny smile tugged at his mouth. I grimaced. How nice that he was amused.

We'd started something this afternoon, he and I. Something I was going to have to finish. I was looking forward to spending more time with Allie (doing something where I was cool); I just wished the impetus for this new endeavor hadn't been my fear that one of Goramesh's minions would decide to pay her a little visit after school one day. I forced myself to ignore that possibility for the moment and focus only on the upside of the situation. Bonding with my kid and getting some exercise to boot. There's nothing like a little demon activity to get a girl back in shape, I always say. And after a few heavy-duty training sessions, I should be able to squeeze back into my size-eight jeans. That's a perk, right?

I mean, really. Who needs Pilates when you've got a town full of demons?

After much rapturous bounding around the living room, the girls finally settled down and the afternoon took a right turn toward normalcy. Stuart and Larson adjourned to the kitchen, and I suppressed my urge to follow and eavesdrop. If things went down the way we expected, I was going to be trusting Larson with my life; the least I could do was trust him to keep his mouth shut around my husband.

Besides, Laura's whole purpose in suggesting this little get-together was to check on my mental health in the wake of my Eric-dreams and my lunch with Eric's "friend." I could hardly abandon her for the political babble going on in my kitchen.

"Is that him?" she asked, while the girls were upstairs putting on outfit number one for the First Ever Crowe-Dupont Gala Fashion Show.

"Him who?"

"Eric's friend. Is Judge Larson the one you had lunch with?"

"Oh." I quickly debated what the best lie was, realizing as I did so that in the space of twenty-four hours, my ability to bullshit had improved dramatically. "Yeah, that's him."

"You didn't tell me he knew Stuart."

"I'm still processing the coincidence. He was just your average lawyer when Eric knew him. Now he's a federal judge."

"Great for Stuart," she said, giving me a sideways look.

"Oh, absolutely," I agreed. "These days, Stuart's all about the endorsements."

"Not so great for you, though, huh?"

I knew what she meant, of course. "I'll deal. It's not like I don't think about Eric every day anyway. I mean, I see his face every time I look at Allie." That much was true; the resemblance was remarkable. What I couldn't tell Laura was that seeing Larson (well, Larson plus the whole demon-Goramesh-end-of-life-as-we-know-it thing) had prompted more than just memories of my first husband; it also brought into sharp relief the void in my relationship with Stuart. Eric and I had been partners in every sense of the word. He knew me from the inside out, and I him. With Stuart, there were shadows between us—my past life (suddenly my present life), and the day-to-day details of his law practice. I didn't really understand what he did when he went to the office, and although I tried—really I did—when he told me stories about his work life, my eyes tended to glaze over.

I wouldn't have known how to tell Laura any of that

even if I'd wanted to. Fortunately, I was saved from commenting by the thunderous footsteps of the girls down the stairs.

Laura and I exchanged amused glances as they skidded to a halt just beyond our view. I'd put Tim down for his late and desperately needed nap about ten minutes earlier, and now I crossed my fingers, hoping their noise wouldn't wake him.

The fashion extravaganza lasted forty-five minutes, the girls strutting their stuff while Laura and I cheered them on (quietly, though, so as to not wake the munchkin). In the end, I had to admit that (notwithstanding the earlier outfit) Allie had picked out clothes that met with the Mom Seal of Approval.

"You two will be the best-dressed freshmen at Coronado High," I said as they took their final bows.

They looked at each other, neither one looking particularly happy.

"What?" Laura and I asked in unison.

"Freshmen," Allie said.

"We're stuck back on the bottom again."

"We were the top in junior high. We were eighth graders. Now we're pond scum."

And to think there were times when I actually regretted missing out on a public school education. Amazing. This was one of those mothering moments where you have to stifle the urge to say, "Don't sweat it. In twenty years none of this will matter." Right then, in my daughter's fourteen-year-old mind, it did matter. It mattered in a big way.

"You'll do great," I said. "And in just three short years, you'll be the seniors again."

"Three years," Allie repeated morosely. She turned to Mindy. "We've *so* got to make cheerleader."

Mindy nodded, her expression equally serious. "Definitely."

I made a point of not looking at Laura, afraid if I did I'd

laugh. My instinct was to leap to my feet and give my girl a hug. (When did she turn fourteen anyway? I swear just last Wednesday she was learning to walk.) I suppressed the urge, knowing that I'd be rewarded with a stiff back and an *Oh, Mo-ther.*

"Okay, girls," I said. "Why don't you take the clothes back to Allie's room? Did you totally pig out at the mall, or are you ready to order dinner?"

"I'm starving," Allie said. "Can we get one with extra cheese and breadsticks?"

"Sure. Why not?" I turned to Laura. "Should we order enough for Paul?"

I thought I saw a shadow in her eyes, but it vanished before I could be sure.

"Daddy's working late," Mindy said.

"Then it'll be a girls' night," I said. "Unless Stuart surprises me. He's spent the last couple of nights eating at his computer and catching up on work. As soon as he and Larson finish schmoozing, he'll probably go back there again." I had a feeling this was a portent of things to come if Stuart actually won the election. Stuart locked away in his study, emerging only for coffee and Timmy's bedtime. I wasn't crazy about the picture, but I also couldn't bring myself to drop an ultimatum. This was the man's dream, after all.

As it turns out, I was right. As soon as Larson headed out (catching my eye only once before taking his leave), Stuart kissed Allie good night, then disappeared to the back of the house. The group dynamic shifted when Tim woke up, but we figured a prepubescent male didn't alter the hormonal makeup of our little gal fest. Besides, Tim made for great entertainment, doing the hokeypokey ad nauseam with the girls until both Mindy and Allie begged him to stop and we finally had to distract him with a handful of Teddy Grahams.

Once he was more or less tuckered out, the girls debated the possible selections from our DVD collection (taking into account all the various parameters I'd outlined, the most important being that the first movie be toddler-friendly). While they debated like Ebert and Roeper, I gathered the pizza boxes and headed for the back door.

"Need a hand?" Laura asked.

"Not here. But if you start a pot of coffee, I'll love you forever." I'd had two glasses of wine with my pizza, and already my head was swimming.

"Does Stuart know you're such a cheap date?"

"Why do you think he married me?"

As she headed off to the kitchen, I crossed the back patio, then followed the path to the side of the house where we keep the trash cans. San Diablo is a holdout to the ugly, plastic, wheeled contraptions so many towns have switched to. We have old-fashioned metal trash cans, the kind that are so bright and shiny in the hardware store that you really can't imagine filling it with your potato peels and sacks of poopy diapers. Call me nuts, but I think the trash cans add to the town's charm.

I'd just lifted the lid when I smelled it, that putrid odor that wasn't coming from the trash. I whipped around to face this new demon foe (a teenager, no less!), but he was expecting my move, managing to block my blow and land his own against my upper thigh. I went down with a yelp, the trash can lid clattering against the cement, and my not-yet-a-size-eight butt cushioning my fall.

Immediately I pressed my hands back against the sidewalk to lever myself back up, but he was on top of me, one knee against my chest and a hunting knife against my throat.

The icy steel of the blade matched the ice that filled my veins. Yesterday that ice had been tainted by fear. Not anymore. Kate Connor, Level Four Demon Hunter, was back in business, and she was pissed off. That ice was adrenaline and determination and years of training sweeping (hopefully) through my body. I was going to kick the shit out of this scum-puppy. No doubt about it. He was going down.

All I had to do was figure out how.

Eight

"It's over, Hunter," he said, his mouth curling into a sneer. "My master is moving in, and this town isn't big enough for the two of you."

Were the situation not so dire, I would have laughed at the cliché. With his red hair and freckled face, demon-boy reminded me of a young Ron Howard, and I was having a hard time reconciling my memories of Richie Cunning-ham with this killing machine who now threatened my life.

I took a breath, then took a chance. "What do you want?"

"I want what my master wants." He grinned, all boy-next-door with a blade. He leaned in closer, and I almost gagged after inhaling a whiff of his breath. "He'll find it, you know. If it's in San Diablo, he'll find it. And the bones will be his."

"Bones?"

He made a shushing noise, then moved the knife from my neck to my lips, laying it flat across my mouth. I fought an involuntary shiver and lost. He saw the movement and his eyes lit with victory. "That's right, Hunter. Be afraid. Because when my master's army rises, you will be among the first to fall. And by the time he's done, you'll wish you'd died a whole lot sooner."

"I'm beginning to wish you'd get it over with now," I hissed, my lips moving against the cold blade.

His face contorted and I held my breath, suddenly afraid I'd made a big mistake. I was ninety-nine percent sure that he was under orders *not* to kill me; it was that left-over one percent that suddenly had me sweating.

But the knife didn't move and my neck stayed intact, and I took that as a good sign. This boy was a messenger, his purpose to scare me, to let me know that Goramesh was here, that he intended to get what he came for, and that he wasn't going to take kindly to me meddling in his affairs.

Of course, killing and maiming were two different things, and from the way demon-boy was now staring at me, I feared he was thinking much the same thing. Since I'm rather fond of all my various limbs, and would like to keep them intact and unmolested, I started to spit out a purely self-serving apology. That's when I heard the back door slam open and then Allie's call of "Mom? Did you get lost or what?"

I met the demon's eyes, and he nodded, raising the blade just millimeters off my lips. I cleared my throat, but still ended up sounding squeaky. "I'm fine," I said. "I just got sidetracked."

"With the *trash*?"

"Recycling. There was glass mixed with the plastic. I sorted it all out."

She didn't answer, but I heard the door close and—though I couldn't be certain—I thought I heard an exasperated *Mo-ther.*

"She'll be back," I said. "She's probably just getting a flashlight to help me." A major piece of bullshit if ever there was one, but it seemed to work. Demon-boy climbed off me, the knife held in front of him, ready to impale me if

I made a wrong move. Not damn likely. He'd been sitting on my chest for so long, I wasn't even certain my internal organs were still functioning. This was one demon I wouldn't be chasing down tonight. He was, however, on my list.

He turned and ran toward the street, and I soon lost sight of him in the shadows. I sat up feeling like an idiot. There was a reason so many Hunters retired young, and I was feeling that reason in my size-ten butt. Just a few days ago thirty-eight seemed so young. I mean, I don't even have crow's-feet. "Old and creaky" may be insulting, but I feared it might also be true.

I stood and dusted my tush off, then replaced the lid on the trash can. My performance this evening definitely wasn't going to win any *Forza Scura* accolades, but at least I wasn't dead. And I had a plan. Two plans, actually. One: work out like a maniac and restore my stellar reflexes. And two: admit that Larson won the demons-in-San-Diablo argument and start in full time helping him figure out what trinket Goramesh was searching for—laundry, dirty dishes, and toilet bowls be damned.

As I walked back toward the house, I rubbed a hand across my bruised bottom and replayed the conversation in my head. Bones, he'd said. But *whose* bones?

I hoped Larson had a clue, because I had no ideas at all.

"Bones," Larson repeated, his voice tinny across the phone line.

"A relic?" I pondered. "One of the saints in the cathedral?" Sometimes demons will instruct their minions to steal first-class relics (like the bones or hair of saints). These relics are anathema to the demons, and the demons will order their human followers to destroy the relics in hideous demonic rituals.

"Possibly," Larson said. "Let me think a moment."

I crossed my legs under me and tugged the guest bed pillow into my lap, trying to make myself more comfortable while he did his academic *alimentatore* thing. Hopefully his thing wouldn't take too long. It was three in the morning, and I was dead tired.

Stuart had stayed up until two working, and I'd stayed up with him, ostensibly succumbing to the urge to clean house (like *that's* not a flimsy excuse) but really just wanting to outlast him. When he finally did crash, I cited a fresh load of laundry that needed to be folded if we didn't want to suffer the absolute shame of wrinkled shirts and jeans. Fortunately Stuart was either tired enough or preoccupied enough not to notice my personality change. (For the record, housework does not keep me up at night any more than worrying about the national deficit. I figure they'll both be there in the morning, so why should I lose sleep?)

As soon as I was sure he was tapped out, I'd shut our bedroom door, crept into the guest bedroom, and shut that door as well. Then I'd dialed the number Larson had given me earlier. He answered on the first ring, surprising me. At three a.m. I'd expected his machine, not the perfectly poised, completely awake voice that answered.

After the usual greetings, I'd given him the rundown of the evening, trying to remember verbatim what demon-boy had said.

Now I could hear Larson breathing into the phone. "Bones," he repeated. "Are you sure?"

I'd been sure, but I was rapidly losing confidence. "I think so. He was talking low, but I think I heard him right. I mean, I suppose I could be wrong. . . ."

He made a dismissive noise. "We'll assume you heard correctly. So far, that's the best lead we have."

I leaned forward, pressing my elbows into the pillow as I kept the phone cradled against my ear. "What leads *do* we have? Father Corletti didn't tell me, and we got interrupted by Stuart and the kids before you had a chance to fill me in."

"Two years ago the altar of a small church in Larnaca was defaced with several Satanic symbols, the most prominent being three intersecting sixes."

"Oh." I pressed my lips together, not really wanting to reveal my ignorance. I didn't have a choice, though, so I took the plunge. "Refresh my recollection. Where's Larnaca?"

"Greece, Kate."

"Right. I remember now. Defaced, huh?"

"Spray paint," he said. "The police assumed it was teenage hooligans."

"But the Vatican knew better?"

"Not at all. The Vatican assumed the same. But then the same symbol began turning up in other locations, and the damage was much, much worse."

I shook my head. "What do you mean?"

"The offices of a cathedral in Mexico were ravaged."

"The *offices*?"

"Correct," he said, his voice grave. "The altar was spray-painted, but it was the offices that were truly destroyed. Records taken or destroyed."

"What kinds of records?"

"The pastor and staff were murdered," Larson said, "so we do not know in great detail. But we can assume the usual."

I nodded, understanding. Demons—or their human minions—have been known to infiltrate a parish's records searching for evidence of the fallen faithful. There's little a demon likes better than to corrupt a once pious soul. And who better to prey on than a soul who is faltering or doubting his or her faith. Which means every time there's a scandal in the Church, demons dance in the streets. Metaphorically speaking, of course.

I pondered the information for a moment. "Just records?" I asked. "No relics?"

"Not that we're aware of."

"Really?" That was odd. As a general rule, a demon's more keen on action (destroying relics) than on research (reading Church records). "Weird," I said.

"Indeed," Larson said. "And there's more. About four months ago a small Benedictine monastery in the Tuscan hills was decimated. Ripped apart stone by stone. Only the monks' cells, though. The chapel itself was barely damaged."

"Good God," I said. "And the monks?"

"Dead. All but one murdered."

I cocked my head. "And the one?"

"Suicide," he said.

I put my hand to my mouth. "You're not serious."

"I'm afraid I am. He threw himself from a window."

I swallowed, trying to focus. Suicide was a mortal sin. What could possibly drive a monk to take his own life? "And we know that Goramesh was behind it?"

"We knew nothing at the time," Larson said. "The local *polizia* were called, but the area is very rural and the investigation was slipshod. The crime was attributed to roving gangs—hoodlums—and the case was closed."

"But not over."

"A young woman turned up a week later in a hospital in Florence. The police learned that she'd been staying in the monastery stables as she backpacked through Europe. She saw nothing of the attack, but in the wee hours of the morning, she took a walk to the chapel, planning to attend matins. That is when she was attacked. She managed to get to the hospital, but the police obtained no useful information from her."

"But?" I just knew there was a *but* coming.

"The Vatican heard about the woman and sent inspectors to visit her in the hospital."

I hugged the pillow, pretty sure I knew where this story was going. "She was a Hunter."

"Very good," he said, as if I was a prize pupil. "By the

time she entered, all the monks were already dead. She interrupted a demon rampaging through the chapel—"

"The *chapel*?" Demons can walk on holy ground, but it hurts like, well, hell. That's one of the first things they teach you when you sign on with *Forza*—if a demon enters a church, his true nature will be revealed; the pain is simply unbearable. That's why holy ground makes for such a great demon test.

"Apparently she is the reason the chapel remained essentially unharmed. According to the woman, he was in a blind fury, probably borne of the torment of his presence in the church. She believed he was looking for something. Presumably he had not anticipated encountering a human, much less a Hunter."

"He attacked her?"

"He did, and they fought. Because of his weakened state, she was able to easily subdue him. She was a clever thing, though, and prior to releasing him from the body he'd claimed, she forced him to reveal his mission. Or, at least, his master."

"Goramesh."

"Indeed. The demon's last words were cryptic, but the Hunter believed the demon described San Diablo as his next target. The Hunter, of course, prevented the demon from doing any more mischief."

"More power to her," I said, sending up a mental cheer for the girl on the front lines. "But did she find out what Goramesh was searching for?"

"She did not."

"Oh." I ran my teeth over my lower lip. "Well, is there some connection between the locations? Other than the nature of the attacks, I mean."

"At the moment I've been unable to find a connection, though I intend to do more research this evening. As for your review of the Church archives, perhaps you can see if any of the Church relics hail from any of those locations."

"Okay. No problem. I can do that." I frowned, hoping I *could* do that. My frown deepened as another thought occurred to me. "What about the girl? The Hunter? It sounds like she was on the case. So why didn't *Forza* send *her* here? I mean, if she already had a bead on the situation, why wait until demons start crashing through my windows? And why keep her out of the loop?"

"She's dead. She prevailed against Goramesh's minion, but she was mortally wounded in the process. She died six hours after telling her story to her *alimentatore*."

He spoke without emotion, but his voice was too tight, too controlled, and the story ripped my guts out. "She was yours," I whispered.

"She was, indeed."

"How old was she?"

"Eighteen."

I closed my eyes, my throat full of tears, as I mourned that girl I'd never known. That girl who—once upon a time—could have been me.

I thought of Timmy and Allie and Stuart, and fear settled over me, cold and clingy. *It still could be me.*

At eighteen, death hadn't scared me. But leaving my kids alone in the world? Not being there when they needed me most?

I buried my head in my pillow and cried.

It's amazing what a few demons will do for one's level of piety. I confess I'd been less than diligent in making sure we all went to Mass on Sundays, but this morning I rustled everyone up, and we managed to make the eleven o'clock service.

Allie had surprised me by not protesting too violently when I hauled her and Mindy out of bed at nine. Mindy had taken a pass on joining us, and although Allie's expression had turned wistful at Mindy's plans to do nothing but "veg out" on the last day before school, in the end my daughter came willingly (*willingly* being a relative term where fourteen-year-olds are concerned). Even Stuart hadn't protested too much, though he had insisted on taking both cars so that he could head to the office immediately following the service. Now that the Mass had ended, I kissed him good-bye, then sent Allie off to get Tim from the nursery while I hung back, wanting to talk to Father Ben.

I'd called Delores earlier that morning, and she'd been so ecstatic that I was ninety-nine percent certain she would have already snagged Father Ben and relayed the good news.

I loitered in front of the annex while he did the meet-and-greet routine with all the parishioners. When the crowd cleared away, he saw me and his already bright smile doubled in intensity. Nothing makes Father Ben happier than an enthusiastic volunteer.

"Kate, I was hoping I'd see you. Delores told me you're going to start going through the in-kind donations."

"Absolutely," I said. Honestly, I wanted to tell him the truth, but I'd been too well trained to break *Forza*'s strict rules. "I wanted to pitch in with more than just typing. I mean, I know there's quite a lot of work to be done."

"That's putting it mildly," he said.

"Always happy to help." I sounded way too perky for someone offering to sit in a dark room and wade through dusty boxes probably filled with spiders. I couldn't seem to rein in my tone, though.

Fortunately, Father Ben either didn't notice or didn't find my enthusiasm odd. Then again, even if he did, why comment? As it was, he was about to pick up a slave laborer. Why insult her by telling her she's nuts?

We arranged a time to meet on Monday, and were just wrapping up our conversation when Allie and Timmy scrambled up. (In all fairness, Timmy was doing the scrambling. Allie was tagging behind him, her face a familiar mix of irritation and amusement. I knew that expression; it used to be mine.)

"Mom! Grab him, already!"

I reached out and managed to snag my runaway munchkin with a quick shift to the left. "Gotcha!"

He erupted into peals of giggles and went limp, falling to the ground and squealing "No tickling, Mommy" when he very clearly wanted desperately to be tickled. I complied, managing to avoid flailing feet as I caught him in one big tickle extravaganza. While he squealed, I scooped him up and let him hang upside down as I said good-bye to Father Ben and promised to see him in the morning.

Only after Allie and I were heading toward the car—me with a limp bundle of boy—did I realize that I could hardly spend the day plowing through church records with a toddler clinging to my thigh. I could barely sit down long enough to check my e-mail without Timmy throwing a fit. Several hours in a basement expecting him to behave just wasn't feasible.

I frowned, considering my options. I could count on Laura to watch him once or twice, but unless I was extremely lucky (doubtful considering the direction of my luck lately), I wasn't going to find the answer by Wednesday.

Bottom line? I was going to have to find a day care, not to mention pay for it. That was something I couldn't keep secret from Stuart, and the thought of discussing it with him made my stomach hurt almost as much as the idea of leaving my baby in someone else's charge during the day.

Allie must have caught my expression as I was strapping Tim into his car seat. She frowned, then started to say something, but seemed to think better of it. Then, being fourteen, she changed her mind again. "Mom?"

"Yeah, hon?"

"Oh, nothing. No big."

I could tell from her voice that it wasn't nothing, but in a particularly bad mommy moment, I pretended to be too caught up with my toddler to notice. I gave Tim's straps a tug, handed him his sippy cup and Boo Bear, then trotted around the van to the driver's side. By the time I slid behind the wheel, Allie was already buckled in. She looked fine, but she was picking at her fingernails, peeling away the purple glitter polish she and Mindy had so carefully applied last night.

Damn.

I dreaded answering questions that I didn't want voiced, but at the same time, I couldn't really assume this was all about me. For all I knew, Allie had a deep and desperate crush on one of the altar boys.

I waited until I'd maneuvered the winding road that led from the cathedral back down to the Pacific Coast Highway. Then I headed north toward our neighborhood, the Pacific Ocean on my left and my daughter—moody and quiet—on my right.

"Anything you want to talk about?"

Her shoulders lifted. "Uhdunna."

I thought about that for a second, then interpreted it as *I don't know.* Ah-ha! Progress.

"Are you worried about school tomorrow?"

Another shrug, this one accompanied with an "I guess."

It was an opening, and I grabbed it. I was pretty sure school wasn't on her mind at the moment, but since I didn't have any other leads, I jumped in with both feet. "You're going to be fine. You have, what, three classes with Mindy? And most of your junior-high friends are going to Coronado. Give it a month, and you'll forget you were ever worried."

Behind us, Timmy was carrying on a serious conversation with Boo Bear. I glanced toward the backseat, and he flashed me a sleepy grin, then pulled the bedraggled bear closer. I didn't need to look at my watch to tell it was getting close to naptime.

"I know," she said, still picking at her fingernails. "It's not that."

"Boys?"

"Mo-*ther!*" She arched her back and tossed her head, letting loose a sigh of exasperation. Now, *this* was the kid I knew. "It's not like I *always* think about boys."

"That's good to know," I said. I kept my eyes fixed on the road, afraid that if I looked at my daughter, I'd crack a smile. "I'm very happy to hear that."

From the corner of my eye, I could see her shaking her head, completely exasperated with the pain-in-the-butt who was her mother.

I was out of options, so I kept my mouth shut over the next few miles. At least she wasn't brooding anymore, so I counted that as a minor victory. Unfortunately, if she really wasn't worried about school or boys, then that left family. Or some other completely unrelated problem that I knew nothing about.

Neither possibility appealed to me.

Timmy's soft snores drifted to the front of the van, and I realized I'd missed my window of naptime opportunity. I should have gunned the van all the way home and gotten him into his crib right after Mass. Now that he was asleep, this was it. Never once had I managed to transfer him from the car to the house without waking him, and once he wakes up, he's good to go for the rest of the day.

I love my little boy, but I love him even more after a two-hour nap. Trust me. Fifteen-minute naps result in rampant crankiness. And that goes for both toddler and Mommy.

I considered my options, then tapped the brakes as we approached California Avenue, the main east-west thoroughfare that divides San Diablo. I made a right turn and headed east, following the road as it cut through the canyons before leveling out when we hit San Diablo proper.

"Where are we going?" Allie asked. I understood her confusion. Our house is in a subdivision off of Rialto, the road just north of California Avenue. While the city planners should have put in a few more cross streets, they didn't, making it impossible to get to our house from the avenue without going through half the town and then doubling back on Highway 101.

"How does the mall sound?"

She eyed me suspiciously. "Why?"

"Tim's asleep. We go home now, and we've got Terror Toddler on our hands."

"So you're just going to let me shop while you sit in the van with Tim?" From her voice, I could tell she was expecting a punch line.

"Either that or we can stay in the van together, and you can drive it around the parking lot until Tim wakes up."

That got her attention. "No way! Really? You'd let me drive the van?"

"Slowly, in a parking lot, with me in the passenger seat. But yeah. Under those conditions, yes, you can drive the van."

The legal driving age in California is sixteen (with an adult in the passenger seat), but kids can get a learner's permit at fifteen, so we've got eleven months to go. I'd already told Stuart that I wanted Allie licensed up and comfortable behind the wheel as early as was legally possible. While I'm not crazy about the idea of my daughter manipulating three thousand pounds of metal while going sixty-five miles an hour, I'm resigned to the fact that eventually, yes, she will be a licensed driver. I figure practice makes perfect.

My current plan to go joyriding in the half-empty mall parking lot wasn't exactly legal, but I didn't care. Timmy would get to finish his nap and Allie would have a blast. Besides, I drove all over Rome at fourteen. Allie'd had a different kind of life (thank God), but she was still a competent and responsible kid.

At the moment my competent and responsible child was

gaping open-mouthed at me. "Who are you, and what have you done with my mother?"

"Very funny," I said. "Very original."

"You really mean it?"

"No, I'm lying to you in a pathetically involved scheme to torture you throughout your adolescence so that when you're older you can write a tell-all book, make a million dollars, and retire comfortably. But I'm doing it all for love."

"You're weird, Mom."

"So I've been told."

We'd reached the mall entrance, and I turned in, passing the Grecian columns that in my opinion look positively ridiculous in the California coastal landscape. The developers, however, hadn't bothered to ask my opinion, and the whole mall was built around some ridiculous Olympian theme.

As I'd expected, the parking lot near the food court was full, but the lot that faced the south entrance was mostly empty—just a smattering of cars near the doors and a few farther out, most likely employees. I pulled into a spot, left the engine running, and got out. As I walked around the van to the passenger side, Allie lifted the armrest, then scrambled into the driver's seat and settled herself behind the wheel. As I slid back inside, she was busily adjusting her mirrors.

"Good to go?" I asked.

"Yeah. This is great. Mindy's going to be so jealous."

"Let's focus on operating the extremely heavy motor vehicle and worry about gloating later, okay?"

"Sure, Mom," she said, perfectly happy.

I unfastened my seat belt and turned around, facing backward so I could check out Timmy. I leaned all the way over, reaching out to grab one of his straps. I gave it a little tug, just to make sure. He was in tight, and seemed down for the count. I readjusted myself in the seat and, as I was fastening my seat belt, caught sight of Allie rolling her eyes.

"Parental license," I said. "Even if you're the best driver on the planet, I'm allowed to worry."

She didn't even bother to respond, instead reaching down to crank the engine. Since the van was already idling, the Odyssey didn't take too kindly to the maneuver, spitting back a growling, gear-burning kind of sound that made my daughter jump.

"It's okay," I said. "I do that all the time."

Attempt number two went smoother, and she pulled forward, a little hesitant at first, but then getting into a groove. "Not bad," I said. "I think you've done this before."

Her grin was wide, and I knew she was proud of herself. "Not recently," she said. "And you've never let me drive the van."

That much was true. Before we bought the Infiniti, Stuart and I used to occasionally let her drive the old Corolla around the high school parking lot. But until the new-car smell faded, I doubted Allie would get much of a chance to drive Stuart's pride and joy.

I pointed her toward a wide-open area, and she drove in circles for a while, then laid out a few figure eights, and finally put the van in reverse and started to drive a straight line going backward.

"Show-off," I said, but I know she could tell I was proud.

She brought the van to a stop, then shifted again, accelerating until she reached a twenty-mile-an-hour cruising speed. Her eyes were fixed on the road when she spoke, so softly that at first I didn't even realize she was talking. "Daddy used to let me drive."

"What?" I'd heard the words, but I hadn't quite processed them.

"Daddy used to let me drive," she said, this time more loudly. Defiant, almost, as if she were daring me to challenge her.

I tugged at the shoulder strap of my seat belt, pushing

it away from my neck as I turned in my seat. "When did he do that?" My voice was measured, but my heart was beating fast, and not just from the mention of Eric. I'm not sure how I knew—her tone maybe, her mannerisms—but we'd moved on to whatever had been bothering her earlier. This was it. Mom was on deck, and she had to get it right.

"When I was little. About six, I think. He used to put me in his lap. He'd do the pedals since I couldn't reach, but I got to steer. He said it was our little secret."

"Eric," I whispered with a little shake of my head. "You nut." Eric loved to share secrets like that. Little things that only he and you had. Our marriage had been like that—three months before our official retirement, we'd been married in a small church in Cluny. We'd told no one, but those months before our "real" wedding had been precious.

He did other little things, too. Secret notes, anonymous presents. Those memories had always been special, but after Eric died, they became cherished. And I'd always been a little sad to think that he'd died before he could share secrets with his daughter.

But he hadn't. I should have known that Eric would never have gone and died without leaving one or two special memories for Allie. That just wouldn't be like him.

"Mom?" She tapped the brakes, slowing to a stop.

I realized I was crying and brushed a tear away. "Sorry, sweetie. I just always loved your daddy's secrets. I'm glad he shared one with you."

Her lips pressed together, and for a second I thought she was going to cry, too. When she didn't, I realized that the corner of her mouth was twitching just slightly, and that her cheeks were a soft shade of pink. I knew then that the driving was only one secret, and I fought my own smile as I said a silent thank-you to Eric. He'd left us unexpectedly, but he'd still managed to leave a little legacy for his daughter.

I reached over and squeezed her hand. She squeezed

back, then tentatively tugged her hand away. When she started picking at the nail polish again, I realized we hadn't yet gotten to the meat of things. I stayed quiet. Sooner or later she'd tell me what was her mind.

When she started to shift the van back into drive, I realized it would probably be later. But then she let go of the gearshift, leaving the van in Park and the engine running. "Does he have something to do with this? Daddy, I mean?"

Not a question I'd expected, and I was grateful she'd spoken to the steering wheel rather than to me. "With this? What's this?"

"You know. The self-defense stuff. And Mass. You haven't dragged me along in a while, and then all of a sudden . . ."

No dummy, that kid of mine. "What makes you think it has something to do with your daddy?"

"Dunno," she said, even though she obviously did. "I mean, I'm super-psyched about the kickboxing stuff, but . . ." She trailed off with a shrug.

I squinted at her, trying without success to read my daughter's mind. "What?"

"You used to do all that stuff with Daddy," she said. "But yesterday you were doing it with *him*."

My chest tightened and I raised my hand to my throat. "You remember that?" My voice was barely a whisper. Eric and I used to spar a bit when Allie was Timmy's age, maybe a little older. As she grew up, though—and as we became complacent, living demon-free—we'd fallen out of the habit. Chasing a toddler was exercise enough, and we were having too much fun being parents to keep up with our training.

"Sorta," she said. "I remember sometimes you guys would let me play, too. I had my own sword and everything."

I knew my voice would tremble, but I had to answer. "You still do." A plastic saber Eric had found at a toy store one afternoon. "I packed it away with my equipment. It's in the storage shed somewhere."

She crossed her arms over her chest, hugging herself. "So why start up again now? And why with him?"

"He's a friend, and he's got some experience. That's all." At least I knew now why Allie had seemed so cold to Larson. I reached over and stroked her arm. "As for taking the classes in the first place, I thought it would be nice for us to do something like this together. And your dad would like knowing you can take care of yourself." I avoided answering her basic question: *why*. I didn't want to lie to my daughter any more than I had to. "Believe me, baby, I'd never do anything to mess up your memories of your daddy."

"I know." She snuffled loudly. "I just miss him."

"I know, baby," I said. "I miss him, too."

The afternoon played out like pretty much any Sunday, though I will say that both Allie and I were a bit more attentive than usual to Stuart. Guilt will do that to a person.

After dinner Tim played on his xylophone while Allie accompanied him on a bongo drum. Stuart and I filled in backup using Tim's somewhat slobbery harmonicas. (I confess we were trying to avoid being part of the act, but Timmy's "you play, too, Mommy" is hard to resist.) After playing, bathing, and reading *Chicka Chicka Boom Boom* (twice), *How Do Dinosaurs Say Good Night?* (once), and *Goodnight Moon* (three times), we finally convinced Tim that he was Super Jammie Man, and it was time for him, his jammies, and Boo Bear to head off to bed, where they could fight for truth, justice, and the rest of it in his dreams.

Silliness works well in our house.

Allie stayed up with us for a while, dividing her time between her room and the living room, with each trip bringing a different ensemble for me to comment on. Despite having lugged home bags of fancy new clothes, in the end she decided on her favorite jeans, a plain white T-shirt, and a cute little pink sweater (The Gap, 75% off) to top off the outfit. The internal wrangling before she reached this key decision took approximately two and one-half hours.

After she headed off to bed—with a halfhearted promise not to call Mindy in the dark and stay up all night anticipating the next morning—Stuart and I opened a bottle of Merlot, popped *Patton* into the DVD player, and curled up on the couch. (He picked it. I'd agreed out of residual guilt. Now I was stuck.)

His arm curled around me and I snuggled against him. "I'm sorry I've been so busy lately," he said. "It's just going to get worse."

"I know. It's okay." More than okay, actually. I was counting on Stuart being busy enough not to notice his wife's newly reacquired extracurricular activities. I shifted, then arched up to kiss him. "This is important to you."

He stroked my hair. "You're the best, you know that, right?"

I laughed, the sound a little forced. "I'm *not* the best, but I promise I'll try. I'll never be Suzy Homemaker, but if we're lucky, I won't completely torpedo your chances of getting elected."

"Won't happen," he said. "One day out of the gate and you've already won Larson over."

"Yeah, well, I guess we just clicked."

"Who wouldn't click with you?"

I didn't answer that one, pretending instead to be suddenly fascinated by Patton pulling out a pistol and opening fire against a German plane. Stuart followed my lead, and we settled in to watch the rest of the movie.

I was cozy and comfortable and actually ended up enjoying the movie (go figure), but I still couldn't quite relax. Things were happening out there in the real world, but it all seemed to be off camera. Just outside my peripheral vision. If only I could somehow turn my head and see the bigger picture—

"Hey." Stuart's voice was soft as he smoothed my hair. "Where are you tonight?"

"Sorry. Just distracted. Allie. High school. My baby growing up." Another lie. That made how many? I'd lost track, and I couldn't help but wonder how many more would follow.

My worlds were colliding, and I wanted to keep the world with Stuart safe and secure. Tucked away in a little box like a treasured Christmas ornament. But my old life kept peeking in, and I was so afraid that Stuart would look at me one morning and catch a glimpse of my secret. Or, worse, that one morning he'd wake up and catch a glimpse of a demon.

I twisted in his arms and kissed him, hard at first, and then softer, until I felt him relax under me and open his mouth to mine. His hands tightened around me, and he pulled me close. I wanted to be even closer. I wanted to curl up, lost inside this man. I wanted him to take care of me. At the very least, I wanted to forget my responsibilities and my promises and my past.

"To what do I owe the pleasure?" he asked, his tone suggesting that he was amenable to more of the same.

"Can't I seduce my husband?"

"Any time, any place."

"Here," I said. "And now."

A familiar spark flashed in his eyes, the kind every man gets when he realizes he's going to get lucky. And then he pulled me close, *Patton* all but forgotten.

I'm not stupid. I knew this wouldn't solve my problem, wouldn't make my worries or the boogeyman go away. Wouldn't even erase my thoughts of Eric.

I wanted it, though. Wanted Stuart. *This* husband. *This* life.

I needed to feel my present tight around me, soft and warm like a blanket. Because bits and pieces of my past kept picking at the loose threads, and I was so afraid that, if I wasn't careful, the perfect life Stuart and I had built together would unravel in an instant.

And then, I had to wonder, where would I be?

For that matter, *who* would I be?

Nine

Good sex warps a woman's mind. I realize that now. But when Stuart asked me if I could throw together *another* quick cocktail party, I was still lost in that sated morning-after glow. Apparently, one of the paralegals was supposed to host the thing that evening, but she'd come down with something. I murmured *yes* and then buried my head back under the covers, happy, content, and full of orgasm-induced confidence.

It wasn't until my alarm went off five minutes later that I realized my mistake.

By that time Stuart was already pulling out of the drive, probably practicing his cocktail party banter as he drove to the gym for an early-morning workout. I toyed briefly with dialing his cell phone and backing out, but then abandoned the idea. It wasn't a huge shindig. Only five couples. And this was what I was supposed to be doing—helping my husband, stepping in during a crisis, being a good wife and mom. Yes, he may have cheated a bit by asking when my body still tingled, but I'd said yes, and now I was stuck.

And considering I had to get two kids up and dressed—and then drive Allie and three other kids to school before the 7:45 warning bell—I really didn't have time to sit around regretting my decision.

I tossed on a pair of sweats and a T-shirt, then pulled my hair back into a ponytail without bothering to brush it. Allie's a bear to wake up before seven, so I headed for her room first, pounding on the door and calling, "Up, up, up."

Her muffled response filtered through the door, and although I couldn't understand the words, the tone was loud and clear—*Go away, Mom, you're bothering me*.

"First day of school, Allie, remember? Come on. We're running late." A lie, but I figured that might get her moving faster.

Next, I headed for Timmy's room. This was about the time he usually woke up—six-fifteen—and I could hear him whispering to himself. I pushed the door open with a cheery, "Good morning, Mr. Tim."

"MOMMA, MOMMA, MOMMA!"

(Now *there's* a proper morning greeting.) I headed over to his crib and soaked up the light from his toothy grin. He held up Boo Bear. "He sleepy," he said.

"Me, too." I took the bear, gave it a big kiss, and then very seriously spoke to his little bear face. "Boo Bear, we need to get Timmy up. What do you think? Time for a fresh diaper?"

I didn't give the bear (or the boy) time to answer. Just schlepped them both the short distance to the changing table. Less than two minutes later (I've been doing this for a few years) Timmy had on a fresh diaper and clean clothes and we were heading into the living room. I plunked him on the couch, turned on *JoJo's Circus*, and continued toward the kitchen to heat up a sippy cup of milk.

Forty-five seconds later Timmy was holding the cup in his chubby little hands, I had my cordless phone cradled at my ear, and I was heading back up the stairs to pound at Allie's door once again.

"Dupont Mental Institution," Laura said, obviously having checked her caller ID.

"How are things at your end?"

"The inmates are restless," she said.

"At least yours is up and moving." I pounded on Allie's door again. "*Now*, Allie. If you're not dressed at 7:20, I'm leaving without you." The first day of car pool is always a challenge, and Karen and Emily were unknown commodities. If they were the kind who ran late—where you ended up sitting on the street, engine running, laying on the horn—I wanted a little padding in the schedule.

I switched my attention back to the phone. "What have you got going this morning?"

"Laundry," she said, sounding about as excited as if she were having a root canal. "Carla refuses to step up to the plate." Carla came in twice a month to do Laura's heavy cleaning. This is a point of great envy on my part. One day I'm hoping Carla can be cloned. "And bills. I could be talked into procrastinating," she added. "If you've got a better offer, I mean."

"Not exactly," I said as I headed back downstairs. "I was hoping to bum a favor."

"Oh, dear."

"Now that Mindy's a teenager, don't you miss the pitter-patter of little feet?"

"You're killing me here," she said, but I could hear amusement in her voice, and said a silent thank-you. "Just spit it out."

"I need a babysitter."

"Oh, really?" Her voice rose with interest. "And what fabulous dalliance have you got scheduled?"

"Nothing as fabulous as all that." I gave her the short-but-incomplete truth—that I was going to be doing some work at the church.

She made curious noises, but didn't ask and I didn't volunteer. As soon as she agreed to watch the munchkin, I swore to do her bidding for the rest of eternity. "You can probably just treat me to dessert at the Cheesecake Factory," she said, "and we'll call it even." A pause. "Or is this more than a one-day crisis?"

"Hopefully just one or two," I said, making one of those *I'm-guilty-but-please-help-anyway* faces even though she couldn't see me through the phone line. "I'm hoping I can find a day care."

"Really?" Her surprise made sense. I'd told her over and over that I love doing the stay-at-home-mom thing (I do). "Two days, two desserts," she said, playing babysitting hardball.

"Done. I'll drop him by after I offload the girls." We hung up and I stood silent for a moment, listening for Allie. I heard the shower running. A good sign. At least I wouldn't have to race back up the stairs and drag her bodily into the bathroom.

"More milk," Timmy said as I headed toward the kitchen. "Chocolate milk, Mommy. Chocolate."

"I don't think so, kiddo."

I took the sippy cup and filled it with boring white milk, then I ripped open a packet of oatmeal, dumped it into a bowl with what looked like the right amount of water, shoved the bowl into the microwave, and set the timer. I was already pushing it with Laura; I couldn't expect her to feed the kid breakfast, too.

Two minutes later I had Tim happily settled in his booster seat poking at tepid, gloppy oatmeal with his spoon. Hopefully one or two bites would actually make it into his mouth.

Allie barreled down the stairs and into the kitchen a few minutes later, eyed the packet of oatmeal on the counter, and shot me a look of disdain. "I'll just have coffee," she said.

"You'll eat breakfast," I said, keeping a proprietary grip on my own mug. We'd compromised on the coffee thing midsummer (that's when she'd claimed to be a true high-schooler). Minimal guilt on my part, though, particularly when I discovered that my daughter takes a little coffee with her milk rather than vice versa. Breakfast, however, I was holding fast on.

"Fine. Whatever." She grabbed a Nutri-Grain bar from a box on top of the fridge, then disappeared back upstairs to finish the getting-dressed ritual. "Makeup?" she called down.

"Mascara and lip gloss," I said.

"Mo-om!"

"I'm not having this conversation again, Allie. I'm deaf to your protests until you're sixteen." The real score? I knew she'd continue to bug me and I'd eventually cave. But I was holding fast for at least a month.

No response, but I did hear a lot of stomping going on up there.

"Makeup, Momma!" Timmy howled. "*My* makeup."

"I don't think so, bud. Not even when you're sixteen."

In lieu of pouting, he threw a glob of oatmeal across the room. I watched it land with a plop near the missing window, knowing I should go clean it up. For that matter, I should get on the phone and find a glazier to fix the damn thing. Instead, I drained my coffee and poured myself a fresh cup. Procrastination, thy name is Kate.

Allie made it back down the stairs just before Mindy rapped on the back door. I ushered the lot of us to the van, the girls carrying their brand-new day packs, me sporting a toddler, a purse, and a diaper bag.

We caught a lucky break and both Karen and Emily were ready when I honked at their houses. Emily was last, and as soon as she piled in, I headed to the high school, where I lined up behind a dozen other vans and SUVs. I caught a glimpse of some of the other moms (and a few of the dads). From what I could tell, I was the only one pulling car-pool duty sans shower, with my hair yanked carelessly back, the T-shirt I'd slept in tucked into ratty old sweats. I slumped down in the driver's seat and made a mental note to get up fifteen minutes earlier on car-pool day.

When the line of cars had moved enough so that we were in the driveway, Emily slid the door open and the girls started piling out. I reminded them that Karen's mom had pickup duty, then put the van in drive. I couldn't get out of there fast enough.

"But not for me and Mindy," Allie said, her hand on the sliding door. "Remember? We're staying after to talk to Ms. Carlson about cheerleading."

"Right," I said. "I remember." I hadn't, of course. (And what are they doing scheduling a cheerleading meeting on the first day of school, anyway?) I mentally rearranged my schedule, realized it was completely impossible, but figured I'd manage somehow. "Call me on the cell when the meeting starts and let me know what time it's supposed to be over. We're having some of Stuart's political folks over for drinks tonight, so Mrs. Dupont may end up picking you guys up."

"Whatever," Allie said. It really was unfair. I'd give myself an ulcer trying to work out who was picking who up and when, and all she had to say was *whatever*.

I sighed. Whatever.

Ten minutes later I was seated at Laura's kitchen table, a fresh mug of coffee tight in my hand. I nodded toward my munchkin, who was seated across from me, his nose even with the tabletop since Laura had long ago packed away her booster seat. "You're sure you don't mind?"

"Honestly. It's fine." She was already dressed to the nines, which made me feel even grimier.

I nodded at her outfit. "You look like you had plans."

She made a dismissive gesture. "Oh, no. Not really. Paul's just working late again tonight, and I thought it might be nice to, you know, look extra special for him."

I thought about how I'd looked that morning as Stuart

had headed off—how I looked now, for that matter—and shrugged. "I'm sure he appreciated the gesture," I said.

I expected her to give me some dish or make a snarky comment. Instead, she just looked embarrassed and started unloading her dishwasher. I decided to change subjects. "If he gives you any trouble at all, just call my cell. And for nap, just plunk him in the middle of your bed and put some pillows around him. He won't roll out." I tried to think what else to tell her. "There're sippy cups and diapers in the bag, but if you need—"

She held up her hand, laughing. "Kate, you aren't heading to Australia. And I have a key to your house. We'll be fine."

I looked at Tim, who was happily shredding a napkin into smaller and smaller pieces. "You going to be okay with Aunt Laura? Mommy's got to go run some errands."

He didn't even slow down with the shredding. "Bye-bye, Mommy. Bye-bye."

Laura and I exchanged glances, and I could tell she was trying hard not to laugh. So much for my guilt about leaving him.

When I actually reached the door, Timmy's tune changed. Not a full-blown fit, mind you, but enough whining to soothe my mommy ego. I gave him a couple of big hugs, some sloppy kisses, and a promise to be back soon.

I'd left the van in Laura's driveway, and as she herded Tim back inside, I settled behind the wheel, then mentally ran over my list of things to do today. Shower, find day care, buy groceries, arrange afternoon car pool, gas up van—the usual stuff. In fact, except for two items—enroll in kickboxing class and review cathedral archives to determine object coveted by vile demon—the list wasn't that different from a typical day's to-do list. I'd always managed to tackle my tasks, and today would be no exception. Just a list of errands and me, supermom extraordinaire. No problemo.

I glanced at my watch. Eight-fifty. Just nine and a half hours until the cocktail hordes descended on my house.

I cranked the engine. Dawdling was over. It was time to get moving. Goramesh might have invaded San Diablo, but he was going to regret it. I was Kate Connor, demon-hunting supermom. And I was going to take him down.

Two hours later I was Kate Connor, discouraged toddler mom. Apparently, enrolling one's toddler in day care requires an act of Congress. The three facilities that I'd noticed in the neighborhood were maxed out on their kid quotient. KidSpace (inconveniently located on the opposite side of town) had a full-time opening in the two-year-old class, and that for a tuition payment that made my blood run cold. I was only looking for part-time, and I turned it down. The woman had made a *cluck, cluck* noise as she asked if I was sure, offering to hold the spot overnight if I wanted to give her a fifty-dollar deposit, charged conveniently to my credit card over the telephone.

I said no.

A dozen phone calls later I realized the magnitude of that mistake. I'd have better luck enrolling the kid in Harvard. And I knew then that the only way Timmy was getting into day care was if I latched on to any opening—no matter how inconvenient or expensive. So far, only one location had fit that description—being both inconvenient and expensive. I practically burned my fingers dialing the KidSpace lady back.

Was the slot still available? Yes, it was, but they'd had three other inquiries. Those moms were coming by to scope the place out. But they hadn't put down a deposit, and she could still hold it for me if I wanted. . . .

I wanted. I whipped out a credit card so fast it would have made Stuart's head spin. So what if I hadn't seen the place? It was full and in demand, right? That had to say something. Besides, if it was a dump, they could keep the fifty dollars. A small price to pay for being on what I was now referring to as The List.

I told Nadine (the KidSpace assistant director, with whom I suddenly felt a close and personal bond) that Timmy and I would come by tomorrow to check the place out and meet his teacher, and that Timmy would start on Wednesday. She told us to drop by anytime, and I considered that another good sign—a toddler crack house would, after all, surely not want "anytime" visitors.

By now it was almost lunchtime, and half of my day was already shot. Despite my looming list of tasks, I still felt an overarching sense of accomplishment. Absurd, really, when all I'd actually done was make some phone calls and spend fifty dollars against the promise of forking out eight hundred and twenty-five more every month.

Stuart was going to kill me.

I decided not to dwell on that little reality and instead moved on to my next, most basic task—getting dressed. I hadn't yet eaten, so I rummaged in the back of the freezer until I found a box of last year's Thin Mints. Since I hadn't eaten breakfast or lunch, I took an entire sleeve out and schlepped it upstairs to the bathroom, along with a can of Diet Coke.

The cookies thawed a bit while I was in the shower, and I snarfed down six, washing the crumbly goodness down with a swig of soda. I didn't bother to do much with my hair, just ran a comb through it and slicked on a tiny bit of gel to keep the frizzies at bay once it air-dried. (Except for the occasional ponytail, I never do much with my hair. There's no point. It's dirty blond and hangs just past my shoulders. I can curl it, spray it, coax it into styles, and two hours later, it's back to being dirty blond, straight, and hanging just past my shoulders. For those special evenings out, I'll pile it up on top of my head with a rhinestone-studded clip. Not fancy, but it works for me.)

I pulled on jeans, a sleeveless sweater and matching cardigan, then shoved my feet into loafers. After a moment's hesitation I changed out of the loafers and into an old pair of Reeboks. The chances of bumping into a demon today were slim considering I intended to spend most of my time in the cathedral archives, but it's best to be prepared. If I did meet another one of Goramesh's flunkies, I wanted traction—and lots of it.

When I headed back downstairs, I remembered the window (the gaping hole in the kitchen jogged my memory). I glanced at my watch, made an unhappy little noise, and sat back down at the kitchen table, where the phone book was still open to the yellow page listings for Day Care Centers.

I flipped to the G's and scanned the pages, running my finger down the thin yellow paper until I found a display ad that seemed nicely laid out and not too cheesy. Not the most responsible method of choosing a repairman, I know, but I was in a hurry. The receptionist answered on the first ring, had a pleasant phone voice, and seemed to know what I was talking about when I described the oversize window in our breakfast area. Impressed as I was by such blatant professionalism, I asked if someone could fix it today.

I heard the receptionist *tap-tapping* at a keyboard. After a moment she came back with the verdict—today was doable, but only if I could be available at four and was willing to pay the rush service charge. Sure, I said, why not? We made all the arrangements, and only then did I think to ask for a rough estimate.

She hedged the response with the caveat that the final cost would be determined on site, then quoted me a number that had me grasping my chest. For two seconds I considered hanging up and letting my fingers do the walking a little bit longer. I nixed that idea fast enough, though. I didn't have the time to juggle estimates, and Stuart wanted the window fixed by the cocktail party (which was scheduled for six-thirty, according to the note he'd left by the coffeemaker). If Stuart said something about the cost, I'd do a *mea culpa* then. At least the window would be intact.

I relayed all the necessary info, promised to be home at four, and hung up, mentally congratulating myself for having accomplished yet another task.

At this rate I'd have Goramesh figured out and conquered before the first guest showed up. I was, after all, on a roll.

I arrived at the cathedral invigorated, optimistic, and raring to go. I found Father Ben in his office reviewing his notes for that evening's homily, and after the usual small talk—the weather, my family, the progress of the restoration project—we headed toward the cathedral.

After a brief pause while I once again refilled my holy water vial, I followed him over the sanctuary toward the sacristy and the stairs leading to the basement archives. From the outside, the cathedral looks old but well preserved. From this new perspective, though, I could tell just how time-ravaged the building really was.

Father twisted a large skeleton key, causing a dingy brass lock to creak. There was no doorknob, and once the lock had disengaged, he pushed on the wood—now smooth from centuries of just such pressure. The door swung inward, ornate hinges creaking with the effort. "Mind your step," Father said, moving over the threshold.

As I followed, he reached to his side and flipped a switch, the light from five low-watt bulbs suddenly illuminating our path. The bulbs were strung along an ancient bit of wire tacked into the stone wall that lined the staircase on one side. I looked up and could just make out a faint streak of black on the low stone roof above my head. Father had turned back to make sure I was coming, and he saw the direction of my gaze.

"Smoke," he said. "Before electricity the priests lit their way down these steps with torches."

"Cool," I said, then realized I sounded like my daughter. I was enjoying this, though. It reminded me of the churches and crypts that Eric and I had prowled back in our glory days.

The stairs made a sharp turn to the right, and the temperature seemed to drop at least ten degrees. I started thinking about earthquakes, and sincerely hoped California didn't decide to do the shaking thing now.

"I can't tell you how much the Church appreciates our volunteers. We're paying an archivist to catalog the noteworthy items, of course, but having volunteers help organize the material is certainly helping to keep our budget in line."

"The cathedral's well known for its holy relics," I said. "Presumably some are already archived and cataloged?"

"Absolutely," Father Ben confirmed. "Although until the restoration is complete, most of the relics are packed up and stored in the basement vault."

"Really? Seems a shame they're tucked away like that." My interest was piqued and I was feeling a trifle smug. I'd get a list of the relics, look for anything that sounded like "bones" or came from any of the ravaged locations. Easy squeezy.

"It is a shame," he agreed, without looking at me. The narrow stone stairs we were maneuvering weren't exactly up to code, and he and I were both picking our way down, careful not to misstep and land in a heap at the bottom. "Of course, some are still in their display cases, and are available for viewing on a limited schedule. We simply moved the cases to the basement to keep them safe during the restoration." He shook his head. "The collection was on display for years in the cathedral foyer. I've only been here a relatively short time, but even to me it seemed like the end of an era when we moved the pieces down here."

My earlier smugness started to crack. "How long were the pieces on display?" If the bones Goramesh wanted were known to be in San Diablo, there was hardly any reason to rampage through Italy, Greece, and Mexico searching for them.

"That depends on the particular relic," Father said. "Some came with Father Aceveda when he founded the cathedral centuries ago. Others arrived as gifts over the last few centuries. The bishop has done an extraordinary job ensuring that the temporary removal of the relics isn't felt too deeply. As soon as the restoration is complete, the items will once again be displayed upstairs. In the meantime, a few items are set out each week in the Bishop's Hall, and the entire collection is available to view on the Internet."

I was now pretty sure I'd find nothing of interest to Goramesh among the already cataloged items, but it wouldn't hurt to check. Frankly, I was assuming that the bones were a recent acquisition. That would explain Goramesh's sudden interest in San Diablo. Something that had recently been donated, but had some connection to Mexico, Greece, or Italy. Or all three.

He'd reached the bottom stair, and now he stepped onto the dingy wooden floor, stopping to wait as I continued to pick my way down. As soon as I joined Father on the floor, I immediately saw the dimly lit display cases that lined two walls of the cavernous room. I wandered to one and gazed through the glass at a row of six cloth bags, each about the size of a half-pound of coffee and labeled with calligraphy so ornate I couldn't easily read the text. In the next case I saw two gold crucifixes and a Bible that looked as though it would fall apart if anyone dared to breathe on it. Other miscellaneous relics and artifacts filled the case, and I turned back to Father Ben, fascinated.

"Impressive, isn't it?" he asked.

I agreed that it was. "Even this basement is impressive."

The space had rough stone walls into which metal holders protruded. Once they'd held torches; now dim electric bulbs dangled from each, filling the room with an incandescent glow that did little to penetrate the shadows.

He laughed. "It does have a certain atmosphere." He waved toward another wooden door—this one with a solid-looking padlock. "All the relics are noteworthy, of course, but the truly priceless pieces are locked in the vault."

I frowned, thinking that an ancient door and one rusty padlock wouldn't keep out a determined thief.

He must have read my expression, because he laughed. "We tried to maintain the character of the basement. There's a stainless steel, alarm-rigged vault behind that door. I assure you, the treasures are quite safe."

"Good to know," I said. And potentially bad for me. I said a fervent prayer that the bones weren't locked back there. I could pick a lock (or I could at one time), but breaking into professional vaults? That was out of my bailiwick.

Another question occurred to me, and I looked back up at Father. "Why keep the collection here and not in the Vatican?"

Father Ben grinned, and all his youth seemed to reflect in that smile. "Would you like to hear what I was told when I came to St. Mary's? Or would you like to hear my theory?"

"Yours, of course," I said, liking Father Ben more and more.

"PR," he said, then watched, as if waiting for me to jump all over that brilliant revelation. I just shrugged, probably disappointing him mightily.

He sighed. "Sadly, it's all about the money. Even for a church. And that requires donations, pledges—"

"Which flow more freely when the church has some cache," I finished, getting the picture.

"Exactly. And while almost all parishes possess some relics, the collection at St. Mary's is truly extraordinary."

"Has it worked? The PR, I mean."

"Apparently so," he said. "That's essentially why you're here."

Light dawned. "The uncataloged material."

"Boxes of relics, family heirlooms, old baptismal records. Correspondence between the priests who founded the California missions. Correspondence between lovers married in the church. A mishmash. All of it interesting. Only some of it worth retaining. Very little of it organized."

Already, I was feeling overwhelmed. "How much exactly?"

"About three hundred bankers' boxes of documents, and another two hundred or so crates filled with a variety of items."

I swallowed.

I think a flicker of amusement flashed across his face, but I could be wrong about that. The light down there was terrible. "How much time do you have?" he asked.

"Today?" I glanced at my watch. "Until two. Then I have to rescue my babysitter from my child." I had more than that on my plate, but I doubted Father Ben would be interested in my rundown of errands.

"That gives you an hour and a half to get your feet wet and get your bearings," he said. I noticed he didn't need to check his watch to figure that out. "Actually, that's probably about right for your first go-round." He glanced at me, and this time I'm certain I saw a smile. "It's really not as bad as it sounds. There may be three hundred boxes of records, but they represent the gifts of only about thirty-five benefactors. And of those, only about ten donated major gifts."

"Okay . . ." I trailed off, not sure what his point was. Ten was a much smaller number, yes, but those three hundred boxes were still stacked in the basement, just waiting for me to scour them, hoping some vague reference would pop out and bring the Goramesh mystery into focus.

He took pity on me and explained. "The major donors wanted their tax write-off, so each donation was accompanied by a brief description of the items." He held up a hand as if to ward off my (totally nonexistent) protests. "These were pious men, don't get me wrong. The donations were made because they wanted to benefit the Church. But even while one is looking toward Heaven, one's feet are still of this earth."

"Render to Caesar," I said.

"Exactly."

Made perfect sense to me. At the moment, I was feeling pretty charitable toward the IRS myself. I'd change my tune come April 15, but in the meantime, I was perfectly happy to settle down in front of each benefactor's tax records and see if I could discern any sort of relic that seemed remotely connected to my purpose. Who knows, maybe the first item on my list would be a big box of bones.

Father Ben explained that the boxes were already somewhat organized. Anything of obvious value—including first-class relics like bones—had been set aside and locked in the vault for the archivist to review. The remaining boxes—filled with miscellaneous papers that, presumably, would include a reference to any relics that had been pulled and locked away—were stacked in this basement area, pending review, sorting, and transfer of the delicate items to a more paper-friendly environment. I felt a twinge of guilt. This really was an important project, and I fully intended to abandon it as soon as I learned what I came for.

The boxes lined the far wall of the cavernous basement. The other walls were lined with either the display cabinets or what appeared to be relatively modern card catalogs alternating with deep wooden shelves on which rested oversize leather-bound books, each about four inches thick, and which may have dated back to the Middle Ages—though I'm not a historian, so I could be way off base with that. The room sported a rough-hewn wooden floor topped with five long wooden tables. I imagined monks sitting there, clad in brown robes and sipping soup from carved wooden bowls. Today, I'd sit, clad in denim, riffling through boxes of papers, and hoping for a reference to bones that was somehow tied to Greece, Mexico, or Italy.

The boxes were numbered and lettered, each letter representing a benefactor, and each number representing a box in that donor's collection. The paperwork for each donation should (and Father Ben stressed the *should*) be in the first box of each letter set.

He hauled Box A1 to the middle table for me, made sure I was settled, then headed back up the stairs. Without Father, the room seemed even more dark and shadowy. Were this not part of the church and were I not a Demon Hunter, I'd probably have been spooked. As it was, I made a concerted effort to ignore the heebie-jeebies as I pulled the lid off the box, then groaned in frustration when I realized the entire box was packed tight with manila folders, each of which was, in turn, packed full of paper.

I tugged the first folder out, laid it on the table, opened it, then yelped as a dozen multilegged critters scattered. I was on my feet in an instant, patting myself down vigorously. Yuck, yuck, yuck! Demons, dirty diapers, even last-minute dinner parties I could handle. But bugs? I don't think so.

I tapped the folder a few times with the edge of the notepad Father Ben had lent me. When nothing else living emerged, I decided it was safe to resume working. I sat back down and skimmed the first page. The Last Will and Testament of Cecil Curtis. I carefully flipped the pages, kicking up dust as I did so, but couldn't find any itemized list of the bequest to the Church.

My eyes itched, and I let out with a violent succession of sneezes. Gee, this was fun.

I shoved the folder back into the box, sneezed again, then pulled out the next dusty collection of papers. I held the sheath at arm's length and shook it. No bugs. I decided it was clear and plunked it on the table. I checked my watch. Exactly seven minutes had elapsed since Father Ben had left me.

With a sigh of resignation, I opened the folder. It was filled with onionskin paper covered in fragile-looking type, as if each page were the third sheet of a carbon produced on an ancient manual typewriter. Each and every page was full of single-spaced print, and—since Larson would never let me live it down if I missed a clue—I squinted to read every word. After about ten sheets my eyes burned and my head ached, and for the first time in my life, I actually wished I wore reading glasses.

This wasn't fun. Important, yes, but not fun.

There was a reason I was a Hunter and not an *alimentatore*. I don't have the patience for this shit. I'm not a detective, I don't want to be a detective, and I was unreasonably pissed off at Larson for sitting in a dust-free courtroom while I was locked in the church dungeon with a bunch of bug-infested papers.

I didn't want to research; I just wanted to hit something.

Unfortunately, there's never a demon around when you really need one.

Ten

After saying all the necessary good-byes to Father Ben, I headed from the cathedral straight to the gas station, my fingers crossed the entire time as I hoped the Odyssey would maneuver okay burning nothing but fumes.

I'd just started pumping gas when my cell phone rang. "Hello?"

"Mom! We're done, we're done! Can you come get us?"

"You're done?" I stared at my watch. Not even two forty-five. "Why are you done?"

"Mo-*om*. Half day, remember?"

I didn't remember, but wasn't about to confess to Allie that her mother was a space case. Instead, I made a non-committal grunting noise. Allie didn't seem to notice.

"And we had our cheerleading meeting and I have about a billion forms you and Stuart have to sign and we already have *homework*. I mean, it's only day one. And it wasn't even a full day, so what's up with *that*?"

"The fiends," I said.

"Yeah. Exactly. So, like, can you come get us?"

"Sure. I'll be there in ten minutes. You'll have to finish some errands with me."

I could practically hear her making a face. "We'll wait in the car," she said.

I smiled. "Whatever."

I found the girls loitering on the steps leading up to the main entrance of the school. They were sitting with three other girls, and a group of four boys was camped out on the far side of the steps. From my vantage point, I could see the girls whispering and casting surreptitious glances toward the boys, who didn't appear to notice.

"So who are the guys?" I asked as Mindy and Allie piled into the van.

"Huh?" Allie asked.

"Your companions on the stairs," I said, pointing back in that direction.

"Oh, them," Allie said, sounding just a little too bored. "Seniors."

"And football players," Mindy added.

"Don't even know you're alive, huh?" I said.

I glanced in the rearview mirror and saw the girls exchange a glance. "No," Allie finally said. "They don't talk to freshman girls."

In my head I raised a silent cheer. My little girl hardly needed to be fraternizing with the football players. Out loud I put on a supportive mom face. "You won't be freshmen forever."

The girls just grunted. I tried to stifle my smile as I maneuvered the van back toward our neighborhood.

"So where are we going?"

"Kickboxing class and then the grocery store."

"Oh, cool," Mindy said.

"Do we get to take a class today?" Allie asked.

"Not today. I'm just going to find a class and sign us up."

Without the possibility of imminent fighting, the girls lost interest, ignoring me in favor of the copy of *Enter-*

tainment Weekly that Allie pulled out of her backpack.

There's probably a more scientific method for choosing a martial arts class, but I relied on the old P & P method— proximity and presentation. Basically, what I wanted was something close to the house that didn't look (or smell) like a total dive.

When Eric and I had first moved to San Diablo, it had a true small-town feel. Local businesses lined Main Street, which hosted (and still hosts) a local market day fair the first Friday of every month. Surrounding this downtown area are neighborhoods overflowing with tall trees and wide, shady streets. Over the years the time-worn houses have been renovated into sparkling jewels. Small, but sparkling.

Eric and I had lived in such a gem when we'd moved to San Diablo. The lack of space in the house for Allie's toys (not to mention the dearth of kids in the neighborhood for Allie to play with) had made us start to eye the outlying subdivisions greedily. About the time Eric was killed, we'd been seriously thinking about moving. With Stuart, my stint in suburbia officially began.

While downtown San Diablo retains its quaint old-world charm, the rest of the city has become truly California-ized, with strip mall after strip mall and a Starbucks on every corner. (A slight exaggeration. And since I'm a frequent and willing patron, I can hardly complain.)

As far as I can tell, the Universal Code for the Creation of Strip Malls requires each to have a dry cleaner, an insurance agent, a pizza-delivery joint, and a martial arts studio. By my count, there are six malls dotting the landscape between the high school and the entrance to my subdivision.

From my quick glance as I drove by, each studio appeared to be a clone of the one before it. Nothing unappealing, but nothing that screamed exceptional quality, either. In the end the only criteria I cared about was proximity, and I pulled up in front of the Victor Leung Martial Arts Academy, which shared a wall with my neighborhood 7-Eleven. (They know me well in there; it's where I go when I run out of milk for Tim or realize that whatever I'm trying to make for dinner requires butter or cream or some other item that is sadly absent from my larder.)

"What do you think?" I asked the girls.

Allie shrugged. Mindy mumbled something I couldn't understand. And with that rousing endorsement, we piled out of the car and headed toward the door.

From the outside the place seemed clean enough, and through the glass (which listed in vibrant red paint everything from karate to kickboxing), I could see a group of kids mingling, their faces bright as they gathered personal belongings from the piles of shoes and backpacks against the far wall. I considered the presence of children a good sign—I may not have done my homework, but presumably some other mother had. Today, I would happily coast on her anonymous coattails.

I pushed the door open, setting a little bell to jingle, and the three of us entered. The kids and a few adults all looked in my direction, but no one moved to greet me. Mindy and Allie took off toward the back of the studio, where someone had hung a collection of black-and-white pictures taken during various tournaments. I couldn't hear everything they said, but I definitely picked up an "Oh, look at *him*" and a "Do you think we'll learn how to do *that*?"

I grinned. They could pretend nonchalance, but I knew the truth. The girls were looking forward to this. And, in truth, so was I.

At the moment, though, it wasn't excitement I was feeling, it was annoyance. Proximity notwithstanding, if someone didn't offer to help me soon, we were going to get out of there and find some other class. I was just on the verge of gathering the girls when a set of swinging doors at the back of the studio slammed inward and a thirty-something man stepped through wearing a uniform cinched with a black belt. His hair, almost as dark as the belt, was pulled back from his head in a ponytail. He sported a day-old beard along with an aura of controlled danger. Honestly, he reminded me of Steven Seagal in *Under Siege*, one of Stuart's favorite movies. The urge to ask him if he knew how to cook was almost overwhelming.

"Victor Leung?" I asked as he approached me, his hand held out in greeting.

"Sean Tyler," he said. "Cutter to my friends," he added with a smile as he looked me up and down. His fingers were warm against mine, and I realized too late I was blushing. *Shit*. What was the matter with me?

I tugged my hand away. "Nice to meet you, Mr. Tyler. I was hoping to talk to the owner."

"You are." I must have looked confused, because he continued, lowering his voice so none of the lingering students could hear. "There is no Victor Leung. It's all about—"

"PR. Yeah, I've heard this one before."

He rocked back on his heels, his eyes dark and his mouth curled in the slightest of smiles, as if I amused him. "So how can I help you, Miss . . . ?"

"Mrs.," I said, probably too quickly. "Kate Connor." I drew myself up to my full height. "I need a trainer." I went into more detail, explaining that I wanted some one-on-one training in addition to a class that Allie and I (and Mindy) could take together. I pointed the girls out to him, and they immediately blushed and tittered, then finally turned back to the wall again, as if the pictures were the most fascinating thing ever. Apparently, I'd been right—Cutter was a hottie.

I expected him to rattle off a list of class times. Instead, he said, "Someone stalking you?"

Not a question I'd been expecting, and I grappled for an answer, obviously not finding a good one since I blurted out, "Not exactly."

He laughed. "Is that like being a little bit pregnant?"

I stared at him, trying to decide if he was an obnoxious jerk or a charming rogue.

"Don't worry," he said, as if reading my mind. He grinned, all white teeth and charm. "You get used to me."

About that, I believed him. Cutter seemed like the kind of guy who would grow on you, and I followed as he started across the room toward a heavy oak desk covered with papers. The other parents and students had left, leaving just the four of us in the studio. "So do I get the story?" he asked as he walked. "Or do you like the role of mysterious suburban beauty?"

(I should point out that I'm not naïve. He was a cute guy—amendment, a *hot* guy—running a martial arts studio less than a mile from the entrance to one of the nicer San Diablo neighborhoods. Of course he sucked up to the local moms. If he didn't, some other instructor would be teaching the neighborhood tots to kick and lunge and jab. I knew all that, and yet I still perked up a bit at the "beauty" comment. There's a lesson in there somewhere, but at the moment, I wasn't inclined to look for it.)

He turned and looked at me, silently prompting me to answer his question.

"Years ago I used to be pretty good at this stuff," I said, as if it was no big deal. "I realized how out of practice I am, and I want a refresher. And someone to train with."

"And your daughters?"

"Daughter," I said. "And her best friend." I shrugged. "I can't always be there to watch their backs." I couldn't help the edge in my voice. If he noticed, he didn't show it.

"Fair enough," he said. "I don't have any more classes today," he said. "Why don't you show me what you've got?"

"Oh," I said stupidly. I looked at my watch. I'd expected

to just run down the formalities today. And I wasn't that excited about the idea of showing Cutter what I had in front of Allie. "I don't think that's such a good—"

"Just dump your things over there." He pointed to the far wall. "Hey, girls," he called. "Come on over here for a minute. Your mom and I have a little demonstration for you."

"Cutter," I hissed.

"What? You're going to be taking classes with your kid. Don't tell me you're embarrassed to fight in front of her. That's gonna make class a little cumbersome."

"Fine." I glared at him again, feeling a bit like we were having a marital spat. My fights with Stuart just never involved actual fighting. "We'll spar." There really wasn't any reason not to. I'd get a feel for his skills, and I figured I could tone my own skills down a bit for Allie's sake. Besides, Cutter was right. Allie would get the full sense of what Mom could do soon enough.

As the girls sat cross-legged at the edge of the mat, I headed toward the wall to drop off my purse and shoes like Cutter had suggested. The studio walls were mirrored, so I have no excuse for not seeing him coming. All I knew was that a split second after I passed him, he grabbed me around the waist, one hand going over my mouth to prevent me from screaming.

What the hell?

I could hear Allie yelling in the background, but I couldn't focus on her. All thoughts had faded from my head, replaced only with a deep desire to nail Cutter's sorry ass. I wasn't thinking, I was just *doing*—and I'll admit it felt good.

I got both my hands on his one over my mouth, then tugged downward, managing to sink my teeth into the soft flesh beside his thumb. As I did that, I twisted, but his arm held fast around my waist despite his howl of protest. I slammed my left arm back, leading with my elbow, and caught him just under the rib cage. He exhaled with a *whoof*, and his arm loosened just enough for me to twist to the side, hook my leg under his, and send him sprawling backward onto the mat.

"Mom! Mom! Wow, Mom, that was *awesome*!"

A split second later I was straddling him, my hands tight around his neck, thumbs against his windpipe. "What do you think you're doing?" I asked as Mindy and Allie raced toward us.

Blood pounded in my ears, and although I wanted to twist around and flash a reassuring smile at my daughter, I couldn't quite manage. All of my attention was still focused on Cutter. "Why did you jump me?" I demanded.

"You said you used to be good," he said. I could feel the tremor of his vocal cords beneath my hands. "I just wanted to see how good. Sorry, I should have asked."

"Yes, you should have." I was being tested a lot lately, and I didn't much like it. So far I'd done better defending myself than I'd expected. For that, at least, I gave myself Brownie points.

"Are you gonna get off him, Mrs. Connor?"

"Why should she?" Allie answered. "She totally nailed him. That was so awesome."

"Pretty awesome," Cutter said, agreeably. "Not that this isn't cozy, but if she got off me, maybe we could show you two a few more maneuvers."

"Will you, Mom?"

"Not today, hon," I said. My adrenaline rush was fading, replaced by the keen awareness that I was sitting on the chest of one very good-looking man. At least, I hoped he was a man. At the moment I was leaving nothing to chance.

"Oh, come on, Mom!"

"Sorry, kid. We have to get to the grocery store next."

"Oh, good," Cutter said. "A reprieve."

I made a face as Mindy leaned over us. "Can you teach us how to do that? Flip guys, I mean."

"Sure, kiddo. That's why we're taking classes, remember?"

Allie circled me and Cutter, her finger pressed to her mouth, her expression serious. "I dunno, Mom. Should we take lessons from *him*? Maybe we should find someone better."

"Oh, for crying out—" Cutter began. "Your mom definitely knows how to defend herself. I promise I can teach you girls the same thing."

"Hmmm," Allie said. I tried to hide my amusement as she turned to Mindy. "What do you think?"

Mindy shrugged. "He's got all sorts of awards and stuff hanging on the back wall. He'll probably be okay."

"Tough consumers," Cutter said. "Not that this isn't fun—you sitting on me, I mean—but do you think I could get up now?" He met my eyes, his dark with amusement and something else I wasn't inclined to examine too closely. "Or we could just stay like this indefinitely."

"Very funny." I climbed off of him, but stayed at the ready, standing over him while he looked up, bemused, from a prone position. The truth was, I did need him alone. Just not for *that* reason. Demon-testing was not for the faint of heart. Neither was it for my daughter to see. "Girls, run over to 7-Eleven and get me a soda, would you?"

"A soda?" Mindy repeated.

"She just wants to get rid of us," Allie said. "She's going to chew him out."

"Smart kid," I said. "I'll meet you two outside in a minute."

"Alone at last," Cutter said as soon as the door shut behind the girls.

I glared at him.

"Hey, a beautiful woman just laid me out flat. All I've got left is my sense of humor."

I had to admit that, on the whole, he was being a pretty good sport. "You spooked me," I said simply.

"I guess so. So how long before you get unspooked and quit looking at me like that?"

A very good question. I suppose he could have been a demon, lying in wait in the off chance I decided to train at Victor-cum-Cutter's studio—but I had to admit the odds were slim. Of course, three days ago I would have said the odds of a demon catapulting himself through my window were nil.

I didn't intend to take chances.

My purse was still looped over my shoulder, and now I stuck one hand inside so I could rummage in its depths. I found the vial of holy water and managed to open it one-handed. With my hand still inside the purse, I drenched my hand (not to mention my checkbook, pens, makeup, and wallet). "Come here," I said.

He squinted at me, but complied, and as soon as he was close enough, I reached out and patted his cheek with my damp hand. Nothing happened. (Okay, that's not exactly true. Cutter muttered a few obscenities and asked the room in general if I was a psychopath.)

I backed off. "Sorry about that."

I expected him to tell me to get out of his studio. Instead, he just wiped the water off his face with the back of his hand and stared at me. "Any chance you'll tell me what that was about?"

"Any chance you'll train with me?" I shot back. "Or teach my daughter's class?" I hoped he would. Now that I knew he wasn't a demon, I had to admit I liked the guy. He had gumption, and he didn't mind (too much) that a woman had bested him. He was also conveniently located near my house, and, as an added benefit, he was easy on the eyes (yes, I know, I'm shallow).

"Lady, you don't look like you need the training."

"I do," I insisted. "My reflexes are better than I thought,

but my instincts are all off. I should have realized you were coming. You never should have got your hand around my mouth. It took me way too long to bring you down. And to top it all off, my whole body feels sore and bruised."

"From laying me out?"

I made a noncommittal noise. I was hardly going to tell him I'd been in three fights in so many days. Allie might be impressed by my ability to bring down attacking martial arts instructors, but that was a long way from laying waste to demons. I needed to be at the top of my game, and I wasn't. Not yet. "I'm not in the shape I need to be," I said with a shrug. Simple as that.

"Need to be," he repeated. "For what?"

"For me." Fighting demons is only part skill and strength, the rest is confidence. My reflexes might still be there, hiding just under the surface, but until my head believed that, I was vulnerable. "I just need to know I can do it."

In the end I'm not sure if Cutter agreed because I'd nailed him, because he believed I was sincere about getting back in sparring shape, or because he thought I was a (somewhat dangerous) nut he had to humor. Honestly, I didn't much care. I'd come to pencil in times, and I was walking away with a sparring schedule for me (nine-thirty a.m., every day until I cried uncle) and a Wednesday/Friday afternoon class for me, Allie, and Mindy.

Mission accomplished. One more item crossed off my to-do list.

Of course, I'd ended up talking with Cutter way too long. (I chalked it up to male insecurity. As we were filling out the necessary paperwork, he launched into his résumé, telling me about his military service, along with the myriad awards and accolades he'd received over the years at various martial arts tournaments. I'll admit, the guy sounded more than qualified.)

I found the girls outside of 7-Eleven, sucking down Popsicles ("the fruit ones have like *no* calories") and describing to each other in minute detail how I'd managed to get Cutter down on the mat.

"That was so stellar, Mrs. Connor," Mindy said. "I don't think my mom could ever do anything that cool."

"My mom kicks butt," Allie said.

"*Allie.*" I used my Shocked Mom voice, but I'll confess to a secret thrill—my kid thought I was cool! "Okay, everyone in the van."

As the girls and I got back in the van, the digital clock read 3:35. I confirmed that with a glance at my watch (as if somewhere I'd hidden an extra half-hour), but apparently all my various timepieces were in sync.

So much for my supermom routine. There was no way I could get the stuff for the cocktail party and get home in time to meet the glazier. *Damn.*

I debated my options as I pulled out onto Rialto, still not sure if I was heading to Laura's, home, or the grocery store. I pulled out my cell phone, punched in Laura's speed-dial number, and stopped at a red light.

Her machine kicked on and I cursed out loud. I waited through the beep. "Laura? Pick up. It's me."

I heard the clatter of the phone and then Laura's breathless "Hey. Sorry. I was changing a diaper."

"I've got Mindy and Allie," I said. "But could I add one more dessert to our tally?"

I swear I could hear her smile. "What do you need?"

I explained about the glass and asked if she and Timmy could finish out their playdate at my house.

"Playdate, huh?"

I cleared my throat, and she laughed.

"Sure. No problem."

"I owe you," I said.

"You have no idea," she said agreeably.

That task accomplished, I turned into a parking lot and reemerged on Rialto heading the opposite direction toward Gelson's (the kind of high-end grocery store where after you valet park, you might actually spy a celebrity—or, more likely, the celebrity's butler).

This is not my usual grocery store.

Once inside, I bemoaned the fact that we weren't rolling in the dough. If an overflowing bank account meant that I could shop regularly in a place like this, I might actually learn to cook a few meals other than the old standbys like meat loaf and chicken with rice.

The girls peeled off, ostensibly to check out the produce section, but I expected they'd end up at the dessert counter. I continued on to the back of the store, where a fifty-something woman in a hairnet asked what she could do for me today. I wasn't shy, immediately revealing my sad tale of woe (I'm a terrible cook and was expected to host a cocktail party in approximately three hours).

Lorraine (I caught a glimpse of her name tag) rose to the challenge, and less than twenty minutes later I was in the checkout lane writing a check for a clump of caviar (and the accompanying sour cream and little potato puffs on which to dab it), foie gras, some fancy crackers that put my usual Saltines to shame, cheese puffs, spinach dip in a carved-out bowl of bread, champagne grapes, and my old standby Brie. (A social *faux pas* since I'd served it last Friday, but I figured I'd survive the shame). I also had a few bottles of wine (recommended by the store's sommelier), the basic supplies for various flavored martinis, and two outrageously large slices of chocolate cake that the girls dubbed their reward for surviving the first day of high school.

After writing a check roughly the size of our mortgage, I followed the clerk out to the van and watched as he loaded my purchases, all the while thinking that I could get used to this. A few minutes later we were turning into Laura's driveway, and I was feeling more than a little pleased with myself.

"Your mom will be back soon," I told Mindy, who didn't look like it much mattered to her. "And you," I said to Allie, "aren't staying overnight. Come back home by ten."

"Sure, Mom."

I waited to make sure the girls got inside all right, then circled the block, heading toward my own house. I parked in the garage, then grabbed a bag before climbing out. I backtracked down the driveway to fetch the morning paper, then headed inside. Laura met me at the door, my phone pressed to her ear.

She held up a finger as I pushed inside, signaling for me to wait. "It's Stuart," she said.

I took the phone from her, cradling it between my shoulder and ear as I dumped my bag by the refrigerator. Timmy had heard me come in, and now he was racing to me, his cries of "Momma!" drowning out pretty much every other sound.

"What, hon?" I yelled. "Say again?" I bent down to collect my son in a bear hug, and he immediately reached for the phone. "Timmy talk! Timmy talk!"

"Kate?"

"Go ahead." I wrestled the phone back from Tim with a stern "No, Mommy's talking." To my husband, I said, "I'm listening."

"I was just calling to check in. You got my note? Six-thirty?"

"We're all set," I said. "I just got back from the grocery store." Behind me, I heard the door open and close, and I turned to see Laura traipsing in with the last of my bags. I mouthed a silent *thank you*.

"You're the best," he said. "I'll be home by six to help you out."

"Sounds good . . ." I trailed off, looking at my watch as I shifted Timmy's weight in my arms. I was thinking about all I needed to do in order to get me and the house ready for company, and wondering if I shouldn't make Stuart come home at five. Too late. Before I got the words out, he'd said the requisite "I love you" and hung up.

Great.

"Lady, you got dry rot."

And it just kept getting better and better.

I'd moved through the kitchen, and now I looked up to see a scarecrow of a man in coveralls and a baseball cap picking at the window frame with what looked like a putty knife.

"Oh," I said. He kept looking at me, and so I said the only other thing that came to mind. "I'm sorry?"

He exhaled (loudly). "Yeah, well, what do you want me to do about it?"

"You talking, Momma?" Timmy said. "You talking on the phone?"

"No, sweetie. Mommy's done on the phone."

"Lady?"

"Hold on a second," I said. I headed into the living room and passed Timmy off to Laura, who'd been going through the motions of picking up what appeared to be every single toy Timmy owns.

"The girls?"

"Your place," I said.

"I figured as much. You want me to keep Allie until after your party?"

Considering I'd already told Allie as much, Laura's offer couldn't have been more perfect. "You're a saint, you know that, right?"

She found Boo Bear under an askew sofa cushion and passed it to Timmy, who clutched it greedily. "Flattery will get you everywhere," she said.

"I'll remember that. And I think we're up to four

desserts, now. With the next favor, I'll buy you a gym membership."

She grimaced. "And here I thought you *appreciated* my help."

I thanked her again, and as she headed out the back door to go supervise the girls, I put Timmy down. He headed straight for the laundry basket where Laura had been collecting his toys and proceeded to rescatter them across the living room. Next on list: straighten house.

I moved back into the kitchen, and ten minutes later knew more than I ever wanted to know about dry rot. After a lot of technical mumbo jumbo, we hit the bottom line—he could do a temporary fix, but we needed to get someone in to replace the frame, at which time the new glass could be reinserted and better sealed. He'd be happy to handle the full job, of course, and assured me that his prices were competitive.

I debated the probability of Stuart siphoning enough time to handle this himself against the likelihood that he'd pawn the job off to me, expecting me only to run the estimates by him after all the bids were in. Since Option Number Two was the more likely—and since I couldn't see fitting home-repair estimates into my already full schedule—I told the repairman he had the job. What Stuart didn't know wouldn't hurt him. (And to ensure that Stuart *didn't* know, I made a mental note to pay the bills for the next two months, even though it was technically Stuart's turn to handle the checkbook.)

He promised to have the temporary glass inserted within the hour, and I raced back out into the living room to try to straighten the house up. Fortunately, Timmy helped, and that made the whole process go a lot faster. (For those of you who might have missed it, that's commonly referred to as sarcasm.)

Once the toys were cleared away, I settled Tim on the couch with Boo Bear, his harmonica, a coloring book, and some (washable) crayons, then headed up the stairs to change. Since Stuart had given me no advance warning, choosing an outfit was easy. I wore the only thing in my closet that hadn't succumbed to wrinkles—a navy blue pantsuit that I'd bought on a whim at a 75-percent-off sale, still sporting the tags from Kohl's.

I did a quick makeup job, fastened my hair on top of my head with a clip, doused it with hairspray, doused the rest of me with apple-scented body mist (to hide the hairspray smell), then headed back downstairs just in time to sign the invoice and write an extremely rubber check to the Atlas Glass Company. (Note to self: Transfer money from savings.)

After that I got down to the really important work—moving all my various purchases to my own dishes, and reheating the quiches and cheese puffs until a) they were warm, and b) the kitchen smelled like I'd actually cooked the things. Just for effect, I tossed a few pans, mixing bowls, and other utensils into the dishwasher and turned it on. Early arrivals would assume I was just wrapping up a day of cooking.

Devious, yes. But it calmed my fear that the entire political community would assume that Stuart was married to an incompetent. ("She stays home all day with her little boy, but her house is always a mess, and she can't cook to save her life. I mean, really. *What* does he see in her?") Paranoid, maybe. But I was willing to put on the act just in case.

At ten after six I walked back into the house after dropping Timmy at Laura's for the duration of the party (she really is a saint). I expected to find Stuart puttering around, sampling all the food he wasn't supposed to be touching.

No Stuart. I frowned, more than a little irritated. This was his party, after all. The least he could do was show up when he promised.

I puttered for a few more minutes, straightening the trays of food, twisting the open bottles of wine on the buffet so that the labels were perfectly aligned. I even fanned out the cocktail napkins (there were still some left in the buffet, just where Stuart had said they were last Friday). The timer binged, and I retrieved the batch of cheese puffs, then arranged them artfully on a bright yellow Fiestaware plate.

Still no Stuart.

I fluffed the pillows on the couch and was just about to retrieve a piece of lint from the carpet (how shocking! how gauche!) when I heard the front door rattle. *Finally!*

I headed for the foyer and pulled open the door.

No one. Just a flyer for pizza delivery. *Okay, fine.* I tamped down my anger, reminding myself that red, blotchy skin would clash with my carefully applied makeup. There were still fifteen minutes before the party was supposed to start; surely Stuart would be here shortly.

In an effort to appear calm and collected, I grabbed the *Herald* from the basket we keep in the foyer, then unfolded it as I walked back toward the kitchen. I poured myself a glass of wine (the better for remaining calm) and spread out the paper, flipping idly through the sections.

When I hit the "Local Interest" section, my hand froze, my gaze glued to the page. There, front and center, was a full-color picture of my Richie Cunningham demon, smiling at the camera and looking oh-so-innocent. Underneath the picture was a short article:

> *English major Todd Stanton Greer narrowly survived an attack by a vicious dog Saturday evening. "It was awful," said classmate Sarah Black, who witnessed the attack. "It just came out of nowhere." Local animal-control authorities had no explanation for the origin of the dog. Citizens with information are requested to contact authorities at 555-3698. Greer was admitted to Diablo County Medical Center in critical condition, but was discharged the following evening. "There was no point in holding him," stated Dr. Louis Sachs. "His recovery was remarkable."*

There was a bit more to the article, but I couldn't read it. My hands were shaking too badly.

Roving dog my ass. The local SPCA might think so, but I knew better. The dog was a demon manifestation, vile and cold-blooded. And the only reason it had to roam the streets of San Diablo would be to attack and kill—and gain human form for the demon who controlled it.

Todd Greer hadn't miraculously survived. He'd died Saturday night. And Sunday evening, a demon had walked out of that hospital, headed to my neighborhood, and attacked me by the trash. So much for my nice, safe neighborhood.

San Diablo wasn't demon-free anymore. Worse, everything I'd seen pointed to an aggressive and virulent demon invasion. *Forza* needed to be out there, fighting the good fight. But at the moment I was the only Hunter on deck.

And I was knee-deep in cheese puffs and Brie.

Eleven

With the exception of Stuart's continued absence, the party was a roaring success. It had expanded beyond the original guest list, and now the living room and den overflowed with politicos, all standing around talking about funding and candidates, with the occasional praise of my cheese puffs thrown in for good measure.

I smiled and nodded and tried not to look at the clock every three minutes. Not easy. I saw Clark cross to the bar, and I tagged along behind him, waiting patiently while he finished up a conversation with a stern-looking woman in a black-on-black suit. "Eminent domain is not a power to be tossed around willy-nilly," she said. "Be careful, Mr. Curtis, or we *will* see you in court."

Had she not sounded so serious, I would have smiled at the phrase *willy-nilly* coming from the lips of such a buttoned-up woman. As it was, though, I wasn't laughing. "What was that about?" I asked as soon as she'd gone.

"The county's looking to acquire some land for expansion of the college. Unfortunately, the land we want is already occupied by some nice little clapboard houses." He lit a cigarette and looked so miserable I didn't even remind him that we don't allow smoking in the house. "Sometimes I hate my job," he said.

"Sometimes I hate your job, too," I said. "Is that the reason Stuart's late? Do you have him working away on some land deal?"

"Stuart's my candidate, Kate. Do you really think I'd keep him away from his own party?"

I didn't, but I'd secretly hoped. Otherwise, I didn't know what to think.

I mingled a bit more, keeping my political-wife smile firmly plastered on my face, but only half-listening to the conversations going on around me. When I heard the front door open and close, I hurried in that direction, expecting to see Stuart, but instead finding Judge Larson.

"Thank God you're here," I said, leading him into the relative privacy of the kitchen. "I'm going crazy."

"What's wrong?"

"Everything," I said.

"That bad?"

"Stuart's not here. He's half an hour late for his own party. And there are demon hordes roaming the streets near the community college."

"Oh, dear," Larson said. He poured himself a drink. "Let's examine those one at a time. Have you called him?"

"Twice. I just get his voice mail."

"There was an accident on the 101. He's probably stuck in traffic."

"For his sake, I hope so." Throwing these parties was painful enough. Throwing them without Stuart was positively torture.

"About the demon hordes?" Larson prompted.

"Right," I said, pitching my voice lower. "Look at this." I pulled out the newspaper article, then let Larson read in peace as I puttered around, piling more cheese puffs and baby quiches onto a cookie sheet, then shoving them into the oven.

After that I made a quick hostess run through the living room and den with a newly opened bottle of red wine. Everyone seemed to be having a good time, I didn't catch anyone looking at their watch with a frown, and everyone was polite enough not to mention Stuart's absence. When I got back to Larson, he was leaning over the table, each hand on either side of the paper, literally shaking with rage.

"Larson?" My voice was barely a whisper, but he heard me. He turned his head up to face me, and the anger I saw there made me take a step back. "Judge? What is it? Did you know him?"

He shook his head. By the time he spoke, he seemed remarkably calmer. "No. No, I didn't know the boy. I am just—" He cut himself off, and I watched as he clenched his fists, all his attention focused once again on the newspaper. "This should not be happening."

"I know," I said, then sighed. I'd already done the anger and fear thing. Now I'd succumbed to a feeling of cold inevitability. I figured Larson would get there, too, soon enough. "San Diablo has always been demon-free. At least, I always *thought* it was. Maybe I was just blind."

Larson waved a hand. "The past doesn't matter. Did you have any luck in the archives?"

I shook my head. "There's a lot of information down there," I said. "It's going to take a while to go through it."

He nodded, but didn't look happy. Him and me both. I was the one battling bugs. "We must work swiftly," he said. "It is imperative we learn what Goramesh seeks."

We were talking in low whispers, but apparently not low enough. Someone I didn't recognize walked into the kitchen, leading with an empty martini glass. "Don't know this Goramesh fellow. Is he seeking the county attorney seat? Stuart's gonna shit a brick if there's some contender out there he doesn't know about."

I stared at him, not sure what I was more astounded by—the fact that he'd overheard us, or the fact that he was running around a party using the kind of language I always swore would earn Allie a monthlong grounding.

"Something altogether different," I said in my best hostess voice as I grabbed him by the elbow and steered him back toward the living room.

"Wait, wait," he protested, then held up his glass. "Gin?"

"Sure. No problem." I retrieved a fresh bottle from the pantry, then made sure my newfound friend made his way back to the party. I was mentally calculating the cost of calling taxis for all the overindulgent guests as I led Larson into the garage. There, at least, I thought we'd have some privacy.

"I need to be out there," I said. "Or *Forza* needs to get on the stick and wrestle up some more Hunters. I can't do all of this. I can't scour the cathedral archives *and* stay up all night racing around to fight demon-dog hordes *and* get my laundry done and my kids to school and my family fed." I paused, not because I was finished talking but because I needed to breathe. "This is bad, Larson. This is really, really bad."

"Deep breaths, Kate."

I held up a hand. "I know. I'm fine. I'm just pissed. That boy couldn't have been more than eighteen. In a few years Allie could have been *dating* him. He's not supposed to be ravaged by demons! He's supposed to be fighting acne and studying for midterms." I ran my fingers through my hair, a bad move since I managed to totally dislodge it from the clip, creating what was surely a less than stellar party look.

I took another deep breath and closed my eyes. Once upon a time I wouldn't have even blinked at the idea of teenagers getting picked off by rampant demons running amok in the city streets. That had been par for the course. But that was a long time ago, before I'd had a teenager of my own. And now the idea of anyone—*anyone*—messing with my kids terrified me.

"I'll do a quick run through town after everyone's in bed," I said. "It's not ideal, but it's better than nothing, right? And you can talk to *Forza*, and maybe Father Corletti can send someone else along. We can beg, right? Even a recent trainee. I don't care. Just tell him we can use some help here."

"Kate." He had his hand on my shoulder. "Focus on the key. Goramesh. Find what he seeks. *That* is where your attention needs to lie."

I stared at him. "You're kidding, right?"

"I'm not."

"But"—I waved a hand back toward my kitchen, which presumably he interpreted as the newspaper article—"demon dogs! Demons in my kitchen! Demons at my trash can! This is nasty stuff, Larson. And it's not going to go away. I can't be camped out in the church basement, knee-deep in moldy old paper. I need to be out there. *Doing* something."

"Kate, listen to me." His voice was sharp, commanding. It worked. I listened. "You are a Hunter, yes, and you're a good one. But do you really want to come fully out of retirement? Now, when you have your children and your husband? *Forza* called you in to help with one specific threat—Goramesh. Are you really willing to turn your back on your family and return to the life of a Hunter? A life they can never know about?"

"I . . . but . . . No." I wasn't willing. Even the thought made me queasy. But years ago I'd accepted the obligation. Could I turn my back on that simply because I'd retired? "I don't want to," I said. "But who else—"

"Katherine, please. You better than anyone should know that demons are always around. The truth is demons roam the world. They always have, and they always will."

I gaped at him. "So, what? You're saying give up? Give in? I don't think so."

"I'm saying do the job you were brought back in to do."

"I wasn't 'brought back in,' remember? A demon came barreling through my window."

"Katherine . . ."

"Fine. Make your point."

"Stop Goramesh. The rest will follow. You need to focus on that task."

"But those kids?" I waved generally in the direction of the community college.

"Perhaps it was an isolated event to serve Goramesh's purpose."

"And maybe pigs fly." Yes, I was being surly. I figured I had cause.

He didn't miss a beat. "And even if it wasn't isolated, more will die if you don't stop Goramesh. Are you prepared to do it all? *Can* you do it all?"

My flippant response was that I was already doing it all—a lot more than I'd anticipated and certainly more than I'd wanted. But I didn't say anything. I just took a few breaths and nodded. He had a point. I didn't like it, but I understood it. We pick our battles. And we pick the battles that will reap the biggest victory. Still, though, those kids were vulnerable. . . .

I opened my mouth, but he cut me off with a wave of his hand.

"Kate," he said. "Your heart is in the right place. But *Forza* needs you sharp. *I* need you sharp."

We were saved any more arguing by the sudden *thwunk* of the garage door opener as it began churning. *Stuart!*

I sprinted across the garage (not an easy task in two-inch heels) and waited impatiently while the door (slowly) rose. As soon as it was three feet off the floor, I ducked under, then ran around the car to the passenger side and tugged the door open. I was just about to chew Stuart out when I saw his face.

"My God, Stuart. Are you okay?" I leaned over and pressed my hand against his chest; it was covered with caked blood. "What on earth happened? Have you seen a doctor? Why didn't you call?"

"It's not as bad as it looks," he said.

The door finished its trek to the top, and Stuart pulled inside, the light from the garage illuminating the inside of the car.

"It looks terrible," I said, tossing subtlety to the wind.

He grimaced, then reached to open the driver's door. I reached over just as fast and snagged his other arm. "Hold on a second there, buddy. Where do you think you're going?"

"Cocktail party," he said, and although he really didn't sound groggy at all, in my mind I imagined him slurring his words and stumbling into the kitchen in a bloody, political mess.

"Let's just sit here for a minute and make sure you're okay." I glanced through the front windshield and noticed that Larson was gone. Presumably he'd stepped back inside. I hoped he didn't announce Stuart's arrival. I really didn't want half the political world to see my husband covered with a quart of blood.

Blood!

I tried again to get some answers. "Once more. What happened?" I did a quick up-and-down scan, wincing as I did so. "Your head, sweetie. You're going to need stitches."

He reached up and dabbed an abrasion on his forehead. "It's not deep. Head wounds just bleed a lot."

"So I see." I squeezed his hand. "Tell me. For that matter, convince me you're okay, or we're going to screw the party, back the car up, and get you to the hospital."

"Paramedics already checked me out. I'm fine. Really, it looks worse than it is. A cut on my forehead and a bloody nose."

I wasn't convinced, but I knew Stuart well enough to know I wasn't getting him to the hospital. "Fine. How'd you get the cut and the bloody nose?"

"Sideswiped turning onto California," he said. "The driver's side is mangled. I don't know if they can repair it."

"What?" I looked around, realizing suddenly that front and side airbags were hanging limp, decorating the car like some sort of perverse drapery. Apparently, I'd been too pissed—and then too worried—to notice. "My God, Stuart. How fast was he going? Did you get his license plate? Insurance? *And are you sure you're okay?*"

Stuart took my hand, then lifted it to his lips and kissed my palms. Normally, I love it when he does that. Talk about an erogenous zone. Tonight, I wasn't loving it. I felt too numb.

"Stuart . . ."

"Hush, sweetheart. It's all right. I'm fine. I promise. I got a nasty bump on my head, a busted nose, and a sore wrist, but overall, I got off lucky. I was a little woozy for a while, but I'm fine now."

I reached out, brushing his cheek. "You're sure? Why didn't you call?"

He leaned over, then picked half of a Motorola flip phone off the passenger floorboard. "Busted."

"So I see."

He rubbed his temple. "I didn't think to have the paramedic call." His smile was tentative. "Forgive me?"

I wanted to chew him out for scaring the hell out of me, but since he'd apologized first, I'd come off looking like a bitch. Instead, I dodged the question. "You're sure you're okay? That had to have been some accident."

"Paramedic gave me a clean bill of health. No concussion. No nothing. I told you—I got lucky. I'm good to go."

I frowned, not quite ready to come down from my current level of frantic wifedom. "Your clothes aren't," I said.

He actually laughed at that. "No, probably not. I've got a clean shirt in my briefcase. Grab me one?"

I considered debating, wanting to keep him there, safe with me in the garage. But I could tell he was itching to go play politician. Mentally I sighed. At least there was no question but that my husband was enjoying the political limelight.

I climbed into the backseat and fetched his briefcase, then popped out of the car and climbed into the van, returning with my emergency stash of baby wipes. Stuart stepped out of the car, then peeled his shirt off. I swabbed his face, cringing as I cleaned the gash on his forehead although my ministrations didn't seem to bother him at all. He shrugged into the clean shirt and started to button it. "Am I presentable?"

I thought about arguing some more, trying to talk him out of the party. But I didn't. Instead, I smiled and helped him adjust his tie. "Yeah," I said. "You'll do."

With that endorsement, he headed inside. I waited a moment and then followed, ·wallowing in the harsh, sad truth—even if I destroyed all the demons in the world, I still couldn't keep my family safe.

In the end Stuart's cocktail party went over like a dream, fractured skull notwithstanding. (And, yeah, I know it was just an abrasion. So I exaggerate.) In deference to my tendency to overworry, Stuart refrained from drinking, and once all the guests left, he actually sat back and let me shine a flashlight at his pupils. Both shrank and dilated just like they're supposed to do, and I felt infinitesimally better.

Stuart, in contrast, strutted around like the king of the castle, injuries all but forgotten; at least three people, including one very prominent restaurateur, had committed to backing his campaign. Stuart chalked this up to his considerable political presence and savvy. I laid full credit with the cheese puffs.

Allie came back at ten, pushing a sleeping Timmy in his stroller. While I put him to bed (he woke up once, demanded Boo Bear, then fell back to sleep), Allie and Stuart gathered all the leftover food, saving what we could in those disposable containers that cost a small fortune but are worth every penny.

That, at least, was the plan. When I came back down, the containers were empty and the two of them were seated at the table, a smorgasbord of leftover finger food fanned out in front of them. "You're supposed to be cleaning up," I said.

"If we eat it, then there's nothing to clean," Allie said.

I considered that, decided she had a point, then snarfed down another cheese puff myself. We did the family thing for about half an hour—Allie giving us the details of her day at school (where fourteen-year-olds are concerned, "details" is a rather amorphous concept), Stuart describing his car accident to Allie's oohs and aahs, and me sitting back and wondering if there were demonic dogs out wandering the town—and what I could do about it if there were.

"Mom?"

My head snapped up. "Hmmm?"

Allie laughed. "You falling asleep?"

"It is getting late," I said. "And I had a long day." I fixed her with a motherly gaze. "So did you. Don't you think it's time for bed?"

"No," she said, but then she yawned, totally destroying the effect. "Okay, maybe."

She kissed us both good night, then headed upstairs, my "and don't call Mindy" echoing behind her. I turned to Stuart next. "You should get in bed, too. If anyone's had a busy day, it's you, and I'm guessing you're not going to call in sick tomorrow, no matter how much I beg."

"You're right," he said. "Major land-use project in the

works. If I called in, I'd just be dropping a mess in Clark's lap, and I don't think that's the way to keep his love and admiration."

"You were in a car accident."

"After which I mingled at a cocktail party for two hours."

"At least go to bed, then. No news. No *Letterman*. Just sleep."

For a second, I thought he'd argue, but then he nodded and kissed me good night. "Actually, that's not a bad idea."

"Finally," I said, "the voice of reason."

I accompanied him upstairs, where my husband graciously succumbed to my worrisome ways as I checked his pupils once more, felt his forehead for fever, dabbed some Neosporin on the cut on his forehead (then topped it with a Big Bird Band-Aid), brought him a glass of water, and finally tucked him into bed. His mouth was twitching as I leaned in to kiss him good night. "Don't say a word," I said. "Just humor me."

He made a zipping lips motion, then pulled me in for a kiss and a whispered thanks. "Don't you stay up too late, either," he said.

"Oh, I won't," I said breezily. "I just want to clean up a bit."

I consoled myself with the fact that I'd told no lies. I did want to clean up—my living room and the entire demon population. Since I could hardly handle the latter that night, I decided to focus on the living room, and I puttered around the house until I was pretty sure both Allie and Stuart were asleep. Then I headed for the guest room and picked up the telephone.

I held it a minute before dialing, wondering what exactly I intended to do. Larson was right, of course. I couldn't just emerge from retirement to go searching out demons in dark corners. I had a family to consider. A family that needed me alive and well.

If there was a specific threat—like, oh, a demon bursting through my window—then I'd happily put it out of my misery. But I could hardly go looking for trouble.

Despite all of that, I still found myself dialing the number for the police station.

"San Diablo Police Department. How may I direct your call?"

I cleared my throat, feeling a little silly. "Hi. I'm trying to find out if anyone has reported any dogs on the loose tonight." I told myself I just needed reassurance. No dogs could mean that Todd Greer was a one-time thing. Not great (especially for Todd), but at least I'd have the comfort of knowing there probably weren't demon hoards roaming the streets.

"One moment, please. I'll transfer you."

I had a vision of being transferred to the demon-dog division, then realized I'd had pathetic little sleep. An officer clicked on the line with a curt, "Metro division. Sergeant Daley." I explained why I was calling, then waited for him to reassure me. He didn't. "Normally, I'd tell you to call animal control in the morning, but it just so happens I got a report in about ten minutes ago."

"You did?" Anger that the demon still prowled surged through me, but it was tinged with a wash of excitement. *This is what you do*, a little voice said, and I didn't bother to correct the voice—this is what I *did*. I drew in a breath, then posed the next question. "Can you tell me where?"

"Lady, what's your interest in this?"

I pulled another lie out of my pocket and told him that my sister owned an aggressive dog that had gotten loose, and I was trying to track it down again.

He harrumphed in my ear. "If this is your dog, it's going to be put down. We think it attacked a college student a few days ago."

"Believe me," I said, "putting it down's exactly what we have in mind."

I think he decided I was basically harmless, because he gave me the location and told me that one of the professors had fought off an angry dog by throwing rocks. I wondered if that professor realized just how lucky he was.

I thanked the officer, hung up, then pulled the pillow into my lap in a gesture that was becoming familiar. Ten minutes ago a dog that fit the description of Todd Greer's demonic canine had attacked near the college. The attack had been thwarted. To me, that meant it would try again.

What should I do?

The odds were good there was nothing I *could* do. The dog had probably already found another victim. Right now it was undoubtedly curled up asleep, flush from the hunt, while a new human-looking demon wandered the campus.

But what if it wasn't?

What if it was still prowling?

And what if I could stop it?

Shit.

I hugged the pillow tighter, letting my gaze drift to the door. I thought about what lay beyond it—my husband, my daughter, my baby boy. A fist seemed to clutch my heart and squeeze. I knew what I *should* do. I should go to the college. Look for the dog. See if I could save an innocent victim. I was a Hunter, after all. I had responsibilities.

I was a wife and mom, too. And those responsibilities counted for a lot. Not getting myself dead was pretty high on my priority list.

But that dog was out there. And nobody but me knew what they were dealing with.

I closed my eyes and counted to ten, the certainty of what I was going to do settling over me. The bottom line was that I could never live with myself if some kid died that I could have saved.

Slowly I crept into Tim's room. He was sleeping soundly, and I pressed a soft kiss to his cheek. He shifted under his blanket, and I held my breath, wondering if he'd wake up. He didn't, and so I said a silent promise to return soon, then tiptoed out of the room.

Allie and Stuart were much lighter sleepers, so I didn't risk a kiss. Instead, I let my fingers trail over each of their closed doors as I passed. Once downstairs, I hit the button for the garage door opener. The thing makes such a racket that I stood stock-still in the kitchen the entire time it was climbing, waiting to see if anyone would wake up.

No one did, so I wrote a note for Stuart saying I'd gone to buy milk (first I dumped the last of our milk down the drain), then I headed into the garage. I climbed into the van and cranked the engine. I debated for a bit, but finally pulled out my cell phone and dialed Larson's number. I knew he disapproved, but he was my *alimentatore*, and he should at least be aware of what I was doing.

I let the engine idle as the phone rang—once, twice, three times. And no machine. I frowned. That was annoying. I tried again, this time calling his cell phone. Again, no Larson, but at least I got his voice mail. "Hey," I said. "It's me. Kate. I, uh, just wanted to let you know that I'm going to do a drive around the college. I got a lead that the demon dog might be there. So, well, there you go. That's why I called. Bye."

I hung up, feeling a bit like a teenager staying out after curfew. I fidgeted in my seat, turning the cell phone in my hand as if it were one of those worry stones. Like every good Catholic, I have a close personal relationship with guilt. And I hated the idea of going without Larson's okay. But I hated more the idea of not going tonight. If some other kid got nailed . . . well, *that* would be guilt.

Since Larson wasn't available, I did the next best thing. I called the Vatican. (I will admit, that's one of the cool things about being a Hunter. With how many jobs is dialing the Vatican for assistance an option?) I hadn't thought to calculate the time, but the operator put me through right away, and I almost sagged with relief when I heard Father Corletti's voice.

"Katherine, *mia cara. Com'é bello sentire la tua voce!*"

"It's good to hear your voice, too, Father."

"What brings you to call? Has something happened?"

"No . . . yes . . . I mean, no, we don't know any more about Goramesh, but yes, something's happened." I gave him the quick-and-dirty rundown. "I know I'm breaking protocol by calling you now that I have an *alimentatore*, but Larson's unavailable and I need to move now if I'm going to check it out," I continued. "I want to, but I'm afraid Larson will think it's a bad idea. Or, at least, a futile one."

"I see . . ." He trailed off, but I stayed silent. I knew Father well enough to know he was considering all options. "You cannot ignore your instincts, child. Your *alimentatore* is your mentor, your adviser, but he is not your superior. In the end, you must follow your own path."

I exhaled then, not realizing I'd been holding my breath. Vindication is a wonderful thing. "Thanks. Wilson used to tell me the same thing."

I heard the deep rumble of his laugh. "As would your current *alimentatore*."

"Larson said they knew each other."

"So they did. Their professional relationship was strong, but their friendship was stronger."

"Thanks for telling me." Somehow, knowing that Larson was close to Wilson made me feel even closer to Larson. Silly, but there's no accounting for emotions.

"And since I do have you on the line, tell me, has Edward proved to be of any use to you?"

Edward? "Who the he—heck is Edward?"

"A retired Hunter," Father said, surprise in his voice. "A brilliant mind, and he has as much skill as a fighter. He has, of course, been unavailable for much time now. I had hope, though, that he would have thoughts on the Goramesh problem."

"A Hunter? I thought you said there weren't any."

"Larson only recently became aware that Edward had moved to your area. He sent word to me immediately, of course. I assumed you were also acquainted with the man. I take it that is not so?"

"No," I said, a knot forming in my gut. "Edward and I haven't been formally introduced." But at the moment I really—*really*—wanted to meet the man.

Twelve

Considering how agitated I was, it's a wonder *I* didn't have a car accident racing from the house to the college. *Another Hunter? Why wouldn't Larson have told me?*

I couldn't think of any answers, so the same questions just kept bouncing through my head, distracting me, and, frankly, upping my blood pressure. I dialed Larson's cell phone number and his home number—both twice—but got no answer in either case. This time, not even voice mail. I was feeling very *persona non grata* and my attention span was shot. I knew I needed to focus, but I was having a hard time shifting from irritation to concentration. I had to, though. If that damn (and damned) dog slipped by me unnoticed, I might as well have just stayed home.

Come on, Kate. Quit obsessing.

Good advice. After all, there were any number of reasons Larson might not have hooked me up with this Edward person. Maybe Edward had moved on to L.A. or San Francisco or some place equally geographically undesirable. Or maybe Edward, unlike me, wasn't about to be sucked out of retirement, and he'd told Larson to take a flying leap.

For all I knew, the elusive Edward could be dead.

I was cruising up and down the darkened streets that surrounded the small community college campus. Built in a warehouse district, the college had a particularly abandoned feel at night. I slowed down, moving my gaze purposefully from one side of the street to the other as I forced myself to think only about the surroundings and not about the Edward mystery.

I rolled down my window, listening for screams, howls, footfalls, anything. But I heard nothing. Come the weekend, I knew, I'd hear a deep bass thrum, highlighted by a cacophony of voices as students traipsed to the various empty warehouses in search of the next rave party. San Diablo may be sleepy, but it isn't dead (the recent influx of demonic fiends notwithstanding).

Tonight, though, I didn't even hear the scuttle of rats in the alleys. Most likely, the demon dog had moved on. A lot of time had passed since the police received the report. For all I knew, the dog could be all the way on the north side of town by now.

I was part relieved and part irritated. I'd come all this way, and I hated the thought that some kid up north might end up being a victim. But I couldn't be two places at once and, frankly, I probably shouldn't be here at all. I ought to be home, with my husband and kids.

And I was just about to turn the van around and go back there when I heard it—a soft scrape of metal against metal. And then, farther away, a jumble of voices. Students, maybe? Working late in the labs and walking home together?

There was nothing particularly ominous about either of the sounds. Even so, the air itself seemed off. Tainted. *Evil.* (Okay, okay, so maybe that's a tad melodramatic. But I did have a bad feeling.) I had no specific reason to think the demon dog was still around, but I wasn't going to leave without warning those kids, and telling them to take the party inside.

I reached up and switched the overhead light to the Off position, then pulled the keys out of the ignition. I didn't want the van lighting up like a birthday cake any more than I wanted its annoying *bing bong* to announce to the world that Kate Connor was about to go strolling down a dark alley.

I slid my purse under the seat, but only after first retrieving the little spritzer bottle I'd filled with holy water and the barbeque skewer I'd swiped from our backyard grill.

I pushed the door open and slid out of the van. I'd changed back into jeans and running shoes, and now I bounced a little in my Reeboks. If there was a demon out there, this time I was the one doing the hunting, and I hadn't experienced the thrill of the hunt in a long, long time.

Two long rows of boarded-up warehouses sat perpendicular to the street, a narrow alleyway running between them. I headed that way, drawn by the low buzz of voices in the distance. Just past midnight and the students were sitting around partying, which is exactly what college kids should be able to do. Party and stay up all night and drink and cram for exams and generally go a little wild—all *without* the overhanging worry that a demonic band of roving dogs might suddenly decide to call them lunch.

I hurried forward, intending to tell them in my best maternal voice to quit hanging around dark alleys and move their party inside. I thought I heard footsteps behind me— and was about to whip around to take a look—when I heard a new sound. A low, guttural howl, like a wolf in pain. Screams followed, and I raced forward, ignoring whoever might be following me. I found the source of the screams in a parking area, huddled behind a Dumpster. Three kids, probably students, backed into a corner by a giant black mastiff, its bare teeth gleaming with drool.

"Oh, God, lady," one of the guys called, his voice rough with fear. "*Do* something. Get it away from us." From the way the dog was eyeing that guy, I assumed he was the primary target. One look at the fear-frozen girl told me why—she wore a gold cross as a necklace. Might just be fashion, but the demon wouldn't want to take that chance. If she were devout, killing her wouldn't do any good. Her soul would leave, but the demon wouldn't be able to get inside. The other guy had pressed himself so far into the shadows I could barely get a look at him, and I wondered if he wore a cross as well.

"Come here, puppy," I called in a sickly sweet tone. "Come on. Don't you know who I am? A much tastier morsel . . ." I wasn't actually talking to the dog, of course. Somewhere up there, hovering in the ether, was its demonic master. As soon as the dog killed, the demon would swoop in, taking over the body just as pretty as you please.

The dog cocked his head, just enough to bring me into his view without giving the kids any room to run. He snarled, and when I saw his eyes, my heart pounded in my chest, adrenaline surging in a primal effort to get me to flee, to run, to get out of that place once and for all.

Looking into his eyes was like looking into Hell. Red on black, and behind that a maelstrom of evil so thick it seemed to coagulate like blood. I said a silent apology to dogs everywhere. This was no dog. This was simply . . . *bad*. Not a demon itself, but a manifestation of pure evil conjured by a demon to do its bidding.

The thing growled, low in its throat, and I saw muscles tensing beneath the sleek, black fur. I held up the holy-water spritzer as I tried to look fearless. But I wasn't. At the moment I was scared out of my mind.

As the beast lunged at me, I knew with sudden clarity that Larson was right. I wasn't back in fighting shape, and I had no business pretending I was seventeen again.

Too late now.

I sprang forward, squirting with one hand and jabbing the barbeque skewer with the other. The dog howled as the mist settled on its fur, but kept coming. As the distance between us closed, my head no longer filled with self-recrimination but with the desire to stay alive and to kill this creature. "*Run!*" I screamed to the kids. "Get out of here *now!*"

I didn't waste time watching to see if they did, I was too busy being knocked to the ground by two hundred pounds of dog. The holy water went flying, and it was all I could do to keep the dog off all my soft, vulnerable parts.

As its jaws clamped down, I rolled to the right, just in time to feel its teeth sink into my jeans rather than my ankle. I reared back with the other leg and kicked, but that only seemed to piss it off more. It growled and snarled and snapped at my face, as all the while I scrabbled backward on the asphalt, tiny rocks digging into my back and shoulders.

The belly of the beast pressed against my foot, and its weight pushed my leg and knee against my chest, bringing the animal closer despite my efforts to keep him at a distance. I struggled to straighten my leg and toss him off, but I couldn't do it. Not at this angle. And, sadly, not in my current shape.

Shit.

I still had the skewer, and I slashed at the beast, the protrusion a sufficient threat to keep him at bay for now, but probably not for long. I needed to get close enough to sink the skewer into his head, neck, *anywhere*. I really wasn't picky. (Unlike a demon, stabbing through the eye or actual beheading wasn't necessary. I just had to kill the thing.)

Beside me, I heard a scuffle where I should be hearing nothing—the kids should be long gone by now. I lashed out with the skewer, rocking back at the same time and kicking sideways with my free leg. The beast backed off again, and that gave me a split second to look to my right. The girl was gone, but the two guys were still there—one with a knife pressed to the other one's breast.

Shit, shit, shit!

"Fun's over, bud," I said to the beast, with more bravado than I actually felt. I had one shot left before my strength—not to mention my luck—ran out. And I needed it to work if I was going to help that kid.

This time, when the beast lunged, I rose to meet it, rolling forward as if we were doing some perverse dance and sinking the skewer deep into the only place I could actually reach—the dog's nose. The creature howled, shaking his head in a violent motion to dislodge the skewer. I rolled back, tucking both knees into my chest and then thrusting them out again with every ounce of strength I possessed.

I caught the beast just at the breastbone, and it toppled backward, still unsteady from the stick in its nose. I scrambled to my knees, not wasting a moment as I lunged for the skewer, yanked it out, then thrust it down again—hard—through the creature's heart.

There was no blood. Instead, the creature oozed a thick oil that ignited, bursting into black and orange flames that seemed to consume the beast, until all that was left was the echo of its howls.

I scrabbled away, breathing hard, then rolled over and climbed to my feet, ready to race toward the men.

Too late.

I saw the attacker draw his arm back, preparing to gain enough momentum to thrust it up between his victim's rib cage. I cried out—a totally useless response. Far more helpful was the silver blade, spinning through the air, seemingly from out of nowhere. A split second later the metal pierced the attacker's eye. The body sagged, and I saw a familiar shimmer in the air as the demon escaped to the ether.

The knife he'd been holding clattered to the ground. The terrified student still stood there, breathing hard. He looked at me, looked at the body on the pavement, then ran off into the night.

"A demon," I said, speaking to no one. "That boy was a demon."

"You would have realized eventually," Larson said, emerging from the shadows. He reached down, offering a hand to help me up. "But by then the other boy would have been dead, his body a vessel for the demon controlling the beast."

I ignored his hand, content to keep my butt on the ground, nursing my sore thighs and my bruised confidence. "I never got a good look at him. The dog had them cornered. It didn't even occur to me to think. I blew it. I completely blew it." And I was going to continue kicking myself about that for a while. If Larson hadn't been there, that boy would have been toast. And so, frankly, would I. Already tired out by battling the demon's best friend, I don't know that I could have subdued the knifing demon, much less survived once demon number two inhabited the knifed boy's body.

"You *were* otherwise engaged," Larson said, calmly unwrapping a piece of Nicorette and popping it into his mouth. I grimaced, empathizing a bit. I didn't smoke, but after that encounter even I could have used a cigarette.

With a hefty grunt, I got up and dusted my butt off.

"In truth, I can't take credit for having exercised any particular skill in the identification of demons," he said.

I'll admit I cracked a smile at that. The man was too formal by half. "Well, you showed more particular skill than I have."

"The demon revealed itself."

That caught my attention. "What?" Once in human form, a demon rarely shows off any of the bells and whistles that look, well, demonish. (You know, the theatrical stuff like horns or glowing orange eyes or a pig nose. The effort it takes for a demon to manifest itself like that is extreme unless the location is particularly evil—your basic spooky mansion built over a portal to Hell, for example. Otherwise, a revealed demon is a ninety-eight–pound weakling. And in that form, once killed, a demon is really and truly dead.)

"Why would he reveal himself?" I asked.

"Sorry," Larson said drolly, "I didn't think to ask before I killed him. Perhaps he was new to the form, and the excitement of his first kill was more than he could bear and his true revelation appeared unintentionally. Or perhaps he controlled the mastiff, and hadn't yet learned to speak to it from his human guise. The next time we're in such a situation, I'll remember to make that query so we can satisfy your curiosity."

"Thanks. I'd appreciate that."

"But we won't have a situation like this again, will we?"

My wounded pride was fast recovering, especially now that he was reminding me of why I was here in the first place. "No," I said, "we won't. In the future I'll keep you better informed, and you'll keep me better informed. Won't you?"

He lifted his eyebrows as he looked at me over the curve of his nose. "You're referring to Mr. Lohmann, I presume?"

"*Edward* Lohmann? Retired Hunter? Living in San Diablo? Yeah," I said snippily. "I'm referring to him."

"Go home, Kate," he said, which really wasn't the response I was looking for. "I assure you I withheld no useful information from you."

"Larson—"

He held up a hand and I shut up, but continued to glare at him, feeling a bit like a petulant child. "I'll tell you everything I know about Eddie Lohmann tomorrow. Right now, it's late. I have a trial commencing at nine, and I'd like to conduct a bit of research before I turn in. Besides, you have a family to attend to in the morning. I presume you'd like to sleep."

I crossed my arms over my chest. He was right, but I wasn't going to say it out loud.

"Trust me, Kate," he said. "Edward Lohmann is at least forty years your senior, feeble, and of no use to anyone, much less himself. I'm happy to give you the details tomorrow, but right now I think we should leave."

I nodded, albeit somewhat grudgingly.

"Good. And I suppose I don't need to say that you shouldn't have come tonight. That your skills are not up to snuff and that you could have come to harm."

"No," I said. "You don't need to say that."

Despite the shadows, I'm pretty sure I saw him smile.

I cocked my head toward the demon carcass. "What shall we do with that?"

He waved a hand. "I'll take care of it. Go. Go home, Kate."

I swallowed, wanting to argue, but somehow not finding the words. I left him to deal with the body and headed back through the dark to the van. I drove home on autopilot, not even thinking about where I was going, and when I pulled into my garage twenty minutes later, his words still echoed in my head.

He was right, of course. My skills sucked (although I think I've been doing pretty darn well). But I'd had no other choice. Knowing the dog was out there, I couldn't have not come.

I parked the van and reached over to grab my purse, pausing in mid-reach as I realized I'd forgotten to pick up milk to replace the gallon I'd dumped down the drain. *Damn.* I was just about to start the van up again and head down to the 7-Eleven when there was a tap at the passenger window. I actually yelped, wondering what I was going to tell Stuart.

Turns out it wasn't a problem. Laura, not Stuart, was standing next to the van. I turned automatically to look behind me, and for the first time noticed her car parked across the street. How long had she been waiting there?

I clicked the lock and waited for her to climb in, concerned by the expression on her face. Not anger or fear. Betrayal, maybe? "Laura? What is it?"

She lifted her eyes to meet mine, and my heart skipped a beat.

"That boy," she whispered, and I realized she'd been following me. "Oh, God, Kate. Judge Larson killed that boy."

As soon as I had Laura seated on the sofa in Stuart's study, I poured us each a glass of red wine, then shut the door, taking one last listen to the house before I did so. All quiet. Good.

I turned back to her and passed her the glass. She downed half of it, then closed her eyes. For a moment I thought she'd fallen asleep on me (it *was* almost two), but then she lifted her head and drew in a breath. "What's going on, Kate?"

"It's kind of complicated." I squinted at her. "Why were you there?"

"Kate! I saw a boy murdered. *What in the hell is going on?*"

"Right," I said. "You're right." I ran my fingers through my hair, not sure where to begin. "Why don't you tell me what you saw?"

She shook her head just slightly. "Oh, no. I want the whole story. I can't just sit back and—"

"You'll get it," I said. "I promise." I meant it, too. Now that my initial shock had worn off, I realized I wanted to tell her. More than that, I think I *needed* to tell her. I needed a confidante, a friend. Larson couldn't really fill that role, and for a lot of reasons, I couldn't turn to Stuart. I didn't want him to look at me and see a woman who wrestled demons; I just wanted him to see his wife.

Laura didn't look convinced. I took a seat next to her and held her hand. "I promise," I repeated, in the same calm and reassuring voice I'd used when I'd had the sex talk with Allie. "I just need to know where to begin. Why were you even there?"

"I followed you," she said after a brief hesitation.

"I guessed as much," I said. "But why?"

She turned away, as if suddenly fascinated by the collection of windup toys Stuart kept on the end table. "I don't know, exactly. You've been acting off, I guess. That fighting thing with the judge. And thinking more and more about Eric. And . . ." She trailed off with a shrug. "I don't know. It doesn't matter." I thought it probably mattered a lot, but I didn't interrupt. "But then I was coming over here earlier, and I saw you backing out—"

"Wait." I held up a hand, interrupting. "You were coming here? In the middle of the night? Why?"

Her cheeks flushed. "I was on my way to 7-Eleven to get some ice cream." She avoided my eyes, and her cheeks seemed to flame even more. "I decided to swing by and see if your light was on, and right as I pulled up, you pulled out. I thought you might be going to the 7-Eleven yourself, so I followed, and then when you kept going, so did I. Mindy and Paul were already asleep, so I figured why not."

I stifled a wince. If I hadn't been so lost in thoughts about Eddie Lohmann, I surely would have noticed I had a tail. As it was, Laura's were probably the footsteps I'd heard—then forgotten about the second I heard the screams.

"Okay," I said. "I understand how you got to the alley, but I still don't understand why you followed in the first place."

She answered, but her voice was so low I couldn't hear her.

"Come on, Laura. You know you can tell me anything. Just spit it out."

"I-thought-you-were-having-an-affair," she said, so fast her words almost sounded foreign.

"An affair?" I turned the word over in my head. "What is it with you? That's the *second* time you've said that, and *no*. What started this?"

She picked at a threadbare spot on her jeans. "Late nights out of the house. Change in behavior. You know."

"You saw me doing the fighting thing *once*. I left the house late at night *once*." My voice was getting shrill, but I couldn't seem to bring it down a notch. "That's hardly a pattern. Why did 'affair' suddenly pop into your brain? It's not as if—"

And that's when I realized. I sat back. "Oh, no, don't tell me. Is Paul . . . ?" I trailed off. I couldn't bear to ask the question.

"I think so," she whispered. She drew in a breath, then rubbed the back of her hand under her eyes. After a second she flashed me a shaky smile. "Of course, I haven't managed to catch the bastard yet. He's too clever a businessman for that. But a woman knows these things."

"You could be wrong," I said. "You were wrong about me."

"Yes, but I'm not sleeping with you." She laughed then, the sound harsh. "Of course, I'm not sleeping with Paul, either. And as for you, you might not be having an affair, but you are up to something. What?"

"Laura, come on." I shifted on the couch, crossing one leg under me so that I was facing her straight on. "I said I'd tell you, and I will. But if you need to talk . . ."

"No." She shook her head as if she needed to reinforce the idea. "No, I don't think so. I've already talked about it to myself ad nauseum. All I want now is something that will take my mind off of it. Honestly, I think the story behind a federal judge murdering a boy in an alley will do the trick. Add in the fact that my best friend was right there wrestling some freak-of-nature dog, and I'm perfectly willing to believe I won't give a shit about Paul or his little whore for at least twelve more hours."

"Actually," I said, "the judge didn't murder a boy. It's something completely different. In fact, I think my story may well earn you a full twenty-four hours of non-Paul thoughts. Maybe even more."

"At last," she said, "some good news. Bring it on." And for the first time that night, Laura actually smiled.

By the time I finished telling her my story, Laura was no longer smiling. In fact, she looked a little shell-shocked. Also, though, she looked intrigued. "You're kidding me, right?"

I shook my head. "Sorry."

She closed her eyes and drew in a breath, then let it out slowly.

"Laura?"

"I'm okay. I just . . ." She shook her head. "So that shimmer I saw above the boy? That was the demon leaving?"

I nodded.

"Wow." She licked her lips. "When that dog—that thing—died . . . I guess I knew then that something pretty freaky was going on."

I wasn't sure what to say. I'd lived with this knowledge almost my whole life, and I'd never told anyone before. To me, this was just the status quo, and while I tried to see this new reality through Laura's eyes, I was pretty sure I was failing miserably.

She pulled her feet up onto the couch and hugged her knees. "So Judge Larson is a Demon Hunter, too?"

"Not exactly. He's like a mentor. He does the research while I do the dirty work." I grimaced, thinking of the bugs in the cathedral basement. So long as Larson kept his day job, my definition of "dirty work" was expanding.

Her brows lifted. "He looked pretty down and dirty in the alley."

She had a point. "Some *alimentatores* have the street

skills to go along with the book skills. I guess Larson's of that ilk."

"You guess? Haven't you worked with him before?"

I shook my head. "I only met him after the demon came through my window." I made an apology face. "I lied about meeting one of Eric's friends. As far as I know, Eric never laid eyes on Larson."

She didn't seem too perturbed by the lie. "Okay, so the guy that Larson killed was a demon living in the body of a dead person."

"Right." I'd given her the brief rundown of how it works, and now she was giving it back to me just like a prize pupil.

"And you were fighting with what?"

"Mythology calls them hellhounds. Huge mastiffs that do a demon's bidding. Nasty creatures. Smell bad, too."

"When you stabbed it . . ." She trailed off with a shiver. "Laura?"

"I'm fine." She finished off her wine. I filled her glass back up. "It's all a little much."

"For me, too," I said. "I thought the most I'd have to deal with this year was boyfriends and potty training."

"God, I don't know which is worse. Demons, or trying to get a toddler out of diapers without losing your sanity." She half-laughed, but it died quickly enough. "That dog . . . um, where exactly did it go when it . . . when it . . ." She waved her hand. "You know. When it went away."

I knew what she meant. The dog had disappeared in a swirl of flame. No ashes. No charred bones. Just gone. "I'm not sure. Hell, I assume. Thankfully, I have no personal knowledge."

Her laugh sounded a little nervous. "Yeah. That's good."

"Laura." I took a sip of my wine before taking a deep breath. "Are we okay? I mean, Stuart doesn't know because . . . well, because it's a rule that I'm not supposed to tell. But obviously, I'm not strictly adhering to the rules here. I just don't want him to see me as some sort of ninja mom, you know? And I don't want you to see me that way, either. You're my best friend. Without you I'd have no one to talk to during the days except a two-year-old, and all my cultural references would be from Disney or Nickelodeon."

"Nice to know where I rate," she said, but she was smiling.

"You know what I mean."

"We're fine," she said. She took my hand and squeezed. "This is going to take some getting used to, but you're still the same Kate. Although . . ."

"What?" I asked, instantly alarmed.

Her smile was devious. "You're no longer a stay-at-home mom. Kate Connor, you have a day job." She frowned. "Or a night job. I'm not really sure about that."

"Either," I said. "Demons come out during the day, too. They just like the night better. Besides, I'm filling the days with research."

"Right. To figure out what Gildamish is looking for."

"Goramesh."

"Yeah, him. Do you have any leads?"

"Nothing concrete. We know the other locations Goramesh ravaged looking for whatever. And we think that bones may be involved. We just don't know exactly what 'whatever' is."

"I could help."

I raised my eyebrows. "What? How? For that matter, why?"

"I want to," she said. "I need a day job, too. Otherwise, what else am I going to do all day except sit around thinking up creative ways to castrate Paul?"

She had a point. "I don't know what you could do," I said. "I could use the research help, sure, but if you go with me to the archives, I'm afraid . . ." I shrugged, not wanting to voice my fear.

"What?"

I paused, then took a deep breath. "I'm afraid he'll realize you're helping me. And that he'll try to hurt you."

She nodded slowly. "I can still help," she said. "From home, even. No one has to know I'm on the case. I can be like that ten-year-old kid who stays at the computer and sends Kim Possible on all her missions."

I wasn't sure whether to laugh or cry about the fact that she'd just compared my life to that of a Disney Channel cartoon character. "Uh—"

"I'm serious. I can make phone calls. I can go to the library. Better yet, I can do Internet research. Find out about the cathedrals he wrecked. Maybe get a clue."

I had to admit, it wasn't a bad idea. But I still hated dragging her in. "I don't know," I hedged. "I'd hate for anything to happen."

"So would I," she said. "But from what you're telling me, if this Goramesh guy has his way, my kid could be a demon-sized Happy Meal. No, thank you. I want to help, Kate. Let me help you stop him. I can do most everything from home, and there's nothing suspicious about going to the library."

I'll admit I wasn't hard to convince. I told myself it would be good for her, keeping her mind off Paul. In truth, I think I was more selfish than that. I wasn't inclined to examine my motives, though. Not when her proposal was dead-on perfect. I did need help with the research, after all. "You're sure you're up for it?"

She waved a hand. "Hell, yes. I spend hours and hours on eBay. My Internet skills are sharp."

I narrowed my eyes.

"Kidding," she said. "Don't worry. I've helped Paul do research on locations and stuff. I know my way around Google and Dogpile and Vivisimo and a dozen others. Come on. At the very least I can punch in the towns and stuff where the attacks occurred. Larnaca, you said?"

I nodded. "I don't know the town in Mexico or Tuscany, but I can find out."

"So I can help?"

Since she'd lost me after Google, I decided she was qualified. "Okay," I said. "I think." I frowned. "Let me think about it overnight. It's late and my head is mush." But I knew the answer would be yes. I think she knew so, too.

I walked with her to the door and gave her a hug. "You're okay?" I was talking about Paul, but the question pretty much covered all bases.

"Yeah. Thanks. It's rough, but we'll get through it. I mostly feel bad for Mindy. If he is screwing around . . . Well, I'll worry about that when it happens. You need to get some sleep."

She was right. I was scheduled to fight with Cutter the next morning, and I had to get Timmy over to the day care before then. He wasn't supposed to start until Wednesday, but I was hoping that if I begged, they'd let him start tomorrow. I was optimistic. Groveling, I've discovered, can be a very effective tool. And I intended to do as much groveling as was necessary.

I opened the door for her, but she paused at the threshold. "So there are demons out there, huh?"

I stood behind her, looking out over my front yard and the oh-so-familiar street, trying to see the world through her new perspective. "I'll drive with you," I said.

"Oh, no. It's okay. You don't have to do that. Really."

There was no way I was letting her go that distance alone. Not tonight, when I knew she'd see a demon around every corner.

"Actually, I really do," I said. She turned to me, and I shrugged. "As it turns out, I need to borrow some milk."

Thirteen

As bizarre as Monday had been, it was almost disconcerting to wake up so normally on Tuesday morning. Normal, that is, except for the fact that I'd had only three hours of sleep, and my entire body felt like it had been pounded by a football team—and not in a good way.

The alarm clock chirped promptly at six o'clock. I rolled over, muttering rude things about its parentage, and slapped the snooze button. *There*. Guess I told it.

Beside me, Stuart muttered something that sounded like "jump through the hobbits," but which I mentally translated as "just a few more minutes." I muttered an agreement, tugged the covers up under my chin, and spooned against him. Nanoseconds later the alarm chirped again. (The digital readout assured me that seven full minutes had elapsed. I was not convinced.)

I slapped the alarm senseless again, then rolled over to shake Stuart's shoulder. "Up," I said. "Go. Earn money." This is my contribution to making sure the family bank account stays liquid.

He groaned again, then rolled over so that he was facing me. Slowly he opened his eyes. Even more slowly he smiled. "Hey, gorgeous."

Since I am particularly ungorgeous in the morning, these kinds of endearments simply embarrass me. I rolled away with a mumbled "Stuart . . ."

He slid closer, then wrapped his arm around my hips, pulling himself closer until he was nuzzling my neck. Even half-comatose, I know better than to shun a nuzzle. "You're perky this morning," I said.

"Why not?" He tugged me back around so that he was leaning over me, one finger tracing the neckline of the plain white T-shirt I'd slept in. "I survived a car crash, locked in some campaign support, and woke up next to a beautiful woman."

He nibbled at my neck again and I laughed. "You're such a politician."

"Public servant," he shot back. He grinned, then, his mouth lifting with his own private joke.

"What?" I said, amused.

"Nothing." His smile broadened. "Let's just say I had a shot of confidence last night."

"The party? It did go pretty well, all things considered."

"The party," he confirmed, "and . . ."

"What?"

He shifted, raising one shoulder in a slight shrug as he trailed his fingertip up and down my arm. "Nothing important. Let's just say I found a new perspective on things. I'm thinking positively, and I'm positive that this election is all locked up." He pushed a strand of hair behind my ear. "You're looking at the next county attorney, sweetheart. I'm sure of it."

"Well, *I* never doubted you for a minute. I mean, why would the voters want anyone else? You're the perfect candidate."

"A man for the people," he said. His eyes roamed over

me, his expression shifted from amused to heated. "A man for one woman . . ."

He kissed me then, slow and long, and I tried to get my head around the fact that my rush-out-the-door-to-work husband wanted morning sex. (He also had morning breath, which is unusual for Stuart, but I chalked it up to too much party food.) Any potential for an amorous morning adventure, however, fizzled when Timmy's cries of "Momma, Momma, Momma. Where you at, Momma?" blared from the baby monitor perched on the dresser.

"He'll be fine for a few minutes," Stuart murmured, the invitation clear in his voice.

"MOMMA!"

"He sounds pretty determined," I said. And (true confessions moment here) I was secretly glad. Not only was my entire body sore and achy, but my mind was already spinning with all the stuff I had to do, all the little details that had to be handled in order to keep my dual life running (somewhat) smoothly. "I should probably get him."

Stuart muttered something incoherent, but rolled back so that I could sit up. I swung my legs over the side of the bed as I reached for a pair of sweats, then dragged myself down the hall to my howling offspring.

It took me a good twenty minutes to get the munchkin up and dressed and myself decked out in jeans and a San Diablo Junior High PTA T-shirt. By the time I got back downstairs, Stuart was already dressed, his hair damp from the shower, the scent of aftershave clinging to him in a way I found both familiar and slightly erotic. I pushed away a twang of regret for not taking him up on his suggestion of a morning tryst.

Allie barreled into the room, as much as one can barrel in spiked-heel slides and skin-tight jeans. I glanced pointedly at her shoes, then up at her face. "Oh, Mom," she said. "Jenny Marston wears heels to school."

There were a lot of things about Jenny Marston I didn't

want Allie emulating. Now I had shoes to add to the list. I pointed toward the stairs. "Go," I said. "Change."

She exhaled so loudly that Timmy looked up, pointed, and starting puffing up his cheeks and blowing air out with a *whoosh, whoosh*.

"Allie," I said, injecting a warning note into my voice.

"Mind your mother," Stuart added, from somewhere behind the morning paper.

"Fine. Whatever," she said, then huffed back upstairs.

I looked at Timmy. "Shoes, at least, are a problem we'll never have with you," I said.

"Not until he wants some cool celebrity sneaker, anyway," Stuart said.

I grimaced, imagining a future where I'd gone undefeated against demons, but had been laid flat by my own children's insidious shoe demands. Not a pretty picture.

After two more cups of coffee Stuart kissed me and Timmy, called a good-bye up the stairs to Allie, then headed into the garage. A few moments later I heard the garage door begin its slow, creaky climb. I yelled at Allie to hurry or else she'd miss her car pool. She clattered back down the stairs and screeched to a halt in front of the refrigerator, this time in neon-pink high-top sneakers and a matching T-shirt. As my daughter would say, whatever.

"Lunch or money?" she said.

Since I'd gone on a wild-demon chase last night instead of staying home to care for my family like I should have done (guilt, guilt, guilt), I hadn't fixed her a lunch. I found my purse, rummaged until I came up with a twenty, and handed it to her. Her eyes widened, but she was smart enough not to say anything.

She planted a quick kiss on my cheek, then raced out the front door, just as Emily's mom tooted her horn. As the door banged shut, I remembered what I'd forgotten, but by the time I reached the end of the sidewalk, the car was already gone. Well, damn.

I'd completely forgotten to tell Allie that we had our first class with Cutter Wednesday afternoon, and to not sign up for any extracurriculars. Now I was going to have to call the school and leave a message for her. The process had been a huge hassle in junior high, and I didn't anticipate it getting any easier now. Allie's voice seemed to whisper in my ear—*Mo-om . . . just get me a cell phone! Fine*, I said to the voice. *I'll get one today.*

I'm not normally in the habit of succumbing to the will of voices in my head, but the cell phone thing had been one of Allie's most persistent battles, with her adamant that she needed one, and me just as adamant that she didn't. Now that I knew there were demons roaming the town, though, my perspective had shifted one hundred and eighty degrees. Anything to keep my baby safer, and if that meant slapping a cell phone into her hot little hand so she could dial 911 at the drop of a hat, well, so be it.

"Allie go to work?" Timmy asked as I came back inside and took a seat at the table next to him. He held a spoon in one chubby fist, and was sticking it repeatedly into a cup of peach yogurt.

"Allie went to school," I said. "Daddy went to work."

"Mommy go to work?"

"As a matter of fact, yes." I took the spoon (amazed that this didn't prompt a huge tantrum) and aimed a bite of yogurt toward his mouth. "Does Timmy want to go to school like Allie?"

"No," he said, giving me the puppy-dog eyes and shaking his head hard enough that there was no way the yogurt was going to make it inside. "No school." A little-boy-lost whine had crept into his voice, and my heart twisted in my chest. Stay firm, I told myself. It's only temporary. Thousands of kids are in day care every day without detriment to the kid or the parent.

Still . . .

I kept a perky smile plastered on my face. "No school?"

I asked, feigning amazement. "But school is great! You'll get to play with messy things like paint, and you'll make all sorts of friends. And songs," I said, pulling out all the stops. "I bet they sing 'Happy and You Know It' at school all the time."

"No, Momma," he said. He shook his head once more. "*You* go to school."

"Wish that I could, kiddo." I fed him the last spoonful of yogurt, then got a paper towel to wipe the bulk of his breakfast off his chin, the table, and the floor. "Would you give it a shot?" I asked. "For Mommy? School sounds pretty exciting to me. Lots of fun, and you get to play games."

Since I had the spoon, he stabbed his finger into the yogurt, then proceeded to draw a line of goop on the tabletop. *Come on, Tim*, I mentally urged. *Say yes and make Mommy feel less guilty.*

"Buddy?" I asked. "What do you say?"

"Okay, Mommy." He sounded much perkier than he had only moments before, and I wondered if in his little two-year-old brain, he was already off on some other topic. I wasn't about to ask, though. His blessing (such that it was) assuaged my guilt, and I headed into the living room to pack up our things.

Tim was his typical cheery self the entire ride to the day care center. I plastered on a happy face, told him this was *his* school, then proceeded to list off all the wonderful and exciting things he'd do that day. He eyed me warily, my only clue that he might be less than keen on this plan the thumb that went automatically into his mouth.

I got out and walked around the car to let him out. He was sitting there, quietly sucking away, when I slid the door open. "You're going to have so much fun at school," I said. "Aren't you, buddy?"

The thumb emerged, followed by a brief nod and an "Okay, Mommy." I called that a victory, then proceeded to unstrap him from the car seat. I helped him down, then held his hand as we walked inside. So far, all was well.

I found Nadine behind a reception counter. I'd called her from the road and begged to start Timmy today instead of tomorrow. She promised to arrange it all, and sure enough, as soon as I arrived, she passed me a variety of papers to sign and asked for the balance due on the month's tuition. Timmy behaved throughout this entire process. But the moment I handed over the check, he started to howl. It may have taken him a while to figure out exactly what was going on here, but now that he'd clued in, he was having none of it.

"No," he howled. "No school. No, no school. Go home. Go. *Home."* Big tears rolled down his cheeks, and I tried to get a grip, reminding myself that this was for his own good—without day care, demons might take over the town, and then where would we be?

I felt my cheeks flame, embarrassment battling with an almost physical need to pick up my child and cuddle him. Nadine, of course, had seen this before, and she passed Tim a toy truck from her desk, at the same time offering me a reassuring smile. "He'll be in the Explorers classroom with Miss Sally. They're on the playground right now. I bet that will help Tim get over his first-day jitters."

As it turned out, she was right. After a few more minutes of clinging and shouting "No, Momma, no!" at the top of his lungs, Tim discovered the sandbox and soon settled in to shovel a beach worth's of sand next to a little boy in Bob the Builder overalls.

Nadine tapped my arm. "We should head back inside while he's occupied." I nodded, but didn't move. My heart was all twisted in my chest, and my stomach hurt. How could I leave? What kind of a mother was I?

A mother who needs to stop a High Demon from raising an army and killing off the population of San Diablo, I answered myself.

At the moment, though, as I left my baby in the care of strangers, that really didn't seem good enough.

I worked off my guilt sparring with Cutter. We started with a few basic stretches, but quickly moved on to the full meal deal, focusing on jabs and crosses, parrying kicks and quartering, and my favorite—spinning back kicks.

This time Cutter was ready for me, and I had to work my tail off just to keep from getting pummeled. I still fully intended to nail him. I just needed to find the right opportunity.

"You're good," I said, parrying an expertly executed cross-behind side kick. "I came to the right place."

"I'm motivated," he said. "Can't get shown up by a skirt twice."

"A skirt? Who are you, Phillip Marlowe?"

"Think of me as your worst nightmare, sweetheart," he said, in a full-on Humphrey Bogart voice. I laughed, and he used my distraction to lash out and send me sprawling. "Concentration, Connor. Gotta work on concentration."

I glared at him from my ignominious position on the mat. "I'll keep that in mind," I said. I reached a hand up, and he took it, more than happy to help me to my feet. *Sucker.* I yanked him down, leaping up as he took my place on the floor.

"Not bad," he said from his new perspective.

"I've still got a few tricks."

He climbed to his feet and looked me up and down. "Yeah, I think you do."

I tried to stand there under his scrutiny without wincing. Not easy. I'm pretty sure every inch of my body was bruised (all the more reason to avoid romantic encounters with my husband, at least during the daylight hours) and I hated feeling on display. "We've still got a good forty-five minutes," I said. "You aren't quitting on me yet, are you?"

His grin was slow and confident. "You're not getting off that easy, Connor." He held his arm out, wrist bent, as he waggled his fingers, Matrix style. "You ready?"

"Always," I said.

We covered the basic territory for the rest of the hour, giving me the chance to practice a variety of moves, both offensive and defensive. By the time we finished, I was wishing I'd let Stuart talk me into putting a hot tub in our backyard. But sore as I was, I felt pretty damn cocky. Even after all these years I still had some pretty good moves.

Breathless, I dug a towel out of my duffel bag and draped it around my neck.

"You done good," Cutter said. "I guess I'll see you and your kid tomorrow." He took a gulp of Gatorade and wiped his mouth. "It'll be a trip showing the class what you've got."

I shook my head. "Tomorrow, you're going to find a significantly less skilled Kate. Blow my cover, and I promise you'll pay for it the next morning."

"I consider myself warned." He stared at me for a moment, and in his eyes I saw a hint of the naval officer he used to be. "You ever going to tell me your story?" he asked.

"Don't hold your breath," I said. And when he smiled, I knew that Cutter wouldn't hold my secrets against me. I also knew that he'd keep trying to figure me out.

The idea of sitting in the cathedral basement with hundreds of pages still to review lacked appeal, but I knew I had to do it. At the same time I was curious about Eddie, even though Larson had assured me the retired Hunter wouldn't be an asset. In the end, procrastination and curiosity won out over bugs and responsibility, and I called Larson's chambers from the car to let him know I was coming.

Since his clerk told me he'd be on the bench for at least

another hour, I decided to use that time to run errands, pretending all the while that my life was just as normal and mundane as it had always been. I hit the dry cleaners, bank, and post office, then decided to go ahead and buy Allie's cell phone before heading toward the government complex.

By the time I parked, I felt good. Centered. My Hunter life had snuck back up on me, true, but that didn't mean my family wouldn't have cash, stamps, or freshly pressed clothes.

I've been to the complex dozens of times to meet Stuart for lunch, but he worked in the county attorney's office, and Judge Larson was in the courthouse. I got a bit turned around, and ended up in Stuart's part of the complex.

I was just about to pop my head into an office and ask directions when I heard Stuart's voice. I froze.

"I have the proposed zoning changes on my desk," he was saying, his voice growing louder as he approached the corner. I darted into the first office I saw, my heart pounding wildly. I had no reason to be down there. What would I tell Stuart if I saw him? I hadn't even told him about Timmy's day care yet. I could hardly explain a lunchtime encounter with Judge Larson.

I kept my ear pressed to the closed door, listening as footsteps approached, then receded. Only when I could hear nothing did I let myself breathe again.

"Excuse me?" a voice behind me asked. "May I help you?"

I spun around, feeling incredibly foolish, even more so when I saw the woman behind the reception desk staring at me, concern all over her face.

"Are you okay?" From her tone, I think she thought I was running from a deranged killer. Either that, or I was the deranged killer and I was running from the cops.

"Sorry," I said. "My boss. I'm not supposed to be taking a break. I didn't want him to see me."

Considering I was wearing stretchy yoga pants, sneakers, and a plain blue T-shirt, I'm surprised this approach worked. The girl didn't question me, though (perhaps she simply wanted me gone), and I slipped back out the door and into the hall. It was only after I'd gone five paces that I realized I still had no idea where to find Larson.

After a few more false starts, I found someone to ask, and arrived at Larson's courtroom just as he was finishing up a bunch of pretrial rigmarole. I went and sat on the wooden seats in the galleys, watching him rule on the various motions and objections. Hard to believe the same man was my *alimentatore*. That just last night he'd destroyed a demon.

The last pair of attorneys finished battling it out (metaphorically speaking), and the bailiff did the "all rise" thing. I caught Larson's eye as he stood to leave, and he nodded at me, the movement almost imperceptible. As soon as he'd disappeared into his chamber, I approached the bailiff. Less than a minute later I was escorted back into the hallway.

Compared to the pristine, awe-inspiring federal courtroom, the backroom area was downright bland. Larson's office kicked it up a notch—a huge mahogany desk, matching credenza, framed gold photos, and even a Waterford dish filled with hard candy—but even that room was so piled with papers and briefs that he had to clear a chair off just so I had someplace to sit. At least now I knew why he had no time to schlep through buggy boxes with me.

"You want to know more about Eddie," he said, a small smile playing around his mouth.

I shrugged. "What can I say? I'm persistent."

"One of your finest qualities," he said. "I told you he was infirm, but the more I think about it, the more I think you may as well talk to him. It certainly can't hurt, and you being a Hunter might bring him out of his funk." He spread his hands. "Perhaps Eddie will have insight, perhaps he won't. But it can't hurt to try, right?"

"Sure," I said. From the way he described the old man, I wasn't going to get my hopes up.

Larson moved around his desk to lean against it in front of me, his forehead creased. "By the way, how is Stuart?"

"He's fine. Wasn't crazy about being nursemaided to death, but he'll survive. Once I washed away all the dried blood, there really wasn't much under there except a few nicks and scratches."

"When he drove up, you were on the verge of telling me what you'd discovered in the archives."

I stifled a snort of derisive laughter. "You mean what I didn't find. There are eighty million boxes down there, all crammed full of paper and uncataloged gifts. There's a tiny bit of organization, but it's going to take me a while to get my bearings." I gave him the rundown of what I'd done so far, such that it was. I almost told him I was going to let Laura help me out, too, but in the end I held my tongue. I'd broken rules by dragging her in, and I didn't really want to admit my guilt. If Laura discovered something amazing, then I'd tell him. In the meantime, I figured ignorance was bliss.

Larson rubbed his chin, obviously processing the information. "I see your problem. The IRS lists provide some help, but the playing field is still large."

"And teeming with bugs," I added.

"I can't do anything about the vermin, but I've been doing some research on my end, and I think I may be able to narrow your search."

"Great," I said. "How?"

"Apparently, the monk whose cell was the most destroyed was Brother Michael."

"Should that mean something to me?"

"No, but Brother Michael is the monk who committed suicide."

"That *is* interesting," I said. "I still can't figure out why a monk would commit suicide." I was talking more to myself than Larson, and I answered myself, too. "He wouldn't. Not unless he'd lost his faith or believed it was for the greater glory of God. Or if the death was indirect and he wasn't really looking to kill himself. Like someone running into a burning building to save a baby, even though he knows he probably won't get out." I met Larson's eyes. "Or someone running who leaps from a building to escape demons, perhaps?"

"Most likely," he agreed.

"Or maybe it was more proactive," I said. "What if the thing Goramesh was looking for wasn't in his cell? And what if the monk was afraid he'd reveal the location if he were tortured?"

"And so he killed himself rather than reveal it?" Larson frowned thoughtfully. "Possible. Definitely possible."

"Yeah," I said, warming to the idea. "The demon tortured him, and Brother Michael broke, revealing San Diablo. But rather than spill the rest of it, he threw himself from the window."

"Very good," Larson said, nodding slowly. "Yes, yes, I believe you're on to something."

I sighed, proud and frustrated all at the same time. "Not enough. We already knew it was in San Diablo, and we're not any closer to knowing what *it* is."

"Patience, Kate. When you next review the archives, keep an eye out for donations from Italy. Or anything that could have a connection to Brother Michael."

"Right," I said, making a mental list. Benedictine, Florence, monasteries. I'd try to find out the monk's family name, and Laura could try to track down relatives in California, or see if Brother Michael had any connection to Larnaca, or that cathedral in Mexico. You never knew. "At least we have a little bit more of a plan." I still didn't relish the detective end, but at least I could see some tiny bit of progress.

He glanced at his watch. "We should wrap this up. I have a status conference in a criminal case schedule in fifteen minutes."

"Sure," I said. "No problem. But you haven't told me where Eddie is yet."

"Of course, of course," he said. "He's currently living out his days at the Coastal Mists Nursing Home." Something flashed across his face. Worry, perhaps? "I hope he'll be of some help, but we shouldn't get our hopes up. My understanding is that on a bad day he makes no sense, and on a good day he rattles on about decapitating demons in his youth. The staff thinks he's crazy." Larson met my eyes. "I'm more inclined to think he has Alzheimer's and is reliving his glory days."

I didn't say anything, but I felt oddly defeated. Larson had already told me Eddie was feeble, so nothing had changed in that regard, but now another worry nagged at me—would that be me one day? Alone at the end of my days, senile and yammering on about my escapades with Eric?

No. I had a family. I had kids. I had a husband who loved me. Unlike Eddie Lohmann, I wasn't alone. I closed my eyes then and said a silent prayer for Eddie. I'd never met the man, but still we shared a bond.

I'd pay him a visit. It was, after all, the least I could do.

Fourteen

I stopped by Laura's before heading to Coastal Mists and found her perched at her kitchen table, her laptop open, her fingers tapping at her keyboard. I moved to stand behind her and found myself looking down at the Web site for the Larnaca tourist bureau.

"I'm trying to impress you with my resourcefulness," she said. "How am I doing so far?"

"Not bad."

"Good. Because the only location you told me about was Larnaca, so after this, I'm stumped. Although I did do some research on the cathedral earlier this morning."

I'd begun to read over her shoulder (the site raved about Larnaca's easygoing pace coupled with its fascinating links to the ancient past), but at that I looked up. "St. Mary's Cathedral?"

"Yeah. Since you said that Goramesh is looking here now, I figured I could start by researching the cathedral."

"Pretty interesting history, don't you think?" I asked.

"Did you read about the saints' ashes used in the mortar?"

I could practically see her face fall. "You already knew about that? I thought I'd be telling you something new."

"Sorry. Old news. That's why Eric and I used to think this town had so few demons." I snorted. "So much for that theory."

"Well, demon-free or not, the cathedral sure has a lot of tragedy."

"What do you mean?"

"Five of the original missionaries were murdered. *Martyred* I guess is the word. They were burned on individual pyres. Just horrific stuff."

"Wow," I said. "I had no idea."

"Really?" She brightened considerably. "You really didn't know?"

"I really didn't. Tell me."

"Well, the yuck part was that they were burned, but the fascinating part is that the cathedral still has their remains. The church kept the ashes in bags, saving them in case any of the martyrs were sainted."

"I've seen them," I said, remembering the coffee-sized bags in the display case. "So, *were* any of them sainted?"

She shook her head. "No, but one of them was beatified. That's the first step, right?"

I nodded. "I doubt any of that's helpful to us, though. The martyrs are part of the cathedral's formal collection, so they've been on the Web site forever. Goramesh wouldn't have to sneak around to find them."

"Oh." She leaned back, her enthusiasm fading. "At least it makes a good story."

"Come on, Laura. I haven't even asked you to help yet, and already you're doing great." I said all this in the same voice I use to tell Allie that her math homework was going really, really well. As uneasy as I'd been about Laura help-ing me originally, now I was keen on the idea. I didn't want her to get discouraged and distracted, moving on to other more consuming things such as closet reorganizing or dust-bunny wrangling.

"Yeah, I guess."

"So tell me about this," I said, focusing again on the Web site about Larnaca and sounding more chipper than I felt.

"I just pulled it up," she said. "I haven't even read it yet myself."

"Look," I said, noticing a paragraph in the middle of the page. "It says that Larnaca is where Lazarus lived."

"Rising-from-the-dead Lazarus?"

"I think so." I leaned over her and pointed to a link labeled Places to See. "Click there."

She did, and a list of tourist attractions came up.

"There," I said. "Lazarus came to Larnaca after he was resurrected, and a church was built on the spot where his remains were said to be found."

"A church," Laura repeated. "Do you think that's where the shrine was? The one that was spray-painted?"

"Could be, I guess."

"But what's the connection to Mexico or Italy? Or to San Diablo, for that matter?"

"I don't know." I chewed on the side of my lip, then paced her kitchen as an idea started to form. "Both the demons that attacked me talked about an army rising. So maybe the desecration of the shrine and the various cathedrals is symbolic. Jesus and Lazarus rose through the power of God, and the demons are going to rise through the power of Satan?" It sounded like a B-movie plot, but it was the only idea I had.

"Maybe," Laura said. She sounded as dubious as me.

"This is all so frustrating," I said. "And what does any of it have to do with bones?"

"Could be symbolic, too. You know, like 'Dem bones gonna rise again.' " Laura's voice was singsong. I just stared at her. She exhaled. "The song," she said. "You know."

I didn't know, and told her as much.

"Didn't you go to church camp?"

Obviously Laura hadn't completely assimilated my description of my childhood. "I lived at the Vatican, Laura," I said. "There wasn't a lot of singing around the campfire going on."

"Right. Sure. Of course." She laughed nervously. This was going to take a while for her to get her head around. "So, I guess you probably didn't sit around with the other Hunters telling ghost stories, huh?"

"Sure we did," I said. "Only they weren't stories. They were object lessons in how to survive." I could still vividly remember how Eric and Katrina and Devin and I would huddle in the alcove between the boys' and girls' dorms. We'd share our own escapades along with any other stories we'd picked up from older, more experienced Hunters. Like Allie now did at her slumber parties, we'd stay up into the wee hours talking. But we weren't doing it for fun. It was work. Survival. Knowledge, after all, is power.

"Your childhood sucked," she said.

"Pretty much." But even though I said the words with feeling, a part of me knew that—given the choice—I wouldn't have lived my life any other way.

"I can see why you retired early," she said. "Probably extended your life expectancy by decades."

I didn't answer. Thoughts of Eric spilled into my head. Retiring hadn't saved him. Death had wanted him, and it had taken him. And even with all of Eric's fighting skills, when it was his time, he'd still lost the battle.

". . . you okay?"

I shook my head, dispelling my thoughts. "What?"

"I asked if you were okay?"

"Fine," I said. I moved to the table and grabbed my purse. "I've got some more information you can plug into Google," I said. "Want to come with me to see Eddie Lohmann? I'll give you the rundown on the way."

Her brows rose. "Come with you? Real sidekick stuff? I wouldn't miss it for the world."

"Don't get used to it," I said, giving her a stern glare. I'm pretty sure, though, that my smile destroyed the effect.

As soon as we were on the road, I relayed my conversation with Larson, giving her all the key words to plug into her next search, and telling her in particular about Brother Michael. I also told her what Larson had said about Eddie's condition.

"That's a shame," she said. "I was hoping you'd have some help."

"I have you," I said.

"I was thinking more along the lines of help that wouldn't squeal like a girl and run the other way at the sight of a spider, much less a demon." Her smile, however, told me how pleased she was by the comment. "So where's the turnoff?"

We spent the next ten minutes trying to find the poorly marked driveway for Coastal Mists Nursing Home and Eddie Lohmann. I pushed thoughts of Laura and the cathedral and Lazarus out of my head, my attention focused solely on my newly founded Adopt a Geriatric Hunter program.

"So what exactly are we doing here?" Laura asked as I pulled into one of the many empty parking spaces. I had the feeling the residents of Coastal Mists weren't inundated with visitors.

"I'm not exactly sure." If he had all his marbles, I wanted to run the situation by Eddie and get his opinion. But the Goramesh problem notwithstanding, I just wanted to meet Eddie. I didn't know the man, and yet I already felt a connection to him. Melancholy mixed with nostalgia, I'm sure. There were no other Hunters in my life. Eddie was a Hunter. *Ergo*, I'd latched on.

Pretty transparent pop psychology, but sometimes the most obvious answer really is the truth.

The entire front of the building was landscaped, with native plants lining the walkway, giving the place the external appearance of a fine hotel. The moment we stepped inside, the illusion faded, replaced by a hollow, antiseptic scent, as if the home's administrators were trying just a little too hard to hide the fact that there was dying going on here.

I realized I'd stopped in the foyer and was hugging myself. Beside me, Laura didn't seem the least bit perturbed. Mentally, I chastised myself. I'd seen all sorts of death and fought all sorts of demons. If the scent of a nursing home didn't bother Laura, I sure as heck wasn't going to let it bother me.

The hallway opened up into a large foyer, the focal point of which was a round nursing station that apparently doubled as a reception desk. A woman in an old-fashioned nursing uniform, complete with starched white hat, greeted us with a thin smile. "Can I help you?" she asked abruptly, even before we'd completely approached the desk.

Her tone caught me by surprise, and I started. I caught Laura's gaze, and her eyes widened a bit, letting me know that it wasn't just my imagination. I chalked it up to PMS and plowed on. "We're here to see Eddie Lohmann. Can you tell me what room he's in?"

She stared at me for so long I began to wonder if there was something gross on my face. I was just about to ask again (I am nothing if not optimistic) when she peered at me over the rim of her half-glasses and sniffed.

"Your name, please?" She shoved a registry in my direction.

"Kate Connor," I said. "And this is Laura Dupont." I started to sign in.

"Relatives?"

"By marriage," I said, not missing a beat as I scrawled my name and Laura's in the appropriate column.

I glanced at Laura long enough to see her brows rise almost imperceptibly. Then I pushed the registry back toward Nurse Ratched. Her lips pursed as she read our names, then she lifted her chin and surveyed me once again through narrowed eyes. I was beginning to feel downright paranoid, and I can't say I particularly enjoyed the sensation.

"By marriage," she repeated.

"He's related to my husband," I said, the lie coming naturally. "Why? Is there a problem?"

"Visiting hours for nonrelatives end in five minutes. If you're family—"

"We are," I said firmly.

I expected her to argue, but instead she raised a hand and a twenty-something girl in a candy-striper uniform came trotting over, her name tag introducing her as Jenny. "See these ladies to the media room. They're visiting Mr. Lohmann." To us, she said, "I'm surprised we haven't seen you here before."

"A long story," I said. "We just found out that Eddie was here."

"Hmmm. Well, I hope you have better luck with him than we do." And with that cryptic remark, she returned her attention to the papers on her desk, leaving Laura and me to follow our candy striper down a long, dim hallway.

Most of the doors were open, and as I peered into the rooms, I could see twin beds and various other bits of furniture and personal belongings. The rooms reminded me of the tiny monk cells that had doubled as dorm rooms in my youth, and I wondered if in some way Eddie hadn't come full circle.

I noticed that most of the rooms were empty, and when I asked our guide, she explained that most of the residents were in the television parlor, which happened to be where we were going. "I'm so glad you're here to visit him," Jenny said. "He never gets visitors and it's such a shame."

"How long has he been here?"

"About three months. At first he was really disoriented,

but I think he's starting to get used to the place. A little clearer, you know?"

"That's great," I said, but my mind was elsewhere. Weird that the Vatican had just learned he was here. At the very least, I was surprised the diocese didn't send a volunteer around to chat with him and a priest to give Communion.

I didn't have time to ponder those things, however, because we'd arrived. The hallway opened out into a second foyer that I presumed had been a secondary entrance at one time but now obviously served as the famous media room. Two threadbare couches sat in front of a small television currently displaying *Jerry Springer* in grainy black-and-white. *What was this? The Dark Ages?*

The residents sprawled on the two couches, and the old man at the end kept shouting "You tell 'em, Jerry!" at the television. The other two didn't even flinch, and I took a guess that this was considered normal behavior in these parts. In addition, the room sported two card tables (surrounded by four old men playing cards, one of whom was trailing an IV rack) and a single rocking chair. A blue-haired lady with a hump in her back stood by the rocker, methodically whapping the end of her cane against the thigh of the old man seated there as she mumbled incoherently. (As I circled around, I realized the cause of the mumbling—she'd removed her teeth. The old man just ignored her, eyes glued to the television.)

I leaned closer to Jenny. "Which one is Eddie?"

"DEMONS!"

I jumped, then identified the howler as the same old man who'd been egging Jerry on. Now he was shaking his fist at the television screen. I looked in that direction and had to admit his assessment had some merit. The kid Jerry was interviewing had so many pins and tattoos that he looked like something out of a *Hellraiser* movie.

"THEY'RE EVERYWHERE. IN OUR TELEVI-

SIONS. UNDER OUR BEDS. IN MY RICE KRISPIES. SNAP CRACKLE, THEY SAY. SNAP CRACKLE!" He whipped out a spritzer bottle and took aim, spraying fine mist toward the television, but mostly only dampening Jenny, who was slowly moving toward him.

Laura took a step backward. I grabbed her arm. She'd volunteered, after all. And I wasn't too keen on facing Eddie by myself. (And, yeah, for a second I considered backing out, too. But I'd come to see Eddie, and see him, I would.)

"Hush, now, Mr. Lohmann. We can hear you without shouting." Jenny crouched in front of him as I inched sideways, wanting to get a look at his face.

The man was eighty-five if he was a day, with a grizzled face that seemed as gray as the unkempt bush of hair on his head. His lips had disappeared with age, and the untrimmed gray mustache he sported seemed to float unanchored on his face. His skin was timeworn and leathery, and now that I saw his face, I knew I would have recognized Eddie Lohmann without Jenny's help. This man had fought battles. Fought and won. Now, I wondered if he was fighting his first losing battle.

His chin lifted suddenly, and he peered at me from under droopy lids. I could see enough of his eyes, though, to see the intelligence under there. Eddie Lohmann might be strange, but I'd lay odds he wasn't senile. Not yet.

"Who's that one?" he asked, talking to Jenny, but nodding to me.

"She's here to visit you," Jenny said. "Can't you be nice?"

His nose twitched. "Is she a demon?"

The other residents looked up from their various activities and peered at me. I stood up straighter and fought the urge to adjust my blouse.

Jenny sighed, then rolled her eyes toward me, which pretty much clued me in to what she thought of the whole demon thing. I took heart that his rantings went unheeded. Still, I didn't like the idea that Eddie was spouting off to the residents and staff.

Jenny was still focused on Eddie, her manner calm and patient. "She's not a demon. There aren't any demons, remember? We use holy water in the mop bucket. They can't walk on our floors." This time she gave a wink in my direction.

"Damn dastardly demons," Eddie mumbled. He looked up at me, his eyes eagle sharp as he crooked a bony finger. "You there. Come here."

Behind me, I heard Laura take a few steps backward, her desire to get out of there so thick I could almost feel it. I moved forward slowly, then speeded up the moment one of the other men (who'd stayed quiet during Eddie's entire tirade) shouted at me to quit blocking the television before he took a cane to me. Nice man. Not exactly the grandfatherly type.

I stopped in front of Eddie and let him take a look at me. He fumbled a pair of half-glasses out of a front shirt pocket and put them on. As Jenny backed off, I stood like a statue, waiting for some signal from him.

"I don't know you," he finally said. He pointed a bony finger. "Get thee hence, Satan's harlot!"

I bristled and stifled the urge to defend my reputation. I shot a glance at Laura, and she shrugged. Eddie had returned his attention to the television. I waited for a commercial, then tried again.

"Mr. Lohmann?"

He looked up at me, no recognition at all in his eyes. "Are you a new one they're trying?" His eyes narrowed as he smacked his lips. "You won't get anything from me."

"My name's Kate," I said, trying for soft and reassuring. I gestured across the room to where Laura had faded into a corner. "That's Laura. We came to visit with you."

He kept his attention on me, not even bothering to look

Laura's direction. "Are you one of them?" He seemed grandfatherly, and yet there was an icy edge in his eyes, and I'd noticed that his muscles had tightened as I approached, as if he still had the power to defend himself should I attack.

He crooked his finger again, urging me even closer. I bent down, not at all surprised when his nostrils flared. "My breath okay?" I asked.

He snorted. "Could be faking," he said. Then he reached into his pocket, pulled out his bottle, and sprayed me straight in the face. I sputtered and wiped my eyes, probably rubbing mascara everywhere.

He sat back, obviously satisfied. "You'll do," he said. "Unless you're working for them." He leaned forward, peering at me.

"I'm not," I said, fighting another wave of indignation.

He stared at me for so long, I feared he'd forgotten again and we'd have to start all over. Finally he spoke. "What do you want?"

I glanced around at the other residents. This wasn't exactly the best place. "I was hoping to talk to you. Do you think we could go somewhere?"

He waved at the television, his expression turning surly. "*Jerry Springer.* Five minutes."

I started to argue, realized that would do no good whatsoever, then perched myself on the arm of the couch right next to him. For the next five minutes I watched the wrapup and Jerry's final words (we all need to try to really listen to one another, in case you were wondering). True to his word, as soon as the program ended, Eddie hoisted himself up with the help of an ornately carved cane, then started shuffling toward the back of the room. I followed, silently urging Laura along, and ignoring Eddie's instruction to "Get a move on there, girls."

Since we were moving at glacial speed, it took another five minutes to make it the fifty or so yards to Eddie's room. Once we got there, I closed the door and Eddie sank down into a dingy gray recliner that I have a feeling started out some other color.

"Have we met?" he asked, his eyes unfocused. "Where'd you come from?"

"We just met in there," I said patiently. "I work for *Forza*." I'm not sure what kind of reaction I expected, but I didn't get anything. Not a blink, not a twitch, not even a nervous tic. He just stared at me, then calmly turned toward Laura.

"Her?"

"A friend. Not a Hunter. But she knows."

His fingers inched toward the spritzer now peeking out of his breast pocket, but then he paused. His eyes narrowed as he looked at me. "You vouch for her?"

"With my life," I said.

The fingers moved away, and he clasped his hands in his lap. "She can stay."

I wasn't sure what to say then. I'd come to meet this retired Hunter, but what did I really want from him? Now that I'd met him, my mind was blank and I stood there, feeling a bit like the star of one of those naked dreams—standing unclothed onstage while everyone waited for me to sing an aria or perform magnificent acrobatic feats.

"Did you come to kill them?" he asked. "I would. But the old body just doesn't work right anymore."

"Kill them," I repeated. "Kill who?"

"Demons," he said as the door opened to reveal a nurse decked out in teddy-bear scrubs. "There are demons everywhere."

"Now, Mr. Lohmann," she said, "don't go starting up with that again." She was balancing a tray of lunch dishes, and as I watched, she moved expertly to the table and slid the tray on. "He's a Demon Hunter, you know," she said to me, her voice both conversational and condescending.

"Oh," I said stupidly. "How nice."

The nurse looked up from her tray and winked at me. "Well, we think so. Such an interesting career. And the stories he tells. I mean, really. He's certainly had some adventures."

She crossed the room to Eddie and turned the light on beside his chair. In the harsh illumination he seemed smaller somehow, his features shriveled, as if the light had somehow stolen his energy. "Have you seen any demons today, Eddie?"

"They're everywhere," he said, but his voice lacked the conviction it had earlier with me.

"Well, then, I'd better refill your holy water," she said. "We wouldn't want any getting in here when you aren't looking."

As I watched, she grabbed his little bottle, winked at me, then headed into the bathroom. I heard the water running, then she returned and tucked the bottle back into his pocket. "There you go. That should keep those nasty demons away."

"Good Melinda," he said. "You're the only one here who's good to me."

"Do you do that for him every day?" I asked.

"Oh, sure," she said. "Otherwise, the demons might get him."

"She understands," Eddie says. "Melinda believes me."

"Right now, though, it's time for your medicine." She turned to me. "Are you going to visit much longer? I can wait if you want. The meds make him pretty loopy."

"That's okay," I said. "We were just leaving." Not entirely true, but I did need to get moving.

She shook a handful of multicolored pills out of a tiny paper cup, then handed them to Eddie, who took them without question. He popped the pills dry with one hand, holding out his other arm for the injection that Melinda was administering. As soon as she withdrew the needle, his head lolled back. Almost instantly I could see the tension drain from his body.

"Eddie?"

He looked up at me, but the Eddie Lohmann I'd met in the television room was gone.

"I-don't-know-you," he said, his words slurring together in one big jumble of sound. "Do-I-know-you?"

"We just met," I said gently. "But we'll come back later." It didn't matter what I said. He was already drifting off to sleep.

Laura and I followed Melinda out of the room. "What's with the medicine cabinet?" I asked.

Melinda's cheeks flamed. "Oh, golly," she said. "You heard him. It's demon this and vampire that all the time if we don't load him up with drugs. He went too long today, actually, because he spit out his pills. That's why Dr. Parker ordered the injection." She leaned closer. "It's kinda creepy. I think he really believes all of that."

"No way," I said, trying hard to keep my face straight.

"No, truly," she said. "I don't think he's like dangerous or anything, but—" She cut herself off, her forehead crinkling.

"But what?"

"Actually, maybe he is. Once he totally jumped another resident. And the poor guy had just had a massive coronary the night before. It was a scene. There's Eddie leaping on Sam, and he was going at him with this tongue depressor and trying to shove it into his eye. Took two orderlies and Mrs. Tabor to get him off."

"Wow," I said. "You saw all that?"

"Yeah. Gave me the willies."

"How's Sam?" Laura asked.

"Great," she said. "Can you believe? Two days after a heart attack and he discharged himself. Said he was going to get an apartment in Sun City."

I fought a grimace. Unless I missed my guess, Sam was the codger who'd flown through my window and was now cooling his heels in the county dump. "Sam discharged himself?" I asked. "He could do that?"

"Oh, sure," she said. "The residents here are all voluntary. It's not like they're committed or anything. Most just don't have anyplace else to go or their families can't take care of them. Special needs and all. I mean, like Eddie. What if you took him home and he decided you were a demon or something?" She cocked her head as she looked at me. "You said you're family, right?"

"Absolutely," I said.

"Hard to see a family member spiral down like that," she said. "I really sympathize." She shook her head. "Demons," she said with a snort. "As if."

I dropped Laura back at her house before heading on to the cathedral. We didn't talk. I think both of us were thinking about Eddie, stuck in that nursing home, keeping a watchful eye out for demons in his Rice Krispies.

The thing was, I believed him. (Well, not about the cereal.) Especially after the Sam story, I'd be stupid not to. But what could I do? If any of the old people I'd seen had been inhabited by Goramesh's minions, then we probably didn't have much to worry about in the fate-of-the-world department—none of them had seemed particularly interested in a Hunter's presence on the premises. If anything, they'd seemed more interested in five-card draw and *Jerry Springer*. Not my choice of programming, but hardly demonic.

I was still buried deep in my Eddie thoughts as I pulled open the heavy wooden doors leading into the cathedral. I'd expected silence, but a creaking sound echoed through the room, and as I listened, I recognized it as the sound of a door swinging on rusty hinges. I couldn't see anyone, but I assumed Father Ben was coming out of the sacristy, and I increased my pace to catch up to him. I wanted to get his thoughts on narrowing my search of the records. (Anything to shorten my time in the basement archives!) But as my silent companion stepped out from behind the partition, I stopped cold. Not Father Ben—*Stuart*.

I froze, guilt swelling. He had to be here looking for me. And when he found me without Timmy . . . well, I was going to have to come clean or come up with a fancy fabrication.

Not inclined to do either, I dropped to one knee, my head down as I genuflected. Then I moved into a pew, toed down the kneeler and put my head in my hands, the very image of a pious woman deep in prayer. With any luck, he wouldn't notice me.

His footsteps increased, his tempo hurried, and he headed down the steps off the sanctuary and then down the aisle. After a moment I heard the heavy clunk of the door falling shut behind him.

I stayed in that position. At first my mind was blank, but then I think I sank into prayer, thanking God for not letting Stuart notice me, for keeping my secret safe until I was ready to share it with my family, for keeping me alive despite my—

A hand closed on my shoulder and I screamed, my voice filling the cathedral with as much power as the Sunday morning cantor's did.

"Oh, Kate, I'm so sorry!"

I relaxed, my hand reflexively patting my chest. *Father Ben.* "Father. Sorry. You scared me."

"Please, I should be apologizing. But I wanted to let you know that we'll be closing the cathedral early today and tomorrow, so that the workers can sand the floors. I thought you might want to know so that your time in the archives isn't cut short."

"Thanks," I said. "I do appreciate that." I stood, and he followed suit. "I saw that Stuart was down there," I said, hoping my voice sounded casual. "Was he looking for me?"

"I don't think so. My understanding is he's working on some project of his own."

"Oh." Not the answer I'd expected. And I couldn't

imagine what interest my less-than-devout husband could possibly have in musty old church records. "Do you know what?"

"I'm afraid I don't. He made arrangements with the bishop."

I blinked, getting more and more curious, but I just waved the comment away. "No big deal," I said. "I'll ask him tonight."

We were at the door to the sacristy now, and I tugged it open.

"Since the construction will cut your time short today and tomorrow, would you like for me to arrange access for you Friday evening after the fair?"

"The fair?" I repeated, suddenly feeling like we weren't talking the same language.

"Didn't I see that you were signed up to help with the parish fair on Friday?"

"Oh, right. Of course." *Oops*. I'd completely forgotten. "Yes, if you could keep the archives open late, I'd very much appreciate it." I smiled, hoping I looked charming and helpful as I made a mental note to myself: figure out what I signed up to do at the fair.

I kept Father Ben detained for a few more minutes as I drilled him about the donations' organization. The answer, unfortunately, was that there really was no organization. What I saw was what I got. Which meant I was back to where I'd started. This time, at least, I could try to find some regional connection.

I settled myself at the table, opened the first box (gingerly, in case of more bugs), and dug back into my project. An hour later all I had to show for my efforts was a backache. Okay, that wasn't entirely true. I did learn some things. I found out, for example, that Cecil Curtis was Clark Curtis's father, which meant I was reading documents about Stuart's boss's family. (Which did make the job slightly more interesting. Basic human nosiness, I guess.) As I'd discovered yesterday, he'd left all of his land (and we're talking a *lot* of land) and worldly possessions to the Church, specifically excluding his "spouse or issue," a little fact that I imagine pissed off Clark (not to mention his mom and siblings).

I learned that Thomas Petrie had won a church-sponsored scholarship and had gone to St. Thomas Aquinas College. He ended up being famous for his series of books that revolved around a mystery-solving priest, and after he started to hit the *New York Times* list regularly, he made frequent contributions to the Church. Since the donations weren't monetary (one year he gave a wooden Madonna-and-child statute), I assume he was donating things that he'd acquired researching each of his various books.

I skimmed through the other benefactors, too, but didn't find much of interest. Mike Florence caught my eye simply because of the Italian town, but from what I could tell, he'd donated nothing more interesting than a six-inch-square gold box with a beautiful carved crucifix affixed to the lid. The receipt accompanied the donation, though, and unless Goramesh was on the hunt for a box sold at Macy's in the 1950s, then I doubted I was on the right track. (I'll admit I was a little curious to see the thing, but it was in a container at the bottom of the stack and all the way at the back. That's what we in the archive-reviewing biz call "geographically undesirable.")

With a sigh of resignation, I pushed aside the last item-ized list. My options now were to review every single piece of paper in each donor's file, or start in on the cool stuff in the boxes. Since I doubted I'd recognize what I was looking for if I saw it, the smart thing would be to review letters and correspondence. But I only had a half-hour left in the basement, my eyes hurt, and I was bored.

Besides, something in my gut told me we were running out of time, and at the moment all I could do was put my faith in God (and Larson and Laura). I was in a cathedral after all. If divine inspiration was going to hit, surely I was in the right place.

I pulled over the first box, but didn't haul it up to the table. It weighed a ton. Instead, I kept it by my feet, then toed off the lid, keeping a safe distance in case a flock of beasties came zipping out.

None did, and I peered down, dismayed to see that the box was filled with decaying leather-bound Bibles. Thousands of pages, any of which could have a note inscribed on them. And each Bible began with page after page of family histories scrawled in terrible handwriting that I was going to have to decipher.

Oh, joy.

I pulled the first Bible, fighting a sneeze as I reminded myself why I'd never started a family Bible for my own family—they get old and rotten and decrepit, and then what do you do? If you're the Oliveras family, apparently you donate it to the Church so a slob like me can wade through the pages later. And why not? It's not like you can dump it in the trash can. There's no Thou Shalt Not, but it still seems to me that tossing a Bible would score you some serious demerits on your permanent Record.

I managed to decipher the handwriting on the family-tree portions (nothing interesting), then paged slowly through the book (no handwritten phrases or underlined verses). I paid particular attention to John 11:17, the chapter and verse about Lazarus, but there didn't appear to be any notes in the margin, any tipped-in sheets of paper, any messages scrawled with invisible ink. I even inspected every centimeter of the leather binding, searching for treasure maps hidden in the spine. Nothing. As far as I could tell, this was a family Bible and nothing more.

When I put the Bible aside, it was almost four o'clock. The cathedral was closing, and I needed to get Timmy. Of course, as soon as I stepped into the real world, all my real-world problems lined up behind me. While I'd been in the basement, Eddie and Stuart had been forgotten. Now, though, they were front and center again.

Stuart, I assumed, had a reason for going to the cathedral, and had I not done my impression of the world's most pious Catholic, perhaps he would have noticed me and explained. Since it was stupid to speculate, I forced myself off the subject. Surely he'd tell me tonight. And if he didn't . . . well, then I'd just have to ask.

Eddie was a harder subject. And as I turned into the parking lot at Timmy's school, I still didn't know what to do about him. More, I didn't know why I'd suddenly become obsessed with the idea of doing anything at all.

At the moment, though, Eddie was the least of my problems. Just beyond those doors was a two-year-old who (I hoped) hadn't been scarred for life by his first experience in non-parental child care.

I parked the car and got out, realizing only then how much my stomach was churning. I'd kept my cell phone on all day with no frantic calls from Nadine or Miss Sally. So I knew (hoped) that no horrible accident had befallen my child.

But it wasn't horrible accidents I was worried about. I was terrified of the expression I'd see in his eyes when I picked him up. An expression that said "Where have you been, Mommy, and why did you leave me with strangers?" As a Demon Hunter, I had a great answer to that. As a mom, I couldn't think of a thing to say.

"He did great," Nadine said as I passed the reception desk on my way to the Explorers classroom. I almost stopped and cross-examined her (What is "great"? Are you just saying that to make me feel better? Will my son ever forgive me for dumping him off on you people?), but I fought the urge and soldiered on.

One nice thing KidSpace does is put windows in the doors to all the classrooms. From a mommy perspective, this is a good thing, and I took the opportunity to peer in at my little munchkin. There he was, my little man, playing on the floor with a plastic dump truck, right alongside another little boy, this one pushing a dinosaur in a wheelbarrow.

He was smiling. He was happy. And from my perspective, this was a minor miracle. I'd made a good decision. My sweet little boy wasn't traumatized. He didn't need therapy. He wouldn't run to Oprah in twenty years and rat me out. If anything, he seemed to be having a great time.

Life was good.

I opened the door, held out my arms to him . . . then watched with desperation as Timmy burst into tears.

"Mommamommamomma!" The truck was forgotten as he raced to me. I caught him on the fly and scooped him up, hugging him and patting his back. So much for my rampant lauding of my parental decisions; this was one stressed-out little boy.

"He really did fine today," Miss Sally said as I rubbed circles between his shoulders and murmured nice-sounding words. "This is very normal."

I believed her (well, I sort of believed her), but that didn't lessen the guilt. I shifted Timmy so that I could see his face. "Hey, little man. You ready to go home?"

He nodded, thumb now permanently entrenched in his mouth.

"Did you have fun today?"

Another reluctant nod, but at least it eased my guilt.

"Before you go, though, I need you to sign this form." Miss Sally pushed a clipboard toward me. I shifted Timmy's weight on my hip and squinted at the preprinted page. "Accident Report."

"What happened? Is he hurt?" I looked down at Timmy. "Are you hurt?"

"No, Mommy," he said. "No biting Cody. No. Biting."

My cheeks warmed. "He *bit* someone?"

"Just a little bite," Miss Sally assured me. "The tooth impression has already faded, and he and Cody have been playing together all afternoon."

"He bit hard enough to leave a mark?" I could hear my voice rise, but I was having trouble getting my head around this. My son was a biter? My little boy was a problem child? "But Nadine said he did great."

"Oh, he did. Truly. This isn't that unusual for new students. And it won't be a problem unless it happens again. Or unless Cody's parents complain." She held up a hand. "But they won't. Cody was a biter, too."

There it was. That label. *Biter.* I had a biter.

After a few more minutes of guilt on my part and reassurance on Sally's part, I started to believe that the day really hadn't been a total disaster. In addition to taking a taste of his schoolmate, Timmy had made friends, sang songs, and spent a full hour playing with finger paints. What more could a toddler want?

In the end we trotted down the hall hand-in-hand, and as we reached the door, he lifted his little face, and those big brown eyes sucked me in. "I love you, Mommy," he said, and I melted on the spot. He might be a biter, but he was my baby. "Home, Mommy? We go home?"

"Soon, sport," I said. "We have one more quick errand." I hadn't even realized I'd made up my mind until I said those words, but something about seeing Timmy in the care of others had fueled my decision. I couldn't leave Eddie all alone. In his condition he might accidentally blow the lid off *Forza*, and that was something I simply couldn't let happen.

Plus, I feared that Eddie was right—there were demons walking the halls of Coastal Mists. And any one of those dark creatures would be more than interested to know all the delicious little *Forza* facts that were locked in Eddie's head. Facts that might get Eddie—or me or my family—

killed. Besides, Hunters protected other Hunters. I'd always lived by that code, and even now, retired, I couldn't back away from it.

So Timmy and I were going back to get the man. What I'd do with him once I had him . . . well, that was anybody's guess.

Fifteen

"**He's *who*?**" Stuart's voice, though whispered, seemed to fill the kitchen. I made a frantic pressing motion, as if I were snuffing flames, hoping Eddie hadn't heard.

No such luck.

"I'm your grandfather, sonny," Eddie called from the living room. (At least we knew his hearing worked well.) "Mind your manners there, boy."

As Stuart's eyes widened, I closed my own, counted to ten, then opened them again with the secret wish that everything would be calm and wonderful, all my problems would be solved, and my family (real and fake) would be living in peaceful harmony.

No go.

"Kate . . ." Stuart's voice was calm, but no-nonsense. I sighed, resigned to telling him some version of the truth.

"He was in a nursing home," I said. (Truth.) "And they were keeping him all drugged up." (Also truth.) "Plus, I think he has Alzheimer's." (Sorta truth. I wasn't sure what was wrong with Eddie. All I knew from my brief time with him was that truth and fiction were mixed up in his head, and either one might come spewing out without any warning at all.)

"I sympathize," Stuart said. "But why is he now in our living room? Both my grandfathers have been dead for years. And the man dropping potato chip crumbs onto our living room carpet is very much not dead. Yet."

"Right," I said. "He's not. Dead, I mean."

(Pregnant pause.)

"Kate . . ."

Another sigh from me. I really should have planned this one better. When I'd returned to Coastal Mists, Eddie had been due for another dose of meds. He'd been coherent (more or less) and when I'd explained that I was taking him home with me, I'd expected a bit of a paperwork nightmare. Instead, the whole process had been smooth as silk, as if I were immune to the red tape that normally tied itself around hospitals and the like.

I helped him pack (though since I had Tim with me, the bulk of my help consisted of rescuing his belongings from the fingers of my toddler). Then we started schlepping toward the front desk.

Melinda stopped us on the way out. "Mr. Lohmann," she'd gushed. "You're leaving us?"

He squinted at her, then pointed a wizened finger at me. "She's training the little one to hunt demons," he'd said. "I'm helping."

To which I'd naturally rolled my eyes and—because I'm an idiot—said, "He's coming to live with us."

"Your son must be very excited," Melinda said to Eddie.

"My who?"

Melinda looked at me, clearly confused, which made sense considering I'd earlier given her the long song and dance about how he was related to my husband. In retrospect, I probably should have just let it pass, but since Stuart *does* have a father, and since he is very much alive and coherent, and since I had no idea if Desmond Connor was a close personal friend of the director of Coastal Mists, I announced that Eddie was my first husband's grandfather. No relation to Stuart whatsoever. "Of course I have to take him home with me," I said. "My daughter needs to know her great-grandpa, and I won't be able to sleep knowing I didn't do everything in my power to take care of Eric's grandfather."

Melinda oohed and aahed about how sweet I was, and while I hung my head and tried to look modest and unmartyrlike, Eddie crouched down to Timmy's level. "You can call me Gramps," he said. At which point Tim reached out and yanked Eddie's eyebrow.

"Caterpillar," he said. "Fuzzy caterpillar."

Not being entirely stupid, I figured that was our cue to leave, and we gathered Eddie's things, signed the necessary papers, and headed out the door.

To my relief, Nurse Ratched was nowhere to be seen. I had mental images of her chasing after us, not letting us leave, and hordes of demons descending on us, intent on slaughtering us first, then burying us in the basement. I told myself I was being paranoid, but I knew I really wasn't. I had no doubt that my geriatric demon had been a Coastal Mists resident, and I fully intended to let Larson in on the problem, and he could relay it up the *Forza* chain of command. It wasn't *my* problem, though. My problem was about five-eight, a hundred seventy pounds, with a stubbly gray beard and eyebrows that vaguely resembled caterpillars.

I got both my problems safely into the car. (For those of you keeping track, Eddie was problem number one. Timmy, as a toddler, automatically qualifies as a problem in any situation that involves moving from point A to point B.)

I'd come up with the Eddie-as-grandfather story solely to ease our departure from Coastal Mists, and, frankly, it hadn't occurred to me that Eddie would adopt the story as his own, much less believe it. For that matter, I didn't know if he really *did* believe it. All I knew was that as soon as I got him to the house, he made himself at home (witness the potato chips), tucked Timmy on his lap (who immediately continued his rapt inspection of the eyebrow insects), and told Allie that she looked just like her mother, and was I training her well?

To Allie's credit, she registered less shock at encountering the old man in the living room than I would have expected, and I deflected his questions by sending her upstairs to do homework before dinner. Eddie and I needed to have a talk, that much was for sure.

Unfortunately, Stuart got home before we could have the talk. (In case you're wondering, springing elderly in-laws on unsuspecting spouses—particularly where you're proposing a live-in arrangement of some unknown duration—is not the key to a laid-back evening.)

As usual, Stuart entered through the kitchen, his tie askew and his briefcase weighing heavy in his hand. I could see in his face that all he wanted to do was drop his stuff in his study and change into jeans and a T-shirt. Too bad for him, I wasn't about to let him pass.

I cornered him near the refrigerator. He shot me a "later, honey" look and pushed past. I counted to five. Sure enough, as soon as he rounded the corner and saw Eddie on the couch with Tim, my husband backtracked. "Okay," he said. "Who is he?"

And that, of course, was when I started to regale him with the long-lost-grandfather-in-law story. Never once did I expect Eddie to announce that he was Stuart's grandfather, or for me to gently correct him with, "No, Gramps, *Eric*'s your grandson, remember? Stuart's my second husband."

All of which would have been fine (well, relatively speaking) if Allie hadn't overheard the whole thing. "Daddy's grandpa?" Her tentative whisper sounded from behind me, and I drew in a breath. As I turned around, she moved toward him, then took his gnarled hand in her own. "You're my daddy's grandfather?"

Tears filled my eyes, and as I looked up at Stuart, I saw my own pain reflected there. His parents had been nothing but sweet to Allie, and I know she loved them dearly, but this was blood. A bond with the past that she'd never known existed (in part, of course, because it didn't exist).

I had to tell her the truth, though. Eric and I had both been orphans. We didn't know who our parents were, much less our grandparents. But as I started to take a step toward her, I hesitated. Allie's eyes were bright, her cheeks pink, and when Eddie (who must have been quite the charmer in his day) told her she had her father's eyes, I swear, she melted a little.

This was a lie, yes. But was it really so bad? Allie craved a heritage, after all, and that wasn't something I ever thought I could give her. Somehow, though, I'd managed. I'd brought home a family history. So what if it was an illusion?

Besides, how did I know that Eddie wasn't really Eric's grandfather? Stranger things had happened. I know. They happened to me all the time.

With Allie and Eddie safely (I hoped) ensconced in the living room, Stuart decided it was time to recommence his interrogation of me. "Once again," he said, "how long is Gramps there going to be our houseguest? And why can't he stay at a hotel?"

"Long story," I said, then added a *shhhh*. "Do you want Allie to hear?" This is what's known as a diversionary tactic.

"Don't change the subject on me," he said. (As a lawyer, Stuart's pretty adept at picking up on the nuances of diversion. Too bad for me.)

I made a show of sighing. "I tried to call you," I said. "Just after lunchtime. Your secretary said you'd stepped out." This was where I expected him to take the opening and explain to me why he'd gone to the cathedral.

"Did you try my cell phone?"

"Um, no," I said. That wasn't the comment I'd expected, although his answer did remind me that I had a nicely wrapped phone in the trunk with Allie's name on it. First things first, though, and I came up with a reasonable-sounding fib. "My phone was dead." I knew Stuart would understand. I didn't bother to memorize numbers—I just kept them programmed in my phone. If mine had no juice, there was no way I could call Stuart or anyone else. I figure I'm doing good on any given day to keep track of all my kids' various appointments. Adding the memorization of phone numbers would be cruel and unusual.

"Late lunch," he said. "I met with some members of the zoning commission about a project, and some of them seemed amenable to talking politics—"

"And so you did," I said. I lifted myself up on my toes and kissed his cheek. "Darling Stuart. Always campaigning." My voice might be cheery, but my insides were churning. Not only had my husband *not* volunteered his business at the church, he'd flat out *lied* to me about where he'd been.

I didn't know what that meant.

But I knew that I sure as hell didn't like it.

I spent the next two hours feeding my expanded-by-one family and pondering my own hypocrisy. By the time the meat loaf was gone and the string beans devoured (or, in Timmy's case, mushed into tiny pieces and methodically dropped on the floor), I'd decided that while I had a Get Out of Jail Free card for my lying, my husband did not.

This conclusion, of course, only made me more frustrated.

Stuart wasn't volunteering any information, and my

very subtle hints to extract some ("Why don't you join us for Mass on Sunday, sweetie? You really should go to the cathedral every week") had failed miserably. I should have just asked him outright, but something in the pit of my stomach told me I wouldn't like the answer.

Eddie ate nothing but mashed potatoes, while Allie snarfed down her food and then spent the rest of the meal staring at her newly acquired relative. At one point Eddie leaned over and pinched her upper arm. As Allie squealed, Eddie grunted with satisfaction. "This one can whack a demon. Mark my words. She's a spitfire." He smacked his lips, his eyes focused somewhere over my shoulder. "I knew a spitfire once. Reminds me of our Allie. Long brown hair. Lethal hands. And legs that could drive a man to—"

"*Eddie.*"

He snorted, but shut up. Allie, of course, looked both pleased and curious.

Great.

"Demons?" Stuart said. "What are you talking about?"

"Eddie used to be a cop," I said, lying now coming almost naturally. "He and his friends called the bad guys demons."

"Demons *are* the bad guys," Eddie said. "And believe you me, I've known some bad ones in my time, that's for sure."

I opened my mouth to get a word in, but Eddie rambled on.

"Vile things. And the stench? *Hoo-boy . . .*" He made a waving motion as if to dispel the odor.

Stuart turned to me and mouthed (not very subtly, either) *How long?*

I punted, focusing on Eddie. "You're not on the *force* anymore, Gramps," I said. "And Allie certainly isn't."

Eddie peered at me, his eyes narrow, a smear of mashed potatoes beside his mouth. "Who are you? Where am I? WHERE'S MY HOLY WATER?"

Allie's eyes widened, and I aimed a gentle smile in her direction. "Gramps is getting old, sweetie. Sometimes he loses touch."

"A cop, huh?" Stuart said, clearly trying to lighten the mood.

Allie looked from Eddie to me and back again, worry etched on her face. Finally she drew in a breath. "I could be a cop," she said, in a small voice. "That's cool. And tomorrow Cutter's going to show me how to toss guys over my shoulder." She was gathering steam, her initial trepidation fading. "Right, Mom?"

"Absolutely," I said. Then, in case that just spurred Eddie on, I added, "Self-defense class," for clarification.

Eddie reached over and patted Allie's hand. "You'll knock 'em dead, little girl." And when he flashed a tobacco-stained grin, I couldn't help but cringe. If I had my way, Allie wouldn't ever knock anything dead. And nothing dead would ever knock her, either.

But Eddie's comment had been good, nonetheless, because I could see the discomfort drain away from Allie. She even scooted her chair a little closer. "Did you ever toss anyone over *your* shoulder, Gramps?"

He waved his hand (which, unfortunately, held a forkful of potatoes). "All the time," he said. "Every single day."

I almost called a stop to the conversation, but in the end I decided it was harmless enough. I concentrated on feeding Timmy, half-listening to Eddie and Allie's fast-track bonding experience. They were in their own little world, Stuart and Timmy and me all but forgotten as Eddie offered Allie all sorts of tips for tossing those pesky bad guys over her shoulder.

Stuart shot me a *you-got-us-into-this* look, but I just smiled and pretended like this was the most normal thing in the world. After dinner, while Eddie supervised Allie's clearing of the table, Stuart took my elbow and steered me into his study.

"You still haven't answered me. Why?" he asked. "And how long?"

I couldn't tell him the real truth—*I think he knows something about Goramesh, and I can't risk the demons deciding to kill him off*—and so I told another one. "Because I had to. They were keeping him all drugged up. I couldn't let him go on living like that." As for the other question—*how long?*—for that, I had no answer.

Stuart studied my face for a while, then he reached out and pressed a palm to each of my cheeks, gently turning my face up until I was looking into his eyes. "It means that much to you?"

I nodded, blinking a bit, as tears stung my eyes.

"Okay, then. We'll try and find someplace better suited. In the meantime he can stay here." He turned, glancing toward the general direction of the kitchen. I knew he was thinking of Allie, and my heart melted just a little. I might not know what Stuart had been doing in the cathedral earlier, but I did know that he loved his family.

"Thanks," I whispered.

"You don't have to thank me," he said. "We're a team. I trust your decisions. I just wish I'd known before I came home and found him sprawled on the couch."

"Right," I said. "Sure. Sorry." (At this point you might think I'd tell him about Timmy. The whole "we're a team" speech and all. But did I? No, I didn't. Enrolling his son in day care was going to elicit a much more vigorous response than dragging home old Demon Hunters. And, quite honestly, I just wasn't up for it. Not right then. But I resolved to tell him tomorrow. Or, at the very least, the day after. And maybe by the time I finally got around to confessing, the Goramesh problem would be solved and Kid-Space and I could go our separate ways. I could dream, couldn't I?)

We headed back toward the kitchen, with me hurrying more than Stuart. (I didn't really expect Eddie to say anything too revealing, and even if he did, I knew Allie wouldn't believe him, but I wanted to be around just in case.) Stuart pulled the door open, then flashed me a grin. "I'm glad you signed Allie up for the self-defense classes," he said. "I like knowing she'll be able to protect herself against the demons."

I froze, my mouth hanging open.

But Stuart just winked at me, then shook his head. "Demons," he muttered, his voice tainted with mirth. "I'll say this much for the guy—he's got one hell of an imagination."

"So he really said Eddie could stay?" Laura asked. She was leaning up against the bathroom counter while I sat on the closed toilet seat, my fingers deep in the pile of suds on Timmy's head.

"Bubbles, Momma. Want more bubbles."

"Hold on a sec, sport," I said to Timmy. To Laura, I said, "That's what he said. For now at least."

"And day care? He was cool with that?"

I concentrated on forming a mohawk out of Timmy's lathered hair. Laura, no dummy, leaned back and let out a low whistle. "You're living dangerously."

I shot her a quick glance over my shoulder. "On more than one count."

"Yeah. No kidding. Seen any demons lately?"

"I'm a little curious about Nurse Ratched at the home, but if you mean did any sail through my windows today, then no."

"What are you going to do? Go back and clean out the demons?"

I shook my head, my attention focused on Tim, who was singing "rubber ducky, you're the one" at the top of his lungs. "No," I said. "I got into this for one reason only. I'll do what I can to stop Goramesh, and I'll tell Larson so he can pass it up the food chain, but after that, I'm out of the demon biz." I got out a washcloth and lathered my boy up. "They'll find another Hunter," I said. "They have to. I already have this life, and I'm not giving it up."

I heard Laura moving behind me, adjusting things on the bathroom counter. "Did you find anything in the archives today?"

I gave her the CliffsNotes version, finishing with, "Not much to work with, huh?"

"Not from the demon end, but it rates high on the gossip meter."

By this time I was toweling Timmy off, and I scooped his damp little body up and headed for his room. "Clark Curtis, you mean?" I plunked Timmy on the changing table, then crouched down to fish a diaper out of the bottom drawer.

"Yup. Wild, huh? There were all these rumors a while back that he was going to quit and run for state senate. But then he never did and he just kept running in the local elections."

I shrugged. "That's wild?" I'd expected something juicy. Gossip, in my opinion, needs a little more *oomph*.

"Sure. His father said over and over again how Clark was going to inherit his entire fortune, and then he goes and leaves everything to the Church? That's the stuff of soap operas."

"True," I said. I'd had a similar thought myself. "But he seems perfectly content now," I added. After all, he was doing the political thing and seemed to be making a success of it.

"Hmmm." Laura leaned back against the counter, and I went back to my kid's bottom. The rest of the house was pretty quiet. Stuart was in his study, and Allie and Mindy were camped out at the kitchen table doing homework. My family wasn't my worry, though. I had things to do tomorrow, and I couldn't do them with an eighty-five-year-old shadow.

"Laura," I began, a wheedling tone to my voice.

"Oh, boy," she said. "Here it comes."

"Remember how you'd agreed to watch Timmy for two days? And remember how I took him to KidSpace today, so you only had to watch him for one?"

She crossed her arms over her chest and lifted one eyebrow. "Yeah?"

"Well, I was wondering if I could call in that marker."

"I'm guessing we're not talking a two-year-old."

"About forty times that," I said.

"Eddie."

"Eddie," I confirmed, trying to coax Timmy's kicking feet into a pair of pajama bottoms. "I can't leave him alone here."

Laura took pity on me and dangled a toy over Tim's head. He quit kicking and grabbed for it. "So you want what?"

"You were going to spend tomorrow bouncing around on the Internet, right? Can you do that from here? Set up my laptop at the kitchen table?"

"I *could* do that here," she said. "What exactly do I get out of the deal again?"

I ensnared Timmy in a Bob the Builder pajama top and got it pulled over his head before he had time to howl. "My love and admiration," I said to Laura. "Plus a lifetime of free desserts."

"Sold," she said. "But if he sprays me with holy water, you're going to hear about it."

I lifted Timmy to the ground, then patted his rump. He headed for the living room and story time on the couch. Laura and I followed behind. "Poor guy, believing he had holy water, and all along the nurses were just giving him tap water." Her brow furrowed. "Do you think the nurses were just appeasing an old man? Or do you think they're demons, too?"

Her words hit me with the force of a slap, and I stifled

an urge to thwap the heel of my hand against my forehead. I grabbed her arm and tugged her back toward Timmy's room, all the while hollering down the stairs for Allie to entertain her brother until I got there.

In the room I pulled the door shut. I was almost bouncing with excitement, and I saw my own energy reflected in Laura's face. "What?" she said. "What have you thought of?"

"The nurses aren't demons," I said. "They're pets. Or some of them are."

"Pets," she repeated. "As in Fluffy and Fido?"

"Sort of," I said. "But not really."

"Kate. I'm going to grow old here. . . ."

"Right. Sorry." I ran my hands through my hair and started pacing Timmy's room. "I should have realized this before. We don't just need to be looking for Goramesh's mysterious thing. We need to look for whoever's going to be trying to get it for him."

Laura blinked, and I realized I was going way too fast for her.

"Okay," I said, "here's the deal. Demons use humans. They can inhabit us when we die or they can possess us when we live or they can even move in and share space with us while we're alive."

"Eww!"

"I know. Time-sharing with a demon. Very yuck." I waved my hand, pushing all those little educational tidbits away. "That's not the point. The point is that demons don't always take over humans. Sometimes they'll just recruit people to do their dirty work."

"Why?" she asked.

"Lots of reasons. Maybe they want a relic from a church to use in some gross demonic ritual."

"So they'll send a human to steal it?"

"Exactly," I said. "And I'm betting that the people at the

nursing home—most of them, at least—are just human. Most probably don't even know there's anything weird going on. But the others—"

"Like Nurse Ratched."

I nodded. "—the others are the demons' minions."

She looked positively grossed out. "Why?"

I shrugged. "Who knows? The lure of power? Immortality? Demons lie. The bait could be anything. The point is they do things for the demons. Things the demons can't or won't do."

"But—" I saw it in her face the moment she made the connection. "Oh! So you're saying Goramesh must have someone who's going to schlep into the cathedral and get whatever this thing is that we're looking for."

"Exactly."

"Any ideas?"

"Nope." I frowned. "Well, not a legitimate one anyway."

"I'll settle for illegitimate," she said.

At the moment, frankly, so would I. With nothing concrete to go on, though, conjecture seemed good enough. I hated to even voice the suspicion. I drew a breath. "I was just thinking about Clark. If he *really* was expecting to inherit everything, but his father gave everything to the Church instead . . ." I trailed off, certain Laura would get my drift.

She didn't disappoint. "And you know what they say about politicians—they'd sell their soul for a vote." As soon as the words passed her lips, she gasped, then squeezed her eyes shut, obviously mortified. "Oh, shit, Kate. I didn't mean—"

I shook my head, holding up a hand to ward off her words. The make-it-all-better mom in me wanted to pat her on the shoulder and tell her it was okay. I didn't, though. Instead, I just stood there, her comment about politicians setting my thoughts to humming.

Stuart. The car accident he'd survived. His sudden and

absolute certainty he'd win the election. And the mysterious trip to the cathedral archives.

I fought a shiver and closed my eyes. This couldn't be happening. My husband couldn't be in league with a demon.

Could he?

Sixteen

"It's possible, Kate," Larson said. "I hate to say it, but it is very possible."

I'd arrived at Larson's office a few minutes before eight, wanting to catch him before he took the bench. I'd called and canceled with Cutter, telling him I'd see him this evening with the girls. Now, though, I was almost sorry I'd come. Although Larson was saying words I'd expected, they were still words I didn't want to hear.

"But Stuart? He's hardly even religious. He only goes to Mass when I prod him."

"Is that supposed to be an argument *against* consorting with demons?" he asked. I frowned, but Larson continued. "You're the one who pointed out his quick recovery from the car accident."

"No. No way." I shook my head so hard I almost wrenched my neck. "I was just tilting at windmills, wasn't thinking clearly." I rubbed my head, trying to ward off a massive migraine. "And besides, I saw him in the church *af-*

ter the accident. He didn't die. He was barely even injured."

"Perhaps the injury was minor, but the impact more than you realize. A man can change his thinking when faced with his own mortality."

"A deal with the Devil? *Stuart?* I don't think so."

"Your husband is an ambitious man, Kate. If he thinks that Goramesh can help him . . ." He trailed off, leaving me to draw my own conclusions.

I didn't like the conclusions that were slipping into my head despite all my efforts to keep them out.

"Watch him, Kate. But if the time comes, you must stop him. It's imperative we discover what Goramesh is searching for, and that we get it safely to the Vatican. If Stuart were to get to it first—"

"You're talking as if we're sure he's involved." My heart seemed to tighten in my chest.

"Until we know for sure that he isn't, we have to assume as much."

The bailiff poked his head in then, checking to make sure Larson was ready to take the bench. He left to go work, and I left to . . . what? Sulk? Worry?

No, as much as I wanted to do all of that, I had those damn responsibilities.

I got in my car and headed for the cathedral.

My cell phone rang as I was parking the car, and when I checked the caller ID, I saw that the call was coming from my house. Had Allie missed her ride? Had Eddie come out of his funk? Had Stuart come home? Was he looking for me? Did he know I was on to him? For that matter, was there anything to be on to, or was I just being paranoid, and Larson along with me?

I waited another ring and then pushed the talk button. "Hello?"

"Hey, it's me." Laura's voice. (She would have been my next guess.)

"Do you have news?"

"You-know-who is driving me *nuts*," she said, her voice just a hair above a whisper.

I cringed. "Sorry about that. What's he doing?"

"Hovering," she said. "He's in watching television right now. He just keeps circling me and looking over my shoulder, and then he'll mumble something about demons and go change the channel. It's freaky, Kate."

"Sorry," I said again, uselessly. "Do you want me to come home?"

"No, no. I'll be fine. Did you talk to him before you left this morning?"

"He was still asleep. How's he look?"

"Better, actually. He's driving me nuts, but he's not spouting off as much. I can't put my finger on it, but I think he's clearer."

"Good." Better than good, actually. I needed Eddie not to be nuts. Especially if Larson's (okay, *my*) suspicions about Stuart were true, I couldn't afford to have Eddie revealing secrets. (That train of thought prompted another round of guilt. How could I think that about Stuart? My husband. Timmy's father. The man I'd vowed to love, honor, and cherish. He wasn't *that* ambitious. Was he? *Was he?*)

I drew in a breath and tried to get off that line of thinking. "Was that why you called? To report about Eddie?"

"Nope. Two things. Do you want the good news or the bad news?"

"Oh, please. The good news."

"I found out that Brother Michael used to live at a monastery just outside of Mexico City. And guess what?"

"It's the one that was recently ravaged by demons?" This was good news.

"Yup." I could hear the excitement in her voice. "So that's a connection, right?"

"It's great," I said. I kept my voice enthusiastic, but in

reality, I wasn't sure where to go from there. We already knew there was a connection. This confirmed it, but didn't really add anything new. I wasn't about to burst Laura's bubble, though. "So what's the bad news?"

"You're hosting a playdate. Here. At three—"

"*Shit*." I'd totally forgotten. I *always* check my calendar. Always, always, *always*. Except today.

Damn, what was I thinking? (Actually, I knew the answer to that one. I was thinking about demons, and the possibility that my husband, who I thought I knew so well, had hooked up with one. In the grand scheme of things, I suppose I had an excuse for forgetting a four-child playdate at which I was supposed to provide snacks, but that didn't make me feel a whole lot better.)

"Did I screw up? Should I have canceled for you?"

"No, no. It's my fault. I should have canceled days ago. I just forgot all about it." I wondered vaguely what else I'd forgotten about, but decided it didn't matter. Obviously, all my various obligations would eventually come and knock on my door.

We chatted a few more minutes, and I decided I'd hit the archives for a couple of hours, then the grocery store (cupcakes, Teddy Grahams, fruit, and juice boxes). After that, I'd pick up Timmy and head home. Laura promised to hang around, just in case Eddie decided to slip back into demon paranoia and scare all the kids (or the parents) to death.

As soon as I hit the button to end the call, it rang again. I clicked back on, expecting Laura. "Did you forget something?"

"Nope," Allie said. "This is so amazingly cool, Mom!"

I chuckled. When I'd given her the cell phone, I'd told her it was for emergencies only. But I should have known she couldn't resist one or two calls.

"I'm glad you approve," I said. "But what's the emergency?"

"Huh?"

"Are you supposed to be using the phone without danger to life or limb?"

"Oops."

I should have said something then, but I was too busy trying not to laugh.

"Well, I do sort of have an emergency."

Considering the way my week was going, you'd think I would have tensed at that statement. But I knew my kid well. This emergency was no emergency. This emergency was an excuse to tread the wireless airwaves. "Okay," I said. "I'll bite. What's the emergency?"

"Can me and Mindy go to the mall after school? Please, oh please, oh please?"

"You're kidding, right?"

"No, Mom. *Please?*"

"Alison Crowe, do you even remember our deal?"

(Long silence.)

"Allie . . ."

"Um, what deal is that?"

Would it not have been so painful, I would have beat my head against the steering wheel. "Our deal that self-defense class comes first, and anything else you may have planned gets bumped."

"Oh. *That* deal."

"Mmmm."

"We could go after . . ." That in a small, tentative voice.

I felt myself caving and struggled to remain strong. "What's so important at the mall tonight?"

(Another long silence. This time, I had a feeling I knew why. Boys.)

"Allie . . . ?"

"Stan's gonna be working tonight. We just want to say hi. Maybe have a Coke during his break."

"We?"

"Mindy and me."

I shook my head wearily. Only fourteen, and already

my daughter was tag-teaming boys. Oh, well. At least she wasn't sneaking off by herself. (For that matter, at least she wasn't pregnant. *That* was a boy-girl-adolescent reality I really didn't want to contemplate.)

"Is this the theater concession guy?" If so, I was going to have to say no. He might be a perfectly nice guy, but he had smelly breath, and that made him off limits until I was absolutely sure that it was just halitosis and not rampant demon stench.

"Oh, *Mom.* That's Billy, and he's so not the bomb."

I presumed that meant he wasn't her type. "So who is the guy?"

"He works at The Gap, and he's *so* hot. Please, Mom. *Please?* He asked me specifically if I was going to be there. He *likes* me, Mom."

"Is he a freshman, too?"

Another one of those pauses.

"Allie, believe it or not I have things to do today. Is he in your class?"

"I think he's a senior," she said.

"You think?"

"Well, I've only met him after school, but he hangs with the seniors, and if he likes me, then *I* can hang with them, too, and oh, Mom, you're not going to say no, are you?"

She was talking so fast, I had to slow her words down in my head and replay them. I didn't like the sound of this, but neither did I see an easy out. Parenting is a bit like walking a tightrope. Too little control and you fall right off. Too much, and you overcompensate and can't move at all.

"Fine," I finally said. "You can go. But I'm coming, too."

I expected to hear a *Mo-om*, followed by another protest. Instead, she just sighed, then said, "Okay. Whatever. Thanks."

I smiled, victorious. "Love you, sweetie. And shouldn't you be in class?"

"First period's study hall," she said.

"Then go study something. And don't make any more phone calls unless there's blood or serious bodily injury."

"Whatever, Mom," she said, then hung up.

I glanced at the phone, the full import of what I'd just done settling in. I'd just agreed to spend an evening at the mall.

I think demons would be easier.

Since I didn't have much time in the archives (what with the forgotten playdate), I decided to take a different approach. I figured it was a (relatively) safe bet that Goramesh wasn't looking for papers. And, frankly, I was bored reading them.

Instead, I went through boxes one by one, pulling off each lid, and then moving to the next box if that one held only paper. I probably should have done this from the get-go, but I'd assumed that anything Goramesh might want would have been pulled for the archivist, and my best bet was to scour the paperwork looking for a clue. I hadn't changed my mind about that, but the thought of reviewing more musty paper really didn't appeal to me. I justified my diversion by telling myself that I might get lucky.

As it turned out, I did find some cool things, but nothing that jumped out as demon-worthy. I even found the carton with the little gold box that Mike Florence had donated to the Church. When I'd originally read the description on the IRS list, I'd been keen to look at it, but now that I held it, I wasn't as impressed. When I opened it, I was even less excited. All I found was something that looked like ash. Some weird kind of urn, maybe?

I continued with this extremely scintillating task for another hour. (This weekend I was begging access from Father Ben, and I *was* going to make Larson come down here with me. Fair is fair.) Then, discouraged, I gathered my things. I paused for a minute in front of the archive cases, thinking how much easier it would be if everything in the basement archive was nice and clean and in lighted glass cases. But it wasn't. Oh, well. At least I had it better than those martyrs, now hanging out in their cloth pouches.

Thinking about the martyrs steeled me. *I* wasn't about to end up defeated. Goramesh was not going to win. I was going to stop him. Somehow, I was going to bring this to a close.

Reinvigorated, I headed to the rectory and tracked down Father Ben. I was hoping he'd tell me that Clark had been skulking around the archives as well. But no, apparently the only ones interested in the basement lately were me and Stuart.

This didn't bode well. Not for my plans to defeat Goramesh.

And, more important, it didn't look good for my marriage.

As a Demon Hunter, I've been exposed to some pretty exhausting situations. Days without sleep while I staked out a demon nest. Chasing after vamps down winding alleys in Budapest. All the usual stuff. But I'm here to tell you that none of that compares with the exhaustion and chaos of a playdate for four rambunctious two-year-olds.

An hour in, and the kids finally settled down ("settling down" being defined as "corralled in the den with enough toys to fill a Wal-Mart") and the other moms and I gathered around the kitchen table with coffee and the last few cupcakes that hadn't been poked and prodded by sticky toddler fingers.

I'd just taken my first sip of coffee and was reveling in the normalcy of it all when Timmy's familiar howl echoed from the den. I was on my feet in seconds, my first thought of demons dispelled the moment I entered the room.

There stood my little boy, arms akimbo, head tossed back, mouth wide open. And right beside him, little Danielle Cartright clutched Boo Bear and was grinning like a fiend.

(I'm not big on criticizing kids, but Danielle is a pain in the patoot, and I feel sorry for whatever man she grows up and marries. I blame her mom, of course, and I do feel sorry for her dad. At the moment, though, I just felt sorry for Timmy.)

"Danielle," I said, since her mother was noticeably silent, "why don't you give Timmy back his bear, please."

"NO!" Not only did she scream the response, she ran to the far side of the room, climbed into a chair, and sat on the bear. What a little charmer.

Her mother, Marissa, came up behind me. "She's in a grabby stage," she said, as if this would entirely solve the problem and dry my kid's tears.

"Maybe you could ungrab her," I said, trying very hard not to scream myself. Of course, I did have to scream a little, because Timmy's howls had increased to an eardrum-bursting decibel level, and he'd raced my way. I scooped him up, but even Mommy's presence couldn't stop the tears from flowing.

"He really shouldn't be so attached to a toy," Marissa said.

I bristled, muscles tensing as I imagined her fresh linen suit with a big old footprint about chest level. A hand closed over my shoulder, and a soft, "Hey, Timmy. Calm down, okay?"

Laura. She and Eddie had been on the computer in Stuart's study, and she must have heard the commotion. Me being no dummy, I knew that the "calm down" comment was meant as much for me as it was for Timmy.

"We're calm," I said, aiming a *get-the-bear-back-or-die-you-bitch* smile toward Marissa.

"Let me see if I can convince Danielle that she should give the bear back," Marissa said, apparently sensing danger.

"Great idea," I said.

I then watched in fascinated horror as she spent *fifteen minutes* trying to negotiate with her two-year-old. The end result? No bear.

Play group was officially over by now, and the other

moms (probably smelling blood) said their good-byes and rushed their offspring out. Marissa didn't seem to clue in on either the inconvenience or my irritation. She was, however, still crouched in front of her kid trying gamely to recover Boo Bear. By this time Timmy had cried himself out, and I settled him on the sofa, promising that Boo Bear was just visiting Danielle and would return to him soon.

I wanted to shove Marissa out of the way and tear the bear from Danielle's hot little hands, but I knew that wasn't the Emily Post–approved solution. And so I waited, my fury with Marissa building as she wheedled and needled and generally trained her daughter to grow up to be a selfish little twit (poor kid). Finally, after a period of time resembling the length of your average ice age, Marissa promised the girl ice cream *and* a new toy *and* a pony ride at the zoo. After which, Danielle climbed out of her chair and, just as pretty as you please, marched over to Timmy and shoved Boo Bear in his face.

"Thank you," Timmy said (and *he* said it without prompting, not that she deserved to be thanked).

I played polite hostess all the way to the door, but the second I closed and locked it, I turned to Laura. "That woman is a—"

"You can't kill her."

"If she were a demon, I could." And boy, did I wish she were.

"She's not a demon."

I glanced back to where Timmy was sitting, curled on the couch, thumb in his mouth, a forlorn expression drawn across his face. My heart twisted in my chest. "She is to me," I said. "She sure as hell is to me."

The girls may have gone upstairs together, but only Allie came down dressed to work out. Mindy was still in her school clothes, and both Laura and I examined her quizzically. "Going for the realistic approach?" I asked. "You're more likely to get mugged in your street clothes, but I think you'll learn better in shorts and a T-shirt."

Mindy became suddenly fascinated with my carpeting. "I'm not sure I want to go."

"Not go?" Laura said. "What do you mean you're not going to go?"

Mindy shrugged, her eyes wide, obviously not understanding her mother's sudden fascination with the wonderful world of kickboxing.

Allie had sidled over toward me, and I raised an inquisitive eyebrow. "She's scared of looking stupid in front of Cutter," Allie whispered. "She thinks he's cute."

"Mindy Jo Dupont." Laura prompted. "Kate put a lot of effort into getting you signed up for this class. Now, why don't you want to go?"

"I just have so much homework." She shoved her hands in her pockets. "You know."

"What I know, young lady, is that there are all kinds of creeps and weirdos out there in the world." Laura spoke with a force I barely recognized, but I knew its source well enough. I'd tainted her safe little world. And that was something I could never change back.

"You're going to class and you're going to learn how to defend yourself." She turned around to look at me, her face glowing from her maternal power trip. "In fact, if there's room in the class, I think I'll join you."

Mindy and Allie didn't even attempt to hide their amazement. For my part, I wasn't so much amazed as surprised. I'd been firmly of the belief that neither hell nor high water would get Laura to anything remotely resembling an exercise class.

Apparently I'd been wrong about the hell part of the equation.

"I'm impressed," I whispered to her later as the girls clambered into the van. "You. Exercising. In public."

She made a face. "You laugh, but I know the score. It's always the comic relief who gets nailed. I've seen enough movies to know that." She adjusted her purse on her shoulder. "And this is one sidekick who isn't going down without a fight."

"Good going there, girlie!" From the sidelines, Eddie cheered Allie on. Beside him, Timmy was turning somersaults on a mat Cutter had spread out for him.

After warming up, Cutter had moved on to the nitty-gritty, showing the class how to break free if someone grabs your wrist. Allie managed the maneuver (pulling your arm up and away so that you take advantage of the attacker's thumb, the weakest link) and I was applauding wildly as well.

"Now let's try your mom," Cutter said.

I shook my head. He was baiting me, but I wasn't about to fall for it. As much as I wanted to hit someone (thank you, Marissa), as far as Allie was concerned, I was a novice here, too.

Cutter caught me from behind and I pushed off, using a stance and a move that—had I done it right—would have tossed him over my shoulder and landed him on the mat. Not so today.

"Come on, Mom! You nailed him last time."

"Beginner's luck," I said as Cutter wrestled me down to the mat.

"Beginner's luck, my ass," Cutter said. "I'm going to figure this out, you know."

He spoke in a whisper, and I answered the same way. "Not unless I want you to, you won't."

From his grimace, I knew he believed me. "Focus on the girls and Laura," I said. "I can take care of myself."

To his credit, he did (with Eddie shouting encouragement from the sidelines, including the occasional "Oh, yeah, *that* one'll make one hell of a Hunter"). Fortunately,

Allie was too busy sweating to concentrate on Eddie's bizarre comments. Either that, or she'd learned to take him in stride.

By the end of the hour I thought the girls had a pretty good start. At the very least they'd each gotten the yell down. (Which, actually, is a key component of any self-defense move. The yell strengthens your abs and puts more force behind the kick. It's all about the abs, you know.)

After the lesson the girls were bouncy and glowing (girls glow, boys sweat), chattering on about how cool Cutter was, and how cool they were, and how they'd beat the crap out of anyone who messed with them. Another mom might think this was a bad thing. I was all for it.

Because the glow really was sweat, we had to head home before going to the mall so the girls could shower and primp. Usually the dressing to meet a boy process takes upward of two hours, but since we were working under a deadline here (the mall closes at nine on weekdays), the girls allotted themselves an unheard-of thirty minutes.

Laura and Mindy crossed the yard to their house, and while Timmy watched a *Blue's Clues* video, I waited with Eddie in the kitchen for Allie to come back downstairs. Eddie's outbursts had slowed down, and he seemed less fuzzy. I'd been wanting to ask him questions—What exactly was going on at Coastal Mists? Did he have any expertise on Goramesh? Did he have any clue as to what Goramesh was looking for?—but this was the first time we'd really had any privacy.

I puttered around making tea, trying to figure out the best way to start the conversation.

"Earl Grey," Eddie said. "None of that sissy herbal tea for me."

"No problem."

"Don't know why anyone drinks that stuff," he said, muttering to the tabletop. "Damn pansy-ass drink." He looked up at me. "What are you drinking?"

"Nothing pansy-assed, that's for sure."

"Hmmph." His eyes narrowed, the bushy eyebrows drawing down to form a V over his nose. "No pansy drink, but you got a pansy-ass life."

I started. "Excuse me?"

"You told me you were a Hunter. You're no Hunter. Family. House. All the trappings." He spoke as if that were a bad thing. "I thought it all might be a façade—that you might be training the girl—but no, you're out of the game."

"I'm retired, thank you very much."

He snorted. "Like I said. Pansy-ass."

"Watch it, Lohmann," I said. "I can drive you back to Coastal Mists just as fast as I got you out of there."

He snorted. "You wouldn't."

"Don't tempt me," I said, but there wasn't a lot of force behind my words.

"So why's a retired Hunter looking for me?" He waggled his eyebrows shamelessly. "A little noogie?"

I laughed, my irritation with him fading. "You're a lot of things, Eddie, but boring, you're not."

He adjusted his glasses on his nose, then leaned back in his chair. "Story time, girlie. What are you doing back in the game?"

As openings went, I couldn't really expect much better, and I gave him the rundown, starting with Wal-Mart and moving more or less chronologically to the present. "Any ideas?" I asked after I finished. Above us, the shower had stopped. I'd talked fast, but not that fast. Any minute Allie might magically appear beside us. I hoped he had some answers. Even more, I hoped they were quick.

"Ideas . . ." He trailed off, smacking his lips. "Nope. Not a single idea."

I deflated a bit. I'd been hoping so hard. But at least that answer was quick. "That's okay. It was worth a shot."

He snorted again. "Got ants in your pants, girl? I'm not

finished. I said I don't have an idea, but I don't need one, either. Nope. I don't need ideas because I already know exactly what that damn demon wants."

He shut up, then, and took a sip of his tea.

I wanted to smack the china cup right out of his hand. "What?" I hissed, frantic for answers. "If you know, for God's sake, tell me!"

"The Lazarus Bones," he said, as if that were the only possible answer.

I just looked at him and blinked. What the hell were the Lazarus Bones?

Naturally I didn't have time to ask before Laura and Mindy reappeared. I considered steering Eddie into Stuart's study, closing the door, and demanding answers. But that would have left me open to severe bodily harm by the girls, who were desperate to get to the mall before they missed Stan's break.

Fine. Whatever.

I left a note for Stuart (who was working late on what I no longer necessarily assumed was legal or political stuff), and then we all piled into the van. Because Allie insisted, I parked near the food court and we headed there first. Since I'd had nothing to eat all day except for one overly iced cupcake, the food court sounded pretty darn appealing.

Not that I was going to be allowed food. I soon learned that Timmy, Eddie, Laura, and I were supposed to sit at a faraway table, trying our best not to look toward the girls' table in case Stan realized we were checking him out. "Look casual," Allie said. "Just some shoppers who aren't in the least bit related to us."

"Right," Mindy added. "We don't want him to know we came with our *moms*."

"Perish the thought," Laura said dryly.

"Exactly," Mindy answered, completely serious.

And so we waited. And waited. And waited some more. I wanted to get up to get some French fries, but I was under strict instructions from my daughter to stay where I could keep her and Mindy in view for when Stan came by. I might lack a coolness factor of my own, but she still wanted to show the boy off to me.

I was both bemused and flattered. Mostly, though, I was hungry.

My curiosity, however, was even stronger than my hunger, and since Mindy and Allie were a good five tables away, this seemed like the perfect opportunity to get some answers from Eddie. So far, of course, he hadn't said another word. (Correction, he'd said plenty of words, commenting randomly about anything and everything as we drove from my house to the mall. He had not, however, said another word about the Lazarus Bones.)

Now Eddie was just sitting there, his cane leaning against his thigh, his spritzer bottle of holy water on the table in front of him. Since I wasn't into this coy bullshit, I asked him point blank. "What are the Lazarus Bones?"

Laura looked at me with curiosity, but she didn't interrupt.

"The bones of Lazarus," Eddie said. His face was deadly serious, but I thought I saw a twinkle in his eyes. He might be amused, but I wasn't. I'd long passed the point of finding humor in the situation; I just wanted it over. And fast. And without anyone else (well, anyone human) getting hurt.

"That much I gathered," I said. "Why does Goramesh want them?"

"He told you that," Eddie said. He rested his palm on the top of his cane as he leaned forward. "The real question is for you, girl. Why are *you* looking for it?"

I leaned back, surprised by the question. "Well, to find it before Goramesh does, obviously. And then we'll get it to the Vatican. It'll be safe there."

He nodded, his head bobbing and bobbing until I wasn't quite sure he was going to stop. Then he smacked his lips. "Seems to me it's pretty safe where it is."

"Maybe now, but not for long. Look what Goramesh did to the monastery and that Mexican cathedral."

"Eh." This was accompanied by a very Gallic lifting of the shoulders.

"Eh, nothing," I said. "This is my town. That's my church. I'm not going to stand back and let it—"

"He can't," Eddie said.

"What?"

"If he could, he already would have."

"Goramesh can't attack the cathedral," Laura said. Her voice held a bit of awe, and she was looking at Eddie with new respect. "That makes sense," she said, this time to me. "The saints in the mortar. That's got to be bad news for demons."

She definitely had a point. "But that doesn't mean Goramesh won't find this thing, the Lazarus Bones." It felt strange giving a name to the item. Before it had just been *it* or *the bones.* "He has human minions. We're sure of it." I didn't tell him I feared that my husband might be a minion.

"If it's been hidden, it will stay hidden," he said stubbornly. "Don't go messing with things you know nothing about."

I decided to switch gears. "At least tell me why a High Demon wants the bones."

"I already told you," Eddie said. "What, you need to clean your ears out?"

"Right, right. The army rising up. What's that got to do with Lazarus? Other than that he rose from the dead?"

Eddie reached into his mouth and removed his teeth, then sat them on the table next to the holy water spritzer. "Damn things cut into my gums," he said, his voice now lispish and soft.

"Eddie," I hissed. "Tell me."

"I'm telling," he said. "Don't get your knickers in a snit."

I held out my hands, twirling one in a *come on already* motion.

"Raising the dead," he said. "The Lazarus Bones can raise the dead."

The answer made sense, and I probably should have guessed it, but to hear it spoken out loud. . . . I drew in a sharp breath.

"That's not all," Eddie said. "The bones regenerate the flesh, too."

"My master's army . . ." I trailed off, thinking of the first demon.

"You mean, like *dead* dead?" This from Laura. "Six feet under for God knows how long? Bugs and creepy crawlies? Formaldehyde?"

"Yup," Eddie said. "Fixes 'em right up. Soul's long gone, so the bodies won't put up a fight. And once the body rejuvenates, who's going to know?"

"Holy *shit*," Laura said, which summed up my sentiments nicely.

"But . . . but . . ." I floundered for something to say. This was bad. (How's that for an understatement?) If Goramesh got his hands on the bones, he could become corporeal. His demonic minions could become corporeal. And suddenly they'd be able to do that without waiting for humans to die. Without fighting exiting souls. They just slip inside.

Not good. Not good at all.

"But . . ." I tried again. "But how can you be so sure? Larson never mentioned any Lazarus Bones. And neither did Father Corletti. And I sure as hell have never heard of them."

"No reason you would've," Eddie said. Something shifted in his features, a sadness that washed through him and added another ten years to his face. "I'm the only one alive who knows."

Laura leaned in. "How can that be?"

Eddie looked over at the girls (I admit, I'd pretty much forgotten about Stan). "The boy's still a no-show," he said. "Looks like I've got time to fill you in.

"Back in the fifties," Eddie began, "*Forza* sent me to help pack up relics in a cathedral in New Mexico before the government started atomic testing. Just in case. Typical duty." He nodded at me. "You know."

"Sure." Hunters often do that kind of work. Because demons like to get their hands on relics to use in twisted demonic ceremonies, the Church will send a Hunter whenever a collection is being moved off site.

"I was working out of a cathedral in Mexico when I got assigned to that job. The rest of the team came to Mexico for briefing. Me, a priest, an art historian, and an archivist. We left Mexico for the States, and we were at the New Mexico site for over a month. First week we struck pay dirt. Hidden behind a loose stone in the cathedral sacristy we found a wooden crate and a papyrus note. Took forever for Zachary to translate it, but he did."

"The Lazarus Bones," I said.

He nodded. "Actual bones of Lazarus. I did my research later, found out how Lazarus was buried at Larnaca, then moved to Constantinople. After that, folks lost track. Somehow, the bones made it to the New World."

Laura's eyes were wide. "What happened?"

"Betrayal," Eddie said. He closed his eyes and I saw his chest rise and fall as he composed himself. "I still don't know who or why. All I know is we were attacked. The papyrus was destroyed. Our historian and archivist were killed. Damn bloody battle. Damn bloody demons—"

"But you and the priest? You survived."

"And we had the crate." He shook his head, as if warding off memories. "We were injured, close to dying, but I knew where we had to go. Far away, and someplace secure. Someplace they couldn't get in."

"San Diablo," I said. "The sainted mortar."

He nodded. "I couldn't make it, though. Father Michael took it the rest of the way."

"*Brother* Michael," I whispered. "He revealed San Diablo, but he died rather than tell them exactly where the urn is."

"So where is it?" Laura asked, voicing the question of the hour. "Let's just go get it and get Larson and get it out of this town."

"I don't know," Eddie said. "I never saw or spoke to Michael again. He made it here. But that's all I know."

I frowned, wanting to argue with him, to tell him he *had* to know because I had no clues.

"Leave it be, Kate. It's not meant to be disturbed. And you have other responsibilities." As he spoke, he nodded toward the far side of the food court, and I realized that the elusive Stan had finally joined Allie and Mindy.

I twisted around, wanting to get a good look at this mysterious hunk. And when I did, my breath caught in my throat and fear licked over me like a flame.

There, at the table with my daughter and her best friend, sat my Richie Cunningham demon. Todd Stanton Greer, recently deceased, and looking none the worse for wear.

Seventeen

Shit, shit, SHIT!

I leaped to my feet, ready to pummel the fiend, then immediately sat down again. It was a long way across the food court, and if Greer saw me coming, he might just kill my daughter. I needed a better plan, and I needed one that didn't involve Greer recognizing me.

Shit.

I shifted my chair, putting my back toward the demon. My insides were trembling, and I'm sure I was sweating.

"Kate?" Laura looked at me, concern in her eyes. "Are you okay?"

"That's him. That's the demon who attacked me by my trash cans," I said, my voice a low whisper.

Laura took another look, and I sneaked a peek, too—just as Stan sprayed a burst of Binaca into his mouth. "Holy shit," Laura said.

"No kidding."

"Holey sheet!" Timmy banged a little fist down onto the table. "You got holey sheets, Momma?"

"Something like that, kid," I said, then to Laura and Eddie, "I need to get him away from her. But I can't let him see me. Dammit, dammit, *dammit.*"

"Dammit," Timmy mimicked, but this time I barely even noticed.

"Should I go?" Laura said. "Maybe tell her there's a fifteen-minute-only sale at the Gap? That Tim's sick and we have to go home? What? What should I do?"

I shook my head. "I don't know." I glanced at Eddie, but he'd been completely silent during the whole exchange. For all I knew, he'd drifted back into his own little world. I stifled a sigh and focused on Laura again. "What's he doing now?"

She shifted slightly, peering over my shoulder for a better view. "Still talking to Allie," she said. "But Mindy's on her way over here."

That did it. I plunked Timmy onto the ground and started to rise to my feet. No way was my little girl spending any time alone with that thing.

A gentle tug at my arm stopped me.

Eddie.

"Wait," he said, and then fell silent again.

"*Wait?* Wait for what?" I started to rise again, getting to my feet at the same time Mindy arrived.

"I think he really likes her," she said happily. "Isn't he a cutie?"

I withheld comment.

"Why aren't you over there, too?" Laura asked.

Mindy shrugged. "You know. I was getting a vibe. And three's a crowd."

My blood was boiling and I was sure I must be turning beet red. A vibe? What kind of *vibe*?

Mindy continued to chatter on. "So, like, can I wait for you guys in the bookstore?"

Laura caught my eye and I nodded. "Sure," she said.

"Watch Timmy," I said as soon as Mindy was out of earshot.

I turned on my heel and found myself face-to-face with Eddie. "I'm going to get her," I said, even though he'd obviously already clued in to that fact.

He jabbed his cane down on my foot, hard enough to bruise. "Think, girl."

"*Ow.*" I stifled the urge to kick back. "What do you think you're doing?"

"Handling this." He nodded toward the table. "Now sit down. And when the girl comes, get her out of here fast."

"What are you going to—"

"Sit."

I sat. And although I needed to keep my face hidden from the demon, I had to see what was going on. I put my purse on the table, shifted my chair around, then propped my chin in my palms, so that my fingers covered most of my face.

Across the table Timmy mimicked me, but I was essentially oblivious. Right now Timmy had Laura to watch him, but my little girl only had one partly senile old man to protect her from the bad guys.

I started to rise, but this time it was Laura who pushed me back down. "If the demon starts to walk away with Allie, then go. Otherwise, let the old man do his thing."

She was right. I knew she was right. (They both were.) And so I gave in to that helpless feeling, watching as someone else held my baby's fate in his hands.

"What's he doing?" I asked. Eddie had completely passed their table, heading instead for a cookie stand. He talked to the vendor, gave him some money, and received two cups of soda in return.

I gaped at him, my blood pressure rising. What the *hell* was he doing?

Eddie hooked his cane over his arm and shuffled toward Allie's table. She looked up at him with a smile. I couldn't hear what she was saying, but it was obvious from her hand gestures that she was introducing Eddie as her great-grandfather.

How nice. How charming. *Now hurry up and deal with the demon!*

Apparently, Eddie wasn't receiving my mental commands. He stood there a bit longer, slightly swaying, then held up the sodas as if showing them off. Then he put one in front the demon, and one in front of Allie, patted Allie on the shoulder, then turned back to demon boy. From his stance and expression, I was pretty sure he was making "nice to meet you" small talk.

And then Eddie took a step backward, left the kids' table, and started walking toward me.

I got to my feet.

Laura grabbed my arm and tugged me back down. "Wait," she said. "Just wait."

I gritted my teeth and stifled the urge to slug her.

So far, though, the kids were staying put, so at least I could keep an eye on Allie.

Eddie returned then, and I glared up at him. "*Well?* What was that all about?"

He shot me a hard look, and I had a glimpse of the steel underneath the feeble exterior. "Just wait," he said. "And watch."

I did, trepidation building as the kids talked and sipped their sodas. Allie was leaning forward, her body language practically screaming that she liked this guy. I fidgeted in my seat. If something didn't happen soon, I'd be experiencing massive coronary failure (which, I supposed, would at least shift Allie's attention away from the demon).

Still nothing.

And nothing.

The two of them just kept on chatting and sipping soda. I fisted my hands at my side. What were they talking about? It's not like they had anything in common. Stan was a vile, hell-bound demon, and my daughter was a high school freshman who went to mass semiregularly (and would, I decided, be going a lot more often).

"That's it," I said. I pushed out of my seat and stood up. At the same time I saw Stan's head snap up and his eyes fix on me. There was blood in Stan's eyes, and he was out of his seat, too. Allie followed suit, and I could hear her "Are you okay?" even from all this distance.

He wasn't okay, of course. He was a demon.

He took a step toward my daughter, and I knew Greer wouldn't hesitate to attack in public. And he'd do it out of spite for me.

I lunged forward.

"Kate!" Laura cried, but I didn't hear her. Her words were drowned out completely by the anguished, guttural howl from the demon.

He dropped to his knees, his hands raised and his head thrown back. A rumble—like indigestion on steroids—spilled from his open mouth, and he cursed, Latin invectives spewing forth like fiery bits of vitriol.

Beside him, Allie backed away, her hand to her mouth. He turned and looked at her, his face contorted.

"Holy water in the pop," Eddie said beside me. "Gets 'em every time."

A nice trick, but I didn't have time to think about it. That was one pissed-off demon, and who knew what he'd do. *"Allie!"* I screamed. "Get over here *now*."

"Little bitch!" he howled, his words directed more to me than to Allie. "What have you done to me? *What. Have. You. Done.*"

Allie didn't wait around to hear his question, though. She was already in my arms by the time his last word was out.

With my daughter's head pressed against my chest, I watched with mixed fascination and horror (and, yes, a definite sense of relief and victory) as Stan stumbled to his feet. For a moment I feared he'd come after us, but he lurched toward the exit. I considered following, but I knew it wasn't necessary. Todd Stanton Greer would be dead (again) within hours. The demon gone. And the boy finally buried.

In my arms Allie trembled. "What a total freakazoid," she said. "What was his damage, anyway?"

"I don't know, baby," I said, stroking her hair. "But it's over now."

She sighed. "He seemed so nice."

"Sometimes you just can't tell about people," I said. I took her hand as we walked away. It wasn't a particularly good answer, but right then, it was the only one I had.

I couldn't sleep.

Too much going on in my world. Too many pieces hanging loose in my life. And so I ended up tossing and turning in an empty bed. Stuart was once again working late in his study, and my paranoia had reached epidemic proportions.

I curled up, hugging my pillow and trying not to think about what I would do if the man I'd chosen to spend the rest of my life with was consorting with demons. I couldn't believe I'd been so wrong about the character of the man I loved, but all the evidence pointed to Stuart's turning bad.

I shivered, not wanting to think about that. Instead, I concentrated on other things, like trying to figure out where Brother Michael could have hidden the Lazarus Bones. I had no ideas, but that got me thinking about the bones and bodies rising from the dead and demons taking over San Diablo and the world and the whole thing going to hell (literally) in a handbasket.

Not fun thoughts.

But also not something I intended to let happen.

Unfortunately, I still didn't know where to begin.

At some point I must have drifted off, because the next thing I knew, the bed shifted as Stuart sat down on his side.

I rolled over, then propped myself up on one elbow. "Hey," I said.

"Hey yourself."

"What have you been working on?"

"Land deal," he said. "The usual."

"Oh." I pushed myself up and plumped my pillow against the headboard, then leaned back. "Want to talk about it?"

"It's dull, Kate. And it's late."

"Oh." I pressed my lips together and tried to decide where to go from here. I ended up choosing the direct approach. I didn't have a lot to lose, after all. "Is something on your mind?" I asked. "Something going on you're not telling me about?"

"Why on earth would you say that?" he asked, his tone sounding genuinely perplexed. I would've been fooled, too, except that he adjusted the covers instead of looking at me.

"Usually you talk about your work. Hell, usually you bore me with your work." I didn't say that usually I tuned him out. That was a little too much honesty. "But you've been days without saying a word. I'm afraid something's wrong."

"Nothing's wrong," he said. "Except that I'm tired. Can we go to sleep?"

"Sure. Of course. You can talk to me, you know."

"I know, Kate." Exasperation. He flicked out the lights, and I slid down under the covers. I tensed, expecting his touch and hoping I wouldn't flinch. But the touch never came, and after a moment I rolled on my side, facing away from him.

"What about Clark?" I said.

For a moment Stuart didn't answer. "What do you mean?"

"We haven't talked a lot about him. What's he up to? What's he planning to do after you take over his seat?"

He actually chuckled at that. "At least you said 'when' and not 'if.' "

"Well, you're going to win, aren't you?"

"Undoubtedly," he said, but the way he said it gave me a chill.

"Clark?" I prompted.

"Official retirement. His uncle died and left him a ton of money. He bought a place in Aspen. He's pretty much set for life."

"Great," I said, but I frowned into my pillow. If there really was a rich uncle, that gave Clark much less incentive to try and seek revenge on the Church for diverting his father's dollars. Since I didn't have any other suspects at the moment, that left my husband in the driver's seat. Not particularly scientific, I'll admit. My head knew that there could be dozens of demonic minions in San Diablo, each one willing to do what it took to retrieve the Lazarus Bones. My heart, however, had latched on to Stuart. And because of that, my heart was breaking.

"Are you going to tell me what's really on your mind?" Stuart asked.

The question surprised me so much that I rolled over and faced him. His eyes were bright and clear, and the smile was the one I recognized so well. The man I knew and loved. Was I wrong? Please, please, let me be wrong.

He stroked my cheek. "Come on, Kate. Tell me."

"Okay," I said. "Truth time." Another breath, then, "I'm spending a lot more time at the church doing this archive volunteer project." I paused, in case the mention of the church spurred true confessions on his part.

Silence.

I cleared my throat. "Um, anyway, it's taking up a lot of time, so I, um, I put Timmy in a day care." I realized I'd scooted away, and had curled up into a ball. Not too surprising, really. On this particular point I was expecting my husband's wrath. (And, frankly, I deserved it. If Stuart ever made that kind of parenting decision without my input, he'd never hear the end of it.)

"Day care," he said. "Where?"

I blinked, surprised by his calm tone. "KidSpace," I said. "Over by the mall."

"You checked them out?"

"Of course. And the teacher's really great."

"And this helps you out?"

"Sure. I mean, it's only temporary." I propped myself up again and studied his face. "Stuart, I'm really sorry. I know I should have run this by you, but it's hard to get day care space, and they had the opening, and I needed the extra time, and so I just—"

He pressed a finger to my lips. "Don't worry about it, sweetheart."

It took me a full two seconds to process his words, and even then I didn't believe my ears. "What?"

"I said don't worry about it. You're a great mom. I trust your judgment."

"Oh." I frowned, unsatisfied despite the praise. "So it's okay?"

"It's fine. But it's after one. I need to get some sleep." He leaned over and kissed me on the cheek before rolling back to his side of the bed. I laid there, staring at his back, his white T-shirt phosphorescing in the moonlight.

This was bad. This was very, very bad.

There's no way in hell (bad choice of words) that my Stuart would step calmly out of the decision-making process where Timmy is concerned. This man sharing my bed was not the Stuart I knew.

Tears stung my eyes and I hugged my pillow even tighter, one thought circulating through my head—my husband, the man I loved, really was working for a demon.

• • •

Stuart was gone when I woke up, and I have to admit I was glad.

I'd slept poorly, my dreams filled with demonic images of my husband and my head filled with thoughts of the Lazarus Bones. I know my subconscious had been busily trying to work it out, but at the moment I wished my brain had just kicked back and rested. I was exhausted and grumpy, and in no mood to take any flak from anybody, human or demon.

Laura, trusty sidekick that she is, agreed to watch my two wards so that I could head to Larson's office and catch him before he took the bench at nine. Timmy was wrist deep in oatmeal when she arrived, Allie had already rushed outside to catch her ride, and Eddie was still asleep (I think yesterday's excitement wore him out, although from the way he'd preened after his brilliant maneuver, I'd have to say the exhaustion was worth it).

I abandoned her with a promise to return at ten to rescue her from my brood. I figured I could take Tim to day care, and then schlep Eddie to the cathedral with me. With any luck, he'd spot something I missed.

I'd told Larson I had news, and he was waiting for me when I arrived, a pot of coffee brewing on a book-covered credenza in his office.

"The Lazarus Bones," I said, then leaned back in his leather chair and took a sip of coffee. I'd come bearing the answer to our big question, and I couldn't help but feel a little smug.

"The Lazarus Bones," he repeated. "You mean the bones of Lazarus, raised from the dead by Jesus? The bones that are thought to have the power to regenerate the dead?"

I gaped at him. "You know about the bones?"

"It's folklore. A fairy tale. Fabrication and conjecture."

"I don't think so," I said. "Eddie's seen them. Eddie was betrayed for them."

The doubt that lined Larson's face faded and was replaced by a curious interest. "Really? All right then, enlighten me."

I did, setting out the story just the way Eddie had laid it out for me.

"Interesting." Larson was behind his desk, and now he steepled his fingers, his mouth turning down into a thoughtful frown.

"Eddie wasn't that senile after all," I said. "Eccentric, maybe, but definitely not senile."

"But we still don't know where the Lazarus Bones are? He hasn't been able to tell you that?"

I fidgeted in my seat. "We know they're in the cathedral somewhere."

"But we don't know where." He slammed his fist against his desk and stood. "Dammit, Kate, we need to find them. We need to find them *before* he does."

I licked my lips, wanting to say something, but not certain what his reaction would be.

He eyed me, his shoulders slumping slightly. "What?"

"I was thinking about something Eddie said. The bones are safe now. I mean, they must be since no one can find them. Maybe we should just leave them there."

"Safe," he said. "*Safe?*" He started to pace his office, and I watched him, wide-eyed. He was wigging out. "How can they be safe if Goramesh is intent on finding them? Do you really believe the demon will stop because the task isn't *simple*? Kate, I need you to *think*."

"I *am* thinking!" I shouted the words, but my anger was mostly at myself. He was right, damn him. "But I don't know where the bones are, so what am I supposed to do? All I know is that Brother Michael took them to San Diablo, and then spent the rest of his life in some monastery in Italy. And then suddenly some demons track him down, and rather than reveal the whole secret, he tosses himself out of a window. The secret died with him, Larson. And that's just the way it is." I was on my feet by now, but I stopped cold, rewinding my own words in my head. *That's just the way it is.*

Or was it?

"Mike Florence," I whispered.

Larson shook his head, his expression suggesting he feared I'd lost it.

"Mike—Michael—*Florence*," I said. "Florence, Italy." I ran my fingers through my hair. How could I have been so blind. "Of course. He made a donation. The bones are in the archives, just sitting there, uncataloged in a tiny gold box."

"A gold box?"

"Right," I said. "About so big." I demonstrated with my hands. The box wasn't worth anything, so whoever had pulled out the valuable relics must not have realized the importance of the contents. I frowned, my euphoria fading. "But that can't be right," I said. "Bones couldn't fit in that."

"Not intact," Larson said. "But bones are brittle."

I cocked my head. "Crushed?"

"The dust would still hold the properties, would it not?"

"You're the expert," I said.

"*Go.* Get the box. Bring it back to me and I'll arrange transport with the Vatican."

He didn't have to tell me twice. I was already up and had my purse over my shoulder. "Come with me," I said. "We'll take it to the airport together. I'll make sure you get settled on the plane."

"I can't. This trial." He rubbed his temple, then looked at his watch. "I can recess after an hour, come up with some excuse. I can meet you then."

I wanted to argue, to point out that his responsibilities to his job shouldn't be more important than mine to my family. But there wasn't time, and it wasn't an argument I

could win. "Meet me at my house," I said. "I have to relieve Laura, and maybe Eddie can confirm we've got the
right thing. I'd hate to go running to the Vatican with dear
Uncle Edgar's ashes."

"Good point." He hesitated just a moment, and then
nodded. "Your house. One hour. Now go."

Exactly one hour later Larson, Eddie, and I were huddled
around my dining room table. Rather than take Timmy to
day care, I'd begged Laura to watch him at her house. I
didn't know how long this would take, or what was involved. If I ended up escorting Larson to the Los Angeles
Airport, I'd miss the pickup time for Timmy's day care.

The box sat next to the salt and pepper shakers, and neither Eddie nor Larson had made a move to touch it.

"How do we know?" I asked. "I mean, how can we be
sure?"

Both Larson and I turned to Eddie. "Any idea?" Larson
asked.

"Well, now," Eddie drawled, "I've got lots of ideas."

"About the box, Eddie," I said, gently prodding him. I
doubted Larson was in the mood to put up with Eddie's in-
cessant rambling. I know I wasn't.

"Charlie only read some of the text to Michael and me,"
Eddie said. "Makes sense. Long document, that was." He
blinked, his eyes owlish behind the half-glasses he'd
shoved too far up his nose. "What year was that again? Not
the sixties . . . none of those flower children. The fifties,
maybe?"

"*Eddie.*"

He waved a hand at me. "Sorry. Right. You're right.
Now, then." He blinked, then peered toward Larson. "What
were we talking about?"

Larson pressed both hands to the tabletop and got nose-
to-nose with Eddie. "How do we test the dust?"

"Right. I remember. Sure. Holy water."

I met Larson's eyes, but he looked just as bewildered as me. "Holy water? How?"

"Sprinkle a bit on and you'll see the Lord's flame. Don't recall the exact translation, but the text said something about hubris, and the flame was a warning of how not to use the bones. A reminder, of sorts."

"A reminder?" I asked.

"Matthew 25:41," Eddie said.

I shook my head. My memory of Scripture has never been very good.

"Then he will say to those on his left, 'Depart from me, you who are cursed, into the eternal fire prepared for the devil and his angels.'" Larson looked from Eddie to me. "Apropos, don't you think?"

I nodded, but couldn't speak, the reality of what the bones represented finally settling in. I wanted to test them, and then I wanted to get them out of my house—out of San Diablo altogether. Eddie's spritzer bottle was next to the salt. I passed it to Larson. "Here," I said. "You can have the honors."

He brushed my hand away, nodding instead toward Eddie. "After so many years, I think Mr. Lohmann deserves the full impact of this moment."

"Damn straight, I do." Eddie drew in a breath, his scrawny shoulders rising with his chest, and then he edged the box toward him. He managed to pry the lid off with little difficulty, then he pointed the nozzle at the dust. "Anyone want to sound a drumroll?"

"I may not be your *alimentatore*," Larson said, "but I'm only going to say this once. Cut the crap and get on with it."

Eddie flashed a grin in my direction, his dentures blindingly white. "Ever noticed just how touchy some mentors are?"

"The test, Eddie," I said.

"I'm doing it, I'm doing it." He tapped a bit of the dust onto a napkin, then squeezed the trigger. A fine mist erupted, then drifted down to blanket the dust.

I jumped back, anticipating the flames. But they never came. Instead, we were looking at a pile of slightly soggy dust on a slightly soggy napkin.

Beside me, Larson made a low noise in his throat. "You're sure that was holy water? You told me the staff was filling his vial with tap water."

"I'm sure," I said, wishing I weren't. "Father Ben replenishes the holy water every morning, and I filled Eddie's bottle for him personally."

"Well," Eddie said. "That settles it. I guess we need to keep looking."

"Yes," Larson said, his voice tight. "It appears that we do."

Larson left, leaving Eddie and me sitting at the table, alone in a morose silence.

"I really thought we had it," I said. "I thought we'd figured it out and we were done."

"From my way of looking at things," Eddie said, "we'll never really be done."

"You maybe, but I'll be finished as soon as the Lazarus Bones are safely back in the Vatican."

"That so?" He chewed on the end of a pen.

I waited for him to say something more, and when he didn't, I squirmed in my chair. "I have to think about my family, Eddie. Allie, Timmy, even Stuart." At Stuart, I looked away. I hadn't shared my suspicions with Eddie, and I didn't intend to. Not until I was absolutely certain.

"Well, we all got to do what we got to do, but this town has more problems than just Goramesh. Maybe he started it and maybe he didn't, but none of the bad stuff's going away just because the bones do."

"There are other Hunters," I said, but I knew there weren't many. Father Corletti had already been over that with me. "I'm *retired*. Just like you. You don't really want back in the game, do you?"

He snorted. "I never left the game."

"What?" I blinked at him. "I thought you were retired."

His laugh was harsh and not the least bit feeble. Whatever drugs had been dragging him down had worked their way out of his system.

"I've been a lot of places I haven't wanted to be over the last fifty-some odd years. You ever go fifteen years without a real shower? Not fun, missy, but that's what I did, and I did it for *Forza*. And food? Some of the worst food you can imagine. Not even food, just sludge. Sludge with—"

"Wait." I held up a hand before Eddie got on one of his rolls. "Back up. What's the deal?"

"I already told you the deal, girl," he said, speaking around the pen. "I was betrayed. I didn't retire. I left. Didn't have a choice. Fought some demons in Sri Lanka and a nest of vampires in Nepal. Spent some time in a monastery in South America, and hid out a few years in Borneo."

"Hid out? Since the *fifties*?"

"They were looking for me. Always looking."

"Who? Why?"

"Demons, of course," he said. "They were looking for the Lazarus Bones, and that means they were looking for me."

"So you've been hiding out all that time? Why come back to San Diablo? You knew the bones were here. Didn't you think the demons would figure it out?"

At that, Eddie actually laughed so hard he started choking, turning first beet red, and then an unattractive shade of blue. I leaped to my feet and pounded him on the back, until he held up a hand, signaling that he was okay. He tried to speak, but nothing came out. I got him a glass of water, and he tried again. "I didn't come here, girl. They brought me here."

"*What?*"

"About three months ago."

"That's when Brother Michael committed suicide," I said.

"Yup."

"Well, where were you before that?"

"Six months before that, I was in Algiers, working as a bartender, and taking care of a few of the more preternatural, evil-type clients. Trained some Hunters, too. Under the table, of course. That's the way it's got to be done, you ask me. *Forza*'s moving too slow, and the danger is too strong. Got to get in there and fight. Got to get in there and—"

"*Eddie!*"

His entire body seemed to slump. "They found me there. The demons. Dragged me back to some dump in Inglewood. Pumped me full of drugs. Asked questions. Tried to get answers. I wouldn't tell 'em. I wouldn't tell 'em a thing."

I wanted to cry, but my eyes were surprisingly clear. Fresh anger lashed through my body. I wanted to make it up to this old man who'd given up the better part of his life to protect a secret. I wanted, more than ever, to destroy Goramesh.

"Demons brought you here?" I asked.

"They let up on the drugs when they did, too. Maybe they thought I truly couldn't remember with my head so scrambled. I don't know. And I never knew what prompted them to move me to San Diablo." He looked at me. "Not until you told me your story, anyway."

"As soon as they learned from Brother Michael that the bones were here, they brought you, too?"

"Fat lot of good it did them," he said with a self-satisfied smirk. "I haven't said a word. Never told a soul, actually. And there's not a drug on the planet can make old Eddie talk if he doesn't want to."

My breath hitched. "You talked to me," I said, my voice little more than a whisper. "Why? Why did you trust me?"

"Am I wrong to trust you?"

"No." I shook my head fervently. "No way."

He aimed his toothless grin my way. "In that case, my reasons don't much make a difference, do they?"

Eighteen

In a mere twenty-four hours I went from testing fine white powder with holy water for end-of-the-world potential to serving funnel cakes on the softball field beside St. Mary's Cathedral.

Such is the variety that keeps my life so spicy.

I still didn't know where the Lazarus Bones were any more than I knew (definitively) who was supposed to schlep them out of the cathedral and into Goramesh's hot little demon hands. To say I was frustrated would be an understatement, and if my smile was a little less chipper than it should be for a parish fair, well, you can just chalk it up to the demons.

"Mo-om!" Allie came up, Timmy perched on her hip. "Do I really have to cart him around? I'm not going to meet anyone cool if I've got my brother attached to me."

"It's a church fair, sweetheart, not *The Dating Game*."

She made a face. "I told you," she said. "I don't always think about boys."

"Just on Mondays, Wednesdays, and Fridays?"

"Right," she said, her grin impish. "And on alternating Tuesdays."

"Well, it's Friday," I said. "Who's today's lucky object of your lust?"

"Nobody," she said with a heavy sigh. "All the good ones are weird."

I knew she was thinking about Stan, and my gut twisted. I'd seen a small item in that morning's paper. Todd Greer—who'd so miraculously survived an attack by a vicious dog just a few days ago—had raced out of the mall and run in front of a bus. He'd been killed instantly. Even though I knew he wasn't human, I'd still felt a twinge of sadness. Residual, I suppose, for the boy he used to be.

I smiled at my daughter, the girl I wanted so badly to keep safe. I suppose I should have assured her that there were plenty of nonweird men out there, but I kept my mouth shut. She'd learn soon enough.

"Why don't you see if Laura will watch Tim?" I suggested after serving a funnel cake to a man in a UCLA T-shirt.

"I looked for her. I can't find her anywhere." She aimed the puppy-dog pout my way. "Gramps said he'd watch Tim."

"Leave the baby with Gramps, and you'll find yourself cell phone–less." I could play dirty when I had to.

An anguished moan, followed by "what*ever.*"

"Why don't you wait for Stuart? He promised to be here by six-thirty."

"It's only six, mom. That's another half hour."

"Oh, the torment," I said.

"When do you get off?"

"Now, actually, but I have some things I have to do." Like sneak down into the archives and hope that inspiration hit.

"Mo-*ther.* You're ruining my social life."

"I know. I'm evil." I stepped back to let Tracy Baker take over as the funnel-cake queen, then I slid out of the booth and came around to face my daughter. "Your best bet is Laura. I'm sure she's around here with Mindy, isn't she?"

From Allie's sigh, you'd think I'd just told her she had three weeks to live. "I don't know. I'll go look for them. *Again.*"

She trudged off, Timmy happily batting at her dangly earrings.

Allie may not have found Laura, but I had no problems locating her. Although Laura isn't Catholic, the parish fair is big in the community, and she and I go every year. Usually we scope out the various booths and buy handmade knick-knacks and stupid gifts. This year we were on a quest.

"I can help, you know," she said as we headed for the cathedral.

"No, thanks. If Goramesh is paying attention, he probably already knows you're helping me. But just in case he doesn't, I'd like to keep the illusion going."

"Then what can I do?"

A little finger of guilt wiggled its way up my neck. "Can you relieve Allie? Her brother is cramping her style."

"For Allie, anything."

"Thanks."

"Not a problem. Just one more dessert on the ever-growing tally." We were right outside the doors now, and she paused, shaking her head slightly as she hugged herself, looking at the building before us. "Sad and inspiring all at the same time, don't you think?"

I wasn't thinking about anything except the zillions of boxes still waiting for my review. After having come so close only to be sadly disappointed, I can't say I was too psyched for the experience.

"Kate?"

"Sorry. What?"

"I was just thinking about the cathedral. The bones of saints mixed into the mortar. And those five martyrs in the basement. I mean, on the one hand it's inspiring, but it's also kind of creepy and weird."

I tugged open the door. "I'm not interested in creepy, weird, inspirational, or devotional. All I want are answers, and instead of spending the next two hours having fun buying beaded scarves and tacky earrings with you, I'm going to be huddled down here with vermin-infested boxes. So forgive me if I'm not soaking in the historical wonder of it all."

Her lips twitched, but she nodded gravely. "Right," she said. "Go work."

She headed back toward the playing field, and I paused just past the foyer to dab my finger in the holy water and genuflect. I've never been particularly good at genuflecting (I'm sorry, but the motion is just not natural) and this time I fell on my butt, knocked completely asunder by the thought that had slammed into my head.

Laura said there'd been *five* martyrs, but there were *six* bags of remains. An extra one was in the display case, hiding in plain sight.

A thrill whipped through my body like electricity.

I knew where the Lazarus Bones were.

I ran back outside, pulling my phone out of my purse, then turning in a circle as I waiting for the signal bar to show up. As soon as it did, I punched in Larson's number. "I know where the Bones are," I said, skipping polite preambles.

"Are you certain?" His voice was tight, tense.

"Positive. I think. Where are you?"

"About a mile from the cathedral. Go in, retrieve the bones, and meet me in the parking lot."

"I can wait," I said. "I'd rather we bring them out together."

"No time," he said, his voice urgent. "Goramesh has ears everywhere. You shouldn't even have called me. But since you've spoken of this aloud, you *must* get the bones *now*."

My cheeks burned from the dressing down, and I opened my mouth to defend myself, but nothing came out. Was he right? Had I just put myself—and the bones—in danger?

"I'll be there when you come out, and together we'll take them to the airport. Now go."

I went. I raced down the aisle and took the four steps up to the sanctuary in one leap. I yanked open the door to the sacristy and pounded down the stairs.

And then I stopped short, letting out a little squeak of surprise as I saw the man sitting there.

Stuart.

Oh, dear God, was he waiting for me?

He was seated at one of the long wooden tables, an oversize book with yellowed pages and tiny handwriting open in front of him. He looked up at me, and I could see the surprise on his face. For my part, I felt only fear, betrayal, and an odd sense of hope. Was he still my Stuart? Or was he here to hurt me?

He glanced down at his watch, then frowned before meeting my eyes again. "Am I late? I didn't think you were expecting me until six-thirty."

"What?" The comment was so unexpected, I couldn't quite process it.

"Isn't that why you're here? Looking for me?"

"I—Not exactly."

For a moment confusion colored his face, but then it cleared. "You snuck down here to do a little more work on your project."

"Something like that," I said, still rooted to the spot. "Why are *you* here?"

He closed the book with a *thump* and a cloud of dust. "Doesn't matter. Just a project I'm working on."

I let my head fall back, exasperated despite the surreal circumstances. "What's going on, Stuart? Just tell me. Tell me the truth, okay?" I took the chair opposite him and reached across the table to take his hand. "Please. However bad it is, I can take it."

"Bad? Kate, what's wrong with you lately?"

I leaned back, my eyes wide, and pulled my hands safely back to my side of the table. "*Me?*"

"You're distracted, you bring old men home without asking me, you enroll Tim in a day care without asking me."

"I thought you were okay with that."

"With your judgment, sure. But you didn't even discuss it with me." He shook his head. "I don't know, hon. I can't put my finger on it, but something is definitely up. Is it the old man?" He drew in a breath. "Is it Eric?" he asked, pain filling his voice.

"It's not Eric," I said. I ran my teeth over my lower lip. "It's you."

"Me?"

"I saw you here the other day. But when I asked, you lied to me, Stuart. What's going on? You never lie to me."

His mouth turned up for just a second, flashing an ironic smile. "Looks like we both lose on that count, doesn't it."

But I wasn't going to get drawn into a game of who lied to whom. I just wanted to know. "Why, Stuart? Why are you so sure you'll win the election?"

He actually laughed at that. "Oh, good God, Kate. Do you think I'm taking bribes or something?"

"I—" I closed my mouth, not at all sure what to say.

"I was just excited. And, yes, I do think I have an excellent shot. Jeremy Thomas is taking a job in Washington, and Frank Caldwell is shifting his support to me. I didn't want to tell you until Caldwell made the announcement, just in case something changed. But it's solid."

I couldn't hide my smile. "That's fabulous!" Jeremy Thomas was a prosecuting attorney who also happened to be Stuart's biggest rival for the county attorney seat. Frank Caldwell is the San Diablo county district attorney. His endorsement was worth its weight in gold.

"Pretty sweet, huh?"

"Very," I said. A weight seemed to lift off my heart, but then I looked around at where we were, and felt the familiar squeeze again. "But what are you doing down here?"

"A land buy," he said. "And Clark swore he'd have my neck if I told anyone, including you. If this leaks, we're going to be in a bad position."

I just stared at him. "Land. You're down here to buy land?"

He opened the book and I realized then what it was. Church property records. "I've been trying to track down the title on some church property the county's going to make an offer on. There are political ramifications, so we're keeping it quiet."

"And that's all? That's all you've been up to?"

"Yeah. What did you think? I was having an affair under the cathedral altar?"

I shook my head. "No. Nothing like that."

He stood up, then, holding his yellow legal pad like a shield. I expected him to ask me what I'd been up to, but he didn't. Maybe he didn't want to know. Maybe I was wishing so hard for him to stay silent, that he heard my plea. Instead, he simply said that he needed to go. "I know I said I'd meet you and the kids at six-thirty, but I think I found the missing link just now, and I'd really like to—"

"Go," I said. "Head back to the office and say hi to Clark for me."

He came around the table and kissed me on the cheek. I was so full of guilt I was afraid it was seeping out my pores. Hopefully, he couldn't taste it.

He started toward the door, but I reached out and caught his hand. "We okay?"

His smile lit me all the way to my toes. "The best," he said.

Damn, but I hoped he was right.

I watched him go, then took three deep breaths, forcing

myself not to cry. I didn't have time for that. I needed to get the bones.

I moved to the glass display case, the fear that I was wrong slowing my step. But the moment I looked into the glass, I knew I was right. Five martyrs, but there were six bags of remains.

I opened each, one by one. Dark ash, bits of hair, chips of bone. Each bag. And then I opened the last. "Reginald Talley," the label read, but I was certain I wouldn't find Reginald inside. I pulled apart the drawstring and peered in. Pure white. Bone, crushed to the finest of powder.

Lazarus.

Brother Michael had ground up the bones. The gold box filled with dust hadn't simply been a decoy, it had been a clue. Part of a whole series of clues meant for Eddie. The first clue was the name: Michael Florence. The priest's name, and then the Italian town to make sure Eddie understood that the box was left there by his friend. And Michael had deliberately put dust in the gold box. The dust was the second clue, telling Eddie that the bones had been crushed and ensuring that Eddie knew to look for the powdered remains.

My head told me I didn't need to test the dust, but having been burned once, I wasn't listening to my head. I pulled out the vial of holy water and set it on the table. Then I reached into my back pocket and pulled out one of the napkins from the funnel cake stand. I spread it out and shook out a tiny bit of powder. Then I opened the vial and turned it on its side until a single drop emerged, clinging tenaciously to the rim of the vial.

I held my breath as the drop fell, and then, when a flame of pure blue fire erupted, I dropped the vial and fell to my knees.

This was it. The real deal.

My heart pounded in my chest, and I stayed on my knees until the flame fizzled out. I'd witnessed something amazing just then, the power of God, and I trembled, sure I could still feel His presence in the room with me. He'd guided me here, and now He would guide me out in safety.

After all, it had been easy so far. No human minions threatening my safety. No demon pet rushing to take me down.

Nothing that I'd feared had come to pass, and although I was happy not to have to fight my way out of the cathedral, the situation was a little disconcerting. My instincts weren't bad. Not at all. And I'd been so certain Goramesh would have sent a human.

If not Stuart, then who?

And that's when I knew—the truth so horrible it made me retch.

It had been me all along. *I* was the mortal pet.

Me.

Nineteen

I grabbed the edge of the table to steady myself, something dark and cold filling my stomach.

Goramesh had almost succeeded. *Because of me!* I held the Lazarus Bones in my hand, and I'd been about to take them upstairs and hand them over to—

Oh, shit.

I'd been right that very first day, and I should have trusted my instincts. Larson really was a demon! He'd lied when he said Goramesh wasn't corporeal.

Goramesh had a body, all right. *Larson* was Goramesh.

I sank to the dusty wooden floor, hugging my knees in front of me. Terror and relief enveloped me, and I couldn't do anything more than rock back and forth. I'd almost missed the truth. I'd almost destroyed everything.

Slowly the terror faded, replaced by a cold, hard anger. He wanted the Lazarus Bones? Then he could damn well come down here himself and get them.

I crumpled up the napkin and shoved it in my back pocket along with my vial of holy water, then I retied the drawstring on the sack. I returned it to the case, took a deep breath for courage, then headed up the stairs.

I wasn't sure what I was going to do, but I did know that Larson wasn't getting those bones. As soon as I got outside the cathedral and got a cell phone signal, I'd call Father Corletti. If he didn't have Hunters to spare, that was fine. Send the Swiss Guard. But I wasn't going to back down until those bones were safely out of San Diablo and en route to the Vatican. Eddie could help me guard them in the meantime. Father Ben, too, for that matter; if I had to, I'd even enlist his help.

I burst out of the cathedral at a dead run and ran straight into Laura. "Where's Larson?"

She pulled herself up short, clearly surprised by the tone in my voice.

"Where is he?" I demanded.

"By the ice-cream stand, I assume," Laura said. "What's wrong? The kids will survive a night of really bad food."

The kids? That didn't make any sense. The kids? And then—

I grabbed her by the shoulder. "Where are my kids?"

"They're with Larson." Her brow furrowed. "Paul came by just like he promised he would, but when he told me couldn't stay, I was so furious I almost lost it. I didn't, though, because I was watching the kids, but I think Paul knew I was fuming."

I made a circle motion with my hand, encouraging her to get to the point.

"That's when Larson volunteered to take them to get ice cream." She licked her lips, clearly worried. "He said you okayed it. You didn't?"

"Oh, no. No, I definitely did not." I turned in a circle, then raced toward the ice-cream stand, the Lazarus Bones all but forgotten.

Laura raced after me. "What's going on?" I heard her

heavy breathing beside me as we skidded to a stop in front
of the booth.

"It's Larson," I said. "He's Goramesh."

She paled, and I caught her just as her knees gave way.
"Oh, God, the kids. *Mindy*." Her eyes brimmed with tears.
"If anything happens to them. To her—"

"It won't," I said, my voice like steel.

"What are you going to do?"

"Beat the shit out of him," I said. At the moment that was
the only plan I had. Frankly, I thought it was a good one.

"*Mommy, Mommy, Mom.*"

We both turned at the sound of the voice. "Mindy,"
Laura breathed, the relief in her voice so tangible I could
almost touch it.

My relief was tainted by fear for my own kids, who
were conspicuously not with Mindy.

"What happened?" I said.

Her face was pressed to Laura's chest, her arms tight
around her mom. But I could see part of her tear-stained
face. "He shoved me away," Mindy said. "And Allie had to
stay with him, he said, or else he'd hurt Timmy."

I closed my eyes, too scared to even pray.

My cell phone rang.

I answered it before the echo of the first ring died out.

"Bring me the bones, Kate," Larson said.

"Screw you." I said the words, but my bravado was
false.

"Darling Kate," he said. "Let me put this in words you'll
understand—bring me the Lazarus Bones, or your children
are dead."

"Bastard," I whispered, but he'd already hung up.

I lashed out, wanting to hit something and finding only
Laura. I fell against her, sobbing, as she patted my back and
made soothing noises that I know she didn't really believe.

All along, Larson had been playing a role designed to

fool me. But I wasn't fooled anymore. Larson was Goramesh—a High Demon. The Decimator. And I was truly afraid.

Enough.

I pushed back and wiped my eyes.

"Kate?"

I didn't answer. I couldn't. Instead, I turned away and started back toward the cathedral. Tears spilled down my cheeks, but I knew what I had to do.

These were my kids, after all.

I clutched the cloth bag tight as I raced back up the basement stairs, my mind churning. I should have known. Should have seen the clues. They were all there. His hesitancy to enter the cathedral. His constantly chewing mint-flavored gum. His strength when we fought in the courtyard. His ability to recognize another demon—and to throw a knife so straight and true.

It had been the holy water that had won me over.

But now, as I passed the receptacles, I realized how even that illusion had been easy for him. A demon can enter holy ground even though it pains him. The pillars of holy water are a long way from the sanctuary and its sainted, impenetrable mortar. Goramesh would have simply knocked over the bowls and refilled them with tap water. I recalled the puddle on the floor before our meeting and knew I was right.

There were other clues, too. I didn't want to research, but he'd convinced me. And I'd agreed to up the ante if there was any sign of demons infiltrating San Diablo. That night Todd Greer paid a little visit. I'd called that a sign. It was a sign, all right—I'd just read it wrong. Larson had ordered the hellhound to kill Todd Greer so a demon could move in and convince me to do Larson's research. And then Larson killed the demon in the alley to reinforce his position as one of the good guys.

What a crock.

And then there was Eddie. Larson had been the one who'd "discovered" Eddie's presence here. And no wonder. He'd brought Eddie here himself. I had to meet Eddie, because Eddie was the only one who knew what Goramesh wanted. I'd even bet that Larson ordered the drugs decreased so that Eddie would be able to think more clearly—all the better for him to tell me the truth once he decided he trusted me.

And why not trust me?

I was another Hunter, and even I didn't know that I was bait.

Larson had even fueled my fears about Stuart, probably hoping that pointing me in that direction would keep my mind away from considering him too closely. It had worked, too.

With a foul-mouthed curse, I burst through the cathedral doors. The clues were academic now. All that mattered was getting my kids back.

The descending sun cast long shadows on the ground, giving the world a surreal quality that matched my mood. I shaded my eyes with my hand and scanned the grounds, but I didn't see any sign of Laura or Eddie.

I flipped open my cell phone and started to dial Laura's number, but the squeal of rubber against asphalt caught my attention. I leaped backward, realizing that Larson's Lexus was barreling toward me across the nearly empty parking lot.

It fishtailed, then careened to a halt in front of me. My muscles tensed, ready to pummel him. Between the tinted windows and the distortion from the fading light, I couldn't see Larson, but I was ready for him. I raced to the driver's-side door and yanked it open. "Get out of there, you son of a bitch!"

"Mom!"

Not Larson. *Allie.*

She fumbled for the door and fell out of the car into my arms. I collapsed to the asphalt, holding her against me, crying in earnest now. "Baby, baby, oh baby," I murmured as she cried. I lifted her chin up, then pushed her away so I could get a good look at her. "Did he hurt you? Are you okay?"

She could barely talk through her tears, but she managed a weak "Timmy." Ice flowed in my veins as she struggled to say, "I couldn't get him away. Oh, Mommy, he's still got Timmy."

"Was he hurt? Was he okay when you left?" I wanted to lash out, to run, to fight, to do *something* to make it all better. Adrenaline surged through my body, and I felt a numbing coldness settle over me. A cold practicality. *No emotions, Kate.* Just get in, do the job, and get Timmy back safe.

"He—he was fine. But I'm scared. Oh, Mom, I'm so scared for him."

I gritted my teeth. "Where did he take you?"

"The cemetery," she said, her voice shaky but stronger. "He told us that you'd had to leave and he was taking us for ice cream and then home, but then he went the other way, and when he got to the cemetery, he called you, and I got so scared."

"I know, sweetheart. But you're doing great."

"He made us get out of the car, but he left the keys. And I got away, just like Cutter showed us."

My stomach churned. She'd been lucky on that count, surprise acting in her favor. Larson could have easily caught her and snapped her neck. I tugged her toward me and hugged her close one more time, just to feel her whole and unmolested against me. "You did good, baby," I said. I pulled her up as I climbed to my feet. The car was still idling beside us, and I looked at it grimly.

"Go find Laura and Gramps and tell them what's going on. Stay with them, okay? Don't leave them no matter what."

She nodded, her chin trembling.

I slid behind the wheel. "Where in the cemetery?"

"The big statue," she said. "The big angel."

I nodded. I knew the place. It was one of the older corners of the cemetery, far away from the road. "Go," I said. "Find Laura. It'll be okay. I promise, I'll get your brother back."

She leaned into the car and kissed me. "I love you, Mom," she said, then ran off across the parking lot toward the fair.

I sighed. *I love you, too, baby.*

And then I gunned it.

I didn't bother using the paved roads through the graveyard. Irreverent, I know, but I just aimed the Lexus toward the southeast corner and floored it. Most of the graves were marked with simple plaques, and I swerved around the few interspersed headstones planted in an earlier age.

The angel loomed in front of me, and I swerved to a stop, the back of the car slipping on damp turf.

Larson sat calmly at the angel's feet, my son propped on his knee. "A charming boy," Larson said. "I'm glad you came. I wouldn't have enjoyed killing him." He flashed me a menacing grin. "That was a lie. I think I'd enjoy it very much."

I stood ramrod straight, my hands fisted at my sides. "Give me my son."

"Give me the bones."

I hesitated.

"I'll do it, Kate. You should know by now that I won't even think twice. But there's something I want more than the pleasure of drawing his blood. Give me the bones and I'll give you the boy."

I held out the bag.

"Smart girl." He turned slightly, then called out, "Doug. The bag, please."

A withered old man stepped out from behind the angel. He plodded toward me, then took the bag. I tensed, recognizing his face. The last time I'd seen Doug he'd been playing chess in the Coastal Mists Nursing Home.

I looked up at Larson. "Bastard."

"Nonsense. Doug has gone on to the next plane. Why shouldn't we utilize his body? It would only go to waste. So much waste there at the home," he said, his voice almost wistful. Then he looked me in the eye, his gaze full of malice. "Don't worry. The waste will be much less from now on. Much, much less."

"Not if I can help it."

"But you can't. Poor Kate, you can't even help yourself."

"Give me my son."

"But of course." He stood, then put Timmy on the ground. "I can be generous, too," he said as my baby ran toward me.

"You're going to die, Goramesh," I said. "I'm going to send you back to Hell."

"Big talk," he said. "And why would you do that, anyway, after all you've done to help me? Without you, Eddie would never have revealed the truth. Without you, I could never have breached the cathedral sacristy."

I didn't say a word, just hugged my baby tight.

"Will you stay, then? Stay and witness the rising of my army? I promise your end will come swiftly."

"I'll stay," I said. "I'll stay and stop you."

"You're out of practice, Kate. Have you forgotten that I've sparred with you? I know you. And I will not be defeated."

"When did Larson die? How did you even get here?"

He laughed then, with such mirth it actually startled me out of my red hot fury. "Dead? Whoever said Larson was dead?"

"But . . . *oh, God.*"

"*He* has nothing to do with it. Larson is in here, with me. He has been most cooperative. He will be rewarded."

"Why?"

"Cancer," he said, his voice now pitched slightly higher. "Why succumb when Goramesh could offer me so much more than death. And then, when I learned about the Lazarus Bones from my Hunter in Italy, well, then I had something to bargain with. Goramesh wanted the bones. I wanted to live."

"You're going to die tonight."

"No, Kate. It's you who will die. This part of me is sorry about that. I do like you. Once upon a time, I even liked working for *Forza*. But it was never about the work. Not for me."

"Black arts," I said, remembering. "You were studying the black arts. And Father Corletti never realized—"

"Don't blame the priest," he said. "I can be most persuasive when I want. Now, of course, I'm both persuasive and powerful." He drew in a breath, his chest expanding. His skin seemed to ripple, like the surface of a pond, and beneath the ripples I saw the true demon, red and black and teeming with worms, its glowing eyes burning with hate.

I blinked, and the vision faded, the acrid smell of sulphur the only clue that it had been real.

Timmy smelled it, too, and started squirming in my arms as he whimpered. "Hush, baby," I said. "It's almost over."

"Indeed," Goramesh said. "Stay, Kate. Stay and watch."

Since I had no intention of leaving without first laying waste to Goramesh, I stayed rooted to the spot, Timmy tight in my arms.

Goramesh moved away from the angel to stand on a relatively fresh grave. He spread his arms and looked down at the earth, then began to spew out Latin and Greek, his words coming too fast and furious for me to understand.

I didn't need to understand the words, though, to figure out what was going on. That was clear enough. And when he tugged open the bag and reached in for a handful of powder, I tensed. I was too far away to do anything yet, but

I put my hand in my back pocket anyway, just so the holy water would be at the ready.

He sprinkled the powder over his body, the incantation coming faster and faster. He reached the end, spreading his arms and shouting *"Resurge, mortue!"* That one, I knew. He was commanding the dead to rise.

I held my breath, waiting. The graves didn't tremble. The dead didn't rise.

I'd known they wouldn't, and I couldn't help but smile as I pushed Timmy gently behind me, the vial now in my hand.

"It's over, Goramesh," I said. "You're history."

"Little fool," he spat. "What have you done?"

I didn't answer. I knew he'd realize soon enough exactly what I'd done.

"Bitch!" he howled, his face contorting in pain. I grinned. And so it began.

As I watched, his skin began to blister and his hair fell in clumps to the ground. He screamed, the sound coming straight from the bowels of Hell.

"What have you done? *What have you done to me?"*

"Not me," I said. "The Blessed Mary Martinez, one of San Diablo's five martyrs. May she soon reach sainthood."

His skin bubbled and popped, and I gagged against the smell of sulphur. Mary wasn't a saint yet, but she'd been beatified. I knew that her remains wouldn't kill him, but he was in pain, and I hoped that gave me all the advantage I needed.

I opened the vial and lunged.

"Get her!" he cried, and Doug barreled into me. I fell to the ground with an *oof*, and the holy water vial went flying, shattering against a gravestone, but doing no harm to Doug or Larson. As Doug grappled for me, I lashed out with my legs, trying to pry the spry octogenarian off of me.

He clung fast, though, and I knew that Goramesh would recover soon and come help. Two against one—especially when a High Demon was part of the equation—was not good odds.

As Timmy's screams rang in my ears, I twisted sideways, managing to get on top of Doug. He grappled for me, his clammy fingers brushing my neck. I dodged away, scrambling to grasp a nearby twig.

My fingers closed around it just as his hands closed around my neck. But it was too late. I knew I'd won, and I drove the twig home.

Doug sagged, and that was the end of that.

I leaped off of him, ready to tackle Goramesh, my fury fueling my confidence. My victory was short-lived. When I turned, I'd expected to see the demon. Instead, I saw my baby, Larson's arm tight around his neck. The dust had finished its work, and now he was oozy and gross, but no longer distracted by the pain of burning flesh.

"You *fool*!" he shouted. "You think you can best me? You think you can *trick* me? This boy is going to die here, Kate. Bring me the bones and maybe I'll bring him back for you."

He shifted and I lunged, the reaction purely instinct. "No!" I cried, my voice thick with fear.

I'd barely closed the distance between us when Larson erupted with a guttural howl. Almost simultaneously I realized what had happened.

Timmy had bitten him.

Larson jerked his arm up, releasing his hold on Tim as he struck out with his other hand, sending my baby flying. Timmy crashed to the ground, his little body going limp. I launched myself, tackling Larson with my full weight and sending us both sprawling. He managed to roll on top of me, and as he climbed to his feet, he grabbed my hair, smashing my metal hairclip against my skull as he yanked me to my feet. I winced, but my own pain evaporated when I realized Timmy still hadn't moved. I drew in a strangled breath, fearing the worst. Larson took advantage, shoving me backward so that the small of my back slammed against the base of the angel statue. I screamed, jerking my leg up and trying to knee him as I twisted. I needed to get free, but his fingers had locked on my forearms like clamps.

He was strong. So strong. And try as I might, I couldn't break free.

"He's dead, Kate," he hissed, his breath foul against my face.

"No." I couldn't believe that. *Wouldn't* believe it.

He moved even closer. "Give me the bones, and I'll bring him back for you." His voice was calm, almost soothing. "You can have your baby back, Katie. You can have him alive again. Just bring me the bones."

I was light-headed, unable to draw breath. He held on to my arms, but he might as well have been crushing my windpipe. Hot tears streamed down my cheeks. Was my baby truly dead? And if so, did I have the strength to use the bones to bring him back? More important, did I have the strength *not* to?

I closed my eyes briefly, seeking strength. *"Never,"* I whispered. "I'll never bring you the bones."

His nostrils flared and rage filled his eyes. "Bitch! I'll snap your neck and leave you here!" He leaned in closer, his mouth pressed against my ear. "And know this as life leaves you—I *will* raise the boy. And he will become one of mine. It's over, Kate. And my victory will be even sweeter than I'd imagined."

I struggled as my fear ratcheted up, but he held on, his grip unyielding. Terror clutched me just as tight, and I choked back a sob as fear and regret mixed together. I'd sworn I wouldn't lose, but now I feared I'd made a promise I just couldn't keep.

I sucked in air, trying to fill my lungs as my heart thrummed in my chest. Through the roaring in my ears, I heard the high-pitched wails of sirens.

Sirens?

Would Laura have called the police? Would Eddie have let her?

Goramesh heard them, too. "Time to end this, Hunter," he said. "Wouldn't want the police to discover my little secret, would we?"

He let go of my arm, then started to twist me around. I knew well enough what he was doing; he planned to break my neck.

"NO!" I screamed. I didn't have any weapon, nothing with which I could take him out. So I did the only thing I could. I lashed upward, knocking his arm away from my neck. It worked. And in that split second I yanked the hair clip out of my hair, then thrust it forward.

It hit home, slipping through the demon's eye like a hot knife through butter. He trembled, the air rippling over him and me, and then a sonic burst, like a jet breaking the sound barrier. The body fell, and I was thrown free, landing on my rump on top of the nearest grave, right next to Timmy.

The sirens were closer now, and I rolled over, breathing hard, terrified of finding the worst. I rolled my baby over and patted his little cheek. His eyelids fluttered. "Momma?" he said. I couldn't answer. I could only hold him and cry.

It was over.

I was tired. So tired.

But I'd won. Goramesh was gone. Larson was dead.

And as my boy curled up next to me, I hugged him tight and closed my eyes.

Epilogue

As it turns out, Allie had called the cops. She hadn't been able to find Eddie and Laura right away, so she'd dialed 911 (using the cell phone for exactly the purpose I'd told her she could) and then Stuart. By then, Laura and Eddie had found her, and they raced to the graveyard in Laura's car, arriving just seconds after the police, with Stuart not far behind.

The paramedics took Timmy to the emergency room right away, where he received a clean bill of health. He had bad dreams the first few nights, but the hospital counselor says those will fade in time. Already, he's sleeping through the night again, so I think my baby's going to be just fine.

I spent the next few days nursing my wounds and talking with the police. I'd killed Larson and Doug, no doubt about that, but I was cleared quickly enough. Allie and Laura's statements confirmed my story that Larson had kidnapped my kids and then he and Doug had tried to kill me. And when the police examined Larson's car and found hair and other trace evidence in the trunk tying him to the disappearance of another Coastal Mists resident, that pretty much sealed Larson's fate as a criminal.

After that, life returned pretty much to normal. There were a few changes, of course. Eddie was a permanent fixture at my house now, his bond with Allie having strengthened to the point of unbreakable. One day I'd tell her the truth. But not now. Not yet.

Laura and the girls are still taking self-defense classes with me. Laura swears it's only to work off the calories from the desserts I keep feeding her as payment for services rendered, but I have a secret belief that she actually enjoys the exercise. Either that, or she likes watching Cutter move.

On the home front, Stuart is currently the most pampered husband on the planet. Guilt will do that. And when the guilt stems from having held the particularly vile belief that your husband is in cahoots with demons . . . well, the groveling and pampering can go on pretty much indefinitely.

As for me, I was still keeping secrets from my family, but what else could I do? I knew Goramesh would be back. His disappearance was only temporary, and that was a reality I had to learn to live with. There were still other demons in San Diablo, too. They'd infiltrated the nursing home, for one thing, and as much as I itched to tell Father Corletti to send another Hunter, I knew I wouldn't make that call.

The truth? I'd taken on a responsibility when I'd become a Hunter so many years ago, and I couldn't walk away from it now. Not when so many of the creatures were out walking the streets.

San Diablo needed a Hunter, and I was here. Out of practice, true, but I had Cutter and Eddie to help me. Besides, a hidden little part of me really does love the work.

And, when you get right down to it, what family doesn't have one or two little secrets . . . ?

AVAILABLE FROM BERKLEY

The Secret Life of a
Demon-Hunting Soccer Mom

California Demon

"One of my favorite writers.
Funny and sassy, her books
are a cherished delight."
—SHERRILYN KENYON

Julie Kenner

USA Today Bestselling Author of *Carpe Demon*

0-425-21043-X

Sink your teeth into the
Southern Vampire series by

CHARLAINE HARRIS

Sookie Stackhouse is just a small-time cocktail
waitress in Louisiana. And she can read minds,
which scares off potential boyfriends. Except the
vampires, of course, who don't seem to mind at all.

"RURAL AMERICA FINALLY HAS A VAMPIRE STORY
TO CALL ITS OWN." —TANYA HUFF

Club Dead
0-441-01051-2

Living Dead in Dallas
0-441-00923-9

Dead Until Dark
0-441-00853-4

Dead to the World
0-441-01218-3

Dead as a Doornail
0-441-01333-3

Available in hardcover:
Definitely Dead
0-441-01400-3

Available wherever books are sold or at penguin.com

NOW AVAILABLE IN HARDCOVER!

Penguin Group (USA) Online

What will you be reading tomorrow?

Tom Clancy, Patricia Cornwell, W.E.B. Griffin,
Nora Roberts, William Gibson, Robin Cook,
Brian Jacques, Catherine Coulter, Stephen King,
Dean Koontz, Ken Follett, Clive Cussler,
Eric Jerome Dickey, John Sandford,
Terry McMillan, Sue Monk Kidd, Amy Tan,
John Berendt...

You'll find them all at
penguin.com

Read excerpts and newsletters,
find tour schedules and reading group guides,
and enter contests.

Subscribe to Penguin Group (USA) newsletters
and get an exclusive inside look
at exciting new titles and the authors you love
long before everyone else does.

PENGUIN GROUP (USA)
us.penguingroup.com